The Gorse Blooms Pale

The Gorse Blooms Pale

DAN DAVIN'S
SOUTHLAND STORIES

Edited by Janet Wilson

OTAGO

.

Published by Otago University Press
PO Box 56/Level 1, 398 Cumberland Street, Dunedin, New Zealand
Fax: 64 3 479 8385   Email: university.press@otago.ac.nz
www.otago.ac.nz/press

First published 2007

ISBN 978 1 877372 42 1

Cover illustration: Jenny Cooper

Printed through Condor Production Ltd, Hong Kong

Contents

PART I

From *The Gorse Blooms Pale* (1947)

'Perspective'

PART II

From *Breathing Spaces* (1975)

'The Far-Away Hill'

PART III

Previously Uncollected Stories

'Invercargill Boundary'

'Day's End'

Acknowledgements

MANY PEOPLE have helped me track down stories and other writings by Dan Davin located in New Zealand. I should like to thank Paul Aubin for xeroxing short stories, poems and other works and Claire Deegan for invaluable research in the Davin archives at the Alexander Turnbull Library for unpublished stories and poems. This work could not have been completed without the enormous help of Denis Lenihan in Sydney, who answered queries about Invercargill and Bluff through consulting resources at the State Library of New South Wales, and Peter Lenihan in Invercargill, who provided information drawn from an extensive Southland network. I remain grateful for their generous assistance with local knowledge and resources in what has become a fruitful collaboration. Thanks, too, to Linda Te Au of Information Services, Invercargill City Libraries, for providing photocopies of maps, accounts and directory entries.

Thanks are also due to the following: Ken Arvidson, for explaining the national examination system in the 1920s and 1930s; Denise Beerkens for writing about the Concannon family; Peter Booth of Ohai Coal Company for information about Southland coal mines; Kay Cooke for comments on Orepuki; Anna Davin for commenting on different stories and their contexts; Delia Davin for information about the Davin and Sullivan families; Tony Foster for providing names of New Zealand trees; Jim Geddes, District Curator of Arts and Heritage, Department of Arts and Heritage, Gore, for identifying people and locations in the stories set in Gore; Lawrence Jones for identifying the blind Dunedin poet of the 1930s; Cilla McQueen and another Bluff resident for answering queries about Bluff; Kevin Mechen, Liquor Licensing Coordinator/Projects

Officer, Dunedin City Council, for answering queries about Dunedin pubs; Keith Ovenden for information about dates of composition; Ann Paetz of Features, Radio New Zealand for confirming the broadcast dates of 'Black Diamond'; Lt Col. Chris Pugsley, for discussing the New Zealand Division's tactical sign and for introducing me to *The Diamond Track*; Igor de Rachewiltz, Emeritus Fellow in the Division of Pacific and Asian History at the Australian National University, Canberra, for the translation of 'Too le Mani'. I am indebted to Anna Davin, Delia Davin and Denis Lenihan for their helpful comments on a draft of the chronology and introduction. Finally I remain grateful to Matthew Baddock and Fiona Tolan of the University of Northampton for their assistance in preparing the text and to the School of Arts in the University of Northampton for granting me a period of sabbatical leave to work on this book.

I should like to thank Brigid Sandford Smith, Dan Davin's literary executor, for permission to reprint all the previously published stories in this volume and the Alexander Turnbull Library for permission to publish from the Daniel Marcus Davin literary papers: the poem 'Invercargill Boundary' (MS-Papers-5079-263); the short story, 'Failed Exorcism' (MS-Papers-5079-287); and to quote from the short story, 'The Unjust and the Loving' (MS-Papers-5079-494).

JANET WILSON

Dan Davin Chronology

This chronology of Dan Davin's life and principal publications includes published short stories, novels, poetry, essays, critical studies and memoirs, but not reviews, obituaries, lectures, radio broadcasts and television documentaries. A fuller list of Davin's principal publications can be found in Ovenden, *A Fighting Withdrawal*: *The Life of Dan Davin, Writer, Soldier, Publisher*, pp. 448–75 (hereafter *FW*, see p. 49), to which this chronology is indebted.

1913   1 September: Daniel Marcus Davin born in Invercargill, the fourth child of Patrick and Mary Davin (nee Sullivan), following his sisters, Evelyn (b. 1908) and Molly (b. 1910), and his brother, Tom (b. 1911).

1914–20: Davin family live at Gore.

1914   8 September: Martin Davin born.

1917   15 September: Patrick Davin born.

1918–20: Davin attends St Mary's Convent School on Ardwick Street, Gore.

1920   family move to Invercargill.

1921–9: attends Invercargill Marist Brothers' School.

1928   top in Southland in Public Service Examination.

1929   top in Southland in Matriculation, 15th in New Zealand with special distinction in English, French and Latin. Captain and Dux of school.

1930   attends Sacred Heart College, Auckland, as a boarder on scholarship in sixth form.

1931   attends the University of Otago on a University National Scholarship and meets Winifred Kathleen Gonley ('Winnie').

1932   October: 'Francis Thompson's Prose', Otago University *Review* xlv: 39–41.

——   December: May vacation, and summer vacations 1933–4, 1934–5. Works on the wharves and in the woolsheds at Bluff.

1933   11 May: 'A Modest Proposal': as Jonathan Sloe, *The Critic*, Otago University: 6.

——   22 June: 'A Serious and Useful Scheme for the Benefit of Scholars', ibid: 5.

——   27 July: 'The Aposanctosis', ibid: 7.

—— 5 October: 'Some Considerations of the Present Universal Distress, Together with a Simple and Ready Scheme for the Alleviation Thereof', ibid: 8.

—— October: poem in translation, 'Morpheus in Mentem', Otago University *Review* xlvi: 28.

1934 nominated as candidate for Rhodes Scholarship but not selected.

—— 17 May: 'A Modest Preface', as Simon Bedlam, *The Critic*: 4.

—— 7 June: 'Graduation Ceremony: Professor Hunter's Address', unsigned lead story, ibid: 1–2.

—— 11 October: 'An Apologia for Politics', as Jonathan Sloe, ibid: 6

—— October: 'Apathy', editorial, Otago University *Review* xlvii: 3–5. 'Decadence in English Poetry of the 1890s', ibid: 22–5. poem, 'A Sweet and Gentle Ballad of Youth', ibid: 38.

1935 graduates MA in English with First Class Honours. Wins Rhodes Scholarship to Oxford.

—— 19 April: poem, 'The Compleynt of Football', *The Critic*: 11.

—— September: poems, 'Deity', 'There is about your Silence', 'Sunday', 'Standstill', and short story, 'Prometheus', Otago University *Review* xlviii: 5–6, 27–9.

1936 graduates with Diploma of Honours in Arts (Latin) First Class. Becomes engaged to Winifred Gonley.

—— August: leaves New Zealand and takes up scholarship at Balliol College, Oxford.

1937 25 June: reunited in Toulon with Winifred Gonley from New Zealand. They spend July to September in Paris.

—— December: first visit to Ireland, to his father's brother Michael in Tonegurrane, Galway.

1938 September: poems, 'Knowledge' (later titled 'Perspective'), 'Exiled', 'Galway', '1936', 'The Far-Away Hill', 'Harmony', Otago University *Review* li: 20–1.

1939 June: completes BA at Oxford University with First Class honours.

—— 22 July: marries Winifred Gonley at St Aloysius Church, Oxford. Begins writing novel, *The Mills of God* (later retitled *Cliffs of Fall*).

—— autumn: Davin volunteers, assigned to Royal Warwickshire Regiment.

1940 22 January: short story 'Toby' (early version of 'Death of a Dog'), published in *Manchester Guardian:* 10.

—— 18 May: Davin, at own request, commissioned as second lieutenant into Second New Zealand Expeditionary Force (2NZEF). Appointed in command of 13 Platoon, C. Company, 23 Battalion.

—— 20 July: birth of first daughter, Anna Deirdre Davin.

1941 March 26–9: writes 'The Milk Round' during sea voyage from Alexandria to Piraeus, Greece; with 13 Platoon and NZ Div. in Greece.

—— 20 May–31 July: Davin, as Battalion Intelligence Officer, wounded in

Battle of Maleme and hospitalised in Alexandria.

—— August–September 1942: works for Intelligence at GHQ (British Army) in Cairo.

1942 June: short story, 'Under the Bridge', *Penguin New Writing* 13: 30–4.

—— October: works for 'J' Squadron (Staff Information Service, British Army) in North Africa Campaign.

1943 January: attends Staff College, Sarafand, Palestine. Returns to active service in the 2NZEF as General Staff Officer Grade 3, Intelligence (GSO3 (I)), responsible for Intelligence at divisional level. Completes ten of the stories published in *The Gorse Blooms Pale*.

—— 6 September: returns to England on leave and is reunited with Winnie and Anna in Monmouthshire, where Winnie, a social worker in the Bristol University Settlement, was working temporarily in a hostel.

—— June: poem, 'Night Before Battle', *New Writing & Daylight* 3: 163.

—— September: short story, 'Jaundiced', *Life & Letters Today* 38:72: 132–5.

—— 1 December: birth of Patricia Katarina (Patty), daughter of Davin and Elizabeth Berndt, whom he had met in Cairo.

—— 6 December: departure for NZ Div. HQ in Italy.

1944 January: rejoins the NZ Div at the siege of Monte Cassino as Staff Intelligence Officer answering to GSO 1 and to divisional commander, General Officer Commanding Bernard Freyberg, VC.

—— February: poem, 'Hope against Hope', *Life & Letters Today* 40:78: 85.

—— 10 May: mother, Mary Davin, dies in Seacliff Hospital.

—— 9 June: the Davins' second child, Delia, born at Bath.

—— 15 July: with the NZ Div when 25 Battalion took Monte Lignano, liberating Arezzo.

—— 9 August–June 1945: works for War Office in London as New Zealand representative on the Allied Control Commission for Germany set up to administer the dismantling of Nazi institutions.

—— November: short stories, 'The Vigil' in *Good Housekeeping*: 8, 9, 61; 'Danger's Flower' in *Selected Writing,* Winter: 37–47.

1945 short story, 'Bourbons' in *Bugle Blast: An Anthology from the Services* 3, ed. Jack Aistrop and Reginald Moore (London: Allen & Unwin), pp. 120–6.

—— April: novel, *Cliffs of Fall* (London: Nicholson and Watson), 188 pp.

—— May: offered a job at OUP by Kenneth Sisam, Secretary to the Delegates of the Press.

—— 31 July: released from Military Service. Mentioned in Dispatches for third time for 'gallant and distinguished services in Italy'.

—— 30 September: Davin begins work at OUP in Walton Street, Oxford.

—— October: short story, 'In Transit', *Life & Letters Today* 47: 43–51.

—— 19 November: birth of Davins' third daughter, Katharine Brigid (Brigid).

—— 13 December: awarded the MBE (Military Division).

—— 30 December: Davin and family living in Rose Hill, Oxford.

1946 December: Davins move to 103 Southmoor Road, Oxford where Dan and Winnie live for the rest of their lives.

1947 *An Introduction to English Literature* with John Mulgan (Oxford: Clarendon Press. Reprinted 1950, 1952, 1957, 1961, 1964, and 1969).

—— 27 May: novel, *For the Rest of Our Lives* (Nicholson & Watson. Second edition, London: Michael Joseph; Auckland: Blackwood & Janet Paul Ltd., 1965), 416 pp.

—— November: short stories, *The Gorse Blooms Pale* (London: Nicholson and Watson).

1948 promoted to Assistant Secretary to the Delegates of OUP upon Sisam's retirement.

—— 17 August to 24 September: returns to New Zealand for research on the battle for Crete in the Second World War for the New Zealand Official War History Series.

—— December (?): short story, 'A Return', *Arena*: 1:4 (December 1948?): 72–8.

1949 becomes Director of the New York business of OUP, and makes first visit in 1952.

—— April: novel, *Roads from Home* (London: Michael Joseph), 254 pp.; 2nd edition, edited by Lawrence Jones in the New Zealand fiction series (Auckland: Auckland University Press and OUP, 1976), 250 pp. + xxxiv.

—— September: short story, 'The Quiet One', *Landfall* 3:3: 228–40.

1953 March: short story, 'Presents', *Landfall* 7:1: 19–25.

—— *New Zealand Short Stories*, selected and with an introduction (London: OUP World's Classics series. Reprinted 1954, 1955, 1957, 1961, 1966, and 1970). Reissued as *The Making of a New Zealander*, Short Stories I (Oxford, OUP paperback, 1976; reprinted, 1989).

—— *Katherine Mansfield: Selected Stories*, selected and with an introduction (London: OUP World's Classics series. Reprinted in 1954, 1955, 1957, 1959, 1961, and 1964. Reissued with chronology and bibliography. World's Classics paperback, 1981).

—— August: *Crete,* Official History of New Zealand in the Second World War, 1939–45 (Wellington: War History Branch, Department of Internal Affairs), 547 pp. + xvii.

1954 December: 'The Narrative Technique of Frank Sargeson' in Helen Shaw, ed., *The Puritan and the Waif. A Symposium of Critical Essays on the Work of Frank Sargeson* (Auckland: H.L. Hofmann), pp. 56–71.

1956 *The New Zealand Novel*, Pt 1 and 2, with W.K. Davin (Wellington: Department of Education, Post-Primary School Bulletin, n.d.) 10: 1 and 2, 65 pp.

—— March: poem, 'Winter Galway', *Landfall* 10:1: 11.

—— 14 May: novel, *The Sullen Bell* (London: Michael Joseph), 287 pp.

1958 3 January: death of Patrick Davin, Davin's father, at age of 80.
—— *English Short Stories of Today*, edited with an introduction (London: OUP for the English Association. Reprinted in 1959, 1961, 1964, 1966, 1969, 1972, 1975, and 1978). Reissued as *The Killing Bottle: Classic English Short Stories* (Oxford: OUP paperback, 1988)).
1959 19 January: novel, *No Remittance* (London: Michael Joseph), 224 pp.
—— February(?): *Katherine Mansfield in her Letters* (Wellington: Department of Education, Post-Primary School Bulletin, 20), 24 pp.
—— 5 March–7 April: 'Joyce Cary', the Macmillan Brown lecture series given at the University of Otago, and Victoria and Auckland University Colleges, New Zealand.
1962 Davins purchase cottage at 4 High Street, Dorchester, from now on a weekend writing retreat.
1967 short story, 'Bluff Retrospect', *Landfall* 21:2: 163–7.
1968 April: short story, 'Roof of the World', *Malahat Review* 10: 89–95.
—— December: short story, 'Goosey's Gallic War', *Landfall* 22:4: 387–96.
—— December: memoir, 'Goodnight, Julian, Everywhere', *London Magazine* 9:4: 30–48 (reprinted in *Closing Times*).
1969 March: short story, 'First Flight', *Landfall* 23:1: 12–33.
—— 'The Battle for Crete', in A.J.P. Taylor and J.M. Roberts, eds, *History of the 20th Century* (in 96 weekly parts) (London: BPC Publishing Ltd.), vol. 4, ch, 64, pp. 1771–3.
1970 16 January: novel, *Not Here, Not Now* (London: Robert Hale & Co; New Zealand: Whitcombe & Tombs Ltd.), 330 pp.
—— July–August: the Davins return to New Zealand, partly for centennial celebrations at Otago University, partly on sabbatical leave and partly for OUP business.
—— appointed Deputy Secretary and Academic Publisher, OUP.
1971 April/May: memoir, 'Spoilt [also Spoiled] Priest', *London Magazine* 11:1: 112–29 (reprinted in *Closing Times* as 'At the End of his Whether').
1972 30 June: novel, *Brides of Price* (London: Robert Hale & Co.), 254 pp.
—— August: memoir, 'In a Green Grave: Louis MacNeice (1907–1963)', *Encounter*: 42–9 (reprinted in *Closing Times*).
1973 January: memoir, 'The Chinese Box: Enid Starkie (1897–1970)', *Cornhill Magazine* 1074: 361–84 (reprinted in *Closing Times*).
—— June: short story, 'Psychological Warfare at Cassino', *Meanjin Quarterly* 32:2: 133–47.
1975 April: memoirs, *Closing Times* (London: OUP), 189 pp. + xxii. Reprinted 1985 (Auckland: OUP).
—— June: memoir, 'Five Windows Darken: Recollections of Joyce Cary', *Encounter*: 24–33 (reprinted in *Closing Times*).
—— October: short stories, *Breathing Spaces* (London: Robert Hale & Co.; New Zealand: Whitcoulls), 221 pp.

1976 January: 'My Language and Myself. English as Creative Power', *The Round Table, The Commonwealth Journal of International Affairs* 261: 19–25.

1976 'Early Reading: The Rime of the Ancient Mariner', *Education* 5 (Wellington: Department of Education): 27.

—— 'Freyberg', in Field Marshall Sir Michael Carver, ed., *The War Lords. Military Commanders of the Twentieth Century* (London: Weidenfeld & Nicolson), pp. 582–95.

1978 March: memoir of Frank Sargeson, 'Three Encounters Thirty Years Ago', *Islands* 6:3: 302–6.

1978 26 July–17 September: retirement round the world trip with Winnie, including New Zealand, to farewell OUP offices.

—— 20 September: retirement from OUP, coinciding with the OUP quincentenary celebrations.

1980 poems, 'Cairo Cleopatra', 'Egyptian Madonna', 'Elegy I', 'Elegy II', and 'Grave near Sirte', in Victor Selwyn, Erik de Mauny, Ian Fletcher, G.S. Fraser, and John Waller, eds, *Return to Oasis* (London: Shepheard-Walwyn with Editions Poetry London for the Salamander Trust), pp. 153–5.

—— 23 August: short story, 'The Dog and the Dead', *New Zealand Listener.*

—— November–September 1983: Chairman of the Salamander Oasis Trust, which published work of servicemen from the North African campaigns, 1940–3.

1981 22–5 May: Davins return to Crete for fortieth anniversary celebrations of the Battle of Crete.

—— 'Freyberg, Bernard Cyril', in E.T. Williams and C.S. Nicholls, eds, *Dictionary of National Biography 1961–1970* (Oxford: OUP), pp. 401–5.

—— 'MacNeice, Louis', ibid, pp. 709–12.

—— 11 July: short story, 'Finders and Losers', *New Zealand Listener.*

—— memoir of J.A.W. Bennett, 'The Learned Adviser', in P.L. Heyworth, ed., *Medieval Studies for J.A.W. Bennett, Aetatis Suae LXX* (Oxford: Clarendon Press), pp. 13–9.

—— *Selected Stories,* with an introduction (Wellington: Victoria University of Wellington Press, with Price Milburn & Co.; London: Robert Hale), pp. 319.

1982 'Maurice Duggan's *Summer in the Gravel Pit'*, in Cherry Hankin, ed., *Critical Essays on New Zealand Short Story* (Auckland: Heinemann), pp. 150–65.

—— short story, 'When Mum Died', in Bridget Williams and Roy Parsons, eds, *The Summer Book* (Wellington: Port Nicholson Press), pp. 42–56.

—— 9 September: *Night Attack: Short Stories from the Second World War*, edited with an introduction (Oxford: OUP. Issued as an OUP Paperback, 1984; reprinted in 1989).

1983 with Victor Selwyn, Erik de Mauny and Ian Fletcher, eds, *From Oasis*

      into Italy (London: Shepheard-Walwyn for the Salamander Oasis Trust).
—— 'Norman Davis: The Growth of a Scholar' in Douglas Gray and E.G. Stanley, eds, *Middle English Studies*. Presented to Norman Davis in honour of his Seventieth Birthday. (Oxford: Clarendon Press), pp. 1–15.

1984 January: short story, 'Cassino Casualty', *Stand Magazine* 26:1: 8–19; also published in *Islands* n.s.1:2, November 1984: 105–18.

—— 22 November–12 March 1985: returns to New Zealand with Winnie to receive an Hon. Lit. D. from the University of Otago.

1985 2 March: short story, 'The Albatross', *New Zealand Listener*.

—— December: short story, 'North of the Sangro', *Stand Magazine* 26:4: 42–54.

1986 *The Salamander and the Fire. Collected War Stories*, with an introduction and glossary (Oxford: OUP paperback), 208 pp. + xx.

—— 'Park, Sir Keith Rodney', in Lord Blake and C.S. Nicholls, eds, *Dictionary of National Biography 1971–1980* (Oxford: OUP), pp. 654–5.

—— August: short story, 'Black Diamond', *Islands* 37: 42–8.

—— December: short story, 'Fancy Dress', *London Magazine* 26:9 and 10, December 1986/January 1987: 22–31.

—— 20 December: poem, 'December', *New Zealand Listener*.

1987 1 January: appointed CBE in New Zealand Honours List.

—— 29 August: short story, 'The Black Stranger', *New Zealand Listener*

1988 12 April: death of Patty Watson (previously Tylecote).

—— poems, 'The Irish', 'Infernal Idyll', 'Day's End', in Robert Welch & Suheil Badi Bushrui, eds, *Literature and the Art of Creation: Essays and Poems in Honour of A. Norman Jeffares* (Gerrards Cross, Bucks: Colin Smyth; Totowa: H.J. Barnes & Noble Books), p. 241.

1989 7 January: short story, 'Gardens of Exile', *New Zealand Listener*.

1990 28 September: death of Dan Davin.

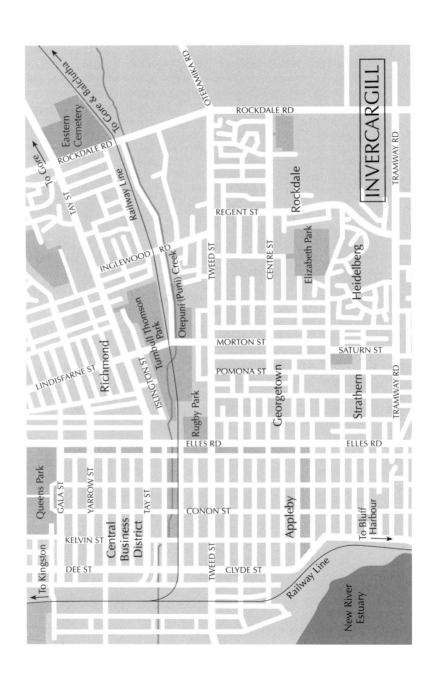

INVERCARGILL

Introduction

I Stories from *The Gorse Blooms Pale* (1947)

No New Zealand writer has set his stamp so definitively upon a particular region as Dan Davin in his short stories of an Irish-Catholic boyhood in Southland. In the first eight stories in this volume, taken from his first collection *The Gorse Blooms Pale,* Davin introduces us to Invercargill of the 1920s, a mainly Protestant town, from the perspective of its most important subculture, the working-class Irish. For his Irish-Catholic family, the Connollys, life centres round their home, a railwayman's house on the edge of town, their garden, animals, gorse hedges and paddocks. For Davin's young protagonist Mick Connolly[1] and his brothers, this microcosm constitutes their world. As they grow older, it opens out to what lies beyond: to the east, a rural hinterland with rolling hills, streams, quarries and fields over which they range with their ferrets on rabbit-hunting trips; to the west, the town itself, with its trams, wide streets, department stores, cinemas, pubs, its invitation to a larger world and a more complex society. This mixed rural-urban topography makes up the landscape of Davin's boyhood. Although he wrote other stories on different topics such as war and stories with more exotic settings, it was to this landscape and this period that he constantly returned and upon which he drew most movingly for his last stories.

The sequence of eight stories which opens *The Gorse Blooms Pale* reveals a remarkable unity of time, place and consciousness.[2] Although written after Davin had left New Zealand, the illusion of immediacy[3] conveyed by the manner of his telling attracted widespread praise in New Zealand and England, giving the whole volume a distinction unequalled in any of his subsequent fictional writings.[4] James Bertram wrote, 'They are simply told and directly told with a natural warmth of dialogue and a general purity of diction which Davin was never to surpass'; E.H. McCormick commented that in this 'superb collection' Davin's art 'is seen in its purest form'.[5] K. John of the *Illustrated London News* responded to the 'transfiguring imagination ... of childhood' and praised their 'shy, secret, pervasive tenderness', while *New Statesman and Nation*'s Walter Allen admired 'the exactness of observation' and 'freshness of the scene' of the childhood stories.[6]

Through Mick Connolly, who registers both familiar and uncharted features of his milieu, Davin takes us to formative moments of childhood. The child's growing awareness is illustrated by minor incidents which acquire either revelationary power – the killing of a bull calf, the death of a favourite dog – or in more comic satiric vein, deflationary power – being called 'the milkboy' by Mrs Crofts' pretty daughter. The homogeneity of the stories comes from the strong family bonds between Mick, his parents and brothers, and Mick's affections for the animals on their rural farmlet, like his dog Jack and the cow Rosy. These anchor his perceptions of the wider world, of neighbours, other boys, Protestant and Catholic, the teachers at the Marist Brothers' School. In later stories they extend to other residents of multicultural Southland, most specifically 'Southland's transplanted Galway'[7] (newly arrived Irish-Catholic migrants whom his father befriended at the wharves or at Church), but also to Chinese, Maori, and black Americans.

Mick's world brims over with natural life and is constantly informed by its rhythms and realities. His empathetic identification with the animals, landscape and changing seasons becomes a kind of intimate occupancy. Observations of seasonal changes in nature are matched to the changes he witnesses in himself: in 'Growing Up' for instance, he 'couldn't help looking up to where framed in the branches the sparrows' nests were, so untidy outside, so neat and downy within. Last year he would have been up there in the branches counting the eggs'. Such precise recognition constitutes an embryonic naturalism that has kinship with Flaubert's. It leads him, albeit reluctantly, to accept the fatedness of life and death as part of a relentless, unavoidable cycle. Particular events take on heightened importance as Mick registers the injustice of fate, epitomising rural life's cruelty: his father's killing of his dog and later a bull calf, the death by drowning of baby rabbits, the loss of a pencil, and in the late short story, 'The Black Stranger', the perplexing discovery by Mick and his brother, in an abandoned barn, of a dead black man.

Mick's enthusiasms, affections and discoveries are interwoven with a gradual loss of innocence, and his consciousness shapes itself in response to these processes. His universe is already a 'Lost Eden': not a place of promise buttressed by the faith taught at mass and in school, but embodying change caused by loss, death and denial. His appreciation of nature as an innocent state is overshadowed by this darker perception of transience. The poem 'Perspective', which prefaces both *The Gorse Blooms Pale* and the *Selected Stories*, is Davin's most powerful articulation of this melancholic awareness. Defining the tensions between the contrasting perspectives which appear in the stories, it states his resignation to betrayal: the promise of arcadian riches for the child, symbolised by God's illumination of the gorse bush, has paled for the adult, just as the father's heroic stature in the eyes of the child has now become life-sized. All is diminished with experience: the child's perception of infinity, the mystery of the unknown, has now shrunk to a hand's span.

In these stories Davin charts the development of an essentially secular outlook predicated on harsh moral realism. This is first evident in Mick's acceptance of his father's attitude to mortality in 'Death of a Dog' and 'Growing Up': death is inevitable, final and should not be mourned. Davin's view that God is either compromised or indifferent sets him apart from his parents and their generation.[8] Mick's questioning of the attitudes of the Catholic nuns and brothers who teach him leads to doubt, anticipating a rejection of the faith in which he has been raised.[9]

Central to Davin's vision and a source of unity is the narrator's growing self-awareness as his individual outlook shapes itself through his responses to events. This is apparent in the first story, 'The Apostate', comparable to Joyce's questioning of belief in *Dubliners*, which introduces through a boyhood incident the scepticism evident in later work. 'The Apostate' explores Mick's epiphany about the divine, that 'God is green and Irish and a Catholic', and homes in on the instrument of writing, the pencil, which in turn leads to an undermining of this religious vision: Mick chooses a red pencil in preference to green in order to avoid simony. But his disappointment at losing the pencil – and God's unpredictable 'answer' to his prayer that he might find it, confirming Sister Mary Xavier's teaching that 'our prayers are not always answered the way we expect them to be' – argues that preferment on religious grounds (that is, for being afraid of the sin of simony) does not necessarily bring its own reward. Disillusioned, Mick concludes: 'There was no God. And He wasn't green either.'

Davin's careful positioning of the child's consciousness within the broader horizons of the Catholic faith, the natural world with which he has such affinity, and the 'indifferent natural universe from which he is estranged',[10] shows the development of his philosophy of self-reliance and sceptical resignation in the face of rural life's harsh realities. On occasion he introduces light-hearted satire, including self-parody, in a fashion reminiscent of Joyce's mock heroics. In 'The Vigil' for instance, Mick's throws a clod of earth at a straying hen, catching her 'a terrific thump'; the action is juxtaposed with his dream of romantic death, a 'young corpse stretched out on the bier. ... a calm, sad expression on his pale, drawn face'. A miniature chivalric gesture occurs in 'Milk Round', where Mrs Crofts chides Mick for delivering milk with dirt in it but he refuses to tell on the girls who had thrown it.

Davin also exposes the dualism which underpins Mick's emerging philosophy. In the 'The Apostate' he saves a small bird from having its neck wrung, although he squirms at being called a softie by the others; in 'Late Snow' he reminds himself when he sees the drowned rabbits, 'His father hated them to cry'; in 'Growing Up' he can't watch as his father brings the mallet down on the calf's head, and takes off into the house. In this last story, conflicting emotions lie behind his consciously off-hand statement, '"It was a bull, so we had to kill it"'. The killing, an irredeemable harsh rural practice, is heightened by the stylistic contrast between the lyrical appreciation of the burgeoning season at the story's beginning and the tenderness with which Mick perceives Rosy ('She was licking the calf and each lick was a caress'). In both these stories masculine modelling is framed by Mick's tangible perception of his father's extraordinary physical strength. His father's arm is 'Like a chunk of red pine' as he raises the mallet to strike: 'The cables of muscle and sinew on the heavy forearms rose and tautened, the biceps bulged against the rolled sleeves'.

A mark of Davin's realism in these stories of initiation is his fidelity to the moment of discovery or revelation (identifications made for both Mick and the reader), what R.A. Copland calls 'winning truths'.[11] Male toughness is acquired to cover up emotion, but emotion is also granted its place. Mick's meditation on spiders in 'The Apostate' concludes that those blessed with crosses on their backs might be entitled to protection from death, although no such superstition is attached to his saving a broken-winged bird later. In 'Death of a Dog' Mick elegiacally bids farewell to his devoted dog Jack, reinforcing both his brothers' laconic appraisal ('"Three bullets it took. ... He was a great dog all right"'), and their denunciation of their mother's betrayal. In the same way, in 'Late Snow' his consciousness of synchronisation as he watches Darkie the rabbit dig through the manure heap ('nostrils and whiskers twitching ... They seemed to keep time with his father's breathing and his own. As if the same breath went in and out of them all') is overtaken by the awareness that he and his father are separated by their different feelings about Darkie.

Throughout the stories are reminders that the family belongs to the underdog Irish-Catholic minority, 'a group that might have felt isolated in a larger community which itself knew isolation'.[12] Hearing the children's playground chant about Catholic frogs and Protestant dogs in 'The Apostate', Mick expects a renewal of Protestant-Catholic hostilities after school; a similar division and the same chant, a light hearted battle-cry, appear in 'Goosey's Gallic War'. The more entrenched attitudes of Mick's parents, a migrant generation, are expressed in the Manichean diction associated with the Irish troubles. The word 'black' is a term of denigration and phrases like 'black Orange Protestant stranger' and 'a black North of Ireland Presbyterian' identify the black-and-white, them-and-us, legacy of Irish factionalism.[13] The Connolly children absorb such sentiments without bitterness – Davin makes comedy of them in 'Goosey's Gallic War'. The New Zealand-Irish generation lacked the same political engagement in Ireland's fate that their parents had: feuding is easily transformed into friendship. In the late story, 'The

Black Stranger', these inherited terms are redefined when other types of alienation and ethnic difference in Southland society surface.

Davin's relationship to his Irish roots, more important in later stories and explored in the novels, preoccupied him throughout his writing career. The preoccupation invites his readers to ask to what extent Davin can also be read from other perspectives: as an historian of the Southland Irish-Catholic community in the early twentieth century (recording their manners and morals at a time when this sub-culture was adjusting to a different world, and before it would disappear, as Akenson claims), or as a philosopher and psychological moralist as Jones claims.[14] Certainly, as M.H. Holcroft suggests, the stories illustrate the cohesive bonds between the different families and groups within this community, and this is one source of their homogeneity. And, as Akenson stresses, no one else writing at that time gives such an insight into the mind-set of the Irish immigrants and their children.[15] He argues for a sociological, rather than purely literary, appreciation of certain stories. 'The Basket', a deftly realised dialogue between Mrs Connolly and her neighbour, the impoverished and elderly Mrs Fox, reveals the plight of women whose husbands fall victim to the demon drink, as well as stressing the importance of horticulture and gardening for basic subsistence.[16] The cadences of Irish-peasant speech are caught in the inflections of Mrs Fox's hypocritical excuses as she arrives unannounced: '"Och, Mrs Connolly, and I won't be coming in interrupting you at all."' In 'Saturday Night', Davin the psychological moralist appears: the local Irish-Catholic brogue is satirically linked to its moral universe through Mrs Fox's sanctimonious comment on Hollywood films, '"Well, and if it isn't a wicked world we're living in!"'[17] Davin has commented on the oral-based storytelling tradition of the *seanchaì* (itinerant Irish storyteller), in which he grew up.[18] The debt is apparent in dialogue and other stylistic features such as the narrator's asides to his audience in 'A Happy New Year' and 'The Albatross'; it has also been identified in his fractured anecdotal style of narration, which celebrates single incidents.[19]

To read Davin as principally a chronicler of Catholic Southland or as a documentary realist is to see one part of the picture at the expense of the whole. This approach risks neglecting Davin's achievements as a realist writer, developed further in his novels: his shaping of events so as to point to a deeper pattern of meaning. Davin himself makes the point that documentary realism can be made to serve the higher aims of literature:

> It is my belief that to be literature, a piece of fiction must combine a passion for the exact, the authentic, detail; some intellectual power which can organise the form and weight it with a central, though not necessarily explicit, thought; and a power of feeling, a spirit, which means that the story while avoiding a moral, is fundamentally moral.[20]

Davin constantly balances the realist elements – 'the exact, the authentic detail' – against fiction's demands for invention. He provides names of real people: neighbours like Mr Pratt in 'Roof of the World', and the Scotts and McGregors in 'The Vigil'. He introduces local settings and family history in 'A Return'. Yet these stories also include fictionalisation and elaboration of events. He sometimes alters facts to move away from non-fiction. In 'Presents', for example, he blurs the layout of Invercargill streets by changing the locations of the Shamrock and Deschlers hotels.[21]

Davin's Southland stories, written outside New Zealand over a period of fifty years, in suggestive ways move beyond the horizons of the migrant Irish-Catholic community in which they are set. For this reason they cannot be labelled as 'provincial'.[22] In the later stories, his themes of exile, home and belonging show strong affinities with the universal preoccupations of diasporic writing. It is a sign of the autobiographical exploration behind the stories that Davin's Irish ethnicity is represented as only one strand of the tapestry, albeit a privileged one. For after Davin left New Zealand he redefined his identity through wider contexts, and particularly in the war came to see himself as a New Zealander. In the 1950s he wrote to Frank Sargeson, 'I feel no wish to write about anyone but NZers – indeed don't feel or don't feel in the same way about anyone else'.[23] The faith, voices and outlook of the older generation of Irish-Catholic peasant migrants provide a point of departure, a set of values against which Mick and his brothers, a more New Zealand-Irish generation, define themselves; the certainties of Irish Catholicism were able to be challenged. Mick's disillusionment in 'The Apostate' anticipates the more secular outlook and interrogative mood of subsequent stories. In 'Death of a Dog', at the Marist Brothers'

School he learns about Cromwell's massacre at Drogheda, studies the 'Pink Catechism', and observes the angelus mechanically; his thoughts are on the fate of his dog. In two late stories, 'Black Diamond' and 'Black Stranger', the narrator-protagonist ponders the nuns' explanation that Tommy Bates drowned in the Mataura River because he went fishing instead of going to Sunday School. Davin's personal quarrel with his Catholic education culminates in his final story, 'Failed Exorcism', where the rebellious young narrator-prodigy challenges the pro-Irish attitudes and disciplinary measures of the Marist Brothers. When the boys are told yet again to rewrite the assertion 'In this year the English conquered Ireland' in their textbooks, *Our Race and Empire,* with 'In this year the Sassenach once again failed to conquer Ireland', he comments, 'I guessed the truth must lie somewhere in between'.

At school the boys sing uplifting Irish nationalistic songs, such as the Clanconnell War Song 'O'Donnell Abu'. The New Zealand-Irish cultural mix of the Connolly household embraces a wider range of family entertainments and musical interludes. Uncle Jack plays the fiddle at a wedding amidst liberal consumption of Hokonui hooch; Mick's sisters are musically accomplished and sing Irish airs like 'She is far from the Land'; and Mick himself yodels 'Mother Machree', his voice breaking on the high notes, in an attempt to get into his mother's good books. In the outback story, 'A Happy New Year', the party entertainments include a bacarolle from Offenbach alongside 'Danny Boy' and 'My Lady of the Boudoir', while the popular dance tune 'I'm Dancing with Tears in my Eyes' features in 'That Golden Time', Davin's story about Otago University.

The flourishing popular culture imported from America and England, prominent in the Mick Connolly stories as a potent influence on younger Invercargillites, contrasts with such genteel pretensions and youthful fashions.[24] Screen idols like Tom Mix, Jean Harlow and William Powell are familiar names. Likewise the pulp fiction which Mick omnivorously devours: 'Deadwood Dicks', dime novels whose heroes include Buffalo Bill and Hopalong Cassidy, monthly magazines like *Chums*, the *Boys' Own Paper*, and *Wide World Magazin*e, the writings of Sax Rohmer. A clash between the piety of the older generation and Hollywood's commercialisation of religious themes is comically presented in 'Saturday

Night', when Mrs Connolly denounces the film *The Golden Calf* for its 'brazen hussies flaunting their bare legs'. Such entertainments blend with the Connolly boys' domestic chores (milking, crushing oyster shells for grit for the hens, digging turnips for mash, bagging potatoes, cleaning out the ferret cage), their gang warfare with other boys (mock battles and games of captivity and torture), and other outdoor pursuits (rabbit-hunting with dogs and ferrets, catching cockabullies and minnows, building forts and huts). An arsenal of weapons and equipment accompanies these activities: shanghais,[25] various guns including Remington rifles, bows and arrows improvised from lancewood, dock grass and nails, Bowie knives, cross-saws and airguns. As Mick grows older, Capstan cigarettes and Westward Ho tobacco are secretly consumed; in 'Failed Exorcism', when he cuts up the bamboo cane with which the boys were punished at school, he tries smoking one of the pieces.

The final four stories in this group from *The Gorse Blooms Pale*, two of which are set at the University of Otago in Dunedin where Davin was a student from 1930–5, differ markedly from the Mick Connolly sequence in mood and subject matter. Less imaginatively engaged, their more academic style is marked by political awareness, self-consciousness as to the role of the artist, scepticism regarding male-female relationships, and knowledge of other literary modes such as classical poetry, First World War poetry, and the bushman's yarn. The world of fallible adulthood is introduced by mature, reflective narrators who comment on the dramatic action, as ironic titles like 'That Golden Time' and 'A Happy New Year' imply. Discussion about war, the British Empire, patriotism, art and morality, or revelations about sex, religion and marriage, replace the earlier intimacies stemming from the close-knit Connolly family and Mick's familiarity with his Southland surroundings. But the focus in these later stories on how humans contrive to bring about their own fates – miniature meditations on the Fall as it is enacted in human affairs – reflects some of Mick's preoccupations translated into more worldly, political contexts.

The two University of Otago stories, 'That Golden Time' and 'Casualties', draw on the structure of a debate and introduce multiple intertexts. Both reflect an engagement with the world of letters and learning as well as with contemporary politics. 'Casualties' concerns a dramatic encounter at a W.E.A. lecture between a conscientious objector and a blind poet (probably C.R Allen, well-known in Dunedin in the 1930s) regarding which view of the war should prevail: the pacifism represented by Siegfried Sassoon, or the heroism which Rupert Brooke advocated. The climax comes with the blind man's revelation that he was unable to act on his principles by enlisting, in contrast to the conscientious objector who did so by not fighting. 'That Golden Time', a meditation on the protagonist's sexual initiation, introduces the theme of the artist's need for sexual freedom. Davin draws a parallel with the licentiousness of the late Republic, in particular the wittily amoral love verse of Catullus, and points out, with reference to the more arid processes of learning through lecture and seminar, that the pagan poet's celebration of Lesbia and her sparrow would hardly be understood in Presbyterian Dunedin.[26] The adult narrative voice and use of classical poetry and First World War poetry which mark Davin's engagement with a university education differentiate these stories from the oral, non-literary character of the Mick Connolly stories, where chance encounters with the world of literature are solemnly observed. Mick reads in the *Tablet* of the scandal surrounding the publication of *Ulysses*; he also discovers a copy of Coleridge's *The Rime of the Ancient Mariner* in the rubbish dump.[27] In fact literariness and the world of letters are self-consciously dismissed in 'The Vigil' but earmarked by Mick as part of his ambitions for the future: 'Some day when he grew up he would read all the books in the world and know all about everything, even about this writer'.

The two stories with rural Southland settings, 'A Happy New Year' and 'A Meeting Half Way', also depart from the Mick Connolly sequence in style and content. Both have been criticised for their distance from the events narrated.[28] Their protagonists are First World War veterans, tragically affected by their war experiences and their themes are marriage and its outcomes. In their moral emphasis on the fates which govern human affairs, they anticipate the tragic dénouement of *Roads from Home* (1949). 'A Happy New Year' is a robust telling in an idiomatic vernacular of the bushman's yarn. Fuelled by copious quantities of raw hokonui, the semi-itinerant narrator, reminiscent of Frank Sargeson's narrators, describes a complex atmosphere divided between the domestic interior world of the women at the New Year's Eve party (marked by the recital of parlour songs and the playing of sheet music) and the men's covert, whisky-driven confessional exchanges in the shed outside, before the final climactic revelation. 'A Meeting Half Way', an early example of 'Southland Gothic',[29] stands out from Davin's other Southland stories by virtue of its emphasis on a male-female impasse and a Protestant heroine. As a study of violent, repressed emotions which explode under pressure, it has affinities with the mainstream tradition of New Zealand writing from Sargeson to Ronald Hugh Morrieson to Maurice Gee, a tradition which explores and critiques the damaging effects of puritanism. The story is reminiscent of Maupassant in its dramatic irony and the fated domestic misalliance between a crude but virile man and his refined but puritanically fastidious wife, although the dramatic nature of the woman's revenge has been compared to Mansfield's story about domestic violence, 'Woman at the Store'.[30] Written predominantly from the point of view of the beleaguered, suffering wife (though also including that of her unfaithful husband), this story like the two university stories shows Davin dealing adroitly with differences in gender, creed and belief. In 'Casualties' the W.E.A. lecturer is a woman whose friend at teacher training college is a communist, and she articulates the view that Marxism, like religion, is another opiate of the masses. In 'That Golden Time', the protagonist is concerned with differentiating the consciousness – and hence the morality – of the artist from that of the student of literature.

These four stories can be linked with three stories with English settings which follow them in the original *The Gorse Blooms Pale*.[31] As narratives of episodes provoked either by political idealism or problematic sexual relations, they do not fit Davin's major themes for this genre: childhood and the war. Instead their focus on sexual betrayal and human folly is taken up and explored more fully in the two novels about Southland which Davin wrote at this time, both of which have tragic denouements, *Cliffs of Fall* (1945) and *Roads from Home* (1949).

Although Davin was writing and publishing fiction and poetry in his later years as a student at the University of Otago, the stories of *The Gorse Blooms Pale* were written after he left New Zealand for Oxford as a Rhodes Scholar in 1936. The earliest publication dates are 1940 for 'Toby' (an early version of 'Death of a Dog') and 1944 for 'The Vigil'.

These and the other Southland stories were written during or just after the Second World War, as were the war stories which also appear in *The Gorse Blooms Pale*.[32] This overlap between the context in which he wrote his short fiction and the earlier periods of his life is partly due to the unexpected homecoming Davin found when he joined the 2nd New Zealand Expeditionary Force. As commander of 13 Platoon, C Company, he met soldiers recruited from Southland – past acquaintances as well as new ones – whose conversation in a colourful but emotionally understated New Zealand vernacular prompted memories of his childhood and university years. He wrote in his diary, 'In parts this battalion is a travelling Invercargill, a peregrinating small town'.[33] Davin's accounts of his war experiences and his earlier Southland experiences run in tandem in his writing and publishing career at this point: his war novel, *For the Rest of Our Lives,* appeared in the same year as *The Gorse Blooms Pale.* But the Southland boyhood stories precede the war stories and novel psychologically and artistically as well as chronologically, for they represent those defining experiences around which Davin's philosophy is based. The fictions about war develop and locate this in a broader political and social framework, but do not substantially change it.

All of Davin's Southland stories, written outside his place of origin, can be identified as expatriate or diasporic writing. In being associated with the circumstances of exile, which he increasingly experienced as 'alienation' from his homeland, they bear comparison with Katherine Mansfield's New Zealand stories and those by James Joyce in *Dubliners* – both of whom at different times influenced Davin. For writers who either choose or are forced to live outside the country of their birth, memories of the formative years of childhood often become a guiding obsession; their imaginative recreation of home is all the more vivid because of geographical separation.[34] Like Mansfield, Davin recaptures the experience of childhood by exploring the impressions and sensations of his youthful protagonists. Like Joyce, he based these recollections on precise details of location and geography: the streets, schools and pubs of Invercargill and its environs, the latter identified topographically and through ownership (Scott's Paddocks, Lyon's Swamp, O'Donnell's Hill).[35] This is also true of Davin's most accomplished novel about Southland, *Roads from Home*.[36]

II Stories from *Breathing Spaces* (1975)

Breathing Spaces, Davin's second volume of short stories, was published in 1975, more than twenty-five years after *The Gorse Blooms Pale*. The eight Southland stories, written between the late 1940s and the 1960s, are grouped into two sections.[37] The five stories of Part One refer to Davin's childhood and adolescence and build on the Mick Connolly sequence; the three stories of Part Two deal with his first return to New Zealand in 1948, and exhibit a change in outlook and approach. Although all eight stories were written following Davin's visit to New Zealand (after twelve years away, at the age of thirty-five), the first group reconstructs the boy protagonist, Mick Connolly, or a slightly older, first-person protagonist-narrator as in 'Goosey's Gallic War' and 'The Quiet One'. The second group, by contrast, introduces a mature protagonist-narrator, close to Davin's age at that time, who registers the changes that he discovers upon returning, finding himself unfamiliar with a world he once knew intimately. These stories define a shift in Davin's fictional topography: from now on the motif of the return will reverberate in his work, becoming a major stimulus for his imagination, forcing him to delve ever deeper into the reserves of memory and the unconscious.[38]

The more reflective tone and expanded scope of all eight stories reveal the passage of time and Davin's greater experience of the world by 1948. His childhood is distant, more a source of nostalgia now that events have shaped his present life in Oxford (married with three children, working for Oxford University Press), in contrast to the Southland milieu in which he grew up. Most dramatically, the war has intervened, but his 'returned' identity as something of a local hero also contributes to the change; he is now an established writer, publisher, and a war veteran, researching for the official New Zealand history of the Second World War in Crete.[39] The loss of innocence and gaining of experience within the unspoiled environment of semi-rural Georgetown, which made the Mick Connolly sequence so intuitively true to its own time and place, is now replaced by accomplished but distanced social observation: the bustling township of Invercargill comes into focus in 'Presents' and 'The Quiet One', while a Protestant family appears in 'Goosey's Gallic War' and the narrator's relatives on his mother's side appear in 'Bluff Retrospect'. Mick's intimacy with the natural world and the narrow compass of his family life in the earlier stories expand into an appreciation of Invercargill society with a sharpened perception of the family's Irish origins and place in that milieu.

In 'Presents', therefore, the boys' father, Mr Connolly, retains his son's admiration, not because of the impressive physical strength observed in 'Late Snow' and 'Growing Up' but because, affected by the railways strike, Mr Connolly compensates for his impecuniousness by shoplifting a Christmas present for his son. Invercargill's trams, its sly-grog pub where Mr Connolly has spent the last of his Christmas money, the vast department store, the Chinese laundry and Chinese crackers which fascinate the boys, all conveying the bustle and confusion of last-minute shopping on Christmas Eve, are linked to the mix of insecurity and exaltation which Mick experiences vicariously through his father's actions.

Other stories develop the moral realism of the earlier sequence as the more mature protagonist acknowledges his part in destroying nature. In 'The Tree', Mick and his brother Ned, in a dangerously enthusiastic mood, imagine they are Tuatapere axemen and cut down a favourite old macrocarpa tree; the same bleak recognition which appears in 'The Apostate' and the poem 'Perspective' dominates the ending. The felled tree, which once 'had challenged the sky', is symbolically aligned to his father as Mick realises the Oedipal implications of his act: 'what had added to his own past was taken from his father's'. 'The Quiet One', commonly recognised as one of Davin's finest stories, powerfully demarcates the boundaries between adolescence and adulthood. With the extended narrative scope of a tale, rather than the vignette style of 'The Tree' or 'The Basket', it opens in high spirits as three lads prowl the town after a band concert, searching for girls. 'The Quiet One' then slows in pace, becoming more sombre in mood when the narrator, Ned, comes across his older, somewhat remote cousin Marty, and finds out that Marty's girlfriend, who has been in hospital following an abortion that went wrong, has just died. Ned realises that he has never been near anyone who 'felt as badly as he [Marty] was feeling'. His epiphany is a complex moral realisation about values: 'we only kid ourselves that we can tell the good things from the bad things when really they're so mixed up that half the time we're thinking one thing, feeling another, and doing something else altogether'.

By contrast, the boys' adventure escapades, 'Goosey's Gallic War' and 'Roof of the World', are nostalgically retrospective. Both show how Davin can transform a single incident with social commentary, dramatic detail, and even provide a symbolic dimension, but they do not develop the moral complexity of the other stories. The ending of 'Goosey's Gallic War' is a tidy reversal, close to wish-fulfilment: the anticipated mixed Catholic-Protestant marriage, celebrated by the two families, would have been frowned upon by Mrs Connolly and the Catholic mothers in *Roads from Home*. In 'Goosey's Gallic War', Davin uses mock heroics in aligning the children's gang-fights with the embattled legions of Rome, but the parallel is not convincingly sustained.[40] In 'Roof of the World', the boys' unrealistic expectations, implied in their experimentation with gravity, are punctured to show excessive bravura overreaching itself. Here, Mick's prayers and invocations to the Blessed Mary, uttered to meet a tense situation, do not halt his inevitable crash to the ground.

The three stories about Davin's return differ in mood and effect. 'A Return' is comic and macabre, while 'First Flight' and 'Bluff Retrospect', which are more reflective, demonstrate some growth in their protagonists' moral awareness. Both 'First Flight' and 'A Return' are based on encounters with family members which force the narrator to weigh up the effects of time passing. In 'A Return', the so-called march of progress is symbolised by the replacement of gorse hedges with wire fences on his cousin's farm and a new roughcast house with electricity;[41] in 'First Flight' the narrator observes the changes to his father's circumstances now that his mother has died. Both stories register deaths in the family: in the former his cousin mimics the voices of the departed family members including his deceased father, bringing the family momentarily back to life; in the latter, the narrator observes the effects of his mother's death on his father and sister, and speculates on his father's future.[42] The third in this sequence, 'Bluff Retrospect', is a fitting conclusion to all the Southland stories published in these two volumes. The narrator, Martin, inspired by memories of childhood, visits Bluff with its impressive coastal views, and reflects on his family's Irish origins and ancestry. He is similar to Martin of 'First Flight' who, after meeting his father's estranged second wife (a widow whom he married after his mother's death), sees him afresh as a Galwayman, 'not quite the stereotype of the New Zealand working man', and still bearing the marks of his peasant Irish culture, 'a dignity, a pride in being a man'. In 'Bluff Retrospect', meditation on the place of Maori in New Zealand society leads the narrator to a comparison with his parents and their migrant community.[43] Gazing across Foveaux Strait from Bluff Hill, Martin recalls the family's earlier Regatta Day visits to Argyle Park and the occasion when a Maori woman admonished his mother and aunt for picnicking on tapu ground. His embarrassment at this incident leads him to consider his parents' attitudes towards Maori, noting the shift of sensibility which separates him from their generation. In revising his own attitudes, he now sees Maori as more like his own family: a dispossessed minority group. In these and the five 'boyhood' stories, the exploration of the protagonists' moral and psychological growth is matched by variation of narrative technique, a more ambitious handling of point of view, and the use of first-person narrators, sometimes with different identities. He is Martin in 'Goosey's Gallic War', 'First Flight' and 'Bluff Retrospect' – the same name as the university student protagonist, Martin Cody, in *Not Here, Not Now* (1960) – and Ned in 'The Quiet One' – the name of Mick's father or older brother in the Mick Connolly stories, and suggestive of the psychological awareness associated with this character.

Although in his *Collected Stories* Davin interleaves some of these stories with earlier ones to suggest a chronologically expanded Mick Connolly sequence,[44] they in fact reinterpret Mick's Southland from the perspectives of the travelled, European-based expatriate. Davin's decision, made about this time, to remain permanently in England creates further distance. 'First Flight' concludes with the sobering realisation that departure from home is final; Martin realises that his father's dream of returning to Galway is one he must avoid: 'I had been warned by books that you could never go back'. 'Bluff Retrospect' also pre-empts the same deluded dream of a return: 'King Arthur never came back'. Its reappraisal of the place of the Irish minority community in New Zealand history and culture is just one strand in the development of Davin's work; in general, moral complexity and psychological reflection develop from the instinctive naturalism of the Mick Connolly stories of *The Gorse Blooms Pale*, making stories of *Breathing Spaces* such as 'Presents', 'The Tree' and 'The Quiet One' examples of Davin's mature art. They must be counted among the best of all his work.

III Uncollected and New Stories: 1934-89

By the time of his retirement in September 1978 as Academic Publisher of Clarendon Press at Oxford University Press, where he had worked since 1945, Davin began to lose the routine which had enabled him to write novels.[45] Instead the short-story format, and that of essays, memoirs, obituaries, reviews and poems, were more congenial.[46] Davin published two more collections of his own, *Selected Stories* (1981)[47] and *The Salamander and the Fire: Collected War Stories* (1986).[48] In the last decade of his life he returned to his childhood and youth and in four of the five war stories published during this time he draws on or invents Southland characters or incidents as alternative settings.[49]

Memories of incidents which occurred in Gore – where the family moved to when he was one and lived until he was seven – and Invercargill – their subsequent home, where Davin lived until he was sixteen – are the basis for four 'Southland' stories, published between 1985 and 1989, and also the manuscript of 'Failed Exorcism'.[50] Also included in the present volume is 'Prometheus', the only story Davin wrote and published before he left New Zealand. It won the Literary Society Competition at the University of Otago in 1934, and was published in the Otago University *Review*. Although a whole career of writing separates 'Prometheus' from the later stories, its setting in Bluff provides a regional parallel to the others set in Otautau/Aparima, Gore, and Invercargill.

'Prometheus', set in the shortages of employment during the Depression, consists of the musings of a mortally ill young man who, because he belongs to the union, has been hired as casual labour on the wharves in Bluff.[51] Morally compromised about getting work due to the protection of the union and his father's influence as a union man, Jack Petrie considers the impasse that his personal circumstances have created: suffering from advanced TB, he could either marry his girlfriend as he would like to and risk infecting her, or he could act unselfishly and abstain, thereby possibly sparing her life. Aptly named, the story hinges on its analogy to the situation of the classical figure Prometheus: of being trapped in a seemingly irresolvable situation. Although brief and undeveloped as a narrative, it anticipates many features of Davin's later work: the vignette style, the representation of a young man's train of thought, precisely observed detail, a working-class vernacular, the male-centred activity and values which resurface in many of the war stories, the psychological dilemma (here represented as an inner struggle correlated to the seemingly mindless activity of unloading the carriages).

The five 'late' stories may be read in the light of Davin's statement in his introduction to *Selected Stories* that 'The stories I have selected here are not only an attempt at repayment but an apologia, a reminder to my country that to leave it physically does not necessarily imply desertion or estrangement'.[52] Davin's Southland childhood remains important for its shaping influence upon him; in different ways the stories pay tribute to those who made him into the person he became. The act of remembering details of places and events appears to be more conscious than in earlier stories which seamlessly represent Mick's sense of wonder and ease of occupancy, but their narrative structures are also more self-consciously retrospective and orally nuanced.[53] This group is morally and thematically complex. Davin uses the experience of childhood to address the problems of age and encroaching death. Distance from his homeland becomes a cipher for a more universal sense of alienation, while his desire for psychological reconnection is confirmed by the meditative approach to the landscapes of his youth. The motif of the return appears in four of the stories, although less explicitly than in 'A Return', 'First Flight' and 'Bluff Retrospect'.[54] Instead the narrator's departure from, then return to, home and family is an organisational principle, a framing device. In all except 'Failed Exorcism', the voice is that of an unnamed young boy, although typically it is the older narrator telling the story who controls its subjectivity. In commenting on and evaluating the experiences of his younger self, Davin also 'returns home' again without making the geographical journey. These are small acts of reconciliation; he reconnects with his parents, acknowledges their values which have shaped his, and through this act of filial homage connects their Irish-Catholic identity with that of other marginal ethnic groups in Southland.

The narrator of 'The Albatross' is an infrequent visitor to the farm near Otautau on which he was raised: 'I ... had fled the coop long before and came back only very seldom.' The story's analeptic opening, 'When we were kids', stresses the time-lag between the occurrence of the incident and the present moment of narration. Davin's difficulty in introducing a narrator who is separate from the protagonist appears in the long opening excursus on the hero – Hawk Metzger, rouseabout and First World War veteran – which delays the narrative proper as the narrator admits, 'I seem to have got a long way from the point'. Davin develops symbolic and thematic links: Metzger is implicitly likened to the wounded albatross because both manage to return to 'base', Hawk during the war after he had shot down the German pilot, and the albatross to the elements once its wing has healed. Davin's further aim in telling of the children who find a wounded albatross, nurse it back to health and then release it, would seem to be to reverse the Coleridgean negative associations of the Ancient Mariner who shoots the albatross and is condemned to a life of unredeemed misery.[55] Not only is a positive outcome hinted at (Hawk later marries the narrator's younger sister), but the Ancient Mariner's trademark 'glittering eye' (which Mick Connnolly observes in his father in 'Late Snow' and which albatross and Hawk share in this story) suggests access to knowledge of a world beyond earthly bounds, experiences which cannot be articulated, and an ability to carry out what had to be done: 'And they'd always know when the right time had come to do whatever it might be.' The narrator's comment as he watches the albatross soar – 'I thought for the first time I might myself glide away some day magically like that' – suggests, however, that the bird symbolises freedom within a non-human realm. The final sentence redefines freedom as paradoxically a loss of human mobility; although Hawk too was free, 'he had done with flying and gliding for ever.' Yet these hints at a deeper meaning in events or even a different reality from that of the farm are not developed further.

The two stories about Gore, 'Black Diamond' and 'The Black Stranger', alongside Davin's last published story, 'Gardens of Exile', share a common structure. In each, the child-protagonist enjoys outdoor adventures with one or more of his brothers but it is the events which occur upon their return home which control the story's meaning. 'Black Diamond', like 'The Albatross', is an anecdotal recounting of a single incident in a reflective, even digressive style but, in extending its central study of the meaning of 'black' in the longer 'The Black Stranger', and in turning to the related theme of exile in the story which follows, 'Gardens of Exile', Davin shows control over a wealth of incident and detail. In these last two stories he relates events to his moral philosophy, defining a metaphysical universe in ways which supersede all earlier narratives.

'The Black Stranger' and 'Black Diamond' overlap in content, theme and setting. In examining the adult world from a child's perspective, the narrator considers how family members have represented worldly affairs. Irish phrases like 'black stranger' refer to the dangers of the world away from home 'outside the light and the family'; similarly families, in order to keep going, dream that things will turn out the better for them, that 'they're going to get to the end of the rainbow'. In 'Black Diamond' the narrator comments that as children they thought 'grown ups were a pretty odd lot'. This story is unique as a retrospective narrative that draws on a Second World War setting and context. Like 'The Albatross', it works through developing significant associations around a central image showing accretions of meaning. It opens in the Western Desert, where the allied troops are moving on Rommel's forces in Tripoli in 1942. The narrator invokes the tactical sign of the New Zealand Division, the 'Black Diamond', to recall an incident when he lived in Gore: he and his brother created a makeshift trolley to collect shards of superior Black Diamond coal for home from the railway yards. The story ends on a note of optimism, with the new-born baby being christened Donal Dhu or Daniel Black: 'Black Diamond'. Davin's technique of concluding on a note of a heightened recognition as in 'The Albatross', rather than exploring the implications of events, means that the story's desert opening does not become an interpretative frame at the end.

'The Black Stranger' develops the meaning of 'black' further. As in 'Black Diamond' the phrase, 'the black stranger', with its negative connotations, is associated with trouble: the narrator's aunt is visiting from Auckland to look after the family who are suffering from the 1918–19 Asian flu pandemic, brought by the troops returning from the Great

War. In both stories the theme of 'the black stranger' recalls the inherited Irish Protestant and Catholic hostilities of Davin's parents' generation, hostilities which are touched upon in 'The Apostate', 'Late Snow', 'Goosey's Gallic War' and *Roads from Home*. But the real black stranger is a negro whom the narrator and his older brother find on their excursion into the countryside; he has caught the flu and crept into a barn to die. This discovery and his parents' reactions provide new contexts by which to redefine these inherited phrases. There are both socio-cultural and emotional contexts: the negro has fought with other Americans in France, and the narrator's mother sees the dead man as an itinerant victim of war, who wanders from door to door trying to sell boot and floor polish, seeking charity from residents ('the black stranger', as she sees herself). Although his father calls the deceased a 'poor old black stranger', his mother has compassion for his plight. Her comment that he had 'not even the black stranger to help him or a priest to confess to, no kith or kin, just like a lonely Protestant' severs the link between black stranger and black Protestant, and expands the semantic implications of the term to include Catholic connotations of mercy, last rites, and sympathy for the suffering of the dying. Davin applies his own experiences of expatriation and dislocation, and feelings which embrace death, desolation and loneliness, to the limited meanings of 'black' and 'stranger' that he encountered as a child; he rewrites the imported Irish diction of his parent's generation into a more universalising synthesis. 'Stranger' comes to refer to other races and ethnic types than the Irish and Celtic; furthermore the term is granted a redemptive value through the compassion of the mother in this story, thereby superseding its origins in political conflict. In the same way in 'Black Diamond', the naming of the baby Donal Dhu reverses the older connotations of Irish 'Dhu' as the outside world of the black stranger, relocating this figure within the home, endowing it with intimacy.

Davin is concerned with social and personal injustice as well as liberty and death in these last stories. The narrator observes through his parents how the Irish-Catholic heritage was adapted to the realities of living in Southland in the early twentieth century, and from this perspective displays a concern for other migrant groups. In 'Gardens of Exile',[56] 'looking back' on his past, he recalls his parents' sympathy for the Chinese market gardeners and launderers in Southland, as a marginal group alienated from their own society in a foreign Anglo-Saxon culture. The narrator identifies them with his father's estrangement from his native Galway – '20 or 30 years … by now' – with its mixed memories. The story's themes can be traced to his early fascination with the sounds of different speakers in Invercargill, of which the Irish were just one:

> I used to marvel at the variety of accents, and variations of locution, in the Scottish, English and Irish voices I heard about me, the differences in the ways my own family spoke, and the speech of my teachers, the Marist Brothers, of priests in the pulpits, of shopkeepers and farmers, and all those others who came and went in our small town.[57]

Like 'The Black Stranger', which begins with the boys leaving home on their adventure, 'Gardens of Exile' opens with the boys on the move again, this time in the middle of their hunting trip, running through the Southland landscape their dogs alongside them. They have gone further than before, spreading out in a wide arc from Waimatua to Rimu, a distance of some fifteen miles (twenty-four kilometres), and are on the homeward run. Despite the boys being laid up by their new ferret and chased by Old Black Jack Fahey in Waimatua, the rabbiting trip is a success in terms of bounty. On the Oteramika Road into town, they meet their father who, while waiting for them, has been a fascinated eavesdropper on Chinese market gardeners talking inside their shack, absorbed in the sounds of their voices. The protagonist ponders this mystery until he finds himself in the same position: listening outside the dining room door to his father speaking Gaelic to the newly arrived Irish from Galway, people he has met at the Basilica and invited home to lunch. Aware for the first time of his father's command of Gaelic and his gifts as a storyteller, he concludes that, as when emerging from a Tom Mix film, you find yourself in two worlds with the one you'd come out of 'somehow more suitable for you'.

Paradoxically, the narrator's father's curiosity about the foreign sounds of Chinese speech suggests greater possibilities – pathways to other peoples and cultures – rather than the outdoor spaces that the boys have traversed on their hunting trip. The narrator realises that these possibilities are mediated by difference: Gaelic speakers like his father would have encountered cultural and linguistic barriers, and the recent arrivals from

Galway are as alien to the English-speaking Southland community as the Chinese are. Language identifies these minority groups as distinct and apart, yet the common experience of cultural dislocation links them. This leads to the narrator's final revelation when he sees his father's loneliness after the Irish depart: 'I know now he understood the inside of what the Chinese were saying, even if he didn't know a word of it.' It encourages him to see that, although his father's knowledge of Gaelic makes him separate from himself, their shared migrant identity binds them: like the Chinese, both live in 'gardens of exile'.[58] This recognition can be linked to Davin's own self-imposed exile, choosing neither to live in New Zealand where he was born, nor in Ireland, home of his ancestors, but instead in England, somewhere between the two. As such the story enacts a return, one which attempts to link together these different journeys.

All four stories show accretions of meaning. This is due to Davin's transformation of his childhood into a space for meditation about his family origins, and his subsequent life as an 'intimate stranger' to that earlier state and to his home in New Zealand. Davin's private concerns are refracted through dualistic narrative structures which show the narrators both 'at home' and simultaneously distant from it. Childhood and adulthood are no longer divided states of innocence and experience but re-form in new configurations as childhood provides the occasion for philosophical meditation. In their metaphysical searching these stories supersede the poem 'Perspective' with its disenchantment at the loss of purity and a childhood arcadia. Davin's spiritual perceptions can be found in metaphoric links made between the species in 'The Albatross', in which 'seagulls were the souls of sailors, but souls of captains became albatrosses', and the meaningful glitter and glare in the eye which associate the albatross with the rouseabout Hawk. The albatross's moment of flight opens up wider horizons: it will go where humans cannot follow. These horizons are matched in the undiscovered realms of Ned's 'deep dream of his own mind' in 'The Black Stranger', by the retrospective resonating of the Black Diamond sign for the narrator of 'Black Diamond', and by the different world which the narrator feels he has entered when overhearing Gaelic in 'Gardens of Exile'.

Two features distinguish 'The Black Stranger' and 'Gardens of Exile' from all other stories: the observation of the passing of the day and the appearance of a cosmology of stars, sun and moon. These can be read respectively as tributes to Davin's mother and father. Their contrasting imagery – the glittering and brittle white frost in the Gore story, and the moon 'a miserable sliver' against the dark shadows in the Invercargill one – together create a chiaroscuro that might be identified as the black and white in Davin's life itself. This light-and-dark contrast also represents his own form of resolution and reconciliation with his origins.

Such a reconciliation comes with a heightened naturalistic appreciation of the indifferent forces of time and death, and a turning away from Catholic ceremony and practice. In 'The Black Stranger', the hint of Christian eschatology informing the mother's response to the stranger's death is stated without narratorial involvement; the dead seagull – which the child thinks of as 'the Holy Ghost, its wings were so beautifully folded' – is followed by an admonition not to be superstitious. When he invokes '"Heavenly Powers"' as protection against the unknown, he quickly adds, 'I was only saying what Mum would have said.' Images of mortality permeate this story about death: the gate which opened onto the railway is 'like an old man who'd got somewhere first, and was still there but no use any more, just staring at whatever passed by'; the dusk 'closed in behind us every step we took, like a dying ghost'. As in 'The Albatross', these images are reinforced by possibilities yet to be realised ('neither of us knew the plot but ... he [Ned] would insist on going through with the action whatever it was'). In 'Gardens of Exile', thoughts of death occur: the narrator's fantasy that Black Jack Fahey would soon be in the Waimatua cemetery is followed by his mother gloomily imagining that the worst had happened to her children. A symbolic reading is also possible: the hinterland beyond Invercargill, the wide arc ranged by the boys and the homeward turn define the trajectory of the mature narrator's life. The sunset and onset of darkness suggest the workings of memory to bring the mind as well as the body toward rest: a shift of perspective to which the boys' unexpected meeting with their father belongs.

Also contributing to the balance between mood and event in 'Gardens of Exile' is the sudden switch into nightmare. The narrator dreams he is bailed up in the cowshed by Billy McNab, an old Chinaman who lived in a hut nearby and who the boys looked upon 'as a pet rather than as a real stranger'. In the dream disguised as Fu Man Chu with moustaches, McNab is wielding a long knife. With him is Jack Fahey with a shillelagh and 'they were coming at me for stealing what they lived by'. His father, a witness, refuses to take sides. This record of the mind's unconscious activity is unique in Davin's Southland stories and the sequence demarcates the narrative turning-point from the boys' return home to the narrator's re-enactment of his father's behaviour, listening outside the door to the sounds of a different language. But the narrator's concluding impression of emerging from an alternative world 'somehow more suitable for you' contrasts to the dream landscape which exposes his guilt in plundering others' resources, so darkening his homecoming. It counterbalances the unconscious fears of menace and risk imposed by unexpected encounters, with the more 'heimlich' connotations of home: of intimacy, containment and harmony.

These final stories count among the 'last things' for Davin, who had renounced Catholicism, confirmed his harshly secular philosophy of life through his experiences of the Second World War, and lived an expatriate life in England. As his mixed memories convert the Southland landscape into a setting for encounters which are both affectionate and problematic, the stories constitute a kind of homecoming. There is a refusal to move towards transcendent values; instead, the warm embrace of the domestic realm is reinforced by what appears to be excluded.

This homecoming is the subject matter of what seems to be Davin's final story, 'Failed Exorcism', written in February 1989. Davin returns to his school days at Marist Brothers' School in Invercargill from Standard Four to his departure after the Fifth Form for Sacred Heart College in Auckland in 1930 and his final departure from Invercargill for Oxford in 1936. Fuelling the narrative is the sense of personal grievance that the narrator experiences at the hands of the Marist Brothers; the psychological humiliations they inflict, such as the treachery by which he is made to expose his brothers' spelling mistake, rankle more than the physical torments suffered in the boys' fight with which the story opens. The title suggests that the story is a retaliation to Brother Tarcisius's demonisation of the protagonist, his resolve to 'drive the devil out of you', after the narrator and his friend Hap despatch the school cane into the fire. The mood is savage and bleak, as cold as the leaking schoolroom, and it matches the Catholic education which demanded rewriting the textbook to foreground Irish victories and insisted on copious demonstrations of piety. Brother Tarcisius is imaged in terms of oppressive political power – black boots 'like a soldier's' and a swishing cassock. The impression of his rigid emotional control is reinforced by his insistence on addressing the narrator with the more formal 'Michael' rather than the affectionate Mick of earlier stories. The narrator's revenge is completed in the final, dismissive sentence; returning some years later to Invercargill before taking up his scholarship overseas – now a local success, farewelling his school friends and family – he reminds Brother Tarcisius of his failure to fulfil his vow. Upon hearing him apologise the narrator comments, 'He didn't explain, and I didn't ask him, whether he was apologising for his bad memory or for his dereliction of duty.'

The unforgiving mood of 'Failed Exorcism' sets it apart from Davin's reconciliations with his family in other stories written during this decade. It can, however, be read as a coda to their themes and concerns: its unrepentant attitude reflects Davin's break with Catholicism after he left New Zealand and suggests some rejection of the culture which supported the faith. No greater contrast with the tender, vulnerable narrator of the opening story 'The Apostate' can be imagined, yet 'Failed Exorcism' exhibits the same scepticism developed through a rigorous exposure of what appear as human flaws in a dubious system. In this scepticism, perpetuated by a mix of high spirits and enraged disappointment, Davin's career as a writer comes full circle.

Davin's Southland short stories are usually considered as the best of his writing. Their blend of intimate affection, despair and moral complexity exhibits the strengths of the mainstream realist tradition of the 1930s and 1940s with which he has been associated as one of the 'Sons of Frank Sargeson'.[59] Certainly his gifts for anecdotal narration and philosophical reflection came together more strongly in the short story than in the novel, for he had mixed success with the ambitious scope and complex plot demands of this latter genre. The positive reception to *The Gorse Blooms Pale* upon its publication in 1947 laid the foundation for a significant post-war reputation in New Zealand and the UK; this was reinforced by Davin's critical judgements and authoritative pronouncements on his craft and the practice of fiction writing in general, as presented in editorials, reviews and articles from the 1950s to the

1980s.[60] But the shift away from realism alongside the perceived decline in Davin's later work – apart from near unanimous praise for his last novel, *Brides of Price* (1972), and his memoir, *Closing Times* (1975) – has led to the view that he did not fulfil his early promise and moreover became out of step with the times.[61] Such perceptions can be revised with a new look at the work itself.

This volume brings his Southland stories up to date by including the six previously uncollected stories in the expectation that they will continue to appeal, that their perceptive portrayals of Southland life in the 1920s and 1930s will remain as relevant today as when they were first written, and that the experiences of his boyhood which so preoccupied Davin will attract new readers. It is hoped that the 'late' works, presented in relation to the achievements of the Mick Connolly sequence and the best stories of *Breathing Spaces*, can be read as evidence of a minor revival. During his last difficult years, Davin's passionate engagement with the locale and events of his early life encouraged him to find ways of expanding the range of the short story as he had originally conceived it. Southland is recreated *sub specie aeternitatis* as he reaches out one last time, across the distance of a lifetime spent half a world away, to recapture his most vivid experiences of growing up.

NOTES

[1] Donald Harman Akenson, an historian of the Irish diaspora, calls this the 'Michael Collins sequence', claiming that the initials M.C. (also in the name, Martin Cody, the protagonist of Davin's novel, *Not Here, Not Now* (1970)) refer to the Irish Republican Army hero. But Ovenden points out that Davin was called McCabe by his brothers and M.C. may equally well be an abbreviation of this family nickname. See Donald Harman Akenson, *Half the World from Home: Perspectives on the Irish in New Zealand, 1850–1950* (Wellington: Victoria University Press, 1990), pp. 96–7; Keith Ovenden, *A Fighting Withdrawal: The Life of Dan Davin, Writer, Soldier, Publisher* (Oxford and New York: OUP, 1996), p. 18.

[2] Akenson, *Half the World from Home*, p. 97.

[3] R.A. Copland in 'The Fictive Picture: Cole, Courage and Davin' says 'he sees the place more with the eyes of a historian, than with those of the original inhabitant ... the effect is of a child being watched'. Copland and also Lawrence Jones in *Barbed Wire and Mirrors* point to the influence of the early James Joyce on Davin's narrative technique. See R.A. Copland, 'The Fictive Picture: Cole, Courage, Davin', in *Critical Essays on the New Zealand Short Story*, ed. Cherry Hankin (Auckland: Heinemann, 1982), p. 73;

Lawrence Jones, *Barbed Wire and Mirrors: Essays on New Zealand Prose* (Dunedin: Otago University Press, 1987), pp. 88–9.

4 See Jones, *Barbed Wire and Mirrors*, p. 18: '*The Gorse Blooms Pale* looks now like one of the most significant of the postwar volumes of New Zealand stories'. Jones also comments (p. 88) that the best of Davin's short stories 'are those dealing with childhood and adolescence in Southland'.

5 James Bertram, *Dan Davin*. Writers and their Work (Auckland: OUP, 1983), p. 14; E.H. McCormick, *New Zealand Literature; A Survey* (London: OUP, 1959), p. 156. John Reece Cole agreed: 'they are acutely realised and clearly conveyed'; *Landfall* 2:2 (June, 1948): 149. The volume was reviewed somewhat critically in the *New Zealand Listener*, 12 March 1948. The reviewer, possibly Oliver Duff, commented that few were stories in the accepted sense but mostly 'sketches and character studies with action'. See Ovenden, *FW*, p. 226.

6 K. John, *Illustrated London News*, 31 January 1948: 132; Walter Allen, *New Statesman and Nation* 35:83: 7 February 1948, p. 119; see also Pamela Hanford Johnson, *John O'London's Weekly*, 20 February 1948.

7 Dan Davin, *Closing Times* (London: OUP, 1975), pp. 47–8.

8 Davin's questioning of the godliness of God appears in the poem 'Deity' which won first prize in the Literary Society's Competition and was published in the Otago University *Review*, 1935. It opens: 'It is a terrible thing to be God;/ Holding the hand of His omnipotence,/ Crushing down pity beneath the weight of destiny;/ To be of infinite mercy, and infinitely strong,/ In the resolve not to intervene/ But to preserve/ The perfection of the great design'.

9 Lawrence Jones argues of the *Selected Stories* in *Barbed Wire and Mirrors* (p. 87) that Davin's sceptical philosophy comes from 'a rejection of Catholicism for a bleak naturalistic vision, of man as conscious creature in an unconscious universe, a victim of the indifferent forces of Sex, Time and Death'. The 'bleak naturalistic vision' is not strongly evident in the childhood stories, which as Denis Lenihan points out are set in the time before Davin's rejection of his faith (in Oxford, sometime between September 1936 and 1939. See Ovenden, *FW,* p. 103); however they are written after that rejection, and either during, or just after he himself had been involved in, war. Their outlook is subtly informed from the standpoint from which they are written. Delia Davin points out that he never wanted to shoot rabbits after the war, though as a child he hunted them constantly.

10 Jones, *Barbed Wire and Mirrors*, p. 86.

11 Copland, 'The Fictive Picture: Cole, Courage, Davin', p. 75.

12 M.H. Holcroft, *Old Invercargill* (John McIndoe: Dunedin, 1976), p. 84.

13 See further, Akenson, *Half the World from Home*, p.103.

14 Akenson, *Half the World from Home*, pp. 90, 121; Jones, *Barbed Wire and Mirrors*, p. 86. Jones (p. 92) also cites Bertram's appreciation of its documentary value in 'Dan Davin: Novelist of Exile' and Michael Beveridge's view of him in *Landfall* 24 (September 1970) as a chronicler of Irish-Catholic Southland.

15 Holcroft, *Old Invercargill*, p. 83; Akenson, *Half the World from Home*, p. 90.

16 To Jones (*Barbed Wire and Mirrors,* p. 89) and Cole (*Landfall:* 149), this story demonstrates Davin's weaknesses of over-plotting and over-writing; but Bertram (*Dan Davin*, p. 15) praises it as a 'brilliant little dialogue piece'.

17 Jones (*Barbed Wire and Mirrors*, p. 86) claims that Davin only fully brings together the social historian, the philosopher and the psychological moralist in the brief vignettes 'Saturday Night' and 'The Quiet One'. But this can also be said of late stories, 'The Black Stranger' and 'Gardens of Exile'.

18 Dan Davin, Introduction to *Selected Stories* (Wellington: Victoria University Press with Price Milburn & Co.; London: Robert Hale, 1981), p. 10.

19 Akenson, *Half the World from Home*, pp. 119–20. Ovenden (FW, pp. 24–5) says the political and cultural tradition at home was oral not literary.

20 Davin, 'Introduction' to *Collected Stories*, p. 14.

21 In his interview with Dave Arthur (unpublished. 15 January 1986), Davin comments 'what you have to do is to set off with a certain set of characters, and they may be based in reality, but unless they subtly alter in accordance with the shape of the story, then it isn't a story, it's autobiography'.

22 Akenson argues in *Half the World from Home* (pp. 106–7) that the social system Davin describes belongs to the 'pure type of national Irish-Catholic pattern'. Jones (*Barbed Wire and Mirrors,* p. 94) points out that Davin's 'personal vision' in the novels enables the provincial society to fit into 'a pattern of human change and struggle.'

23 Dan Davin to Frank Sargeson, 25 September 1955. Cited in Ovenden, *FW,* p. 275.

24 Holcroft (*Old Invercargill*, pp. 125–6) notes that at the beginning of the First World War, comics and boys' magazines flooded into Invercargill from Fleet Street. School boys became avid readers of *Chums*.

25 Also spelt as 'shangeyes'; see *ODNZE*.

26 Copland ('The Fictive Picture', pp. 75–6) complains of the 'false notes' and 'unacceptable pedantry' of this story, but it is partly a rhetorical exercise designed to prove a point about education.

27 Davin, through the good offices of Brother Egbert, won a scholarship which paid a subscription to the Public Library; he also used the Railway library. He makes no reference to his childhood reading of Walter Scott and Dickens in the Mick Connolly stories. See Ovenden, *FW,* p. 30.

28 Jones (*Barbed Wire and Mirrors*, p. 89) claims they rely on 'melodrama from the past', noting that they resemble the overplotting of Davin's novels. Copland ('The Fictive Picture', p. 76) notes a sense of strain in parts of 'A Meeting Half Way'. But 'A Happy New Year' is praised by John Reece Cole for showing 'that which is flat and grey in the New Zealand character and mood' (*Landfall* 2:2 (1948): 150). Davin's interest in Sargeson's style appears in 'The Narrative Technique of Frank Sargeson' in Helen Shaw, ed., *The Puritan and the Waif. A Symposium of Critical Essays on the Work of Frank Sargeson* (Auckland: H.L. Hofmann, 1954), pp. 56–71.

29 The epithet comes from Denis Lenihan.

30 Bertram, *Dan Davin*, p. 16.

31 'Hydra', 'Boarding House Episode' and 'In the Basement'.

32 That is, between July and September 1939, after his Oxford finals; in 1941–2 when in Cairo with GHQ military intelligence; in 1943 when Davin was on leave in the UK; and in 1944 after being seconded to Intelligence in London. See Davin, *Selected Stories*, pp. 12–3. 'Milk Round', written en route from Alexandria to Piraeus in March 1941, is possibly the first of the Connolly sequence (see Ovenden, *FW*, p. 137). The war stories,

'Jaundiced', 'Danger's Flower', 'Under the Bridge', and 'In Transit', were published in English journals 1942–5.

[33] Ovenden, *FW,* p 137.

[34] Davin's introduction to his edition of *Katherine Mansfield: Selected Stories* concludes by acknowledging her universal appeal: 'most ... of us have been children ... and for most the family has at one time been the world'. See Dan Davin, ed., introduction, *Katherine Mansfield: Selected Stories* (London: Oxford World Classics, 1981 [1953]), vii–xvii.

[35] Davin acknowledges this in his discussion of the genre in the introduction to *The Salamander and the Fire* (xiii), saying that due to an historian's training 'I ... found myself unable to name a place or even cite a map reference which was not at least hypothetically compatible with the topographical'.

[36] In his edition (1976) of Davin's *Roads from Home*, Lawrence Jones includes three maps of Invercargill and its environs. See Akenson, *Half the World From Home*, p. 98.

[37] Six were published separately: 'A Return' in c. 1948; 'The Quiet One' in September 1949; 'Presents' in 1953; 'Goosey's Gallic War', 'Roof of the World' and 'First Flight' in 1968–9.

[38] In *Barbed Wire and Mirrors* (p. 88), Jones points to Davin's 'diminishing capital' of memories and lack of firsthand experience of New Zealand after 1936 as major disadvantages. However in the best of the 'late' stories, Davin extends his repertoire with reflection on, and interpretation of, his early experiences.

[39] See Ovenden (*FW*, pp. 241–4), on the events of this visit.

[40] Lawrence Jones, *Barbed Wire and Mirrors,* p. 89; Copland, 'The Fictive Picture', p. 75. Both critique this story for being over-elaborate and literary.

[41] This has been criticised for fragmentariness and overplotting. See Patricia Craig, review of *Selected Stories*, *TLS*, 12 June 1981: 660; Jones, *Barbed Wire and Mirrors*, p. 89.

[42] This was singled out in the review of *Breathing Spaces* by Peter Campbell (*TLS,* 24 October, 1975: 1255) as a 'situation report' by a 'modest observer'.

[43] This story has recently inspired work by other artists with a Bluff connection: by the sculptor, Steve Mulqueen, based around the translation of Orepuki or Papakihau, as 'slapped by the wind', and Brian Potiki whose play, *Motupohue* (2006), opens with Davin writing 'Bluff Retrospect' in his Oxford study.

[44] 'Presents' appears after 'Milk Round' and before 'Late Snow'. 'Roof of the World', 'The Tree' and 'Goosey's Gallic War' are inserted between 'Death of a Dog' and 'The Basket', and 'The Quiet One' between 'Growing Up' and 'That Golden Time'. 'A Return' and 'First Flight' are in Part III which follows the group of war stories in Part II. I have kept them distinct for reasons suggested above.

[45] That is, in retreats in the Scilly Isles where Kenneth Sisam, his mentor from Oxford University Press, lived in retirement. When Sisam died in 1969 these also ended. See Ovenden, *FW*, p. 367.

[46] This had been the case throughout his career. In the Introduction to *The Salamander and the Fire* (xi), Davin writes that the short story was more suitable 'for rapid composition and revision in what little time might be available'.

[47] Its three sections correspond to his major themes in this genre: Southland, the war, and several stories associated with travel: 'A Return', 'First Flight', and the tour de force, 'The Locksmith Laughs Last', set in New York. In 1982 Davin's edition of war stories, *Night Attack: Short Stories from the Second World War*, was published.

[48] Selected from stories published in the two earlier collections and including five additional stories published between 1980 and 1985, with the exception of 'Fancy Dress', which was published in *London Magazine* 26: 9 & 10 (December 1986/January 1987): 22–31.

[49] Memories, or fictionalised accounts of his Southland boyhood, appear in stories set in Italy and the Western Desert: for example 'The Dog and the Dead' (1980), 'Finders and Losers' (1980), 'When Mum Died' (1982) and 'Cassino Casualty' (1984). The only exception is 'North of the Sangro' (1984). 'Black Diamond' (1984) is a singular 'cross-over' story; it opens in the desert, but its real setting is in Gore almost thirty years earlier.

[50] Another unpublished story dating from this time is 'The Unjust and the Loving', an anecdote about a little girl Davin met as his classmate in Gore at the age of five or six.

[51] Davin retells this story in *Not Here, Not Now* (pp. 273–7) from the point of view of his hero, Martin Cody, the 'compassionate labourer', equivalent to the Irish strong man in 'Prometheus' who helps out the enfeebled Jack Petrie. It concludes with the union's moral spoken by Martin's father – that no individual should work more efficiently than any other in order to maintain the same work schedules with management and hence the same rate of pay.

[52] Davin, *Selected Stories*, p.14.

[53] In their memoirs in *Intimate Stranger: Reminiscences of Dan Davin*, both Tom Hogan and Margot Ross comment on Davin's attempts to recover his past whenever he visited New Zealand. From 1969 he corresponded with Natalie Dolamore, a retired librarian, about Gore during the time he lived there. See Janet Wilson, ed., *Intimate Stranger: Reminiscences of Dan Davin* (Wellington: Steele Roberts, 2000), pp. 31, 64.

[54] Davin, with Winnie, visited New Zealand twice during these years: in 1978, as part of a retirement trip of the OUP offices throughout the world, and in 1984, when he was awarded an Honorary Doctorate of Literature by the University of Otago. He had also returned in 1959 and in 1969.

[55] As a boy Davin accidentally killed with his shanghai the drake of a local carrier, Murray. This story may be an attempt to expiate his guilt, and relieve the weight of this metaphorical 'albatross', although Delia Davin points out that this incident was part of Winnie's childhood, not Dan's. See Ovenden, *FW*, p. 28.

[56] Davin thought this was one of his best stories, saying in the interview with Dave Arthur, 'There's some underlying poetic element in it. Everyone that's spoken to me about it has felt this inner depth to it.'

[57] Dan Davin, 'My Language and Myself: English as Creative Power', *The Round Table: The Commonwealth Journal of International Affairs,* 261 (January 1976): 19.

[58] See Louis MacNeice's impression of him: 'I was an antipodean, a topsy-turvy man; an Irishman who was not of Ireland' (Davin, *Closing Times*, p. 47).

[59] See Lydia Wevers, 'The Short Story', in *The Oxford History of New Zealand Literature in English*, ed. Terry Sturm (Auckland: OUP, 1991), p. 230.

[60] Notable is Davin's influential edition of *New Zealand Short Stories*, in the Oxford University Press World's Classics series, first published in 1953 and often reprinted.

[61] See, for example, Lawrence Jones's review of Davin's *Selected Stories*, *Landfall* 36 (1982): 93–9. Jones' review is reprinted in *Barbed Wire and Mirrors*, pp. 86–90. On the reception of *Brides of Price* and *Closing Times*, see Ovenden, *FW*, pp. 338, 349, 353–4.

Works Cited

ABBREVIATIONS

DNZB: *Dictionary of New Zealand Biography,* Vol. 5 (1941–60), ed. Claudia Orange (Wellington: Ministry for Culture and Heritage, 2000), http://www/dnzb.govt.nz.

DSUE: *The New Partridge Dictionary of Slang and Unconventional English*, ed. Tom Dalzell and Terry Victor, 2 vols. (London: Routledge, 2006).

FW: Keith Ovenden. *A Fighting Withdrawal: The Life of Dan Davin, Writer, Soldier, Publisher* (Oxford and New York: OUP, 1996).

IS: *Intimate Stranger: Reminiscences of Dan Davin*, ed. Janet Wilson (Wellington: Steele Roberts, 2000).

ODNZE: *The Dictionary of New Zealand English: A Dictionary of New Zealandisms on Historical Principles*, ed. H.W. Orsman (Auckland: OUP, 1997).

OED: The Compact Edition of the Oxford English Dictionary, 2 vols., (Oxford: OUP, 1971).

OUP: Oxford University Press.

RDNZS: *The Reed Dictionary of New Zealand Slang,* ed. D. McGill (Auckland: Reed, 2003).

RfH: Dan Davin. *Roads from Home*, ed. Lawrence Jones (Auckland: OUP, 1976 [1949]).

Stone's *Directory:* John Stone's *Dunedin and Invercargill Directory* (Dunedin 1920–9).

Wise's *Directory:* Henry Wise's *New Zealand Directory* (Invercargill 1929).

WORKS BY DAN DAVIN

MANUSCRIPTS

'Failed Exorcism', MS-Papers-5079-287, Daniel Marcus Davin literary papers, Alexander Turnbull Library.

'The Unjust and the Loving', MS-Papers-5079-494, Daniel Marcus Davin literary papers, Alexander Turnbull Library.

'Invercargill Boundary', MS-Papers-5079-263, Daniel Marcus Davin literary papers, Alexander Turnbull Library.

Interview with Daniel Marcus Davin and Dave Arthur (typescript), 1 January 1986.

PUBLISHED

'Prometheus', Otago University *Review*, 48 (September 1935): 26–9.

'Knowledge', Otago University *Review*, 51 (September 1938): 20–1.

'Toby', *Manchester Guardian*, 22 January 1940.

'The Vigil', *Good Housekeeping* (November 1944).

The Gorse Blooms Pale (London: Ivor, Nicholson and Watson, 1947)

'A Return', *Arena* 1:4 (December 1948?): 72–8.
Roads from Home (London: Michael Joseph, 1949); 2nd edn, Lawrence Jones, ed. (Auckland: Auckland University Press and OUP, 1976).
'The Quiet One', *Landfall* 3:3 (September 1949): 228–40.
'Presents', *Landfall* 7:1 (March 1953): 19–25.
The Sullen Bell (London: Michael Joseph, 1956).
No Remittance (London: Michael Joseph, 1959).
'Roof of the World', *Malahat Review* 10 (April 1968): 89–95.
'First Flight', *Landfall* 23:1 (March 1969): 12–33.
Not Here, Not Now (London: Robert Hale, New Zealand: Whitcombe & Tombs, 1970).
Closing Times: Memoirs (London: OUP, 1975).
Breathing Spaces (London: Robert Hale & Co.; New Zealand: Whitcoulls Publishers, 1975).
'My Language and Myself: English as Creative Power', *The Round Table: The Commonwealth Journal of International Affairs,* 261 (January 1976): 19–26.
'Early Reading: The Rime of the Ancient Mariner', in *Education* 5 (Wellington: Department of Education, 1976).
Selected Stories (Wellington: Victoria University Press with Price Milburn & Co.; London: Robert Hale, 1981).
'The Albatross', *New Zealand Listener*, 1 March 1985.
The Salamander and the Fire. Collected War Stories, with introduction and glossary (Oxford: OUP, 1986).
'Black Diamond', *Islands* 37, new series 3:1 (August 1986): 42–8.
'The Black Stranger', *New Zealand Listener*, 29 August 1987.
'Gardens of Exile', *New Zealand Listener,* 7 January 1989.

SECONDARY WORKS

Akenson, D.H. *Half the World from Home: Perspectives on the Irish in New Zealand, 1850–1950* (Wellington: Victoria University Press, 1990).
Allen, Walter. Review of *The Gorse Blooms Pale, New Statesman and Nation*, 7 February 1948.
Alexander, Robert Ritchie. 'Hone Tuhawaiki', *Te Ara – the Encyclopaedia of New Zealand* (1966; updated 26 Sept. 2006), http://www.teara.govt.nz/1966/T/TuhawaikiHone/en (accessed 17 Jan 2007).
Apperson, G.L. *English Proverbs and Proverbial Phrases. An Historical Dictionary* (London: Dent, 1929).
Baker, Sidney J. *New Zealand Slang, a dictionary of colloquialisms* (Wellington: Whitcomb & Tombs, [1941]).
Beattie, Herries. *Otago Place names as bestowed by the Pakeha* (Dunedin: Otago Daily Times, 1948).
Beerkens, Denise. *St Patrick's Church Rakauhauka, Southland. The Faith of the Irish Settlers: Centennial 1894–1994* (published by the Centennial Committee, 1994).
Bertram, James. *Dan Davin.* Writers and Their Work series (Auckland: OUP, 1983).
—. 'Dan Davin: Novelist of Exile', in *Flight of the Phoenix: Critical Notes on New Zealand Writers* (Wellington: Victoria University Press, 1985). Reprinted from an article in *Meanjin* 32 (1973).
The Church in Southland. A Brief Historical Survey of Catholicism in the Province.

Invercargill 1856–1956. A Centennial Production. Foreword by the Bishop of Dunedin. the Most Rev. J. Whyte (Invercargill, 1956).

Campbell, Peter. Review of *Breathing Spaces, TLS* 24 (October 1975): 1255.

Cole, John Reece. Review of *The Gorse Blooms Pale, Landfall* 2 (June 1948): 148–51.

Copland, R.A. 'The Fictive Picture: Cole, Courage, Davin', in *Critical Essays on the New Zealand Short Story*, ed. Cherry Hankin (Heinemann: Auckland, 1982), pp. 62–80.

Craig, Patricia. Review of *Selected Stories, TLS* (12 June, 1981): 660.

Davin, Anna. 'Davin, Winifred Kathleen Joan 1909–1995', *DNZB* (updated April 2006) http://www.dnzb.govt.nz (accessed 17 Jan. 2007).

Davin, W.K. 'A Soldier's Wife', in *Women in Wartime: New Zealand Women Tell their Story,* ed. Lauris Edmond and Carolyn Milward (Wellington: Government Printing Office, 1985), pp. 65–76.

de Guignand, Francis. *Operation Victory* (London: Hodder and Stoughton, 1947).

Dictionary of New Zealand Biography, Vol. 5 (1941–60), ed. Claudia Orange (Wellington: Ministry for Culture and Heritage, 2000), http://www/dnzb.govt.nz.

Emerson, G.W., J.A. Dangerfield and A.C. Bellamy. *Coalfields Enterprise: Private Railways of the Ohai District, Southland* (Dunedin: New Zealand Railway and Locomotives Society, 1964).

Encyclopaedia Britannica, 7th edn. 1842, http://www.britannica.com (accessed 17 Jan. 2007).

The Diamond Track: From Egypt to Tunisia with the Second New Zealand Division 1942–1943 (Wellington: Army Board, 1945).

Gallagher, Patrick. *The Marist Brothers in New Zealand, Fiji and Samoa 1876–1976* (Christchurch: Pegasus Press, 1976).

Holcroft, M.H. *Old Invercargill* (John McIndoe: Dunedin, 1976).

The Householders' Annual Index of Useful Information and Directory of Selected Business Firms (Invercargill Southland edition, 1911–1912).

Invercargill. *Jubilee Magazine Marist Brothers' School Invercargill 1897–1947.*

—. *Marist Brothers School, Invercargill, 90th Jubilee, 1897–1987.*

John, K. Review of *The Gorse Blooms Pale, Illustrated London News,* 31 January 1948.

Johnson, Pamela Hansford. Review of *The Gorse Blooms Pale, John O'London's Weekly,* 20 February 1948.

Jones, Lawrence. *Barbed Wire and Mirrors: Essays on New Zealand Prose* (Dunedin: Otago University Press, 1987).

—. 'Dan Davin', in *Great Writers of the English Language,* Vol. II: *English Prose Writers,* ed. James Vinson (London: Macmillan Press, 1979), pp. 300–1.

—. *Picking up the Traces: The Making of New Zealand Literary Culture 1932–1945* (Wellington: Victoria University Press, 2003).

—. Review of Davin's *Selected Stories, Landfall* 36 (1982): 93–9. Reprinted in *Barbed Wire and Mirrors,* pp. 86–90.

Joyce, James. *Dubliners. An Annotated Edition,* ed. John Wyse Jackson and Bernard McGinley (London: Reed Consumer Books, 1993).

Lenihan, Denis. 'Roads Around Home: Dan Davin Revisited', *Kotare*: *New Zealand Notes and Queries* 5.1 (2004).

Lind, Clive A. *Pints, Pubs and People: 50 years of the Invercargill Licensing Trust* (Invercargill: The Trust, 1994).

McCormick, E.H. *New Zealand Literature; A Survey* (London: OUP, 1959)

McNeish, James. *Tavern in the Town* (Wellington: A.H. and A.W. Reed, 1957).

The New Partridge Dictionary of Slang and Unconventional English, ed. Tom Dalzell and Terry Victor, 2 vols. (London: Routledge, 2006).

New, W.H. *Dreams of Speech and Violence: The Art of the Short Story in Canada and New Zealand* (Toronto: University of Toronto Press: 1987).

O'Farrell, Patrick. *Vanished Kingdoms: The Irish in Australia and New Zealand, a Personal Excursion* (Sydney: University of New South Wales Press, 1990).

The Oxford Dictionary of Quotations, ed. Elizabeth Knowles, 5th edn. (Oxford: OUP, 1999).

The Compact Edition of the Oxford English Dictionary, 2 vols. (Oxford: OUP, 1971).

The Oxford Companion to Irish History, ed. Sean Connolly, 2nd edn. (Oxford: OUP, 2002) [1998].

The Oxford Dictionary of New Zealand English: A Dictionary of New Zealandisms on Historical Principles, ed. H.W. Orsman (Auckland: OUP, 1997).

Ovenden, Keith. *A Fighting Withdrawal: The Life of Dan Davin, Writer, Soldier, Publisher* (Oxford and New York: OUP, 1996).

—. 'Davin, Daniel Marcus 1913–1990', in *DNZB* (updated 7 April 2006), http://www.dnzb.govt.nz (accessed 17 Jan. 2007).

Smith, John Meredith. *Southlanders at Heart* (Invercargill: Craig Printing Co. Ltd, 1988).

Stallworthy, Jon. 'Dan Davin', in *The Oxford Dictionary of National Biography*, ed. H.C.G. Matthew and Brian Harrison, 60 vols. (Oxford: OUP, 2004), 15, pp. 424–6, http://www.oxforddnb.com/view/article/40201 (accessed 10 July 2007).

Stone, John. *Dunedin and Invercargill Directory* (Dunedin: 1920–1929).

The Reed Dictionary of New Zealand Slang, ed. David McGill (Auckland: Reed Books, 2003).

Tod, Frank. *Pubs Galore – History of Dunedin Hotels 1848–1984* (Dunedin: Historical Publications, 1984).

Traue, J. 'McNab, Robert, 1864–1917', *DNZB* (updated 7 April 2006), http://dnzb.govt.nz (accessed 17 Jan. 2007).

Watt, J.O.P. *Invercargill Marist Brothers' School 75th Jubilee 1897–1972 Magazine* (1972).

Wevers, Lydia. 'The Short Story', in *The Oxford History of New Zealand Literature in English*, ed. Terry Sturm (Auckland: OUP, 1991), pp. 203–68.

Wilkes, G.A. *A Dictionary of Australian Colloquialisms*, 4th edn. (Sydney: OUP, 1996).

Wilson, Janet, ed. *Intimate Stranger: Reminiscences of Dan Davin* (Wellington: Steele Roberts, 2000).

—. 'Dan M. Davin (1913–1990)', *The Literary Encyclopaedia,* http://www.litencyc.com/php/speople.php?rec=true&UID=1157 (accessed 5 April 2007).

Wise, Henry. *New Zealand Directory* (Invercargill, 1929).

MAPS: BODLEIAN LIBRARY

NZMS 260 E47 D47 Bluff (1983)

NZMS 260 E46. Invercargill (1983)

PART I

From *The Gorse Blooms Pale* (1947)

Perspective

God blazed in every gorsebush
When I was a child.
Forbidden fruits were orchards,
And flowers grew wild.

God is a shadow now.
The gorse blooms pale.
Branches in the orchard bow
With fruits grown stale.

My father was a hero once.
Now he is a man.
The world shrinks from infinity
To my fingers' span.

Why has the mystery gone?
Where is the spell?
I live sadly now.
Once I lived well.

Perspective: first published under the title of 'Knowledge' in Otago University *Review* in 1938, this poem in line six provides the title of Davin's first collection of short stories, *The Gorse Blooms Pale*. The poem is the epigraph to that volume and also to Davin's *Selected Stories* (1981). Davin links gorse with mortality and change in 'Growing Up', 'A Return' and 'The Far-Away Hill'.

1

The Apostate

'GOOD-BYE, MUM,' said Mick from the door.

Mrs Connolly put down her cup and looked up.

'Come here a minute, Mick,' she said. 'Did you clean your ears?'

'I have to go, Mum. I'll be late.'

'Come back and let me have a look at those ears.'

He came back over the coconut matting to her chair in the corner.

She put him between her knees and took his head in both hands. She turned each ear towards the light of the window and looked carefully. Her apron was wet and smelt damp. She had been clearing away their dishes before sitting down to her own breakfast.

'The Lord save us,' she said. 'You could grow a crop of King Edwards in them ears. Come here.'

She got up stiffly. She had been up three hours to make an early start on the washing before getting all the breakfasts. The damp was already in her bones.

In the scullery she wet a piece of the roller towel on her finger under the tap and scoured out each ear in turn. He wriggled impatiently.

'There now,' she said at last. 'We couldn't have you going off to school like that, a disgrace to us all.'

Released, he shot towards the door. She looked after him, smiling.

'Wait a minute,' she said.

He stopped in his tracks. Had she noticed the hole in his stocking?

She reached up to the high mantelpiece and brought down her small black purse. She slipped the two silver knobs of the catch past each other, looked in and sighed. She could feel him watching her. Well, it was little enough pleasure the poor kids had. She took out a penny.

'Here,' she said, and held it out to him.

'Oh, thank you, Mum.'

'Now, don't you go letting on to the others at lunch-time or they'll all be wanting one. And mind you don't spend it on trash.'

She sat down, tasted her tea and found it nearly cold. She reached for the big brown teapot.

Outside, Old Jack got up and wagged his tail, hopefully.

'No, Jack, it's only school today.' A hug of consolation.

At the corner of the house he looked back. Jack had not yet lain down again. He was sitting there on the back verandah, head on one side, brown eyes wistful.

There was no need to hurry at all, really, now that he was out of the house.[1] It was only half-past eight and school didn't go in till nine. The sun was hardly up. As he came along Venus Street[2] he could look straight into it through the five-barred gate of Scott's paddocks,[3] lying low behind the mist.

The mist had made the frost light and there was just the faintest silvering on the footpath. It had kept the sun from getting at the spiderwebs on Basset's macrocarpa hedge, too. There were little wee beads strung along each fine thread.

You could hardly believe they'd been spun there so cleverly just to catch flies. But if you started at the outside and followed the lines they always led into the centre where the little spider was bundled up, waiting for the sun.

Still, there were some good spiders. They had crosses on their backs and they were blessed. Once their great-great-great grandfather had spun a web across the cave to stop the soldiers finding Jesus and His Holy Mother. It just showed you. And you should never kill a spider without looking first to see if it had a cross on its back. Besides, if you killed any sort of spider it always rained afterwards, though it was hard to see why.

Mick got tired of staring at the spiderwebs. He began to run. When he came to his favourite branch, the long one that hung out over the footpath, he jumped the way he always did to see if he could reach it. Today he just managed it. That was a good sign. He laughed as it showered silvery drops over him. It was a pity Paddy wasn't there to see. He couldn't get any way near the branch, though of course he was a year younger.

He looked at the little twig he had snatched. Queer how each little bit fitted so snugly into the others. Like little green knuckles. And what a nice green colour it was.

He crossed the gravel road[4] and came through the cocksfoot[5] to Scott's big gate. The withered heads of cocksfoot were hanging down under the weight of mist.

There was plenty of time so he'd take the short cut today.[6] He reached up to the top bar. It was cold and slippery as if it had been soaped. His fingers left dull, steely ridges across the frost. Right from the top he jumped and landed with a thump. His schoolbag followed anxiously and clumped against his behind a second later.

A narrow track led through the paddock towards the railway bridge.[7] There were no marks on the grass. Nobody had been through today yet. He was an explorer lost in the fog. His feet swooshed over the sheep-cropped grass, leaving patches of dark and sending little sprung showers of silver from the short, proud blades.

On the top of the rise he stopped. The mist was clearing. You could see the dark green gorse hedges meet at the corner just before the bridge.

Under the mist everything was green. He squatted on his haunches to look at everything. The mist of his own breath came out in front of him and melted away. Down in the dip a sheep coughed and the mist of its breath came out in a sharp puff.

The grass under his feet was green, shining where they had rubbed the white moisture off it. The sprig of macrocarpa was still in his hand, green.

He had a revelation. In a flash, like what happened to Saint Paul, only not frightening.

Green was the colour of God. It was the colour of the grass and of the trees and of the sea and of all the best things, of God's things. Green was the colour of Ireland. In Ireland, his father said, everything was green. Even the fairies. Green was Ireland's National Colour. And the Irish were the best people. Even here in New Zealand you knew that. And all the Irish were Catholics. Their colour was green. God's colour was green. That proved it. The Irish were God's green people. So their green God was the real God.

At first he only felt this. It was afterwards that he worked it out. After he had crossed the bridge, not stopping to watch the lines meet in a point this morning, but jumping down over the ditch and then following the creek bank.[8]

Now he was wonderfully glad. He had felt glad before but without knowing why. This was different. He would have liked to have somebody to tell about it. But probably it was better to tell no one. He would just keep it inside him and walk about as if nothing had happened. While all the time inside him he knew that God was green and Irish and a Catholic.

It was still too early. The bell wouldn't go for ages. In the distance he could see the other kids playing outside the school, chasing one another up and down the bank[9] and making slides. Usually he tried to get to school early to do this too. But this morning was different. All that didn't seem right somehow for a boy who'd just found out what he had.

He would walk round the block when he came out of the paddock into Islington Street and come into school by the main gate.[10]

He got through the barbed wire fence and out on to the footpath. It was asphalt although there were still only a few houses in the street. His father said they'd made the road, thinking the town was going to grow there but it had stopped growing.

Up towards the main road[11] houses were thicker. Men were coming out their front gates and getting on their bikes. Mothers were fussing over their kids as they left for school. Most of the kids were Protestants.[12] They'd very likely go to Hell when they died for singing:

Catholic dogs
Jump like frogs,
Don't eat meat on Friday.

Then, when Mick and his friends sang:

Protestant dogs
Jump like frogs,
Do eat meat on Friday.

both sides would pick up stones out of the gravelly road and begin to fight. But, of course, that was only in the evening on the way home from school.

He stopped outside Mrs Peak's store. There were pocket knives in the window, very sharp and shiny. The big blades were right open and the little blades half open. The Nest knives[13] were best with their warm black handles and big blades that had a hollow scooped out of the top near the point and a sharp, lifting edge. When he was old enough to skin a rabbit his father was going to buy him one. His father's knife was very narrow in the blade because every Sunday after dinner he sharpened it on the oilstone[14] to mend their boots. It had string wound round the handle.

The cheapest knives were three-and-six. But he only had the penny. So it was better to look at the pencils. There was a lovely, shiny box full of them, all colours. It didn't say how much they were.

He went into the shop. Mrs Peak leaned over at him, looking as if she'd like to eat him. She was fat and had a sort of musty smell.

'Well, what can I do for you, my little man?' He stiffened. That was no way to talk to a boy who would soon be able to skin a rabbit and knew what God was like.

'How much are the pencils, please?'

'A penny each.'

So was a chocolate fish. Or he could buy a penny's worth of speckled fruit and make the joke about not too many coconuts.[15] Or a penny's worth of rosebuds.[16] If he sucked each one instead of crunching it they would last all morning. Even after he'd given some to Tommy Stafford and Jack Bates. His mouth watered. He didn't really need a pencil.

But Mrs Peak had got the box out of the window.

'What colour would you like? There's a nice green one.'

Mrs Peak was a Protestant. It was like that word in the catechism, simony,[17] for her to sell green pencils. But she couldn't know any better. She couldn't know it was God's colour. So perhaps it was all right.

'Or perhaps you'd like a red one.' She took out the red one and handed it to him. It was a wonderful pencil, round and rich and shiny, the colour of blood. He took it in his hands. He could see it in the glass sharpener twirling and then coming out with the blood-red part ending in a smooth circle and then the reddish wood coming to a sharp, black point.

He sneaked a look at the green pencil again. It seemed a quiet sort of a pencil, not very exciting.

'It's a maroon red,' said Mrs Peak.

'I'll have the maroon one, please,' he heard himself say. Maroon had clinched it. His penny was warm and damp when he handed it over. He had been holding it in his pocket. The bell rang.

He just got to school in time.

At playtime he and Tommy Stafford and Jack Bates raced over to the park.[18] In and out among the pine trees they chased each other. Then they sat down on the pine-needles to get their breath. The pine-needles were lovely and dry and tingly and you could smell them.

'Look what I've found,' said Tommy. He held up a piece of shiny stuff.

'It's only a bit of gum,' said Jack.

'It'll be kauri gum,' said Mick. 'I had an uncle who used to dig for it once up in Auckland. He used to put a long spike into the ground and feel for where it was.'

'Don't be silly,' said Jack, 'kauris don't grow down here.'

'Perhaps they did once and we are the first to know, all through my piece of gum,' said Tommy.

Jack was half persuaded. He got up and began to scuff among the needles to try and find a piece. If he could find any he'd believe it.

Something brown moved at the foot of a big tree. They rushed over. It flew in front of them, in desperate flights, a little distance at a time. It was a young thrush. Mick fell on it and caught it.

'We'll wring its neck,' said Jack. He was angry. First the gum and now the thrush. And he was the biggest, too.

'You'd be too frightened,' said Tommy. 'I wonder what it'd look like when it was dead?'

But Mick had the bird in his hands. He could feel its heart beating. Its eyes were bursting with fear.

'No,' he said. 'We'll let it go.'

'I want to kill it.'

'They do eat the gooseberries,' said Tommy. 'I've seen them.'

'No, we'll let it go. How'd you like to have your neck wrung?'

'Softy,' said Jack.

'Softy,' Tommy said after him. He was the youngest. Mick could see they were going to rush him. 'The bell must have gone ages ago,' he said.

They hesitated. This was only too true. Mick let the bird go. It flew on to a branch and could hardly breathe for relief.

They all watched it for a second. They were glad it was safe now and they could say it was Mick's fault if anyone asked why they didn't wring its neck. They rushed back to school.

'Two cuts each,'[19] said Sister Mary Xavier[20] gravely. But when they told her how they'd caught a bird and let it go she didn't give them very hard ones.

They walked back to their seats with their hands in their armpits, pretending it hurt. The little girls'[21] eyes were big with horror and respect. Little girls never got the cuts. They cried if they were just scolded.

Mick's wrist against his pocket seemed to miss something. He held his breath and tried to fight off the moment when he would know what it was. But he knew already, even before he searched. He had lost his maroon pencil. His eyes filled with tears. He bent his head down. The others would think he was crying because he'd got the cuts. He'd already been called a softy because of the bird. They were very critical about these things. Only poor old Jumbo Jones was expected to cry. That was because he was a real sugar-baby.[22]

Through the moist mist the maroon pencil floated in a vision. The gladness had gone from the day.

But perhaps if he prayed to Saint Anthony, Saint Anthony would talk to God and get it back from him. Three 'Hail Marys' to Saint Anthony, that would do it. 'Hail-Mary-full-of-grace –.' Not so fast or Saint Anthony would be offended. 'Hail Mary, full of grace, the Lord is with Thee, Blessed art Thou amongst women –.'

Religion was the last lesson before lunch. Sister Mary Xavier talked away. But Mick wasn't listening. He couldn't even play the game of seeing faces in the shape made by the damp on the plaster wall behind the nun. All the shapes kept turning into pencils. If only the bell would hurry up and go so that he could tear over to the pine trees and look for it.

What was that she was saying?

'And one of the most glorious of God's saints has said that it has never happened that anyone who prayed with all his heart for what he wished, provided the wish were holy, has had his prayer unanswered.'

Of course he'd find the pencil. Didn't that as good as say so? Better say another three though, to make sure. After all, the saints must be pretty busy. They'd need reminding.

'But, dear children, our prayers are not always answered the way we expect them to be. God who knows everything knows what is best for us. And sometimes he knows that what we pray for with all our hearts is not what is best for the salvation of our immortal souls.'

That was just like grown-ups. His heart began to sink. They always talked like that when they weren't going to give you something. Supposing it was not for the good of his immortal soul?

'But, be sure, my children, the prayer is always answered. If not in the way we expect, then in some other way and in the long run the best way. For God is infinitely good. Don't forget to bring your crayons for drawing this afternoon. Now repeat after me this prayer.'

He came back from the park. No thrush, no red pencil, nothing. Only an old piece of pine-gum.

He sat down in the sun by the porch door and opened his schoolbag. His lunch was wrapped neatly in newspaper. Jam sandwiches. He didn't like the way the jam soaked into the bread, even if it was raspberry. He'd save the corned beef one till last.

The others had all had their lunch and were playing marbles. He was glad he didn't have to talk to anybody.

As he picked the last shred of corned beef from his coat and pushed it down over the lump in his throat something in the pile of sawdust swept from the classroom caught his eye.

The end of a pencil was sticking out of the sawdust. A red pencil. A maroon pencil.

He kept quite still for a moment. Then he leapt.

The pencil was two inches long.

He sat down again. So that was God's answer.

But perhaps it was a punishment for not buying the green one? No, because he'd been afraid of simony and you couldn't get punished for being afraid of a sin. And anyway if it was that why should God give him a red one now?

'Be sure God will always answer your prayers somehow, dear children.'

There was no God. And He wasn't green either. And if that was the best He could do He could keep His rotten old pencil.

He threw the stub back into the sawdust.

The Apostate: although this story was composed later than the others in the 'Mick Connolly' sequence (like 'Late Snow', 'The Vigil', 'Death of a Dog'), Davin placed it first in *The Gorse Blooms Pale,* probably because of Mick's epiphany about God and the opening up of his consciousness to new perspectives. See *FW*, p. 121 and n. A transcript is held in the Alexander Turnbull Library (MS-Group-0319).

NOTES

[1] out of the house: the Davin family, on whom the Connolly family is based, lived at 36 Morton Road, Georgetown. The house was built in 1909, possibly by Patrick Davin, and the family moved there from Gore in 1920. See 'First Flight'.

[2] Venus Street: the street parallel to, and west of, Morton Street.

[3] Scott's paddocks: land owned by Peter Scott, farmer, lying between the north side of Oteramika Road (now Tweed Street) on the corner of Oteramika Road and Lindisfarne Street (not then extended across the park to join up with Morton Road), where Miller Street (not in existence then) and Turnbull Thomson Park now are. Wise's *Directory*, 1929. See 'The Vigil' and 'Death of a Dog'.

[4] the gravel road: Oteramika Road which runs east (now partly renamed as Tweed Street). See 'Death of a Dog', 'Goosey's Gallic War'.

[5] cocksfoot: wild grass that grows on roadside.

[6] the short cut today: instead of walking west along Tweed Street and north up Elles Road North (now Queen's Drive), Mick cuts across Scott's paddocks, crossing over the railway line bridge and Otepuni (Puni) Creek and coming out onto Islington Street. Davin wrote in 1984 how 'he first went [to school] on foot jumping the Puni Creek on the way'. *FW*, p. 21 and n.

[7] the railway bridge: located south of Camden Street and north of Pomona Street in Georgetown, where Puni Creek turns north of the railway line in what is now Turnbull Thomson Park.

[8] the creek bank: Puni Creek.

[9] chasing ... the bank: Puni Creek flowed through the south part of the school playing field. It was straightened by the City Council in 1927 and the grounds were drained by members of the Marist Brothers' Old Boys' Cricket Club. J.O.P Watt, ed., *Marist Brothers' Invercargill 75th Jubilee Magazine, 1897–1972*, pp. 13–4.

[10] Islington Street … main gate: the Marist Brothers' School moved from Clyde Street in 1925 to Mary Street. Mick walks from Islington Street up Camden Street, west along East Road, then to the main gates on Mary Street.

[11] the main road: East Road, now renamed as Tay Street, the main highway from Invercargill to Gore and Dunedin.

[12] Protestants: Protestant and Catholic primary education was segregated in Invercargill. But as there was no Catholic secondary school before 1927 a number of Catholics went to Southland Boys' High School. See 'Failed Exorcism'; *FW*, pp. 27–8; *IS*, p. 228.

[13] Nest knives: possibly knives in a nest or cluster, although Nest might be a brand-name.

[14] oilstone: an oil whetstone.

[15] coconuts: 1920s slang of US origin for black people, notably negroes, but extended to Cook Islanders. The implication is that, in buying speckled fruit, one should avoid pieces that are black all over.

[16] rosebuds: a kind of boiled sweet.

[17] simony: selling or trading in sacred goods. Simon Magus offered the disciples of Jesus payment for the power to perform miracles. It is a key term in James Joyce's *Dubliners*.

[18] the park: possibly the small park on the corner of Elles Road and Tay Street.

[19] Two cuts each: two strokes of the strap or cane.

[20] Sister Mary Xavier: nuns would sometimes have taught in a Marist Brothers' Primary School, although Davin may be thinking of his earlier school days in Gore at St Mary's Convent. This detail suggests that Mick was in the final years of primary education at the Marist Brothers' School before the Secondary Department opened in 1927 (i.e. between 1925–6).

[21] the little girls: Catholic girls would have attended the St Joseph's School for Girls which opened in Tyne Street in 1923.

[22] sugar-baby: easily moved to tears. The phrase was originally said of a child reluctant to go out while raining (i.e. 'You aren't made of sugar, you won't melt'). *DSUE*.

2

The Vigil

IT WAS A LATE SUMMER AFTERNOON. The cows had been milked and were out in the back paddock, lying down and chewing their cud or lazily cropping the short grass. The gorse hedges which ran down two sides of the paddock were a mass of gold and there was a thrush on one singing its heart out. Half-an-hour before, old Mr McGregor, the carter, standing up in his spring-cart had sailed down the road which marked the top end of the paddock to his milking and his tea. No one else would pass along it now.

The hens had been let out through the little square hole that led through the back fence from the fowl run.[1] They were busy poking and scratching about in the dried mud which had been all soft and squelchy and impossible to walk on in the winter. You could still see the deep holes where the cows had walked, dragging their hoofs out of the ooze. But the holes were hard and dry now. Some of the hens were picking away at the very fresh light-green grass that grew round the ruins of the haystack. In the winter the cows used to wear the barbed-wire fence down trying to get at the hay. Now they didn't care and only the hens were interested in scrabbling about among the sticks and logs which had kept the stack off the wet ground.

The back gate leading to the garden was open and Mick sat there to keep the hens from getting in. He had the Catholic weekly[2] and he was reading the 'Smile-raisers'. The best one was about a man writing to his girl to say he'd go through fire and water for her but not to expect him if it rained. At least that was the one that had made his mother laugh.

Then there was a lot of stuff about a writer on the literary page. He must be pretty bad because the editor[3] kept talking about Liffey mud and the disgrace to the glorious literary tradition of Ireland. But it was hard to tell what it was all about. Some day when he grew up he would read all the books in the world and know all about everything, even about this writer.[4]

After a while he got tired of reading about things he couldn't understand and he put the paper down. He began to feel hungry. It must be about tea-time and it was getting a bit cold. He lay on his back and looked up to try and see the lark he could hear singing. Soon he found it, the smallest little black speck in the sky. He watched it for a while and then sat up again to look at the hens.

Every now and then one would try to get past into the garden and he would frighten it with a long stick he had, to save getting up. Some of the hens didn't worry about the garden at all but were quite content where they were. But there were two cunning hens who never moved far from the gate and only pretended to be interested in what they were doing. As soon as he looked away they would make a dash for the gate. Hens as a rule were stupid, but when they were cunning they were even more annoying because somehow they were still stupid but bad as well. He collected some clods and when the two hens made him angry enough he pelted them until they scurried squawking into the gorse hedge.

Rosy, the one his father called the red cow, came up to the water-trough and stood there drinking. It was the trough they scalded the pigs in whenever they had a killing. Afterwards it used to be scrubbed out and brought into the paddock again. It was always a long time before the cows would drink out of it. But they'd got used to it again just now. It held a lot of water but even so it went down by inches when Rosy drank. At first she drank steadily, then more slowly, lifting her head and looking thoughtfully and sadly into nowhere, while long dribbles of water idled their way from her nostrils back into the trough. She was the biggest and boldest of the cows; once she had thrown a young bull which was pestering Strawberry, into a ditch.

It was high time his mother called him for his tea. It must be getting late. They didn't seem to care whether he got anything to eat or not. He tried lying on his stomach to see if he would feel less hungry that way. Then he saw Rosy staring at him sadly and he forgot about being hungry.

How was it that all cows had that sad look? When he had the sulks his mother used to say he had a lip on him like a motherless foal. But probably even a motherless foal couldn't look as sad as a cow, with those great big brown eyes.

Rosy perhaps had a right to look sad, though. Her calves were always bulls and so they were always killed. And even though she seemed to forget about it after a while and the other cows were very sympathetic she must have a sort of idea what would happen by now. And she was due to calve in another month because the last time she went to the bull his father had chalked the date up on the cow-shed wall. It was the same with all the other cows, too, because even when they had heifers they were taken away. They all knew what would happen but they couldn't do anything about it. Rosy was probably telling the two yearling heifers about things like that when she let them lick her.

She was a fine cow; not really red but nearly, and very glossy and shiny now with her summer coat.

It was getting very late and very cold. He could hear the other boys playing away up on the hill but he hadn't had anything to eat and he'd have to stay where he was or else the hens would get into the garden. His mother always said his father would have a fit if the hens got into the garden. That was the worst of having a father who was mad about gardens. Even Jack, the collie, knew better than to go galloping about in there among the potatoes and cabbages.

It was getting dusk as well now. He could hear Mrs Scott[5] away in the distance calling to her kids to come in off the hill. They were lucky not to keep hens and a garden in their family. And there were McGregor's drake and ducks going off down the road from the peat swamp.[6] He hunched himself up against the wall. His knees were so cold they felt all prickly with goose-flesh.

There was nothing more to think about. He had thought about hens and haystacks and larks and cows and gardens, and even if there'd been anything left to think about he was too hungry. The trouble was they'd forgotten all about him. They didn't care whether he went hungry or not. He often used to think he was an adopted child; now he was sure of it.

And his step-parents were trying to be cruel to him. Well, if nobody cared whether he starved or froze he would just starve and freeze. He'd stay sitting here forever and when they found him he would be all stiff and cold and then everyone would be sorry and his mother and father would be very ashamed while people criticised them for their savage cruelty and neglect of their sensitive child.

One of the innocent hens had been getting worried about the time and she now came towards the gate thinking it was the way back into the fowl-run. He threw a clod at her and caught her a terrific thump.

'What a noble-looking boy,' people were saying as they looked down at his young corpse stretched out on the bier. There was a calm, sad expression on his pale, drawn face; as of duty done. 'Some people don't deserve to have children,' one person said. 'What an intelligent, sensitive face,' said another. 'Like the sentinel at Pompeii,'[7] said Father O'Duffy,[8] who used to tell them about Italy. Beside the bier lay his faithful dog, Jack, with his head between his paws. Later on, when they buried him out in the cemetery between the railway and East Road,[9] Jack would lie by his grave, the way Mr Manion's[10] dog Glen did, and stay there fretting till he died.

Still no sign of anyone to call him. They'd be sorry but he wasn't going to let them off. He'd stay by his post. They needn't think he was going to put the hens in himself and come up to tea. If they were going to neglect him it wasn't his place to remind them of their duty to their child. Even if he was only adopted.

Just then Mrs Connolly came through the gate. 'Ah, there you are, sonny,' she said. 'What with getting your father off to his late shift and getting the baby to bed I forgot all about you. Don't bother to shut the hens in. Paddy's had his tea. I'll get him to do it.'

He stalked small and dignified down the path in front of her, so that she wouldn't see him nearly crying.

But when they got up to the warm kitchen she said: 'Now sit down here in your father's chair next the fire and I'll make you a nice piece of toast and boil the brown hen's egg for you.'

As she cleared away the tea things to put back fresh ones he swallowed the lump in his throat and began to forget the tragic drama in which he was to have been the most important figure, though stiff and cold beneath the stars.

The Vigil: a draft of this story was completed by January 1939. It was first published in *Good Housekeeping*, November 1944: 8, 9, 61 (*FW*, p. 449). In revising it for publication in *The Gorse Blooms Pale*, Davin named his anonymous protagonist Mick and his mother Mrs Connolly (see 'Late Snow'); he added local references – names of neighbours (McGregor, Scott, Manion, Father O'Duffy) and places (the East Road cemetery) – identifying Mick's magazine as a Catholic weekly and removing the allusion to James Joyce. He cut the information about how Rosy's bull calves were killed (saving this for the story 'Growing Up'), renamed the dog 'Toby' as 'Jack' to preserve consistency with 'Jack' in 'Death of a Dog' (also previously 'Toby'), and added the classical allusion to the sentinel at Pompeii.

NOTES

1. The hens ... fowl run: the outhouses were separated from the family garden by a fence. Having let the hens out, the protagonist is guarding the back gate along the fence to prevent them from entering.

2. Catholic weekly: the *New Zealand Tablet,* the South Island Catholic weekly, published in Dunedin.

3. the editor: the firebrand Catholic priest, the Reverend Dr James Joseph Kelly (1878– 1939). Kelly edited the *Tablet* from 1917 to 1931.

4. this writer: James Joyce, whose masterpiece *Ulysses* was banned in America until 1933 and in the UK until 1936.

5. Mrs Scott: on Scott's paddocks see 'The Apostate' and 'Death of a Dog'.

6. McGregor's ... swamp: see above reference to McGregor's Flat.

7. the sentinel at Pompeii: the soldier who stayed at his post when the eruption of Vesuvius (A.D. 79), destroyed Pompeii. Pliny the Younger wrote to Tacitus: 'The remains of a soldier were found ... he was performing the office of sentinel. His hand still grasped a lance, and the other military accoutrements worn at the time were found beside him or upon his bones.' ('Vesuvius', *Encyclopaedia Britannica*, 7th edn., 1842, http://www.britannica.com/original/print?content_id=1227 (accessed 17 Jan. 2007)).

8. Father O'Duffy: not known as a Marist Brother.

9. the cemetery ... East Road: Eastern Cemetery, on the corner of East Road and Rockdale Road, leading onto the highway from Invercargill to Gore and Dunedin.

10. Mr Manion's: Manion is also mentioned in 'Death of a Dog' and 'Gardens of Exile'. In 'The Dog and the Dead' (published 1980) a dog called Glen dies at the graveside of his master, Jack Lardner, who lived at Waimatua. This story, set after the Battle of Alamein, also recounts the shooting of a savage Doberman who is guarding a German grave in the sand. The German prisoner with the New Zealand liaison officer says: 'It's Captain Schleicher's dog, Fritz. And it's his grave. This was our position.' (*Salamander,* p. 67). These two episodes of dogs fretting until they die at their masters' graves, with their contrasting dates and settings, show Davin returning to and deepening the vigil theme of this story (cf. James Bertram's argument that the dog's death is a variation on 'Death of a Dog', *Dan Davin*, p. 60).

3

Milk Round

MICK STOOD BACK with the leg rope in his hand, while Ned pulled out the iron bolt from the top bar of the bail and let Strawberry's head free. But she was in no hurry to go out into the cold. She turned her head to look at them and rolled an appraising eye. The wisp of hay hung out on each side of her jaws like a moustache.

'Come on, you old scamp,' said Ned and he slapped her where the canvas cover came down over her shoulder. Strawberry accepted fate, turned fussily in the narrow space, her heels slipping and scraping on the wet concrete, and made for the door.

'Tell Mum I'm just going to put them up in the hill paddock and throw them a few swedes and then I'll be in for tea.'

'Right you are, Ned.'

Ned followed Strawberry out into the mud.

Mick picked up the two buckets. They were light enough for him to carry. Only Dolly and Strawberry were milking now and they were drying off, too.

In the backyard, the light from the kitchen window picked out the puddles in the asphalt. His father hadn't quite got the knack yet when he put it down and the surface was uneven.

Paddy was in the wash-house, doing the separating. He took it very seriously. It was only last Saturday that they had decided he was big enough to turn the handle all the way round and be trusted with the job.

'Just in time,' he said. 'There's hardly any cream coming out now. The bowl must be nearly empty. You'd better go and get Mum to pour it in right away.'

'Who're you ordering about?' said Mick. 'I've got to measure out the milk for the customers first. Then I'll pour it in.'

'But you can't reach that high.'

'Can't I?' Mick swung the two buckets up on to the bench. Their father always made the buckets out of old kerosene tins and the light of the hurricane lantern winked back now from their shiny sides.

The empty treacle tins they used for billies were ranged up alongside, all clean and washed and ready. Mick got the pint-measure out of one and began to dip.

A good full quart for Mrs Campbell because she was a hunchback. And another bit extra because she was a widow and was poor and had four children. Only the bare quart for Mrs Crofts. She was so snooty just because her husband was a bank manager and her daughters took lessons in elocution. A good quart for Mrs Thomas because she had white hair and was always so nice. Well, perhaps a little bit more for Mrs Crofts; it looked a bit mean having her billy so exactly half full. Though she didn't deserve it.

'Hurry up,' said young Paddy. Even the skimmed milk spout was hardly more than a trickle.

Mick didn't answer but pulled the kerosene box up to the separator and began to pour what was left in the two buckets into the bowl. He could feel young Paddy waiting for him to slip.

The new weight on the pans made the handle stiffer to turn and the sound that came from the separator was different. Slowly the two spouts began to thicken again.

Mick had to reach on tiptoe to get the last of the milk out of the bucket. The box swayed dangerously.

'Be careful,' said Paddy.

'Oh, go to hell.'

'What was that I heard?' said Mrs Connolly, entering suddenly from the kitchen. 'I never thought I'd live to see the day when I'd hear one son of mine speak like that to another and the two of them brought up in a good Catholic home.'

Mick grabbed his billies and made for the door. His mother looked after him as he crossed the yard. It was a shame to have to send the poor kid out into a dirty black night like this.

From the corner of the yard Mick shouted back Ned's message. Jack, the collie, heard him and began to rattle his chain by the wood-heap. Mick put down his billies and went back. On the end of the chain Jack leapt and pawed at him. Mick undid the chain from his collar.

Together the two of them came out into the street. Jack raced away up the footpath and disappeared into the dark and the rain. He knew they were going left because they always went that way to save Mrs Thomas's for the last.[1] And he knew he could run ahead for a while because it was two blocks to Mrs Campbell's.[2]

Laden with its precious freight of gold dust the mail-coach moved slowly along through the narrow gully, a cliff on one side and on the other a steep fall to the river. Somewhere in front, Jack, the outrider, was scouting for bushrangers and would come racing back at the slightest suspicion of an ambush.

Behind the front hedges there were lights in the houses they passed. People little thought how out there in the night men were coming and going on dangerous missions so they might eat and sleep warm in their beds.

Jack was waiting for him at the corner by Macdonald's General Store.[3] The shop was closed but by the street-light you could almost read the names of the sixpenny books in the side window. 'Deadwood Dicks',[4] his father always called them, though none of them were ever about Deadwood Dick. They were mostly about how the money was found in Harry Trevor's pocket in the changing-room before the big match with Aston Villa[5] and how it was proved he hadn't taken it after all and he was allowed to play and kicked the winning goal; or about how blood will tell and how Ralph turned out to be the missing heir to the baronetcy and the fortune; or what happened to Bill Cody[6] in Dead Man's Gulch and the valley with the whitening bones.[7]

That was Mrs Campbell's, the little house with the white picket-gate. You could always tell which one it was because she'd made the gate herself when the kids broke the last one swinging on it and the pickets were all different sizes.

They went round past the lighted kitchen window and Mick knocked.

'It's Mick with the milk, Mum,' called little Rose. She kept on holding the door open and smiled at him seriously. She was nearly six and the eldest.

'Come in, Mick,' called Mrs Campbell. 'Come in out of the rain. The boy's as wet as a shag,'[8] she went on when she saw him. 'Won't you sit down there in front of the range while I wash the billy for you? And a good hot cup of tea would do you no harm either.'

'No thank you, Mrs Campbell.' The little room was nice with the range open and the children staring at him over the top of their plates, but he must be getting on.

'You'll have a bit of cake then,' she said. 'Just wait a minute now while I cut you a piece.'

His heart sank. He'd been afraid of this. Her cakes were terrible, all soggy in the middle and no currants. But there was no way of refusing because whatever you said it would really be because you didn't like her cake and that would show in your face.

The piece of cake stuck to the knife like an oyster, but he got it away without breaking it up. 'Thank you very much, Mrs Campbell,' he said. 'I'll eat it on the way.' He couldn't look her in the face as he told her this but she didn't seem to notice. He backed out the door.

'Good-night, Mick, and don't go catching a cold.'

'Good-night, Mrs Campbell and thank you.' But he wasn't quite able to say: for the cake.

Jack was wagging his tail and kept jumping up for his share. But Mick made him wait till they got under the light. He looked at the cake. Its inside was a pale, sticky yellow. He threw it to Jack. Jack leapt and his jaws snapped on it. Then he seemed to think. He laid it down on the footpath and looked up meekly, anxious not to give offence.

'There you are, you see, Jack,' said Mick. 'And now we'll have to pick it up and hide it in Pratt's hedge[9] in case the Campbells find it.'

They were getting near the Morton's place now and they'd have to be careful. Last night those two Morton girls, like the great, stupid lumps they were, had thrown clods of earth at him out of the garden and some of it had splattered into the milk. Tonight he'd be on the watch for them. He bent down and picked up a good-sized stone from the loose gravel at the side of the road.

This was it, the house they were coming to now. Over the front hedge he could see the front door was open and there was a light in the hall. He shifted the two full billies and the empty one into his left hand. Their weight made the wire handles cut into the underside of his fingers. But it was best to have his right hand free. He whistled Jack back to heel.

As he came level with the hedge a clod was thrown over it and fell in the gutter just beyond him. Another followed. He could hear them giggling. They were behind the hedge all right.

'After them, Jack.'

Jack gave his rabbiting yelp and thrust in between the thick holly roots. The girls raced squealing for the door. Jack burst out behind them.

Mick craned over the hedge with his right hand back, ready. They appeared in the light, Molly, the fat one, first. She tripped on the mat and fell sprawling. Dora tripped over her and fell forward on her hands. Mick saw the blue stretch of bloomers and threw. Another angry squeal and tears behind it this time. Girls. He called back Jack and went on.

That meant their brother Howard would be waiting for him tomorrow night. And he was in the Sixth Standard at Georgetown School.[10] Well, let him. He'd fix Howard, too. And Mick's father was twice as big as theirs. Or else he'd get Ned to come along with him. There mightn't even be any need for that. He could see Howard blubbering already and Dora running to the tap with a handkerchief for his nose and Molly saying: You shouldn't have hit him so hard. How was he to know you were so strong?

But Crofts' gate[11] with the big brass number plate and the cold concrete path suddenly came between then and now and he grew down to his ordinary size again. Even the few chrysanthemums that shivered there still in the garden looked as if they only stayed there because they were paid to and couldn't afford to go anywhere else.

A neat little girl about his own age with her hair stretched tightly back over her forehead and a ribbon in her pigtail answered his knock. She looked at him without speaking and called back over her shoulder: 'It's the milkboy, Mummy.' Then she tossed her head and went away.

Milkboy, indeed. If only she knew who he really was she wouldn't talk like that. But the dung on his cow-boots was more faithful and damning than his imagination. The sleeves of his coat were too short.

But long enough to rub the drip from his nose before Mrs Crofts could come. He would have to wait till he grew up. Meantime he looked round to see that Jack wasn't running over the clean matting they had on their verandah. But Jack was skulking back in the shadows. He knew when he was welcome.

Mrs Crofts' bosom appeared in the doorway, a rampart not a haven. Her severe voice spoke from the battlements.

'So there you are. The milk last night wasn't fit for human consumption. It had dirt in it. When you go home tell your mother I'm not paying for dirt in my milk. I hope it's all right tonight.'

No good reminding her it was the best milk in town or she wouldn't be buying it. And what was the good of explaining about the dirt? If it had even been boys –. You couldn't say girls had done it.

He passed over the billy in silence.

The other little daughter peered out while her mother was getting the clean billy. She had dark eyes. Half curious, half derisive, she looked at Mick as if he came from a different world, the place where people who got wages and had dirty fingernails came from.

'Run inside at once, Doris dear,' said Mrs Crofts, coming back. 'You'll get a chill.' Listening to her voice now was like looking into a room with a fire. 'Here's the billy,' she added to Mick in the other voice and the door in that room slammed shut.

A pity about them, them and their chills. Soon she'd be like her sister and able to look at the people who brought their milk without seeing them at all.

Getting outside that gate was like changing out of your good suit when you got home from Mass on Sundays. Jack's tail was up again like a flag. If only those little girls weren't so pretty as well. That was what stopped you being as sorry for them as you'd like to be.

It was raining again and under the next street-lamp the gusty wind shook and swayed the circle of light. The spears struck out of the darkness and through the light, glittering at him. He bent his head and marched on against them, a Greek soldier advancing under the darkness of Persian arrows. They rattled against his armour and he shook the billies exultantly as he pressed on. Jack looked back and saw the gesture and raced on with the standard through the slain.

The corner before Thomas's,[12] two lights swung into the road. A dragon coming with glaring eyes to devour him and his faithful hound. Undismayed he went on to meet it and the glare in its eyes grew more terrible and he could hear its angry roar. But he had his good sword.

Just as it reached him it swerved to one side, unable to brave the certain death that waited in his right arm. By magic it changed itself into Mr Crofts' Chrysler and inside in the magic square of light he could see the magician himself, his hands on the wheel, the thin lips pursed up and the eyes staring on into the darkness beyond the rain.

At Thomas's Jack was waiting for him again. Together they went down the asphalt path with the trellis where they grew such lovely roses in summer on one side and on the other the garden where there nearly always seemed to be flowers. He held Jack by the collar. Solomon, the big black cat, might be sitting behind the lighted window. Last night Jack had left great muddy streaks on the paint trying to get at him but Mrs Thomas had said it didn't matter. Solomon was there again tonight and arched his back as he saw them pass. The stiff hair rose on Jack's back and he growled but let Mick hold him down.

'Ah Mick, what a wet evening it is for you,' said old Mrs Thomas. 'Stand up on the verandah out of the wet and I won't keep you a moment.' Her brown eyes smiling under the white hair made him feel quite warm inside. She went away to get the clean billy. He could hear the big laugh of her son Bob in there. He played for Southland and might be an All Black soon and rode a motor-bike. Alice was laughing, too, though you could hardly hear her, her voice was always so soft. He could tell by the sound of it her boy Geoff must be there. She always said hello to you in the street and wore silk stockings and smelt of scent.

'There you are, Mick,' said Mrs Thomas, handing him the billy. 'And here's something for you.' She stuffed an apple in his pocket.

'Thank you, Mrs Thomas,' he said. It was all right taking things from her because it would have been very nice to give her things, whatever things you gave to old ladies. A teapot, perhaps.

At the front gate again Jack turned round and looked up expectantly.

'I'm sorry, Jack, it's an apple and you know you don't like apples.'

Jack kept on looking, only he shifted his head from one side to the other.

'You know I always give you half if it's anything you like.' Jack kept on watching him sadly.

'It's a terrible waste, Jack.'

Jack didn't move or take his eyes off his face.

Mick took out his knife and cut the apple in half. It was a Cox's Orange. He had to wipe the juice off the blade on his coat.

Jack's eyes were eager. Mick looked at him again, sighed, and threw him his share. Jack's jaws snapped and caught it. He put his head between his paws, mumbling it.[13] Mick began to eat his half, hurriedly.

Jack looked up and walked back to Mick, leaving his half in the gutter. He watched Mick eat his.

'No, Jack. You've had yours. I can't help it if you don't like it, can I?' He hastily swallowed the last of the core.

The two of them went on down the lane past the Ghost House[14] to the barbed wire fence where the short cut started. Through the drops that made little rainbows on his eyelashes Mick could see the light in the kitchen, away across the empty section.[15] Soon he'd be taking off his wet boots in front of the range and his mother would be wrapping her hand in her apron to get something hot for him out of the oven.

'Come on, boy,' he said to Jack who was nosing about in the gorse. 'It's Saturday tomorrow and we'll chase the rabbits then.'

Milk Round: in this story Davin first introduced Mick Connolly and his family. It was composed between 26 February and 9 March 1941 when Davin was sailing as part of the New Zealand Division from Alexandria (Egypt) to Piraeus (Greece). It marks the first appearance of Mick Connolly; 'Late Snow', composed in 1939, also introduces members of the Connolly family, but the names may have been added when Davin revised the story for publication. *FW*, p. 137. A transcript is held in the Alexander Turnbull Library (MS-Group-0319).

NOTES

[1] going left … Mrs Thomas's for the last: she probably lived in Conyers Street, although no one of that name is recorded in either Wise's or Stone's *Directory*. Mick delivered the milk walking anticlockwise from home in Morton Road: south along Morton Road towards Centre Street which bisects it, then one block east along Centre Street to Conyers Street, north along Conyers Street, then cutting across the empty section back into Morton Road.

[2] two blocks to Mrs Campbell's: possibly 81 Morton Road, located beyond Centre Street where Alfred Duncan Campbell, carpenter, resided, according to Stone's *Directory* 1928. Mrs Campbell may have been widowed, yet her husband's name is still listed in the register.

[3] Macdonald's General Store: possibly McKenzie's Store, located on the north-east corner of Centre Street (no. 50) and Morton Road. Wise's *Directory* 1929.

[4] Deadwood Dicks: a character in the 1800s Dime Library novels who became so famous that several men claimed his identity. The name became synonymous with the genre of pulp fiction.

[5] Aston Villa: the Aston Villa Football Club at Villa Park, Birmingham, founded in 1874. During its 'Golden Age', it won both the FA Cup and the League Championship six times.

[6] Bill Cody: William Fred Cody (b. 1846) a.k.a. Buffalo Bill. See 'Failed Exorcism'.

[7] Dead Man's Gulch … bones: a reference to the grisly murders of five prospectors at Slumgullion Pass, later renamed as Dead Man's Gulch, in Colorado in 1874. This event was fictionalised along with legends of Buffalo Bill in the Beadles New York Dime Library in the 1890s.

[8] as wet as a shag: army slang.

[9] Pratt's hedge: Thomas Pratt, ironmonger, who lived at 49 Morton Road according to Stone's *Directory* 1928 and Wise's *Directory* 1929. See 'Roof of the World'.

[10] Georgetown School: probably the public school, St George School, on Pomona Street and Tramway Road in Georgetown, the district south of the railway line, and then on the edge of Invercargill.

[11] Crofts' gate: possibly located in the cross street, Centre Street (the present cross street, Hamilton Street, did not exist until the 1940s). Davin may have used the name of Samuel Crofts, carter, at 54 Morton Road, for his fictional bank manager.

[12] The corner … Thomas's: Mr Crofts must be turning right into Centre Street from Conyers Road.

[13] mumbling: turning over and over without chewing.

[14] the Ghost House: Conyers Road was sparsely settled in the early 1920s. *For the Rest of Our Lives* (p. 252) includes an anecdote about a nearby house, 'more like the ghost of a house', rumoured to be haunted. Empty, 'it was going to rack and ruin'; the boys crept in one night, heard groans, and ran away. Later they heard that on old blind swagman had died there during the night.

[15] the empty section: the Ghost House was accessed by a shortcut 'across the gorse section' (*Lives*, p. 252). This may have been 54 Morton Road, an empty section in the early 1920s (Wise's *Directory* 1929), from where Mick may have seen the kitchen light of the family home at 36. From 1936 Morton Road was renamed Morton Street: evidence of increasing urbanisation and civic pride.

4

Late Snow

NED WAS STILL AWAY at Uncle Tom's[1] and wouldn't be back till Monday. Paddy and young Matt had gone off to see Tom Mix[2] at the Civic.[3] There was no one to tempt Mick out into the uncertain sunlight of the early spring afternoon. Even in the kitchen it was quiet because Nellie and Eileen were away at choir practice and Saturday was always the day that Mrs Connolly went to the Rialto[4] to sit in the old armchairs that never got sold and listen to the auctioneer's jokes and talk with relations in from the country about the price of poultry-food and butter-fat or how young Johnny Nolan was letting his farm go to rack and ruin taking that no-good Calaghan girl to every dance and race-meeting in the country and she no better than a black North of Ireland Presbyterian,[5] and they say she drinks too.

So Mick felt fairly sure of getting in an hour's reading without someone asking him to come and have a look at the watermill he'd made or lend a hand cleaning out the ferret cage or mow the back lawn or run up to the store and buy some seedless raisins and a pound of almonds or whatever else it was people always wanted you to do as soon as they saw you trying to get a bit of time to yourself in peace.

They'd found the books this morning in the rubbish dump at the gravel pit. They all had old Stott the lawyer's name[6] on them so he must have chucked them out when he moved over to the north part of the town where all the nobs lived. They'd been drying on the rack above the range ever since in spite of Mrs Connolly's demands for all that rubbish to be taken out of the way of her cooking. And now one of them, the *Pageant of English Prose*,[7] was nearly dry and this little one, *The Ancient*

Mariner[8] was dry enough to read. Mick had already unstuck most of the pages without tearing them much. He'd always liked the bits they read in *English Extracts*,[9] painted ships upon a painted ocean and we were the first that ever burst into that silent sea and at one stride came the dark. But this was the first time he'd ever come across it all in one piece so now was his chance to see what it was all about.

Curled up here on the sofa by the window he scarcely heard the occasional loud crack of the red pine log in the open grate or the continual sizzling of gum at its ends. Even when the corner of his eye caught the little jumps and starts of the wild kittens under the macrocarpa hedge he didn't consciously look at them. But he could see the long beard and glittering eye of that old man all right and the wedding-guest wanting to get away and wanting to stay at the same time like wanting to go to the lavatory in the middle of a good picture. And all the noise coming out the bridegroom's door like the day Molly Killearn got married, with Uncle Jack's fiddle[10] scraping up inside and the women all gabbling and the men outside in the wash-house tasting the jar of Hokonui[11] that Tom MacDonald had brought.

But he didn't hear his father's boots scraping on the mat out on the back verandah or hear him cross the kitchen until he was nearly at the sitting-room door. And by the time he did hear the door was already opening and it was too late to curse himself for not having thought of this and hidden on the roof or in the hedge where no one would have thought of looking for him. So here was the old man with some job for him, picking over small potatoes for the pigs, chopping up oyster shells for the hens or carrying round the hammer and a tin of staples while they mended a fence.

But, instead of summoning him to any of these or saying: 'There you are with your nose stuck in a book as usual,' his father just called to him and when he looked up beckoned him with his head, as quiet and mysterious as if there was a baby in the house he was afraid of wakening.

What was he up to now? Well, there was nothing to be done about it. The old man could put on a glittering eye,[12] too, when he liked. Mick put the corner of the cushion in the book to mark the place and followed him outside.

By the time he got to the back verandah his father was already halfway across the back yard and turned round only long enough to beckon Mick again. On they went, Mick still a few yards behind. But now he felt like a bather who once the water is over his knees thinks he might as well make a job of it and splashes flat on his belly like the rest. Besides they'd passed the back lawn and the hen-house so it wasn't that. And now they'd passed the potato shed so it wasn't that either. What was the old man up to? They went through the cow-shed and round the big wooden fence that cut the cow paddock off from the back garden.

The old man had fenced off the cow paddock this year and put it down in swedes and potatoes. You could see where he'd been working in the potato drills because some of the earth was freshly turned up and his shovel was still upright in the ground. Some job there then, probably.

About halfway along the back fence his father turned round and put his finger to his lips. Like a girl, thought Mick as he stopped to see what would happen next. But at that moment he stood on an old pile of potato shaws[13] and they crackled under him. His father, who had got down on one knee and was looking through a knot-hole in the fence, turned his head to stare at Mick for a second. Not so like a girl. He got clear of the potato shaws.

But what was it all about? The old man was back at the peep-hole and grinning to himself. He wore no collar but the front stud was still in his shirt and you could see the black-green mark it had made against his neck. Size seventeen in collars he took. There were sweat patches spreading from under each side of his upper arm. With the sleeve rolled up and the thick flannel rolled up underneath so that the big vein on his arm was swollen and green against the muscle. An enormous arm. Like a chunk of red pine. It must be something pretty interesting to make him stop working. You usually had a job to get him away from his shovel till it was dark.

His father moved over to make room and signed to him to have a look. Mick got down and squatted on his heels. He screwed up one eye and peered through.

On the other side of the fence and about ten yards away was the manure heap, all ready to be spread. At the base of it there was a round hole and from the hole little showers of black earth were being thrown back. As Mick watched the showers came faster and thicker and thicker.

Finally the glossy hindquarters of Darkie, the half-tame black rabbit they'd brought home from Waimatua[14] when she was a bunny, appeared. As she worked back out of the opening heaving the earth clear you could see her pads all wet and velvet.

When she was right out she sat up on her hind legs and listened. Mick could see her nostrils and whiskers twitching. They seemed to keep time with his father's breathing and his own. As if the same breath went in and out of them all. Her eye was wilder and more watchful than usual as she looked around the garden.

At last she was satisfied. She looked down at the dark earth heaped around her and set to work distributing it evenly, smoothing it away till the only sign left of her work was the hole.

Mick's father was nudging him. He pretended not to notice. Darkie finished spreading, sat up and looked and listened and then went back into the hole. The earth began to shower out again but this time it fell further inside the opening, almost blocking it.

Another nudge from his father and Mick nearly fell over backwards. His father took his place at the knot-hole.

Suddenly from away on the other side of the garden Mrs Connolly's voice called:

'Ned, are you there, Ned? Would you like a cup of tea?'

'Damn,' said Mr Connolly. He straightened. 'All right, Nellie,' he called back. 'I'm coming.'

'She's frightened Darkie away,' he said to Mick.

They looked over the top of the fence. Darkie was sitting under the wreckage of a winter cabbage. Her nose was twitching but her knees were tucked under her as if she'd been there all the afternoon.

'The cunning of the creatures,' said Mr Connolly. 'She knows it'll be warmer under the manure heap than anywhere else in case there are any more frosts.'

And when Mick came to think of it, often in the sun after a white frost you could see steam coming out of the manure heap.

'Well,' said his father apologetically. 'I thought you might like to see, you being fond of animals. But don't tell your mother about it. You know what she's like about having young animals running round the house.'

It was a few weeks later that the snow came. The night before, Mr Connolly had shaken his head when he came in.

'I don't like the look of it, Nellie. There's a ring round the moon and it's cold enough for snow.'

'But surely it wouldn't go snowing on us now, Ned, with the garden coming along so nicely and the earliest lambing they've had for years.'

'I don't like the look of it all the same. I think one of you boys had better come up with me after tea and we'll put the covers on the cows.'

'It's all right, Dad,' Ned said. 'I didn't like the look of it much either, so Mick and I put them on when we'd finished milking.'

'You did then? Well, good for you, son.' He had his boots and collar and tie off now and sat down in his chair by the fire. His wife had already taken the big plate of steak and onions and fried potato from the oven and set it in his place.

And sure enough, when they woke in the morning it was to snow. Paddy and Matt were delighted and watched it out the window from the bed. They didn't have to get up yet. But it was a different matter for Ned and Mick. They had to get out into it to attend to the cows. In the kitchen Mrs Connolly had been up since six.

'A dirty morning,' she said. 'This'll put the country back a step. I felt sorry for your poor father this morning, up at five to get off on that early shift. Still, he'll be back in time to get a good lunch and it may clear.'

Mick left Ned pulling out turnips from under the snow-covered heap. It was always his job to cut them up for the bran mash while Mick brought the cows down from the hill. This morning they were standing at the gate ready and miserable, with their backs to the driving flakes. They set up a roar when they saw him. No trouble today trying to get them past the fresh grass that grew on the roadsides.

After the milking they decided to leave them in the home paddock with enough hay to keep them going for the morning. Cutting it with the snow slithering in clots from the top of the stack was their last chore of the morning. Then, quite suddenly, they began to enjoy the snow. Before long all the boys of the neighbourhood were there and the cows chewing away at their hay watched the snow-fights thoughtfully and listened to the shouting.

But by afternoon Mick was tired of it. Ned had got him and Paddy out into the back paddock after dinner to make an igloo. It was good fun at first. But once you got the walls over a certain height and wanted to make them curve towards the centre, they kept on falling inwards. It became a back-breaking job instead of a game. Only Ned's determination kept them at it. Even then they gradually began to feel it was his igloo, not theirs. And there was a bitter wind, with a bite of hail in it.

Skinny Dunick came along the back road with his dog, Rover. He was Paddy's great friend.

'Where are you off to, Skinny?'

'Over to Mason's bush to see if we can get a rabbit. We'll be able to see their tracks in the snow. Why don't you come? Bring Jack.'

Ned was squatting on his haunches and frowning as he tried to work out some new way of balancing the blocks. Paddy saw his chance and bolted, Jack after him.

'Hey, come back here, young Paddy, where are you off to?' But it would have been too hard to catch him in that snow.

'No guts, that's the trouble, Mick. A fat lot of rabbits they'll catch, them and their tracking. Any rabbit in his senses'll stay in his hole today.'

And so would anyone else, Mick was thinking. He kept thinking too of that fire in the sitting-room. But how was he going to get there? Poor old Ned was so set on building his igloo. And the more failures he had the more stubborn he got. He'd be there till it was time to get the cows in. But you couldn't very well go away and leave him. He always thought you felt the same way as he did about things. And if you didn't he'd make you. Unless Mick could think of a good excuse he'd be stuck. There was no good trying to make a break for it. Ned would be on the watch now and that two years extra made him faster and stronger.

'Mick! Mick, where are you?' His mother's voice. He could see her over the top of the fence, standing by the woodheap where the gooseberries began.

'Women,' said Ned bitterly. 'Why the blazes can't they leave us alone. Pretend you don't hear.'

'Mick!'

'She can see us,' said Mick. 'I'd better go.'

He set off towards the back gate.

'Come here, Mick,' his mother said, as he crossed the yard. 'Go in and put on your Sunday coat. I've been thinking it's time you had a new one and I might see something nice in town today.'

'Are you going to town in this weather, Mum?' he said when he came back, the jacket looking very clean against his torn shorts and dirty boots.

'I've got to. I promised poor Mrs O'Neill in the hospital I'd see her today and it'll be very miserable for the poor creature there in this weather if no one comes and she so bad with the gallstones. So I might as well stop off in the town, while I'm at it. Now, let's have a look at you. Yes, it's much too small for you, you're coming out in all directions like a squeezed sausage. A size bigger we'll need. Perhaps two sizes.'

'Now, Mum, I don't want all the other kids laughing at me after Mass on Sunday and saying: Is your old man in bed?'

'Don't speak like that about your father. You'll get what I think's good for you. The rate you're growing you need everything too big or it'll be the ruination of us all, keeping you in clothes. It's elastic jackets and leather pants you ought to be wearing.'

But he could tell she'd remember what he'd said all the same.

There was always a great scene before they got her away, what with remembering the buttons to be matched, and the prescription for Eileen's cough, and the final discussion about the new frying pan, and Nellie's new ribbon, and the instructions about keeping a good fire on in the range and not dreaming and letting it go out on them, and the search for the tram time-table and the trial trip out the door and the hurried rush back again and: 'You'll miss that tram, Mum,' and: 'I can't go without my purse, can I, now where did I put it?' But at last they got her safely away.

Mick looked out the window. Sharp against a sky that looked like a bruise he could see Ned toiling in the snow with all the grimness a hopeless job called out in him. He had forgotten all about Mick. He was used in the end to being left alone with the impossible.

Mick dropped back the corner of the curtain and looked round the kitchen. Nellie and Eileen had the cookery books out already. No doubt what they were up to. Making toffee. That'd keep them busy for a while.

All the same, after he'd put a new log on the sitting-room fire, he hid their music under one of the mats just in case they took it into their heads to practise 'Little Brown Bird'[15] or 'She is Far from the Land'[16] again.

And then he shut the door and got out *The Ancient Mariner.* He knew parts of it by heart now. The great thing about it was that it was so easy to remember the bits you liked and they gave you something to think about when you were milking or going head on into the rain as you followed the cows. Every time he came to the albatross he thought of the stuffed albatross in the museum upper gallery[17] and that led on to the lovely hummingbirds in the glass case and all those different-coloured moths you never saw in New Zealand. And then there were the swordfishes and sharks and of course the jawbone of a whale that was hung in the centre and looked like a gigantic wishbone. Or if you read about the wedding-guest that led you on to the time all the kids went to the tin-canning[18] when the Crowe couple came to live opposite – .

They seemed very quiet out in the kitchen all of a sudden. Not a giggle out of them. Then he heard why. The tramp of his father's cow-boots. Coming towards the door, too. By the time he got the window open it'd be too late. Under the sofa? Hopeless, he'd be seen from the door.

The door was open now, anyhow. His father was beckoning him out. Had he ever been to sea? He never talked much about that time just after he left Ireland.[19] What was it this time? There seemed to be a curse on him every time he tried to read. He got up and followed.

In the garden the snow lay heavy, drifted against the fences. Only under the cabbages and the gooseberry bushes, now just turning green, there were wet, black patches. The apple trees seemed sorry they had taken the spring at its word.

But his father didn't look left or right. The first time Mick had ever seen him walk along the path without stopping to look at something and see how it was getting on, or mutter to himself about trying shallots there next time or putting in a bit more lime.

They stopped at the manure heap. Sickly yellow snow covered it, with sodden black corners sticking out here and there. And today you could see the opening to Darkie's burrow. A week or two back after the young ones were born she'd sealed it up and only used to open it for herself. But now either she'd opened it or the weight of snow had broken it in. The opening was full of dirty snow-water, dark, dirty-yellow. The heat of the manure must have melted the snow.

Half on the surface, half under it, floated a baby rabbit, its eyes still closed, drowned before it ever saw the light or knew the colour of snow. The rest of them would be drowned inside.

Mick didn't dare look up. His father hated them to cry.

'Look,' said his father.

Under a desolate cabbage Darkie was crouched on a bare black patch of earth. Her nostrils were twitching and her sides were moving in and out. Her eyes were velvety and dark, the old wildness out of them.

Mr Connolly went over and picked her up. It was the first time she'd let herself be caught for ages.

'I'll take her in and put her by the fire to warm,' he said.

It was very cold. Mick felt embarrassed. As if what they felt about Darkie separated them and they were afraid to look at each other.

He watched his father go towards the house. What was to be done now? He couldn't go back to the albatross. The girls would be talk, talk, talking about Darkie.

He got through the hole in the back fence. Ned was still digging away.

'Where the hell have you been?' Ned said as Mick came up. 'I think I've found the way to do it. Just give us a hand with this bit, will you? We'll have to get it done before milking time. Then it'll freeze solid tonight.'

Late Snow: a draft of this story was completed by January 1939. The entire Connolly family appears here: the boys, Ned, Matt and Paddy, corresponding to Davin's brothers (Tom, Martin and Patrick); Mick to Davin himself; Nellie and Eileen to his older sisters (Evelyn and Molly); Mr and Mrs Connolly, also called Ned and Nellie, to his parents. Davin probably first invented the Connollys in 1941 in 'Milk Round', revising for publication in *The Gorse Blooms Pale* this story and other early stories ('The Vigil', 'Death of a Dog') by renaming the characters. *FW*, pp. 121, 137. A transcript is held in the Alexander Turnbull Library (MS-Group-0319).

NOTES

1   Uncle Tom's: more likely 'Old Tom' – Tom O'Connor, Patrick Davin's friend from Galway who lived in Bluff – than the real Tom Davin, Patrick Davin's younger brother. See 'Bluff Retrospect', 'Prometheus', 'The Black Stranger', *FW*, pp. 3–4, 69.

2   Tom Mix: screen idol (1880–1940), known as 'King of the Cowboys', and first of the escapist motion picture cowboys.

3   the Civic: the Civic Theatre on Tay Street.

⁴ the Rialto: Todd's Rialto which ran through from Don Street to Spey Street, not the Esk Street Rialto owned by McKay. The Rialtos, or Exchange Marts, were businesses concerning auctioneers, commissioning agents and valuers, furniture sales, brokers, importers and dealers in farm produce and fruit. See *RfH*, pp. 3–7 and n.; 'Presents', 'Gardens of Exile'; Holcroft, *Old Invercargill*, p. 54.

⁵ black … Presbyterian: a pejorative reference to a Protestant woman married to a Catholic. See *RfH*, p. 10, 'Black Diamond' and 'The Black Stranger'.

⁶ old Stott … name: according to Ovenden, the books were thrown out by a retired school teacher. *FW*, p. 28.

⁷ Pageant of English Prose: R.M. Leonard, ed., *The pageant of English prose, being five hundred passages by three hundred and twenty-five authors* (London: H. Frowde, 1912).

⁸ *The Ancient Mariner*: see Davin, 'My Language and Myself', p. 20; 'Early Reading', p. 27; *Not Here, Not Now*, p. 93; 'The Albatross'.

⁹ *English Extracts*: R.M. Leonard, ed., *The Pageant of English Poetry, being 1150 poems and extracts by 300 authors* (London and New York: H. Frowde, 1909), pp. 105–8.

¹⁰ Uncle Jack's fiddle: Jack Sullivan, Mary Davin's oldest brother, affected by a head injury he had suffered in an accident. He often visited the family and would play the violin for them (see *FW*, p. 23). Davin's story, 'My Uncle Jack', is among his papers in the Alexander Turnbull Library.

¹¹ Hokonui: Hokonui hooch or moonshine, illicitly distilled or brewed whisky named for the Hokonui Hills in Southland. Invercargill had been voted dry by a local option poll in 1905 and remained so until 1944. See 'A Happy New Year'.

¹² a glittering eye: another allusion to the Ancient Mariner, who stops the wedding guest and 'holds him with his glittering eye', controlling his will by a form of mesmerism.

¹³ potato shaws: stalks and leaves of the plants.

¹⁴ Waimatua: about eight kilometres southeast of Tisbury, Invercargill, on the Gorge Road-Invercargill Highway, the Southern Scenic Route to the Catlins Coast. See 'Gardens of Exile'.

¹⁵ 'Little Brown Bird': A popular old song with these words:

> *All through the night there's a little brown bird singing,*
> *Singing in the hush of the darkness and the dew.*
> *Would that his song through the stillness could go winging,*
> *Could go winging to you,*
> *To you.*
>
> *All through the night-time my lonely heart is singing*
> *Sweeter songs of love than the brown bird ever knew.*
> *Would that the song of my heart could go a-winging,*
> *Could go a-winging to you,*
> *To you.*

¹⁶ 'She is Far from the Land': words to an old Irish air by Thomas Moore (1779–1852), also known as 'Island of Sorrow'.

¹⁷ the stuffed albatross … gallery: there is still today a stuffed albatross in the Southland Museum in Invercargill. See 'The Albatross'.

¹⁸ tin-canning: noisy serenading of newly weds in their new home, climaxing in a storming of the house, forcing the couple to give all their captors a drink. See *RfH*, p. 40 and n.

¹⁹ that time … Ireland: Patrick Davin's rebellion and subsequent flight from school in Galway is told by Ovenden (*FW*, p. 4). Davin himself heard the story from his father's friend from Galway, 'Old Tom'. See 'The Black Stranger'.

5

Death of a Dog

'NOW STOP YOUR ARGUING and get to bed,' said Mrs Connolly. 'It's long past your bedtime already and your father's too tired after his late shift to listen to any more of your nonsense.'

'But it's not nonsense, Mum,' said Ned. 'Jack didn't mean to bite her. It was her own fault for teasing him when he was eating.'

'No, I don't think he really meant to, Mum,' said Eileen. She looked over at the boys placatingly. But they only looked back at her grimly. Too late for that sort of talk now. Why hadn't she left poor old Jack to have his bone in peace? Or if she had to go teasing him why couldn't she shut her mouth instead of rushing up to the house as if all the devils in hell were after her instead of just a bit of a bite on the knee. Anyone'd think it was a rattlesnake the fuss there'd been with their iodine and poultices and all the rest of it. Women!

'It was a nasty bite, though,' said Nellie. Not that she meant any harm. She just liked a fuss and she was too stupid to see it was practically asking for old Jack to be killed, talking like that.

'I don't care what you say, the dog will have to be shot.' Mrs Connolly had made up her mind and nothing could shift her. The worst of it was that if she'd made up her mind the opposite way she'd have been just the same. She'd get it into her head that they thought they could talk her into thinking black was white and once she got that way you couldn't even convince her black was black.

'The neighbours have been complaining long enough,' she went on, 'and the poor postman hardly dares come in the gate. And now he's bitten one of our own there's no telling what he'll do next. He'll be having the law on us, that's what he'll be doing, and before we know where we are we'll be getting a bit of blue paper. The dog'll have to be shot, that's all there is to it. And let that be an end to it.'

The boys looked at their father. He liked Jack. Surely he wouldn't let this happen. There was a silence. He was always slow to speak.

'Now, Ned,' said Mrs Connolly, 'don't you go being soft with those boys. I've told you and told you there's no good bringing dogs home to these boys. A dog with boys for master has no master. They'll always cock him up[1] and end by spoiling him the way they have with Jack. We've been threatened with the law over him already and if you don't do something this time it'll be the law we'll have.'

Mr Connolly turned his chair at right angles to the table and rested his weight on his left forearm as he faced them.

'Your mother's right,' he said. And he looked down at his plate where the fat was already beginning to thicken about the remains of his chop.

That was final. There was no hope that way.

'It's no use,' said Ned, as soon as the lights were out. 'We'll have to find some other way.' Mick and he were sitting up in the double bed they shared. On the other bed Paddy and Matt were sitting up against the wall with the blankets wrapped round them.

'Couldn't we take him out to Manion's farm,'[2] Paddy suggested, 'and get them to look after him till the storm blows over?'

'No good,' Ned decided, after a moment. 'They've only got sheep and he's a heeler.[3] Besides, we couldn't get him out there in time. It's too far.'

'I'll tell you what,' said Mick. 'Why not get up as soon as it's light and take him up to the bush. We could tie him up there and take turns smuggling food to him.'

'That's it,' Paddy broke in. 'And the day after tomorrow's Saturday. We could take him on to Manion's and get young Joe to look after him for us.'

'You know, I think that's it,' said Ned, and they all began to feel suddenly that it was reasonable. For if Ned thought a thing was all right it was all the same whether it was morning or night-time he would do it. He wouldn't forget about it in the morning or say it was hopeless.

'Won't Dad be wild when he finds out,' said Matt. 'I'd like to stay with Jack up in the bush and he could catch rabbits and I'd cook them and there'd be no need to come home or go to school or anything.'

'You shut up, young Matt,' and Paddy jogged him with his elbow. 'This isn't a silly kids' game. It's a matter of life and death.'

Ned and Mick began to feel uncomfortable. This sort of talk made it sound less like common sense.

'All shut up now,' said Ned, 'and get to sleep. You won't have so much to say in the morning.'

The moon had come up. Away in the distance Black's retriever began to bark at it. Then came Jack's bark answering. The last time he fought the retriever Mick had to hold him by the collar while Ned prised his jaws open with the handle of the rabbiting adze. Mick's memory worked back through all that long list of fights and his eyes filled with tears. But they weren't going to let him die.

The retriever had stopped barking. Through the open window you could hear Jack's chain clink as he went back to his kennel.

Thinking he was smothering Mick woke. Ned stopped shaking him but kept his hand over his mouth and gestured towards the other bed.

'We won't wake them,' Ned said. Remembering everything, Mick got that hollow feeling in his stomach again that was always the same no matter what you were sorry or afraid about. It was better to be asleep. But you had to face the day.

'Hurry,' Ned whispered. 'I think I slept in a bit.'

They went out to the kitchen and took their boots from the super-heater cupboard[4] where they'd been drying. They sat down and began to lace them up.

In the bedroom off the kitchen there was a heaving and a long, low yawn like a groan. They looked at each other. But it was too late. Mrs Connolly came out in her nightgown to light the fire.

She looked at them and looked at the kitchen clock. It was not quite six.

'You're early on the go this morning, aren't you?' she said.

'Oh, well, we were awake so we thought we might as well get up and get the cows,' said Mick. He was quicker than Ned at that kind of thing – Ned always went red. Mick could tell he was going red now the way he was bending down over his boots.

While she was getting the kindling out of the oven they slipped out and round by the wood-heap where she couldn't see them.

Jack jumped wildly up at them. But Ned caught at his collar so the chain wouldn't make a noise. 'Down, Jack, down,' he said. He unslipped the chain from the collar. It was to look as if Jack had got free by himself. They'd use an old leg rope to tie him up when they got there.

They followed the line of the gorse hedges so as not to be seen from the kitchen window. Once they were on the grass road[5] it was all right. Jack had calmed down, too, as if he sensed there was something up. He kept quietly in to heel though the dew was full of wild scents and you could smell the spring coming.

But it was taking longer than they thought it would. There was a ghost of mist still loitering in the peat-hollow beyond the frog-pond, though the first roosters had long since had their crow. Ned kept taking out the five bob watch they'd bought out of the rabbit-skin money. It was his turn to wear it this week.

'You know, Mick,' he said. 'We're too late, we'll never make it and get back in time for the milking. It's my fault for sleeping in like that.' But he kept on hurrying on towards the edge of bush, still so remote beyond the mist.[6]

'I'll tell you what, Ned,' said Mick. 'What about the old underground hut? We could tie him up there for today. And then tonight after school one of us could take him on the rest of the way. The old man'll never find him there.'

'I'm not so sure. You know how shrewd he is. But there's nothing else we can do. If we're late back they'll smell a rat anyway. Yes, that's what we'll do.'

They turned half left and climbed towards the clump of gorse on Faraway Hill.[7] The year before they had all set to work digging the underground hut. By the time they had dug down to the yellow clay the others had deserted. But Ned had kept on with the big mattock[8] till it was deep enough. Only by then the summer was already gone and the rain coming. And the very first time they had lit a fire in it to boil eggs and potatoes the roof had caught fire. But the gorse round it had not caught and the place was still well hidden.

They fastened the rope to the heavy manuka pole which had held up the scrub roof. Jack sat down in the middle of the dugout and looked up at them, wagging his tail.

They patted and hugged him and then climbed out. He looked up at them and put his head to one side.

'Good-bye, Jack. We'll be back tonight, so don't worry. You just chew away at that bone and wait for us.'

They set off for home, bringing the cows with them.

It was a longer, drearier morning at school than it had ever been before. Brother Athanasius's[9] jokes had never been so feeble, Mick thought. And though he had no difficulty with the correction of sentences and remembered about Cromwell and the massacre of Drogheda[10] and got his answers to the questions from the Pink Catechism[11] right word for word he was beaten by Dennis Beaton at mental arithmetic. It was easy enough to do things you liked but when it came to long tots[12] it took more effort to be the best. And when you thought of poor old Jack and that winter's night when Dad first came in out of the rain and put down his railway lamp that had a red and a green and an ordinary glass in it and took out of his big overcoat pocket the fat little black and tan puppy, well, it was pretty hard to keep your mind on figures then.

'I don't know what's the matter with you today, Mick. Tell him the right answer, Dennis.'

And there were the times when they came home from the Bluff Regatta[13] or the railway excursion to Queenstown.[14] As the whole family came trudging up to the gate with the empty picnic baskets and their mother wondering if the fire had kept in and if the hens had got into the garden there Jack'd be, waiting for them behind the gate, his nose stuck through the pickets to see if he could get a scent of them coming down the road or hear their voices. And when they opened the gate he'd be nearly frantic with excitement and go running round himself in circles, grinning and trying to catch his own tail. So that even their mother couldn't help showing her smile, though she always pretended not to like dogs, dirty big beasts running all over the house with their great, muddy paws, carrying the Lord only knows what germs.

'Yes, Brother Athanasius. By the four marks of the Church I mean that the Church is one, she is Holy, she is Catholic, she is Apostolic.'[15]

Jack taking them as far as Scott's paddocks[16] on the way to school and looking after them from the gate as they went on, the morning wind stirring in the plume of his tail. Jack on Saturdays watching them pump up the bikes and following them down to the ferret cage when they went to put Snowy in the sugar bag for the day's rabbiting. And trotting home behind them at night, tired and tireless, after the day's wild runs among the biddy-bids and tree stumps, and the splashing in the peat-swamps and the stampedes in the gorse, and sometimes the rewarding snap as the rabbit doubled and the pattings and congratulations, and the flung carcase for him to worry and crunch while they took up the nets and stowed away the skin, stabbing their knives in the crisp, grass-covered ground to clean them. And the hawks hovering overhead, and the sun dropping cold towards the mist which sidled out of the bush and swamp, and at last the ride back with their voices reaching only a little way into the dark and after the head wind and the miles a glimpse of the light in the kitchen window, seen from Oteramika Road[17] across the wetness of McGregor's Flat.[18]

Jack, the great fighter, who walked Georgetown stiff and proud as a boxer and met every strange dog, no matter what his size, with bristling hair and whose teeth came flashing and fast behind his challenge. Jack in whose reputation they could have walked from one side of the town to the other, wrapped in it like a cloak.

And now perhaps they'd already seen the last of him.

'And now all join with me in saying the midday Angelus.'[19]

As they came down the creek and across the paddocks they reassured one another while their hearts sank lower and lower. Whatever happened there'd be trouble, that was certain.

'Now, remember, you kids,' said Ned. 'Not a word out of you whatever he says. He can't kill us. Anyhow, it's me that'll get all the blame, being the eldest. But he might try to worm it out of you. All you two need say, Paddy and Matt, is that you had nothing to do with it. That's not telling a lie, really, because you didn't, you only had something to say about it. But it's me and Mick he'll go for and me mostly, worse luck.'

When they came round the corner of the house the first thing they saw was the rifle. It was leaning at an angle against the kitchen door. Mr Walsh's .32,[20] the one they always borrowed for the pig-killing.

They went in and sat down on the form[21] their father had made to hold the four of them at meal-times. Their mother was rushing to and fro with hot plates. She hardly looked at them and you couldn't tell what she was thinking. Their father must be still down in the garden. They knew his shift ended at ten that morning. No sign of the girls so no way of finding out what was brewing.

They'd planned to say nothing till the subject was mentioned. But as they bent over their soup-plates they didn't have to look to see the rifle still standing at the door. Had he found Jack and shot him? Or had he borrowed the rifle and then not been able to find him?

A shadow darkened the doorway. He wiped his boots on the old potato sack and came in. He crossed to the fireplace and sat down. Mrs Connolly put his soup in front of him. He took up his spoon and began. There was complete silence. Mick felt as if the rifle was leaning on his brain.

And now the stew. He went on eating. He was waiting for them to ask.

At last the strain was too much for him. He finished his meal and stood up. Four pairs of eyes followed him up, fastened on his face where it stood level with the mantelpiece.

'Thanks for digging the grave for Jack,' he said. 'It saved me a lot of trouble, just having to fill it in. You didn't think Mr Walsh was watching you when you went up the road, did you?'

Four pairs of eyes looked down at their plates. Not even Matt whimpered. They weren't going to let him have the satisfaction of seeing any tears. They didn't know the jeer came from a heart as sore as their own. Worse, because it couldn't let itself be sorry.

'I'll say this for him, he was tough. It took three bullets.'

'That'll do now, Ned,' said Mrs Connolly. 'You've killed their dog. Isn't that enough without tormenting them about it?'

He looked at her, astonished and hurt. It wasn't the first time she had acted as if he were wholly responsible for what they had decided on together.

But the boys weren't fooled. No speeches from her would make them forget her part in it. It was just like her, trying to change sides when it was too late. At least you always knew where you were with him.

They trooped out in silence. If they hurried there was time to get up to Faraway Hill before they had to go back to school.

Part of the dug-out was filled in. You could see the fresh yellow clay piled up in one corner. Soon the gorse would grow over Jack and the rabbits would burrow there and he'd never know.

They said nothing to one another and avoided one another's eyes till they were well on their way back down the grass road again. But to themselves they were saying: 'Good-bye, Jack. We won't forget you.'

After they had thrown stones on Mr Walsh's roof there was nothing for it but to go back to school. As they climbed through Scott's big gate one after the other, Ned smiled a bit, suddenly.

'Three bullets it took. And the old man's a good shot. He was a great dog all right.' And that was their first taste of comfort.

Death of a Dog: written in 1938 as 'Toby', this story was first published in the *Manchester Guardian*, 22 January 1940: 10. The original is a much shorter, terse account. In revising it for publication in *The Gorse Blooms Pale* Davin expanded the domestic scenes, adding references to the protagonist's sisters, centring the boys' collective memories of Toby through the mind of the protagonist-narrator, and giving details of the Catholic lessons. To the original ending: 'They threw stones on Mr Lee's roof until they were tired, and then went back to school. There was nothing else to do', he adds Ned's comment and the moral conclusion. Significantly, in 'Toby' the characters are named after Davin's siblings, the 'villain' who betrays the dog's whereabouts is called Mr Lee, and the protagonist is anonymous. Mick Connolly and his family do not appear until 'Milk Round', written in 1941; *FW*, pp. 121 and n. 76, 129, 137. For the impact of this incident on Davin see *FW*, p. 21.

NOTES

[1] cock him up: pamper, indulge him.

[2] Manion's farm: see references to Manion in 'The Vigil' and 'Gardens of Exile'.

[3] heeler: dog trained to control cattle by nipping them in the heel. Blue and Red Heelers are also well-known Australian breeds.

[4] the super-heater: Southland term for a hot water cylinder or cistern. *ODNZE*.

[5] the grass road: the grass origins of one of the roads which now run east off Conyers Street, then the boundary of the town (e.g. Wilfrid Street). It takes them past Mr Walsh's on the corner. See 'Growing Up', 'Invercargill Boundary'.

[6] the edge ... the mist: possibly Metzger's Bush or Paddocks in what is now the Heidelberg area.

7 Faraway Hill: south-east from Oteramika Road and east of Conyers Street and the 'grass road', approximately ten or fifteen minutes away from Morton Road for the boys to go there and get back to school after lunch. See 'The Faraway Hill'.

8 mattock: tool for grubbing with a steel head combining a blade shaped like an adze and sometimes, on the other side, a kind of pick.

9 Brother Athanasius's: possibly the same Brother Athanasius of 'Failed Exorcism'.

10 Cromwell ... Drogheda: Oliver Cromwell's infamous massacre on 11 September 1649 of the garrison of the English Royalist regiment and Irish Confederate troops including Catholic clergy in the besieged town of Drogheda during the Irish Confederate Wars; and thereafter until 1658 'the ruthless suppression of Catholic and royalist resistance, the execution, transportation or imprisonment of substantial numbers of Catholic clergy and the wholesale confiscation of Catholic lands'. S.J. Connolly, ed., *The Oxford Companion to Irish History* (Oxford: OUP, 1998), p. 135. See 'Black Diamond'.

11 the Pink Catechism: the Penny Catechism, so called because of its pink covers. It was used in New Zealand and Australia for instructing young children in the basic precepts of the faith.

12 long tots: lengthy sets of figures for addition. *DSUE*.

13 the Bluff Regatta: an annual event usually held on New Year's Day. See 'Bluff Retrospect'.

14 railway excursion ... Queenstown: outings provided by the railways for their employees and their families, by putting on special trains.

15 four marks ... Apostolic: the four essential marks that characterise the Christian Church as enumerated in the Nicene-Constantinople Creed.

16 Scott's paddocks: see 'The Apostate'.

17 Oteramika Road: the road which runs east from the crossroad, Elles Road. See 'The Apostate'; 'Late Snow'.

18 McGregor's Flat: land owned by the carter, Mr McGregor, neighbouring the Connolly's in Morton Street. See 'The Vigil'.

19 the midday Angelus: Catholic devotions commemorating the Incarnation, through summons by bell at morning, noon and sunset.

20 .32: a larger rifle than the .22, used for small game hunting.

21 form: bench, without a back.

6

The Basket

THEY HEARD THE CLUMP of the wooden latch on the back gate. Mrs Connolly looked up from the range which she was blackleading on her knees.[1] 'Who's that, Nellie?'

Nellie put down the knife she was polishing and looked out behind a corner of the lace window curtain. 'It's Mrs Fox. She's just coming across the back lawn.'

'Blast the woman. Hasn't she got more sense than to be coming round here this time of a Saturday morning, of all mornings, pestering me with her blather[2] and me with the housework to do and the dinner to get ready?'

She got up and flurried into the bathroom.

There was a knock at the back door. Nellie opened.

'Good morning, Mrs Fox. Come in. Mum won't be a minute.'

'Oh, and I won't come in just now with your mother busy and all. I just came over to give her back the basket she lent me to carry the vegetables in the other day.'

'Come in, then, Mrs Fox, come in.' Mrs Connolly had emerged from the bathroom, drying her hands on the roller towel as she came. She had taken off her sugar-bag apron. 'You must excuse the kitchen being in such a state, Mrs Fox, but we were just having a little clean-up.'

'Och, Mrs Connolly, and I won't be coming in interrupting you at all. I just wanted to give you back your basket for fear you might be needing it.'

'Nonsense now, come in and have a cup of tea. You'll be after catching a cold traipsing across those wet paddocks.'

'It's too much of a trouble it would be for you, surely, Mrs Connolly.'

'Not at all, now, not at all. Nellie and I were just going to make one, weren't we, Nellie? Run out and get a little kindling, Nellie, and we'll have the kettle boiling in two shakes of a dead lamb's tail.[3] Sit you down there now, Mrs Fox, and make yourself comfortable.'

'You're too kind altogether, Mrs Connolly. If you're sure I'm not disturbing you?'

'Of course not, woman, of course not. What's the matter with you at all? There now, you see, the kettle's on and it'll be boiling in a moment. And how's Mr Fox?'

'He's well enough. Though he's not the man he was. He's ageing and it's a disease has killed stronger men than him before today. And how's your husband?'

'He's very well, thank God. Sure he's so well that if he gets a cold he thinks he's dying. He's as strong as a man of forty. I wish I was as good on my feet.'

'It's a strong healthy woman you are too, Mrs Connolly.'

'Well, I can still cook him good meals and wash and keep the house clean. There's the kettle boiling now, Nellie. Take it off and make the tea. Is it two teaspoonfuls of sugar you'll be taking, Mrs Fox?'

'Thank you, Mrs Connolly. It's the good cup of tea you make, that's certain.'

'There's no comfort like a cup of good strong tea. It puts strength into your bones.'

'You're right there, Mrs Connolly. Many's the long day I don't know how I'd have got through if it hadn't been for a good cup of tea. And have you heard that young Nellie Flaherty and Johnny Brogan are to be married? And them so young. I don't know what they're going to live on, I'm sure.'

'The Lord will provide, Mrs Fox. Perhaps it's better for the young folk to get married and be happy while they're young. It steadies them too, I always say.'

'And that's true for you now, Mrs Connolly. I was only a slip of a girl myself when I was married and many's the hard trial I had soon after, what with Frank taking to the drink so hard and all.'

'Never mind, Mrs Fox, you can look back now and say: It was a hard life but I lived through it and was true to my man and brought up his children in the love of God.'

'True for you, Mrs Connolly. It's a rare comfort for an old woman to have a chat with you in the butt-end[4] of her days and you with the good heart and the good word always for another's troubles. But I must be going now and getting something ready for Frank to eat when he comes back from the town.'

'No hurry, Mrs Fox, no hurry at all.'

'I must be getting away, just the same and many thanks to you for the good tea and the kind words. It's lucky you are, Nellie, to have such a mother.'

'I'll walk down to the back gate with you, Mrs Fox. Nellie, just be finishing off those knives and have the potatoes on for the men's dinner. And keep an eye on the fire. I'll be back in a minute. We'll walk through the garden way, Mrs Fox.'

They crossed the square of asphalt, went by the wood-heap, still shrunken from last winter's fires and not yet the great mass of roots and red slabs it would be by the onset of the next.

The garden flourished with the vigour of a disciplined jungle. Beans reared massively up their poles into the air like muscular sailors swarming up the rigging, rows of peas dizzy with height twined perilously on to the sticks they had outgrown and stretched their tendrils into space like the hands of greedy children. The cabbages squatted fatly on their stalks each rapt in an intensity of bulging growth. Delicate and succulent the lettuces folded their modesty into tempting balls and complacently awaited ravishment. Beetroot, carrots, parsnips, onions – spring and spanish – alternated their serried parade on either side of the narrow path. Most impressive of all was the rhubarb, whose coarse, veined canopy of leaves almost concealed the huge, red-streaked stalks beneath, through which pumped the rich sap almost visibly.

'Sure, Mrs Connolly, and it's a gift of God your man has for making the world grow. Just look at the wonder of them cabbages.'

'Perhaps you would like a cabbage to take home with you, Mrs Fox?'

'It would be a shame to be cutting down one of God's miracles.'

'That's what Ned is always saying. He spends all his spare time growing things and yet he would have them all flowering away to seed if you would let him, rather than cut them. But we'll take one from the corner there and he won't notice it. That big yellow fellow over there with the heart of a bull on him.'

She felled the giant, cutting him close to the ground and covering over the butt of the stalk with soil, guiltily. But she grew bolder.

'And a few sticks of rhubarb he would never be missing. I don't know why he grows it, I'm sure, since there's only him and me that eat it. None of the others will look at it.'

'It's too good you are, Mrs Connolly.'

'Don't be talking, woman. What good is it if not for the eating?'

The rhubarb also fell to the knife, the broad voluptuous leaves were cut off and left to grow grey in the sun.

'And some carrots and parsnips to mash up for your man's dinner. You can't beat the good, fresh vegetables.'

'There never was woman had such a good neighbour as you, Mrs Connolly.'

'Sure, aren't we all neighbours, Mrs Fox. The good food is all the better for sharing. Perhaps you would like some spuds as well. The King Edwards have done wonders this year.'

'Now, Mrs Connolly, it's too much you have given me already. And haven't we potatoes at home?'

But already the spade was under the roots and the fat white potatoes lay on the upturned ground, naked and born.

'It's poor ground you have over there and the likes of these would be hard to find. Take them if only to try them.'

'Och, Mrs Connolly, and the woman with the heart like yours deserves the grand husband God gave her.'

'Don't be talking now. I'll just run back and get you the basket.'

She came back with the big wicker basket and it was loaded full.

Mrs Fox passed out through the little gate in the fence. 'Goodbye to you now Mrs Connolly, and may the Lord repay you for I can only give you the thanks of a poor old woman.'

'Get away with you now and if ever you're in need of a few vegetables, just be letting me know.'

Mrs Fox went over the paddock picking her way through the cowpats. Mrs Connolly came back by the garden. She was drying her eyes furtively. They were wet with her own generosity and Mrs Fox's poverty.

She came into the kitchen. 'Poor old woman. It's the hard life she's had, Nellie, with that lazy old drunkard of a husband of hers and little enough to show for the long years of slaving for him, now that they're come into the years of old age.'

'Have you been giving away Dad's vegetables again, Mum?'

'And what if I have given her a miserable old cabbage or so that would have gone to seed otherwise? And don't you be telling your father she was here or he'll be down in the garden complaining as if it was murder I'd done. And haven't you done those knives yet, my lady Jane,[5] dreaming here all the morning and doing nothing? The devil take that old wretch of a woman coming round here destroying my morning's work with her blathering, and me with a houseful of men will be home in an hour roaring for their food like a pack of wild things. And bless me if she hasn't gone away again with my basket.'

The Basket: a transcript is held in the Alexander Turnbull Library (MS-Group-0319).

NOTES

[1] range ... blackleading on her knees: Mrs Connolly, kneeling, was cleaning the cooking stove with blacklead (graphite).

[2] blather: voluble, foolish talk.

[3] two shakes of a dead lamb's tail: a variant on the colloquialism 'two shakes of a dog's hind leg'. See 'Presents'.

[4] butt-end: slang for 'tail end'. *DSUE*.

[5] my lady Jane: an idle young girl or woman. See 'A Return'.

7

Growing Up

IT WAS LATE AFTERNOON but the heat had not gone out of the day. Gorse pods still burst occasionally and their abrupt snap seemed to split the moments in two like the halves which went on twisting, the inner sides black and shiny and the outer silky and furred as a bee, even after their seeds had whirled out in an invisible arc to the future. Hidden in the sky the larks exulted, far above the paddocks which concealed their private future, the nest of four pale eggs. And on the edge of Murray's swamp[1] the frogs croaked harsh praise of a world of sun and grass and water.

At Walsh's little house on the corner[2] Mick and his father turned into Grass Road.[3] They could see by the blue smoke curling above the macrocarpa hedge that old Mr Walsh was watching the passing of men and time from his usual ambush. When they came level with the pink-painted picket gate he took the pipe from his mouth and looked at them with faded blue eyes.

'She's had the calf all right,' he said. 'A fine stamp of beast she is, that cow.'

Without looking up Mick shared his father's relief that Rosy was all right, his annoyance that once again old Mr Walsh was there to rob them of surprise.

'Thanks then, Tim,' said his father. 'Yes, she's a fine beast.' He didn't ask whether it was a bull or a heifer and Mick knew why. The old man would have told them already if he'd been up to see. So Mick's father didn't stop but walked on, hands in the trouser pockets he always had made well to the front, old waistcoat unbuttoned but held in place by the weight of nails and staples he always carried in case a fence needed mending. Old Mr Walsh replaced his pipe and continued to look out over the paddocks, rehearsing in his memory unspoken the calvings of the last sixty years.

'You couldn't have a boil on your bottom without that old fellow knowing it,' said Mr Connolly. He spoke aloud but to himself. Yet Mick felt bigger and older as he did the day his father first let him take Rosy to the bull.

They moved on up O'Donnell's hill.[4] Now and then Rob, the new collie,[5] dashed from the golden flare of gorse which crowned the right of the road, looked about till he saw them, waved his tail reassuringly and vanished once more after rabbits.

Away on the left, where the country dropped to the creek and the railway,[6] an engine shrilled triumphantly, its brood of trucks behind it. It would soon be home.

'The four-thirty-five goods,'[7] said Mick.

'That's right,' said his father. He took out his watch, looked at it, snapped back the cover and put it in his pocket again. 'She's up to time,' he added.

They left the road and jumping the dry ditch came to the gate, three strands of barbed wire nailed to three manuka poles.[8] Mr Connolly lifted the wire loop from the head of the pole nearest the straining post.[9] The gate folded back open.

O'Donnell's trees running along the crest of the hill cut the paddock in half and the dropping sun had thrown the nearest side in shade. Rosy would be on the other side of the crest where the grass still basked in warmth.

The macrocarpa trunks were bare as high as Mick's head. The cows had broken off the small branches and twigs, rubbing themselves there on days when the sun was too hot or rain made them take shelter. Wisps of hair clung to the rough bark. And the ground was dry there with little grass since the trees stole the rain. As they passed under Mick couldn't help looking up to where framed in the branches the sparrows' nests were, so untidy outside, so neat and downy within. Last year he would have been up there in the branches, counting the eggs.

Rosy lay on her side, back towards them. She was between them and the calf. She had lost all her winter hair and the sun nestled warmly in the licked whorls of her roan summer coat. She heard them coming and turning her head recognised them. She got slowly to her feet and lowed anxiously. They could see under her belly to the calf, also up now and teetering a little on legs far too long for its body.

'Gosh,' said Mr Connolly, 'the kids didn't take long to find them.'

And sure enough both Rosy and the calf had long daisy-chains draped round their necks in garlands.

Rosy shook her head as they came up and moved round to keep between them and the calf. The calf was licked and clean.

'Well, old girl,' said Mr Connolly, and he slapped her on the shoulder, 'so you made it all right. Just hang on here, Mick and I'll see if I can find her cleaning.[10] If she hasn't eaten it already, the old devil.'

He began to walk about the paddock, searching the grass. Rosy looked from Mick to the calf, all pride and fondness for the calf, confidence and suspicion for Mick.

'It's here, all right, Mick,' called out his father. 'We'll leave her in the home paddock tonight and you bring up a spade and bury it in the morning.'

He came back and looked at the cow and calf.

'A bull,' he said. 'Pity, I hoped we'd get a nice young heifer out of her this time. A strong little beggar he looks too.'

Mick watched Rosy compassionately. She was licking the calf and each lick was a caress. Poor Rosy. She always had bulls.

His father bent over, picked up the calf and slung it over his shoulders. Rosy tossed her head and lowed, her eyes wild. The calf lowed back at her. She rushed round to where the calf's head was and began to lick it.

'It's all right, Rosy,' said Mr Connolly, bending his legs and heaving the calf further up his shoulders. 'We're just going home, that's all.'

They set off for the gate. Rosy followed just behind, lowing anxiously. She walked awkwardly with her full udder.

Rob came scampering over the hill, saw the procession, stopped irresolute, then followed behind Mick, subdued.

As they passed Walsh's house old Mr Walsh was still at the gate. He took out his pipe.

'A fine bag of milk she's got there,' he said. 'A bull, by the look of him. A pity, and him with a touch of the Jersey. It's a good cross for

Southland, the Shorthorn and the Jersey. Well, you'll get five bob on the skin, I suppose.'

Mick glared at him and then looked back at Rosy. She didn't understand, luckily.

At the big wooden gate of the cowshed they stopped.

'We'd better get him in right away,' said Mr Connolly. 'If she gets used to him sucking her there'll be the devil to pay. You open the gate and as soon as I'm through nip in and close it so she can't get through.'

The door clumped to in Rosy's face and Mick slid the wooden bolt.

'That's the style,' said his father.

Rosy's roars came frantically through. The cows in the next paddock began to bellow in sympathy, recognising their common fate.

Mrs Connolly was feeding the hens, her sugar-bag apron caught up with the oats in its fold, her hand strewing out the grain in fistfuls. It fell like a rain of sunlight and the hens scurried about in a frenzy, their heads jerking up and down like the needle of a sewing-machine, their eyes always ahead of their beaks, their greed in advance of their eyes.

'A bull, Nellie,' called Mr Connolly.

'Poor Rosy,' said Mrs Connolly, 'such fine calves and never a one we could rear.' Then, as if ashamed of that softening or frightened of it: 'Well, I suppose the sooner it's killed the sooner we'll have peace and quiet again.' She pursed her lips and went on strewing the oats, mind closed against the sad bellows beyond the wall.

As Mr Connolly came with the calf to the lawn, the Scovy duck[11] retreated with dignity and her family to the hedge. Molly, the ferret, left her young in the darkness of the inner compartment and climbed up the netting of the cage spreadeagled and pink eyes cold and curious.

Mr Connolly set the calf down on the dark of the rich, clipped grass. It stood there, doddering with its awkward grace. It had Rosy's colouring, only at the ends the hair deepened into the Jersey's tannish black. It was still wet from the mother's licking. It shivered a little. It was alone for the first time. Suddenly it gave a strong young bellow, startlingly strong from something so young. Rosy's answering bellow was prompt, desperate with solicitude.

'We'll have to get on with it, Mick,' said Mr Connolly. 'Fetch me the mall.'[12]

Mick dragged the heavy mall from the tool-shed. His father hefted[13] it above his head and put it down again. He liked the mall because it was heavy enough to make him feel his strength. Mick looked at the iron rings which bound each end of the wooden, barrel-shaped head. The calf's eyes were big and dark.

It stood shakily in the square of green. Two hands on the handle of the mall, Mr Connolly was leaning forward, muscles relaxed, watching the calf. His grey eyes were inscrutable. Mick felt the layers of feeling inside his father, the indifference – almost callousness – forced by life which held these necessities, under this the gentleness that puzzled at the necessity, the strength and weakness of man forced by life to give life and take it.

The cables of muscle and sinew on the heavy forearms rose and tautened, the biceps bulged against the rolled sleeves. Mick looked at the mall raised high above and behind his father's head. Would he be able to watch the down stroke? He must if he were to be grown-up.

The mall came swiftly down. Mick looked away. But his ears heard the thud.

When he looked back the calf was down. It had made no sound. There was blood at its ears and nostrils. His father was leaning on the haft[14] of the mall, breathing more heavily. Red hairs, short and curly from the calf's head, red and tannish black, clung in blood not curving but broken to one of the iron rings. Mr Connolly was looking down at the calf.

'Poor little beggar,' he said. And then to Mick: 'I'll show you how to skin him tomorrow. You can have the skin. It's a good skin, worth five bob.'

But Mick was running up the path towards the house.

Mrs Connolly came back from the fowl-run. She looked down at the dead calf.

'It's a shame,' she said. 'But what else can you do? I've fed the pigs.' She went on towards the house.

'Bring the milk bucket back with you,' called Mr Connolly after her. 'She's got a big bag of milk on her and there'll be a nice drop of beastings.'[15]

'I left the bucket in the cowshed,' she replied.

He put the mall back then went to the cowshed and barred off the opening so that Rosy couldn't get through to see her calf. He opened the wooden gate and let her into the bail.

'Poor old girl,' he said as he leg-roped her. But while he milked her, easing the great swollen udder, she kept her head turned towards him in the bail and from time to time she moaned.

'Perhaps you'll have a nice little heifer the next time,' he said.

In the kitchen chops were frying and you couldn't hear Rosy. Mick's young brother came in. 'What was it?' he asked.

'It was a bull so we had to kill it,' said Mick casually.

Growing Up: a transcript is held in the Alexander Turnbull Library (MS-Group-0319).

NOTES

[1] Murray's swamp: Robert Murray, contractor, lived at 40 Conyers Street which ran parallel to Morton Road on the east side (so close to the Davin's home in Morton Street) and which demarcated the town boundary. 'Murray's Paddock', probably the next door section to 40 Conyers Street, may have also been a 'swamp' (see 'Goosey's Gallic War', 'Invercargill Boundary', 'Gardens of Exile'). Wise's *Directory* 1929.

[2] Walsh's … corner: this is the same Mr Walsh who betrays the boys in 'Death of a Dog'.

[3] Grass Road: possibly the same grass road as in 'Death of a Dog', which leads to Faraway Hill. See also 'Invercargill Boundary'.

[4] O'Donnell's hill: south of Oteramika Road and west of Rockdale Road. If located just off Grass Road, then it is probably no more than two blocks away from Morton Road.

[5] the new collie: this story follows chronologically from 'Death of a Dog'. Rob replaces Old Jack; Mick has grown older.

[6] the creek … railway: Puni Creek and the railway line north of Oteramika Road.

[7] The four-thirty-five goods: the goods train coming to Invercargill either from Bluff (a line which was heavily used for freight trains) or from Gore, or one of the branch lines.

[8] three strands … manuka poles: a Taranaki Gate with three battens instead of two. See 'Goosey's Gallic War'.

[9] straining post: large fence post stayed to take the strain of the wire.

[10] cleaning: the placenta of a cow.

[11] Scovy duck: a Muscovy duck.

[12] mall: var. of mallet, or hammer.

[13] hefted: lifted up.

[14] haft: handle.

[15] beastings: first milk drawn from the cow after giving birth.

8

Saturday Night

'YES,' SAID MRS CONNOLLY, '*The Golden Calf*[1] it was called. And so naturally Mick and I thought it was a Bible picture. You know, like *The Ten Commandments* or *Ben Hur*.'

'You're right then,' said Mrs Fox. 'That's what anybody would be thinking.'

'But you'd never guess what it really was.'

'Well, what was it then at all?'

Mrs Connolly lowered her voice and looked at the boy.

'It was about women's legs if you please. *The Golden Calf* was women's legs.' Indignation ousted caution and she raised her voice. 'A pack of brazen hussies flaunting their bare legs.'

The boy did not look up. He was a practised eavesdropper.

'You don't say,' said Mrs Fox, and her spectacles glistened as she leaned over the table. 'Well, and if it isn't a wicked world we're living in!'

'A wicked world indeed. And so that's your pictures for you. Disgusting, wasn't it, Ned?'

Ned started from his doze by the range. 'What's that?'

'That picture we saw, *The Golden Calf*.'

'Disgusting,' said Ned. It was no matter for argument. He settled into his chair again, the cat warm on his broad thigh and under his hand. The cat knew who was the most stable member of the household.

'Yes, them's your pictures for you, not fit for young people to see.' Mrs Connolly raised her voice meaningly and looked across at Mick. He did not lift his head from his book. The hand lifting the heavy tea-cup to his mouth showed no sign.

But the battle was on. It was Saturday night. It was going to be a job now to get the money. His mother had already committed herself by this attack. Especially in front of Mrs Fox. His father would be no use. He could always be silenced with *The Golden Calf.* It was no good Mick's pointing out that he didn't have the slightest desire to see *The Golden Calf,* that there were other films on and in any case he was fourteen and old enough to go out to the pictures at night at least once a week anyway. Logic would be useless once his mother was worked up like this, especially with that silly old gas-bag urging her on.

Nellie came bustling out of the scullery and grabbed his cup. He grabbed it back.

'How much longer are you going to roost there, you and your old book? I've got to get ready for choir practice. Can't wait for you all night.'

He glared at her. On second thoughts better not give her a broadside.[2] Not tonight.

He shut the book, got up and left the room.

In the bedroom he took down his navy-blue suit from the wardrobe, dug out a pair of clean socks, clean shirt and tie and gazed on them with satisfaction. His first suit of longs, all neatly pressed. He'd ironed them himself this morning. Not the sort of job you could trust women with. Socks nice dark blue, shirt light blue, a nice dark red tie. Not at all bad, really. Especially when you'd bought them all yourself out of rabbit-skin money; all except the tie, that is. The curse of it was, now he'd spent the money on the togs,[3] he had to get the picture-money from his mother.

'Where are you going, Mick?'

Eileen had come in behind him.

'What do you want to know for?'

She ignored his crustiness. 'My word, you will look a sheikh. Going to the pictures?'

He was mollified. 'Yes.'

'Where are you going to get the money?'

'Oh, I'll get it.'

'Wish I was going. I get sick of Nellie always dragging me off to these silly old choir practices.'

'Eileen, Eileen!'

'There she goes again.' Eileen shot out the door.

Mick went over to the chest of drawers and opened his drawer. It contained a cross-section of his life history. Doughty marbles, cigarette cards, bits of shanghai as they called their catapults[4] until they began to read *The Boys' Own Paper*,[5] remnants of a fretwork phase and a photographic phase. But the latest stratum was at the bottom. From underneath the litter he drew a packet of 'Westward Ho'[6] and transferred it deftly to the blue suit. From another cavern he produced a ferocious razor and some shaving soap. He inspected the razor affectionately, heritage from Ned, already emancipated, picked up his towel and sauntered out in his shirt-sleeves.

His mother and Mrs Fox were deep in conclave.[7]

'Gallstones,' Mrs Fox was saying. 'They took so many out of me I wonder I hadn't been rattling. I was like a quarry. It must have needed a wheelbarrow to carry them all away.'

Mrs Connolly did not look up as Mick passed. The gallstones story was an old favourite, and she was too comfortable. A person liked to sit quiet for a bit after tea and have a bit of peace.

Mick left the bathroom door ajar. The softening process first. He began to sing:

Like a candle that's set in a window at night
Your fond love has cheered me and guided me right.
Every sorrow and care in the dear days gone by
Was made bright by the light of the smile in your eye.
I kiss the dear fingers
So toilworn for me,
Oh, God bless you and keep you,
Mother Machree.[8]

The voice broke a bit on the high notes. But no harm in that. Showed how grown up he was. Better let it sink in a bit. The razor cut its swathe through the soft fur. Well, even if a man didn't have much of a beard he might as well get into the way of using a razor.

Better let fly again. No getting away from it, mothers were a blasted nuisance. Just wouldn't realise a man couldn't always go on being a boy just to please them. Ned had had just the same trouble. Frightful rows there used to be before she got used to him going out of a night. Mind you, he always took the bull-at-a-gate method.[9] Mother Machree, he flattered himself, was more subtle.

Mo-other Machree-ee.

That should melt a stone.

'It's a beautiful voice the boy has, surely, Mrs Connolly.'

Mrs Connolly bridled. 'Well, of course, he's at the awkward age now, Mrs Fox. Hobbledehoy,[10] neither man nor boy.'

'Sure, and the boy is almost a man already.'

'Yes, they're all growing up on me. I only wish I had another one coming on. They're nicer when they're young. Not so bold.'

'Sure, Mrs Connolly, and it's a lucky woman you are to have such fine sons at all, and so clever they all are. It's a proud woman you must be.'

'Ah, well, and I suppose they might be worse. Though that Mick's a bit of a queer one. I had hopes of making a priest of him. But now I don't know at all, it's hard to know what he's thinking sometimes.'

'Ach, Mrs Connolly, the boy is a good boy and you know it. Many's the time when I've seen him up with the day bringing in the cows and feeding them at the fall of night. I've been thinking to myself: It's a lucky woman you are, Mrs Connolly, to have such fine sons, so clever and so strong, a fine comfort for you when you're old and the nights are long and the winter hard. And it's wishing I am my own Andy had half the respect for his parents that your boys have.'

'Don't be fretting yourself with worry now, Mrs Fox, your own Andy's a good boy for all that. The young men will always be for drinking a drop or two when they're young and the blood's wild.'

'Still and all, Mrs Connolly, you'd be waiting a long time before you'd be hearing him sing the like of young Mick there – for all he has a good voice and all, the like mine was once. Just listen to the boy now.'

Like a candle that's set in a window at night,
Your fond love has cheered me and guided me right.
Sure I love the dear silver that shines in your hair
And the brow that's all furrowed and wrinkled with care.

The bathroom door opened and Mick came out, his face shining, his walk elaborately casual. A quick whip of the eyes and he passed.

When he came back he was arrayed to perfection. He picked up the *Southland Times* and ostentatiously scanned the film advertisements.

'And where are you off to, all cocked up[11] so fine?' his mother asked.

'I thought of going to the pictures,'

'Not to that *Golden Calf*, I hope?'

'Good Heavens, no, not to that rubbish. There's a good film on at the Regent.'[12]

'Well fetch me my purse from the mantelpiece.'

He passed it over, worn, black leather.

'How much will it be?'

'Just a shilling.'

'Well, here's two shillings and you can buy yourself an orange drink.'

A packet of Capstan and still some money to spare!

His father was watching him. He had Mick's face with thirty years of hard work superimposed. You could not see his thoughts and he seldom spoke them.

Mick took the money. 'Thanks very much, Mum,' he said.

'Don't be late,' called Mrs Connolly. But he was already wheeling his bicycle round the corner of the house.

'After all, he's not a bad boy,' said Mrs Connolly.

'A fine strong lad and he is then,' said Mrs Fox.

Ned Connolly got to his feet.

'I'll just see that the cover is on Rosy. She's near calving.' He put on his gum boots.

'He's a sly one, is that fellow,' he said as he went out the door.

Saturday Night: a transcript is held in the Alexander Turnbull Library (MS-Group-0319).

NOTES

1   *The Golden Calf*: a black and white Hollywood movie released 16 March 1930, directed by Millard Webb and starring Jack Mulhall. Now a 'lost movie', its classification as a romantic comedy musical confirms it is not about the biblical story.

2   give ... broadside: 1) the firing of all guns on one side of the ship 2) a strong attack in words. *ODNZE*.

3   togs: clothes. See 'tog' v. 'to dress', *DSUE*.

[4] shanghai … catapults: popular weapons of New Zealand children, made of a wooden prong to which is attached a leather or rubber thong. See 'Roof of the World' and 'Goosey's Gallic War'.

[5] *The Boys' Own Paper*: a British monthly paper, published from 1879 to 1967. It contained fiction, poetry, and 'how to' guides, promoting gallant boyhood and ideal masculinity.

[6] 'Westward Ho': possibly *Westward Ho Smoking Tobacco*, advertised in America during the 1920s in ways which link the tobacco with the call of the west.

[7] deep in conclave: involved in private discussion.

[8] Mother Machree: an Irish classic, composed in 1910 by Ernest R. Ball, with lyrics by Rida Johnson Young.

[9] bull-at-a-gate method: charging headlong at the problem.

[10] Hobbledehoy: a youth between boyhood and manhood, at the awkward age.

[11] all cocked up: colloq. full of airs, preening. In *Roads from Home*, Moira is 'all cocked up' with her convent education (*RfH*, p. 132). See 'Death of a Dog'.

[12] Regent: cinema on Dee Street.

9

That Golden Time[1]

CASTLE STREET[2] WAS EMPTY, as empty as that other space towering vacantly overhead towards the stars. The emptiness, the way his heels rang on the asphalt, was satisfying, emphasised his aloneness. A man alone, alone late at night with no one to say he should be home in bed. A man making his way home from the arms of his mistress. And the clear, frosty night a splendid setting for his solitude.

Mistress, it wasn't quite the word really. It didn't go somehow with a girl you'd met at the Town Hall dance only a week before. She was too far from names like Roxana[3] and Pompadour,[4] the canopied beds, the whisper behind the fan, loud feet on the stairs, the sudden hush of the nightingales and a quick escape into the moonlit garden.[5] No, the slang words suited her better – sheila, skirt, tabby[6] – gin in the dark of the doorway and, distant in the dance-hall, the band playing 'I'm Dancing with Tears in My Eyes'.[7]

Still, she'd fallen for him, and when you didn't know any better you had to take what you could get. She did have a room at least, a flat really. And when they were away from the others she was quite gentle and hadn't laughed at him. Of course he looked older than he was. But it was the first time for him, you couldn't get away from that. She must have noticed.

But he didn't want to think about her. She was only the essential partner in the thing. The important fact was that now he knew. And out here in the lonely silence of the street he could piece into the mosaic this final stone.

So that was what it was like. In itself, nothing so very wonderful. A relief certainly, after the tension and desire. An event really, an epoch. But in itself, nothing so very wonderful. A disappointment? Well, yes, in a way. But an adventure, a stage in knowledge. A step across the threshold. He was closer to being a man. Was a man, in fact. Of course, he wasn't fool enough to think that at seventeen you could know everything. But at least he knew more than he had known. He had had one of a man's experiences, even if it wasn't much, not all it was cracked up to be. He'd been drunk and he'd had a woman. Not too drunk luckily. Or perhaps he had been? Perhaps it would have been better if he hadn't drunk so much? Alcohol was a sort of anaesthetic, wasn't it?

With academic deliberation the university clock boomed a warning note. Like old Prof. Evans clearing his throat to speak. To announce that Catullus, in spite of his sensuality, it could not be denied was a great poet. A pity that in a society as corrupt as that of the late Republic[8] his experience should have been almost necessarily licentious, that the manners, he might say, the mores, of the time made it natural that he should express himself in a licentious way.[9] One might almost grant him the excuse of inevitability since he inevitably reflected the morals of his time. 'To hold the mirror up to Nature –'.[10] And, after all, even in Shakespeare –. And then, also, one must remember that he did not have the benefits of revealed religion.[11] We must make allowances. And he was young. A passionate pagan –.

The Professor sighed, troubled perhaps by a vague resentment that Catullus, in spite of his professors, should be living still, while he, Professor Evans, M.A. of his University, Elder of the Church[12] and confident of everlasting life, should stand here, dead, and forbidden by a lifetime's hebetude to expound the paradox.[13] He sighed again: 'Well, we must get on with the reading. "Lesbia's Sparrow".[14] Will you begin, Miss Macpherson?'

The clock, an old man's echo, struck its three strokes in empty pomp. But its reverberation, a quavering afterthought, still vibrated over Miss Macpherson's well-conned reduction of a light Latin fancy to Presbyterian prose.[15]

Vivamus, mea Lesbia.[16] The waters of the Leith,[17] telling their own less even time, smoothed the rugged jutting of Miss Macpherson's earnest face, abolished her horn-rimmed glasses and Lesbia's passionate paleness burned from the water. Night and the clock's ponderous warning sombred daylight's shallow stream into the depth and passion and mystery of all dark water still and flowing.

Yet, perhaps the Professor and Miss Macpherson were right. Or the sparrow. Tonight's experience had more of his swift flurry in the gutter and casual aftermath of adjustment than it had of Lesbia. Lesbia herself perhaps had only been the hen, lent false feathers and the fine sheen of passion by a poet's frustrated frenzy. And that frenzy itself but a more complex kind of mating call.

Nobis cum semel occidit brevis lux
Nox est perpetua una dormienda.[18]

The night at least was magnificent and, as for the final sunset and the single timeless sleep, that remained to be seen. Or never to be seen.

But he wasn't really being fair to Catullus. Let sparrows observe sparrows. Men must watch the fate of men. The whole point of a love poet lay in the love. And he could hardly claim to have been in love with Lily, God forbid.

So perhaps he still didn't know.

Lesbia had left the water, dismissed to the enigmatic past. Lily's friendly face, pale in the naked overhead light as putty, in the light of the lampshade pink as her own brassieres, passed along its prisoner's walk of expression from anxiety as they tiptoed up the stairs and past the landlady's stertorous room,[19] to nervous and giggling triumph as they sat on the bed and canvassed with a show of argument the inevitable understood, to complicit eagerness which she masked by bending to her shoes and releasing her choked feet to irrelevant cheerfulness, through all these stages till at last, nervous and heart hollow, he saw again under the half-closed lids the eyes fixed across the enormous distances beyond which we see nullity when, alone except for the company of another guilty body, our desires cling to their desperate ecstasy, alone.

Surely he had got some truth out of it then? But if truth were beauty and beauty truth?[20] Too bare an equation surely, when the two were one and that one not beauty. Catullus and Keats were more fortunate than he. Or less impatient? Or were they wrong?

Anyhow, he'd got some truth out of it. Even if one man's truth were another man's poison he knew something he hadn't known before. He could face these poet chaps more on their own ground now. He was different from what he had been. He looked up from the stream, its dark film now empty as the street, to the University's Presbyterian gothic.[21] It might have given him Catullus but he was one up on it now. What would old Bacchus Evans think if he knew where he had been? And all the class which would mouth poetry tomorrow as mechanically as prayers? Masked behind his face he would savour secret laughter.

The clock voiced with the quarter its brief disapprobation. Time to be making for home. A quarter past three. It would be good to be back in his digs, alone in his room, that first base from which he had set out to wrest from the city knowledge and freedom. It was there on many a lonely night that he had pored over the map of the unknown and measured his adversaries, ignorance and fears. He would go back there now and mark in the new line, the new frontier.

He moved on, fingering still the outlines of his experience, minutely scrutinising it for missed significance, suffering already his first intimations of the speed with which the memory of the senses fades, till what is called pleasure depends on the word it first created for reality while the urgent detonation in the nerves can no more be recalled than the dead bones of poets can arch again the pulsing sap from which their passion flowered. And he learnt for the first time the disgust that seeps into the place of passion which, engendered in the brain, passes along the blood, goes and leaves a vacuum untenanted by tenderness or love.

The house stood out white against the dark of the hill.[22] But its whiteness was blank and unlit. The Buchanans were always early to bed. The door was locked. They must have thought he was in bed too. He crept round to his ground floor window. Mrs Buchanan was not tolerant of new moralities. The window was ajar as he had left it. He climbed cautiously in.

He switched on the light. He was breathing a little hard, from climbing in. And this was his moment. There might be no crowd for his triumph but he did not want anyone else. Triumph is better enjoyed unwatched. One's own jealous observation is a sufficient audience, a sufficient adversary. The most formidable even, since here visors are lifted, motives and vanities admitted and disasters plain.

Yet he paused before facing the mirror, as a man pauses before looking to see what cards he has drawn, or before opening a letter long awaited. Now he was to see the lines that drink and debauchery had cut in his face. He was to see what it looked like to have changed. He squared his shoulders and turned to the mirror, to see and confront his manhood.

The face that he saw was young, its imaginary beard carefully shaven and tomorrow's instalment of the fiction not yet visible. The mouth was full but its line firm. The eyes were steady, perplexed, inquiring, very young.

It was the face with which he had set out that evening, nerved for the momentous stride into maturity. It was the face of an intelligent youth of seventeen, only now a little tired.

He studied it a long time. Then he put the mirror down. He felt very tired. It was late. And he had not prepared his Cicero for the morning.

Still, he had done one thing. He was no longer a virgin, anyway. He had the laugh on the rest of them, say what you like. As for the Cicero he didn't need to bother about that old windbag. His tirades were never unpredictable. He could do it at sight, easily.

He picked up the mirror suddenly, as if to catch it off its guard. The face was obstinately the same. He saw what looked like a blackhead and became intent on removing it. Lily had a bad complexion. Fastidiously he banished her memory from the mirror.

The clock struck the half-hour as he got into bed.

That Golden Time: a transcript is held in the Alexander Turnbull Library (MS-Group-0319).

NOTES

[1] That Golden Time: an allusion to proverbial sayings warning either of the illusory nature of a golden age, or of its transience. See G.L. Apperson, *English Proverbs and Proverbial Phrases. An Historical Dictionary* (London: Dent, 1929), p. 255.

[2] Castle Street: a street now bisected by the campus of the University of Otago.

[3] Roxana: the beautiful, upper-class protagonist of Daniel Defoe's novel *Roxana* (1724), who becomes a prostitute in order to save herself from destitution.

[4] Pompadour: the Marquise de Pompadour (b. 1721), the official mistress of Louis XV from 1745–50. She became a patron of the arts, and remained an influential but hated figure in French affairs of state during the Seven Year War with England, until her death in 1764.

[5] the canopied ... garden: stereotypical images from the eighteenth century of an illicit

liaison involving betrayal and escape, suggestive of the licentiousness of affairs with courtesans, mistresses and prostitutes.

6 sheila, skirt, tabby: only 'sheila' is identified by *RDNZS* as indigenous; 'skirt' is late nineteenth-century slang and 'tabby', dating from c. 1700, is an old woman. See *DSUE* s.v. 'Pommy Sheila'; 'The Quiet One'; 'The Albatross'.

7 'I'm Dancing with Tears in My Eyes': a popular song, words and lyrics by Al. Dubin and Joe Burke, which reached no. 1 on the charts in 1930.

8 as corrupt … late Republic: the period from 123 to 23 BC. Gaius Valerius Catullus (c. 84–54 BC) and his circle have been associated with its so-called decadence because of their Epicurean lifestyle, interest in poetry and love, and remoteness from politics. Nevertheless Catullus's life and work belong to the beginning of the great age of Latin poetry in 60 BC.

9 express … licentious way: Professor Evans's 'puritanical' explanation of the erotic wit and sexual innuendo of Catullus' poetry, as a consequence of the late Republic's 'pagan', 'licentious mores', does not account for the inspiration in a personal experience of love, nor the influence of literary tradition.

10 'To hold the mirror up to Nature': Hamlet to Players, *Hamlet*, Act 3, Scene ii.

11 revealed religion: Christianity, a religion based on revelations from the deity which are transcribed into a sacred text.

12 Professor … Elder of the Church: the Professor of Latin at the University of Otago in 1930–5 when Davin was a student was Thomas Dagger Adams, probably a Scot (who had arrived in 1907). The comments attributed to the Professor in the previous paragraph reflect the moral values of Presbyterian puritanism, then the controlling ethos both of the city of Dunedin and the University of Otago.

13 the paradox: i.e. that licentious living can be a source of immortal art in the hands of a supreme artist like Catullus.

14 Lesbia's Sparrow: 'Passer deliciae meae puellae': 'Sparrow, my Lesbia's darling pet'.

15 Presbyterian prose: a barbed comment on the 'reduction' of Catullus' playful wit to the moral sobriety of a Presbyterian translation, here associated with the middle-class Anglican and Protestant students.

16 Vivamus, mea Lesbia: 'Let us live, my Lesbia': The rest of this line – 'atque amemus', i.e. 'and love' – has been deliberately omitted.

17 The waters of the Leith: another pointed allusion to the link between Dunedin and its Scottish Presbyterian heritage. The river which runs through the University campus is named after the Leith in Edinburgh.

18 *Nobis … dormienda*: 'For us when the short light has once set, remains to be slept the sleep of one unbroken night'.

19 stertorous room: a transferred epithet. The room is animated by the sound of the landlady's heavy snoring.

20 But if truth … truth?: Keats' famous line '"Beauty is truth, truth, beauty"' in 'Ode on a Grecian Urn'.

21 University's Presbyterian gothic: Dunedin's growth in the Victorian period coincided with the revival of Gothic architecture. The university's original buildings in this style, including the clock-tower in Leith Street, were designed by Maxwell Bury in 1878.

22 The house … the hill: possible locations are suggested by Davin's lodgings as a student: George Street where he was living in 1932–3 or London Street on City Rise to which he moved in May 1933. *FW,* pp. 63, 69, 71.

10

Casualties

THE LECTURER PAUSED and looked over the top of the reading-desk and out of her circle of light down into the less brightly lit schoolroom. It was the first lecture of her W.E.A.[1] series. She had been nervous, had read too fast perhaps and had not taken the feel of her audience. Not that there were so many of them; and the eyes lifted to hers now seemed humble enough. Too humble, eyes that looked without reproach at the stone you gave them. But what bread could they want, these faded women, this sprinkling of men? What did they expect of books, of poetry at second-hand? What they had not got out of life? But books, like God, give only to those who have.

But it was nearly over: just time to read the verse on which she was to end. Then a few perfunctory questions, a sluggish discussion decently prolonged, and she could hurry away along the wet streets that glistened outside under the lamps to Olive's place and there everyone would be drinking coffee and talking for themselves as if they meant it and not drearily waiting to hear the oracles of others.

'And so it is not unfair to say that, except for Rupert Brooke whose untimely death came before his second thoughts, Siegfried Sassoon speaks for all the war poets I have been discussing when in *The Heart's Journey*[2] he says:

Here was the world's worst wound. And here with pride
"Their name liveth for ever," the Gateway claims.
Was ever an immolation so belied;
As these intolerably nameless names?
Well might the dead who struggled in the slime
Rise and deride this sepulchre of crime.'[3]

The last accusing syllable flung by her voice, clear and mercilessly young, rang against the misted windows and steady rustle of the rain outside. In the ensuing pause there was a shuffling under the children's desks as elderly knees tried to accommodate afresh their aches. Or, she thought, as if they had suddenly felt her, so much their junior, as a teacher taking their generation to task and were uneasily at a loss to know whether their vague resentment sprang from guilt or innocence.

She closed her books and squared her sheaf of papers. All over now except the few, flagging questions the dutiful ones would be bound to ask.

'If anyone has any questions I shall do my best to try and answer.'

The shuffling ceased. In the silence she could feel the timid ladies fearing her eye might light on them. Why did they come at all? Because it was free? Because it was improving? Or because Literature was refined? Perhaps Lee, her communist friend at Training College, was right: you could never fool the real workers with this grey, anaemic pap. They had enough instinct to sense that you couldn't find power, a deeper life, here. This diluted Culture for the Lower Classes was just Church all over again, the old opium. But in weaker solution.

The silence was getting heavier, anxious. Depression sapped at her. How could you get behind those masks? If you did what would you find? More greyness, probably. Or perhaps realities intolerable, a drab, daily horror that forced these drained women and few, devitalised men to scratch at their walls and try and break out into the air of the imagination, an air they thought fresh and free as the sunlight should have been for them and would never be.

A seat at the back squealed on its hinges. A tall, gaunt man got slowly to his feet. He wore dark glasses and did not seem so much to look as to aim his face at her. She recognised him at once. It was Carr,[4] the blind man whose verses, stiff with Literature, were published from time to time in the morning paper. And that was his sister sitting beside him who shared with him the big white house on the hill and went walking with him about the gardens of the city.

'Does not the lecturer think,' he said, 'that these men who call themselves poets and profess to speak for their generation degrade the very name of poetry and trample on the honour bought by the dead with their blood, in polluting with these scrannel verses such a sacrifice?' His accent was more English than is usual among New Zealanders. His voice was low, clear, and trembling. His cheeks were pale with the anger that should have flashed from his eyes.

The lecturer bent her head, flushing. On paper, or from her father at the breakfast table, she would have shrugged off the words with a patronising smile. This was the first time she had met to her face an intensity whose demand for an answer was as imperious as logic. One forgets that argument is only a pleasure when it is with friends whose age, premises and prejudices are the same; for, since it is only in logic that conclusions are ever reached and life is not logical, about these difference is cheerful. But an attack on presuppositions threatens the very pipe from which the bubbles are blown. So gathering her confusions to a desperate rally the girl looked up now to answer.

But she was too late. There was a man in the second row already on his feet. He seemed to have been waiting to catch her eye. Or else his indignation had made it difficult for him to begin. Some sort of working-man, she guessed; not from his clothes but by that social sense mothers foster till in maturity it is intuitive. His anxiety to do the right thing helped. The blind man's politeness like her intuition or a bird's flight had been taught him young.

'He doesn't know what he's talking about, Miss.' His voice was more incoherent than his words and his sincerity, like the other's, was immediately arresting. 'The war poets were right. They knew what they were talking about, don't you worry. We'd know too if we went through what they went through. We should know anyhow, out of our own common sense. It was the world's worst wound, all right. It's terrible and shocking to think of them all lying there dead, nameless names. And what for? For men like that Zaharoff[5] and patriots who stayed at home. While they were out there killing their brothers. Because what's Christianity about if we aren't all brothers? Remember that bit of Wilfred Owen's:

I am the enemy you killed, my friend.
I knew you in the dark: for so you frowned
Yesterday through me as you jabbed and killed.[6]

'He knew what we all ought to know. He'd learnt it all right. It's murder. It's worse, it's fratricide. And I say to these poets: "Good for you." What's a poet for if he doesn't tell the truth?'

He sat down, blushing at his own vehemence. But a convincing and determined man.

The other was up. He tried to lean forward on the low desk to support his trembling hands. But he was too tall for it. He stood straight again. Here was the chance to intervene, to get the meeting back into her control. She saw it but could not take it. The passion between these two men usurped the room. She and the rest of the people in it were as powerless and huddled as sheep under lightning. Only by being there they gave the illusion of being jurors to be fought for. They conducted the fire, and, shabbily afraid, felt elation in its anger.

'What's a poet for if he doesn't tell the whole truth? Why don't they say that behind the temporary scum of a few profiteers there is a great ideal, the British Empire? That was what we fought for, not for the profiteers. And when we fought for that we fought for justice, freedom, democracy. But perhaps our friend doesn't think these things worth fighting for? Or didn't, if as I guess he wasn't one of the soldiers he presumes to speak for.'

Trying to assure herself that it was absurd, like a tennis-match, the lecturer watched the nearer man get up, pale now and stung. That was the way she would tell it later over the fire at Olive's, she knew, like a tennis-match. And the way she would tell it, they would all laugh and then go on to have a serious discussion about pacifism and patriotism and whether that resolution about King and Country they passed away in Oxford[7] the other day was right. And they'd agree it was right. But just now it wasn't really like that and both men were right and truth belonged to whoever could carry it off cupped[8] and helpless in the feelings.

'I fought for what I believed in all right,' the second man was saying. 'And I fought the only way I believed was right. But it wasn't for all that hypocritical tripe about Empire. Or small nations either, which don't include the Indians I suppose, there are too many of them to be small. No, I fought for the brotherhood of man. And I fought by not fighting. I refuse to fight. And it was gentry like you, Mr Patriot, who put me in gaol in spite of my principles, in spite of yours for the matter of that, and sent me off to England and made me leave my poor wife and kids here to starve while I had to load cases of rum on the Liverpool docks so that the poor devils who knew better than to kill their fellow men sober, because they got less out of it than you did, could get their brains sodden enough to do it. That's what I had to do, Mister, I had to send them the cursed drink as if they didn't have enough on their heads already without drunkenness, poor devils. But I did what I could for my principles, which is more than you did, Mister Whoever-you-are. And what's more, I don't think you could have done much fighting yourself, for the matter of that. Unless it was with the tongue. Soldiers are not so free with their words. But Wilfred Owen had words for you and your like and here they are:

> But cursed are dullards whom no cannon stuns,
> That they should be as stones.
> Wretched are they, and mean
> With paucity that never was simplicity.
> By choice they made themselves immune
> To pity and whatever mourns in man
> Before the last sea and the hapless stars:
> Whatever mourns when many leave these shores;
> Whatever shares
> The eternal reciprocity of tears.'[9]

He sat down and stared at his hands on the desk before him, the denied rage in them twisting to get out like a ferret in a bag. But everyone had swivelled, their elbows on the desks behind them, staring at the blind man.

When he got up the anger had gone out of his face. The corners of his mouth were working as the muscles pushed back the grief in his throat. When he spoke across the dead hush his voice came in breaks, the words of a man arguing with himself alone, a bad antagonist and an argument that never ceases.

'I don't think you can realise –.' He stopped and began again. 'There is nothing I should have liked more, I only wish I'd had the chance to give my life for the least of those who were killed. I'd have known what I was dying for, I'd have been proud. Immune, it's they who're immune. And I'm alive. I'd have died, been dead, been like them. Whereas now –. Doth God exact day-labour?'[10]

His voice broke altogether. He groped his way across towards the door, blundered against the jamb and seemed about to fall. His sister, ungainly in her concern, rushed after him and caught his arm. The sound of their slow steps came back, descending the stairs.

The second man had started, his hands clasping, as his mind completed the line of the sonnet. He buried his face in his hands. The old grudges turned to griefs now, no help against the new grief that he had hurt the blind. He sobbed. The last old lady was leaving the room.

The lecturer was still at her reading desk, holding her notes in front of her, the fragments of her own truth scattered. The man looked up and saw her. He spread out his hands.

'I didn't know he was blind,' he said.

'Of course you didn't,' she said.

But the sympathy he saw in her face was no use to him. She had been a child when it mattered. He got up and had disappeared round the curve of the stairs when she came to the last light switch.

Out in the wet street the sparse street lamps swayed uneasily in the wind and as the light shifted the puddles alternated from glistening shallowness to black, bottomless wells deep enough for truth to hide.

Casualties: a transcript is held in the Alexander Turnbull Library (MS-Group-0319).

NOTES

[1] W.E.A.: the Workers Educational Association, founded in the UK in 1903 (NZ 1905).

[2] *The Heart's Journey*: a volume of poetry (published 1928) by Siegfried Sassoon.

[3] Here … crime: the second verse of Sassoon's 'On Passing the New Menin Gate'.

[4] Carr: C.R. Allen, the 'blind clergyman-poet of Dunedin' was praised by Curnow in 1933 as 'one of the few New Zealand poets who can be taken seriously'; but his Georgian, 'genteel' verse quickly dated. Davin has possibly substituted the name of another contemporary minor poet, Clyde Carr. See Lawrence Jones, *Picking up the Traces: The Making of a New Zealand Literary Culture 1932–1945*, pp. 26–7, 32, 67–8.

[5] Zaharoff: Sir Basil Zaharoff (1849–1936), international arms dealer and financier.

[6] I am the enemy … friend: from Wilfred Owen's poem 'Strange Meeting'.

[7] that resolution … Oxford: the famous motion, passed in 1933 by 275 votes to 153, that 'This House will under no circumstances fight for King and Country'.

[8] cupped: hollowed out.

[9] But cursed … stuns: the sixth and final stanza of Wilfred Owen's poem 'Insensibility'.

[10] Doth God … day-labour?: from Milton's sonnet on his blindness, 'When I Consider How My Light is Spent'. Davin found it in an old examination paper ('My Language and Myself', p. 20).

11

A Happy New Year

IT WAS NEW YEAR'S EVE that night so we'd got the milking over early and had tea. Everyone else was up at the house and getting ready for the party. But I never was much of a one for parties. Not that kind of party anyhow where you sit round the sitting-room that the women have suddenly started calling a drawing-room and the girls are all dressed up and it's: 'Will you have a glass of port, Mrs So-and-so?' and: 'You'll take a drop of whisky, I expect, Mr So-and-so,' but the girls never get squiffy[1] and you can't lay hands on enough yourself to get over feeling a sawney[2] and wishing the whole show was over.

So I just sat outside the door of my hut and watched the cows in the front paddock going it[3] to get a good feed in before they settled down for the night. The sun wasn't quite down and the air was as clear as a bell. Away up high you could see some gulls flying as if they were in a hurry to get to wherever gulls go and you could hear quite plainly the sheep calling to one another away behind on the ridge. In fact it was one of those evenings when you begin to feel sorry for yourself in a quiet kind of way and wish you had someone you could explain to about how you really weren't a bad chap. Only it'd have to be a girl because when it comes to that kind of thing a man just laughs.

So in a way it was a kind of distraction whenever my big toe gave a jab where young Jackie Brass put a .22 bullet[4] through it when I took him out on Christmas Day to try his new Winchester[5] on the rabbits. Not that I was worrying much: it was healing up nicely and I'd been on quite a fuss the first few days what with Phyllis Brass coming and smiling at me and bringing me cool drinks and Mrs Brass, who wasn't a bad sort really, feeding me up like a fighting cock and as pleased as

Punch with me because I'd said it wasn't Jackie's fault.

Still, for all that, it was a bit of a curse tonight. If it hadn't been for the old toe I'd have been down in the township at the New Year's Eve Grand Dance and there'd have been plenty of booze going and there was a sheila I had my eye on. So there I sat and I was thinking to myself it was about time I stopped going to all these hops anyhow and never staying put in a job more than a few months and never writing to that nice girl I used to have in North Auckland before I came down South and spending all my dough on what I could drink. After all, a man can't stay a rouseabout[6] all his life on other blokes' farms. What the old man used to say to me about chaps who didn't have a spark of gumption in them except for getting in on a hand of poker or a bottle of whisky or a girl, kept coming back into my head. And I got to thinking of all the other New Years I'd known and how in the old days before the depression a man used to think each New Year was going to be different but now they were all the same. By that time I'd stopped looking at the landscape and was looking down at my feet, one of them in the cow-boot and the other in the old gym-shoe which was turning green at the edges with grass and cow-dung and had a hole cut in it for my sore toe to stick out.

So I didn't see old Jack Brass coming at me and didn't hear him either because he was always a bit of a creeping Jesus the way he walked. Not that he was like that in other ways. It was just that the Missus had put the fear of God into him about walking round the house like a great clodhopper[7] and he'd got into the habit of walking as if the ground would object. He had just enough money to die a few years younger than he might, poor old Jack, from worry. He'd have been all right if he wasn't married. Or perhaps he was better the way he was. Having sheep and cows and land and kids to worry about stops you from worrying about yourself, I suppose. Anyhow, for a boss he wasn't a bad boss. It was pretty hard not to see good in a bloke with a daughter like Phyllis, in any case.

'Hallo, Len,' he said, 'all on your lonesome?'

'Yes,' I said.

'Why don't you come on up to the house? Phyllis has got some girl friends coming and the two young Bretts from across the river are going to come over.'

'Thanks all the same, Jack,' I said. 'Don't feel much like it tonight.'

He took a good look at me and then looked back towards the house. I could see he was up to something.

'Come on over to the stables,' he said.

There was some sort of mystery on but I could see by the way he was purring and frightened at the same time it was a pleasant one.

'OK, Jack,' I said. And I got up and hopped alongside of him. When we got inside he shut the bottom half of the stable door which made it pretty dark because the evening was getting on by now. The big rumps of the team were sticking out from their stalls and you could hear them snorting and blowing their lips about as they dug into their chaff but you couldn't see their heads.

Jack stopped looking out the top half of the door and came over to where the big barrel of chaff was in the corner. I sat down on a heap of sacks. Jack fished a big bottle out of the barrel.

'You know what the Missus is,' he said. 'Been saving this up for a long while.'

I thought I'd better not follow up that one about the Missus so I asked him what it was.

'Just the best, that's all, Len,' he said. 'You know I don't often touch it but what with the party and you looking so down in the mouth I thought a taster wouldn't do us any harm. Here, help yourself.' And he held me out the bottle and a mug.

I poured out a little one on the bottom.

'Go on, man. Make it worth your while.'

Well, I thought, why not? I tipped the bottle and filled up the best part of the mug. More than I meant to, as a matter of fact.

'Drink her down,' he said.

I couldn't see what the colour was in that light and didn't care much anyhow so I just upped the mug and down she went.

He reached for the mug. He had the bottle already.

'What do you think of it?' he said.

I was still getting my breath. It was raw Hokonui,[8] if I'm any judge, and about as strong as anything that ever came out of the bush.

'Pretty good,' I said.

He had put just a bit in the mug, not halfway. I began to feel a bit ashamed at having hogged so much. He drank his down.

'Good stuff,' he said. You couldn't tell whether he knew it was Hokonui or not. He was so innocent in some ways he might have thought it was Scotch. But he was as cunning as a Maori dog,[9] too, and he might have known bloody well but just not be giving anything away unless he had to.

'Have another,' he said.

I took the bottle and the mug. This time I was only going to have a polite one. But then I thought: It's too late to start getting polite now. So I filled her pretty full again. And away it went.

This time I noticed he filled it right up to the top himself.

Well, after that we got to talking and in the end he began to tell me how worried he was about Billie. Billie was his brother. He lived in the hut behind the stables and lent a hand on the farm. Good worker he was too, hard as nails and though he wasn't as big as Jack, who had bones on him like a swamp-plough, he was a tough bit of goods. Only he was a terror for the booze. He wouldn't just go on a lash for a day or two like most of us and then sweat it out. He often kept at it till it laid him on his back in the DT's.

'You haven't seen him at all today, have you?' Jack asked me.

'Not a hair of him.'

'He ought to be home any time now. He's not the man he was and he's been knocking it back since two days before Christmas. I don't know where he's getting the dough from either. He must have spent what I gave him by now.'

This was news to me. I'd always thought Billie had some of his own. He generally seemed to have plenty. What with this and the booze I began to think Jack was a pretty good sort of joker.

'He can't keep off it once he starts, poor old Billie,' said Jack. 'If it hadn't been for that he'd have owned this farm today.'

'That a fact?' I said, not wanting to seem interested.

'Yes,' he said. 'He's older than me, you know, and the old man left him the farm. All of it this side of the river, that is. The rest came with the Missus. I worked the farm for him while he was away at the war. But when he came back and took over things were going to rack and ruin. It was the war changed him, I suppose. He didn't seem to care a brass farthing for anything except the booze and talking about the war with his old cobbers. They were all the same, those returned men. Well, in the end we bought him out with Cissie's money, Cissie and me. We'd just married. Billie went off on the swag[10] for a few years, him and Joe Hoskins who's the baker down in the township now. Then they turned up again and Billie asked if he could stay on. Cissie thought he'd probably do better on his own. But I said yes, of course.'

'Jack! Where are you, Jack?' I could tell Mrs Brass must be standing at the back door. That was the way her voice always came when she called, round the bend of the macrocarpa, with a grinding edge to it like a train.

'Coming, Cissie,' Jack called back. 'You'd better come on up with me,' he went on. He'd got a bit bolder now and he was resting the bottle on the leaf of the door.[11] There was just enough light for me to see it was pretty well cut. So I got up off the sacks and went over to him.

'I don't think I will, thanks all the same,' I said. And all the time I must admit my mind was back fossicking in the chaff barrel to see if there was any more. Bottles are like fleas: where there's one there's two.

'Come on,' he said. 'Phyllis'll be disappointed if you don't.' He was a nice chap all right. But of course, that was the whisky talking. He knew I didn't have a bean. Mind you, the way he liked Phyllis, if she'd been set on having me he'd probably have given in. But the way the Missus liked her was different and she'd have had plenty to say. And she'd have won the way her type always do. Anyhow, that's not the way I do things. I'd sooner be without money than marry for it. Still, it was nice of old Jack. And Phyllis was a nice girl, too.

'All right,' I said. 'I'll be right on up as soon as I've changed my boot and put on a tie.'

It soon turned out I'd guessed right what sort of a party it would be. So there I was stuck in a corner under the picture of a Newfoundland dog Phyllis had painted when she was at school. Mrs Brass was very proud of that picture but you could easily tell Phyllis had never seen a Newfoundland dog. Opposite on the other wall was that picture of the wild horses when they see the lightning. Jimmy and Peter Brett on the sofa underneath it, dressed up to the nines in their blue suits and Christmas-present ties, looked a bit like wild horses themselves the way their eyes goggled at Phyllis. Only they seemed to like their lightning since that was what they'd put on collars for.

Phyllis was full of beans, of course. Who wouldn't be, with the three of us gaping at her and the two girl friends from the next-door farm pretty well chosen so as not to put her in the shade? And Mrs Brass sitting up as straight as a swingletree in a bolster[12] and smiling away as if it was her we were after. So it was in a way, I suppose. Women with daughters are like that, I think, with the glazed look in their eyes and a smile at the corner of their mouths so you can tell by the way they take a gecko[13] from time to time at their own old man that their minds are skipping back twenty years or so and they're having it both ways.

Not that it stopped her from keeping a pretty close eye on things: but then they're all the same and even the youngest of them can take your hand away from her knee, pick up a point from Jean Harlow's[14] hairdo, wish you were William Powell[15] and keep that soulful look in her eye all at the same time. And work out how much you paid for the seats too and decide to marry you at the same time as she's thinking how mean you are and how men are all the same – except William Powell, of course.

So after a while Mrs Brass thinks it's time Phyllis showed off how well they taught her the piano at the convent.

'Won't you play us something, Angela?' she says, knowing very well Angela hasn't brought her music.

Angela swallowed down the bit of seed cake she'd just nibbled. 'I haven't got my music with me or I'd love to. But surely Phyllis will play for us. She plays so beautifully, doesn't she, Jean?'

'Yes,' says Jean, who was a bit better looking and didn't have to be quite such an enthusiastic friend.

Phyllis dickers[16] a bit but of course she finishes by getting up and saying she's going to play a thing called Offenbach's 'Barcarolle'.[17] The Bretts goggle a bit more and Jean, who can't play and has her eye on young Jimmy Brett, looks tight about the mouth. But Mrs Brass is as proud as a full money-box.

I notice old Jack's head has begun to jerk though, and his pipe's gone out and after a while his eyes go dead on him and his head sags like a top-heavy stook.[18] Then up it goes again with a jerk and he stares wide open in front of him as if he daren't look to see if anyone has noticed.

By this time I was feeling pretty desperate for a drink myself and I didn't care much for this kind of game. Too young for me. I wasn't as shook on Phyllis as all that. The trouble was, though, she knew I was the only half-hearted bloke there so it was me she was after. She was pretty young still and it narked[19] her that everyone was eating out of her hand except me. Of course, if I'd been able to kid myself a bit it might have been different. But I knew enough to know that that feeling inside only seemed to be the sort of thing the blokes in the pictures are supposed to feel. I knew bloody well that if her legs and waist and breasts and face had been different I'd have felt different too and I wouldn't be thinking what a lovely character she had. Anyhow, supposing I had begun to play round and get keen, half my attraction would have vanished. And she was only a kid. She wouldn't have to wait round long before a better sort of joker than me would turn up.

Well, she got through the Barcarolle business all right and it wasn't bad either. Sort of suited the way I was feeling. Then there was a lot more polite talk and she began to sing 'Danny Boy' while Angela, who seemed to have got over her caraway seeds and having no music, accompanied.

Just as the song finished we heard a voice outside roaring away at the same song, taking her off. Mrs Brass looked at Jack and Jack looked at her and both looked at me. The Bretts and the two girls looked at their feet and Phyllis pretended to be looking at her music though I could tell she had her eye on me. It was Billie, all right.

This was just my chance. So I got up, looking very indignant, and said 'Excuse me a bit, would you.' And I had the satisfaction of making everyone feel I was being the gentleman and doing them a favour. Only I'm not sure Phyllis was fooled.

Billie stopped roaring as soon as he saw me, which was just as well because he'd just started on 'My Lady of the Boudoir'.[20] He gave me a great whack on the back. 'Thought that'd fetch you,'[21] he said. 'Come on over to the hut.'

As soon as we were in the hut I knew this was a worse jag[22] than I'd ever seen Billie on before. For one thing Joe Hoskins was flat out on one of the two bunks already. When he saw me his eyes gave a roll and his Adam's apple moved up and down under his sunburnt skin like a rat under a sack. But that was about all he could manage. Billie looked better but his grey eyes were bloodshot and had a queer glitter in them and a week's growth didn't help his looks at all. His hands were shaking too, just a little but all the time. Ripe for the DT's, I thought to myself.

'Poor old Joe,' says Billie. 'I put him down here to cool off. He's got to get his pies into the oven before four o'clock tomorrow morning. But can't let a man ride his horse across the river in that state.'

Joe's eyes opened and he said something thickly. Pies was the only word I could catch.

'Poor old Joe,' says Billie. 'He knows I won't let him down. Not after the way you carried me back that night, eh Joe? Me and Joe left together with the first draft and we came back together, too. Good old Joe. Plenty of time for the pies, Joe. Have a drink.'

We were sitting down on the other bunk by this time with a mug each and were hoeing into some Hokonui. Like a real old soldier Billie had fixed himself up pretty comfortable in that hut, rough but snug.

Well, things were pretty good and Billie showed me all over again how he worked his system of strings so that you could switch out the light from the bed and pull a bottle and mug from under it if you had a hangover and didn't like getting up. But then he got to talking about the war which is a thing that always makes me a bit uncomfortable with old soldiers. They get to poking the borax[23] at everyone who was too young to be there and everyone who was old enough but didn't go and they sing songs no one else knows and tell yarns you know are probably lies but you can't say so because it's not the thing to contradict a returned soldier, not with him drunk anyway and as tough a customer as Billie.

And sure enough Billie was no exception, because after he'd pulled out his old kit-bag and shown me the bits of shrapnel they took out of his shoulder and the bullet they'd got out of his leg and the French and German newspapers, yellow as cheese and dated 1918 and full of chaps that only Billie and blokes like him knew about any more, nothing will do but he must make me try on a German helmet he had and as a matter of fact it didn't suit me badly either. But when I said 'Donner und Blitzen' the way my old man used to say it for fun Billie suddenly gets a notion that I'm a German and comes at me with his old bayonet. I didn't like the look in his eye at all and I wasn't too fly[24] on that gammy foot of mine but I took the weight on the other foot and the next minute I had the bayonet and threw him on the floor. Still, things didn't look too good so I said:

'A Jerry could never have done that to you, Billie.'

'By God, you're right,' he said and Joe said 'Pies,' from the bed.

'Don't worry, Joe,' Billie goes on. 'No, Len, it'd take a better man than a Jerry to do that. Why don't you marry Phyllis, Len? You're not a bad sort of joker.'

That knocked me back a bit, especially as girls' names usually bring trouble when chaps are drinking. They get a bit touchy then and they suddenly get shocked and on their high horses about things they know perfectly well when they're sober but don't think about.

By this time Billie was back on the bunk again with his head in his hands. When he took them away I saw there were tears rolling down his cheeks. Jesus, I thought to myself, he's got a crying jag on now.

'What's the trouble, Billie?' I said. 'Have a drink.'

He pours out a drink without saying anything. And then I see he isn't crying any more but working himself into a flaming rage about something. I didn't like to kick the bayonet out of sight for fear of starting him off again, but I kept my eye on it.

'Yes,' he says. 'You ought to marry her. She likes you and you're not a bad joker. Of course, those greedy bastards over at the house would never let you. She'll marry more land if they have their way. But I don't see why I shouldn't have my say, God damn them if I don't.'

'I don't see why I shouldn't have mine either,' I said. 'Nobody's asked me what I think.'

'It's the least I could do for her,' he goes on.

I didn't like the drift of this at all so I changed the subject. 'I don't see why you've got such a down on them,' I said.

That started him off properly.

'No,' he says, 'but I do. No Jerry could do to me the things my own family have done to me, my own bloody family that Joe and me saved from the Jerries back there in the bloody trenches.'

Joe stirred a bit and started muttering about pies again.

But Billie was still chewing the rag.[25] I thought I'd better get out because I could see something was coming and I didn't want to be mixed up in any of this family stuff.

'I reckon I might be able to get Joe on to his horse now,' I said.

'You leave Joe where he is. I'm not letting Joe get buggered about by any bloody fly-by-night rouseabout. Where would he be better off than with his old cobber? Or are you against me too? Are you on the side of those bastards up at the house, lording it with their drawing-rooms and their la-de-da parties?'

'I'm on nobody's side, Billie.'

'That's right and nobody's on my side. Except poor old Joe here and he's in the rats.[26] Just a couple of poor old returned men that nobody wants after we slogged out our guts in the trenches for them.'

'That's all bull, Billie. Everyone likes you.'

'So they bloody well should, the way I've been a door-mat for them all my life.' He took another gulp. You'd have thought he was quite sober if you couldn't see his eyes. 'Look here, Len,' he said. 'You're not a bad joker.'

'Aren't I?' I said.

'No, you're not. But I'll tell you what. You're a bloody fool all the same. Otherwise you'd do what I say and marry that girl. But you're just a bloody fool. I suppose you think Jack's not a bad joker, either?'

'Well, yes.'

'And you think the Missus is all right, too, don't you?'

'Yes,' I said.

'Well, let me tell you something. It's time you knew just who you're dealing with if you're going to marry Phyllis.'

I let that one pass. He'd have forgotten all about it in the morning.

'Well,' he went on, 'when I went off to France I owned this farm. And I was engaged to Cissie.'

'Uh huh,' I said.

'Naturally us boys didn't feel much like settling down when we came back. It seemed pretty tame. Well, we got to boozing round a bit, Joe here and me, and we kept a couple of racehorses. And the next thing we knew I had to take a mortgage on this place. And a bit after that the bastards were going to close on me. Cissie was pretty keen on me but she's no bloody fool, too right she isn't, and she's got some of the skinflint blood of that old man of hers in her. You know how mean he was and how much he left when he died. Well, you don't, but it was a hell of a lot. Anyhow Cissie knew a thing or two and she was dead scared that me and the booze

136

between us would send her dough after mine. To cut a long story short she pointed her gun at Jack instead of me. Of course, he goes down like a rabbit. She had looks in those days. So Joe and I went off on the swag for a while and the end of it all is that she and Jack get married and buy up my mortgage. And so here am I, just the poor bloody drunken relation.'

'Still, Billie, you asked for it. A man's got to grow up. It's every man for himself these days.'

'Perhaps we just didn't grow up out there, some of us. It wasn't every man for himself the night Joe carried me in, my bloody oath it wasn't. But you don't know the half of it.'

He gulps down the rest of his whisky, fills her up again and stares at the floor.

'You don't know the half of it,' he says again. And I can see his mood getting blacker and blacker on him.

Suddenly there's a tap at the window. We looked up and we could see Jack peering in through one of the broken panes.

'Did you take my bottle, Billie?' Jack says. Not nasty at all but just as if he'd like to come in and have a bit of real company. We must have looked better than we felt.

'Of course I took your bloody bottle.' Billie is on his feet and making for the door. 'Why shouldn't I take your bloody bottle? Haven't you taken everything of mine?' All this in a sort of scream.

'For Christ's sake, be quiet, Billie, you fool. They'll hear you up at the house,' Jack said, as he met Billie at the door.

'Let her hear if that's what you're frightened of. There's a thing or two she wouldn't like you to hear.' And at that he takes a swing at Jack, misses and falls back inside.

Jack and I soon had him back on the bunk and tried to quieten him down. The noise had wakened Joe and he was muttering away about his bloody pies. Once we had Billie by an arm each we didn't quite know what to do and I for one felt a bit of a fool sitting there, hanging on to him.

'What do you mean, Billie, there's a thing or two she wouldn't like me to hear?' Jack said then.

Billie looked at him and you could see he was almost out of his mind with rage the way some chaps get with the whisky, especially Hokonui.

'I'll tell you what,' he said. He stopped and then he out with it. 'She wouldn't like you to hear Phyllis was my kid, would she?'

There was a long pause, not really long but it felt long. At the end of it I knew Jack wasn't going to crown him. He let go Billie's arm and you could hear the bunk creak as his weight relaxed on it. You couldn't tell whether it was sheer surprise that had knocked him or whether it was something he'd guessed all along without knowing it.

Nobody said anything or looked at anyone else. Only old Joe kept grumbling in his stupor.

Then Billie spoke and his voice was quite different, sort of flat and dry.

'Yes, Jack,' he said, 'and I never meant to tell you. Cissie was in pod when you married her. She knew it, too, but she knew I'd never be any good. It wasn't her fault. I talked her into it one night when we were still on together. She thought it might help keep me off the booze, I suppose. Anyhow it didn't and she soon thought better of it. She knew you were the better man. So did I, for that matter, and told her so. That's why I pushed off with my swag that time. We never said anything to you about it because we thought you were more likely to be a decent father for Phyllis than I ever would be. So you were. So you are, Jack. As for me, I couldn't even hold my bloody tongue. I'm sorry, Jack.'

'It's all right, Billie,' said Jack. He got up. 'I've had everything of yours,' he said. He looked at the whisky bottle and gave a kind of grin. Then he went out.

'Pies,' Joe was muttering again.

I limped over and started to get him on my back.

'I'll do that,' Billie said. 'At least I can get my old cobber home.'

From the door of my hut I watched him get Joe across the saddle and ride down the tussock slope towards the river.

Things would either remain the same or get better or get worse, I thought. But it would be better for them not to have me still around when I knew so much. Up at the house I could hear Phyllis's high voice calling good night to the girls. The Bretts would be seeing them home.

The next day I'd collect what Jack owed me and get a lift down to the township. I could put up at a pub. New Year's Day was as good a day as any to be on the move again.

A Happy New Year: a transcript is held in the Alexander Turnbull Library (MS-Group-0319).

NOTES

1 squiffy: tipsy, slightly drunk.
2 a sawney: fool, simpleton. See 'The Black Stranger', 'Gardens of Exile'.
3 going it: moving sharply, getting a move on.
4 .22 bullet: from a small-game rifle, often used for shooting rabbits.
5 Winchester: popular brand of breech-loading rifle, capable of firing multiple shots.
6 a rouseabout: general hand, odd jobber, employed in unskilled menial work. *ODNZE*. See 'The Albatross', 'The Black Stranger'.
7 like a great clodhopper: like a clumsy, heavy-footed bumpkin. See 'A Meeting Half Way'.
8 raw Hokonui: illicitly brewed whisky. See 'Late Snow'.
9 as cunning as a Maori dog: very cunning or sly.
10 went off on the swag: took to the road, travelling in the style of a swagger or itinerant in search of work. A swag is a blanket-wrapped roll or bundle of possessions and useful articles, usually held by straps to the back or laid round the neck like a horse collar. See 'The Black Stranger'.
11 the leaf of the door: the door sill or threshold. *OED* s.v. 'door-sill'.
12 as straight as a swingletree in a bolster: farming terms. A swingletree (US whiffletree or singletree) is a cross bar attached to the traces of a draught-horse and to the vehicle or implement it is pulling, often pivoted in the middle to give the animal more movement. A bolster is a pad preventing friction and giving support, fitted to the machine.
13 take a gecko: have a good look at (sometimes 'dekko').
14 Jean Harlow: (1911–37). Movie star and sex symbol of the 1930s.
15 William Powell: (1892–1984). Screen actor from the 1920s to the 60s. He was engaged to Jean Harlow with whom he co-starred in *Reckless* (1935), before she died suddenly of eurethic poisoning in 1937.
16 dickers: haggles, barters; possibly 'dithers'.
17 Offenbach's 'Barcarolle': a folksong with rhythms reminiscent of a gondolier's stroke. The most famous barcarolle by Jacques Offenbach comes from his opera, *The Tales of Hoffman* (1881), but the Can-Can from *Orpheus in the Underworld* (1858) was also popular.
18 stook: sheaves of corn or hay stacked together for drying.
19 narked: annoyed, irritated.
20 'My Lady of the Boudoir': possibly a song from the 1917 film, *The Mystery of My Lady's Boudoir*, directed by Francis J. Grandon.
21 fetch you: attract you, arouse your interest.
22 jag: drinking bout, binge.
23 poking the borax: teasing, ridiculing, taking the mickey out of. *ODNZE*, s.v. 'borak'.
24 fly: nimble, fast.
25 chewing the rag: gossiping.
26 in the rats: hallucinating with the DT's; 'in the dingbats'. See McGill, *RDNZS*, s.v. 'ratbag', 'ratter'.

12

A Meeting Half Way

SHE LAY ALONE in the big double bed, no longer even trying to sleep. The hated house, sheathed in darkness, was awake only in her bitterness and in the unsleeping ghosts of her hopes, never strong and though at each birth of her two children irrationally reborn, today killed finally.

The Minister had refused dinner, embarrassed. He had a long way to ride; if she didn't mind, he would have to be going. It had been a great pleasure to come and with baptism receive the little ones into the Christian life for which she had so well prepared them. But he really must be going.

And he had gone, he and his pious mare, out through the station gate and down the clay road that would lead him as the years had to a light and a fire and a wife whose bed and Christian breast would give a welcome and a sanctuary less troubled to his anaemic certainties.

The Minister had gone, leaving her, the children put to bed, to dine alone with her husband, even his presence a sneer, his moody silence a heavy alternative to mockery. Then he too had got up, knocking his pipe out on the bread-plate and rasping his chair back from the table, and with a grunt for explanation stalked out into a night ragged with cloud and gusty with an east wind barren of rain.

Now, after the tidying-up of the dishes, the banking of the fire, the last look at the sleeping children, the weary ritual of undressing an unloved body, she lay in the double bed alone, awake these several hours, redeemed by no sleep from the misery of hate fed in each hour of nine years of days, hate by nine months older than the boy, her elder child. Outside the wind moaned in the pines, caught at the earth always dry there, stirred on the ground the dead needles and tossed and tore at those which still had sap and something to hold to. The shadows of the thrashing branches darkened the blue roller-blind with a movement as broken and repeated as her own thoughts. She turned on her side, her back to the window. But before her eyes, shut or staring, the exasperating pattern of shadow still played, the familiar accompaniment of so many nights spent like this in flight from the rehearsal of thoughts, stale, bitter and repetitive, thoughts driven over the dry soil of her heart by anger and despair.

It served her right for looking forward to today. She had known him long enough to know better. And she had looked forward to today. It was to have been her triumph after five years of nagging him to have the children baptised instead of letting them grow up round the station like little heathens. The Lord knew she had done her best to be a good mother to them and bring them up well-mannered and God-fearing like gentlemen. And in spite of it all they were growing more like their father ever day, wild and boorish. While she'd been teaching them their prayers they had learnt from him to swear. Everything she'd slaved to do he had undone. Instead of loving her and respecting their father they were afraid of no one, liked their father and even laughed at her. When she got the governess that time he was always following the girl about and pestering her until in the end she simply had to go. He'd made his own wife the laughing stock of every servant they'd ever had in the house. So now for her own self-respect she had to get along without them and keep house herself, she who was used to every refinement.

The station-hands for miles around knew the story of how he'd built that other homestead on Saddle Hill,[1] saying that it was more convenient to the sheepyards for the men and that his wife not being able to keep servants wouldn't be able to cook for them. So, of course, he must put that vulgar, hateful Mrs Fox in as housekeeper there. As if everyone didn't know what his real reason was. And him eating there every day with the hands, coming home only when the fancy took him and then only for a quarrel. His day wasn't complete unless he heaped her with insults and brought her to tears.

Downstairs in the drawing-room the green marble clock, a present from Tuatapere school,[2] where she'd been a teacher when she was single, struck one.

One o'clock and still no sign of him. He was probably lying in bed with that Fox, as coarse and vulgar as himself, sleeping like great brutes, the pair of them, after eating and drinking and wiping their mouths with the backs of their hands. She could just see him sitting there with his whisky in one hand and pawing that woman with the other, the food repeating on him with never a 'Pardon'. Fine treatment to give his wife who'd had a good education and brought into the house its only refinement. And probably he'd be telling her a pack of lies about today, making a great story out of it.

It wouldn't have been so bad if it hadn't been in front of the Minister, who was such a sensitive, refined man too. She'd begged and entreated him to be shaved and clean for once. And then he'd got up late and gone away down to the stables and she'd hoped he'd stay away altogether. She'd caught the children and cleaned them and dressed and drilled them for their parts. Finally, the Minister had come and they'd all had lunch, she having to apologise for the absence of her husband. It must have looked a bit queer him not being there but she'd been so thankful he wasn't, all the same. And then everything was ready and they were all in the drawing-room and the Minister was just beginning the solemn words.

Then who should come tramping in but him. A dark stubble bristled on his jowls. He wore no coat and his old waistcoat was covered in cow-hairs, with a dirty old pipe stinking from the lower left pocket. His dungarees were smeared with stale cow-dung. And his muddy cow-boots were not even laced up. The laces trailed and jerked along the carpet, leaving quick smears. He must have had whisky down in the stables or wherever he'd been for his face was swollen and flushed and the smell of drink came in ahead of him.

There he stood in the middle of her carpet glowering with his bloodshot, angry eyes for all the world like his own bad-tempered Jersey bull. And then in the middle of the Minister's solemn words, in front of his innocent children and his refined wife, he said:

'How long does this bloody monkey-business[3] go on at all?' And he flopped all dirty as he was into her best chair, leaving the Minister still standing.

The Minister blushed and then drew himself up, took his glasses off and put them on again, and went on. But everything was spoiled. She did not dare to watch the christening any more. She stared at his great muddy footprints on the carpet. In front of the Minister and his own children. With those great muddy cow-boots and the laces not even done up.

At least the children had had too much sense of decency to giggle.

The dogs began to bark and out of the darkness she heard his deep voice growl them to silence. The back door rattled and he came tramping along the passage. It was a wonder he bothered to come home at all. The bedroom door opened and he reeled into the room, heavy with whisky. He sat on the bed, on her shiny pink satin quilt, and flung the boots still unlaced on to the floor.

'Can't you think of the children asleep?' she said, 'thumping your great clodhoppers[4] down like that. You've shamed us all once today, in front of the Minister. You and your boots. They weren't even laced up.'

'I came, didn't I? What more do you want?'

'You could at least have had the decency to be properly dressed, shaming me and the children.'

'It was only Saturday, wasn't it? I don't get dressed up for anybody if it's not Sunday, Minister or no Minister, least of all that little goat, bleating there like an imitation Pommie.'

He climbed into bed and soon she had his snores as well to plague her sleeplessness. He lay beside her, his dark, brown hair black against the pillow, his back so broad there and its muscles now quiet under the thick singlet he hadn't bothered to take off. The short sleeve was taut against the bulge of his bicep. This was the body she had first seen nine years ago at the Tuatapere axemen's carnival,[5] where he and his axe had carried off the prizes. Only then it had been exultant and alive. For this she'd fooled herself with the fancy that she'd be able to soften away the roughness and keep for herself the life in him.

Well, the night of the wedding had killed all that. Once or twice after when he was not there she had thought of his body with desire. But the physical reality, the uncouth speech, the sneers at her quivering gentility as soon as he fell back from the impersonal intensity of lust were too much. The only passion he could now rouse in her was hate.

And now he was a threat to her children as well. Today showed that. He mightn't love her, wouldn't even recognise such a thing as love. But he could be jealous of her children. And he would get them in the end, take them from her, just as he slept there now so warm and soundly while it was she, the innocent one who only tried to do her duty, who must lie awake.

In bitter resentment she watched the dark heave of the branches shadowed on the blind and a cold wind of anger blew across the dry soil of her heart, barren of rain and hardening her to face the coming day and do what she now saw she must do.

At breakfast she watched him stealthily as he ate. The children had breakfasted earlier and had just ridden off on their ponies to visit the next station, their shouts lingering with their steamy breaths in the frosty air. Decision masked in her face, she saw him get up at last, shirt open over a hairy chest, and reach down a light rifle from the rack. Without a word he stalked through the doorway into the bright white-frost morning. She ran to the window and pulled the curtain aside. He turned down past the stables. He must be going to the stump paddock to shoot rabbits. She waited till he was through the fence and among the stumps. Then she took the other rifle and keeping to the trees followed down as far as the fence.

He was sitting on a stump in the middle of what had been a piece of swamp-bush. Fire had been through it and now burnt carcasses of trees thrust up gnarled and tortured fingers towards the morning sky. No life pulsed in their roots or drove up their veins to fan out in a delicacy of transparent green and taste the rapture of the air and rain. Their cycle had ended in no fullness of years and slow waning of decay but in minutes and the sharp agony of the flames, the juice of giant and sapling devoured alike that day when fire ravened[6] through their company. Now biddy-biddy grew thick at their feet and, like a nomad tribe camped for a time in the broken columns of a forgotten culture, the rabbits burrowed beneath them.

He watched a stoat, thin and lithe, its head poised listening above a hole. How thin and cold and cunning and like her. Sucking the blood from rabbits. But it's alive and warm and kills quickly and it likes blood. It's not like her. And he lowered the rifle he had half-raised.

Here he was, only forty-five and a young man yet, but like a rabbit at the end of a blind burrow with the shining pink eye of the ferret coming on at him, caught in this blind, barren, monotonous life, he who'd once

144

roamed the whole country. After all the women he'd known to be caught between two, Hetty Fox, fat and warm, stupid and sensual and greedy, but a woman all the same, and his wife, thin and bloodless, giving nothing but possessions and clamping them on to you like handcuffs, gathering things round her like a magpie, whining and nagging, with her best carpets and her Minister and her haw-haw manners.[7] A woman who wouldn't go to bed with the light on even if she were alone. Her silk cushions, her fish-knives and her serviettes. If she'd only pestered herself with her bloody nonsense about the dignity fitting their position it wouldn't have been so bad. But to try and put that snobbish hocus-pocus across on him was going a bit too far. And before long she'd have made the kids as bad as herself. Only yesterday they hadn't had the sense to see the funny side of that goat of a parson and his bloody tomfoolery. The next thing she'd have them taught to feel ashamed of their own father.

How such a bloodless bitch had ever managed to produce such sturdy brats was a mystery, but it was plain enough she'd ruin them if she got the chance. Young Molly now – or Mary as her mother would have it – she had a bit of life in her but the old woman would turn her into the old maid she ought to have been herself. She'd suck the blood out of them all right the way she'd try to turn him into a poor, your-slippers-are-by the-fire-dear sort of spineless hubby. And all that fuss about Hetty and when she couldn't get her own way, the injured looks. If she'd been any good there'd have been no need for Hetty or anyone else. A real bitch in the manger[8] she was, bursting with jealousy because a man went elsewhere for what she hadn't got.

Well, there was nowhere else to go now. It was too bloody late in the day. He'd just have to stick it out and make the best of it and try and stop her turning the kids into complete little milksops.

He got up and walked cautiously on. As he rounded a dead tree he saw a rabbit. He smiled as he saw his hands were quite steady in spite of last night. He fired and the rabbit dropped over sideways and lay kicking. He picked it up by the hind legs, smashed his fist into the back of its neck and looked without seeing as the blood dripped a little from its ears.

The next was a long shot but he got it in the head. He'd been a sniper in the war. Just on twenty years ago. They'd been good days. Better in a way if a man had never come back from them. He picked up the second rabbit and turned back towards the homestead, smiling to himself. The dogs could have them for their breakfast. He could see their tails wagging already. The blood from the rabbits' ears dripped unnoticed down his trouser leg.

Perhaps he was a bit too tough on her after all. That old bitch Fox was getting a bit too pleased with herself. He might send her packing and have another go at making a do of things with his wife. The kids had some guts at any rate and he might be able to make something of them. If he could hold himself in he might manage all right. If only she had a bit more blood in her and a bit less education and could forget these notions about the dignity of a station-owner's wife. If he got rid of Fox at any rate she should be ready to meet him halfway.

There was a thrush singing in the gorse as he made his way to the fence. He did not see the white thin face of his wife watching him along the line of the rifle barrel. He did not hear her repeating in the silence of her mind: 'In front of the Minister.' They were looking at different and incompatible futures.

He threw the two rabbits across the fence and bent to put his leg between the wires. His foot came through, the laces dangling loose, wet and shining with the dew. The bullet took him in the head and he fell heavily through the fence on his side, the rifle toppling ahead of him. His right leg caught on the barbed wire; the trouser leg ripped slowly to the seam and the torn piece hung there grotesque and breaking the pattern of his body.

She ran forward, wiped her rifle with her apron and put it under the palm of his right hand, still warm and flexible. She picked up his rifle and then stood over him, looking down without seeing at the blood which welled from his ears.

As she slipped back through the trees to the homestead, she was already planning where they would go when the station was sold and how the children would love her as the best of mothers and one of them would be a minister and both would wear shoes.

A Meeting Half Way: a transcript is held in the Alexander Turnbull Library (MS-Group-0319).

NOTES

1 Saddle Hill: possibly a land form of the same name which lies to the east of the Takitimu mountains.
2 Tuatapere school: Tuatapere is a small town eighty-eight kilometres west of Invercargill on the Waiau River.
3 monkey-business: tomfoolery.
4 clodhoppers: big, heavy shoes or boots. See 'A Happy New Year'.
5 Tuatapere axemen's carnival: the Tuatapere annual sports events held on New Year's Day at which the crosscut-saw competitions attracted attention. See 'The Tree'.
6 ravened: raged voraciously.
7 haw-haw manners: affected manners.
8 bitch in the manger: spiteful and meanspirited. A variant of the colloquialism, 'dog in the manger'. See 'The Quiet One'.

PART II

From *Breathing Spaces* (1975)

The Far-Away Hill

A small boy in the cold east wind
Seated on that bleak hill I thought
Time and my mounting strength would yet deliver me.
Now Time's gone and on that bleak hill
I see the green grass shoot, the hares hide
And the east wind brings the peat smell,
And the lark's song. Sitting on that hill I gaze
Across the sun-born gorse, see the gold and the gladness
And wish I could believe that this
Was being that small boy.

Paris 1937

The Far-Away Hill: this poem was first published in the Otago University *Review* (September 1938: 20). It was written on Dan Davin and Winifred Gonley's first visit to Paris in 1937 after Winnie's arrival at Toulon from New Zealand in June. They stayed from July to September in rooms at 3 Square de Port-Royal and liked Paris so much they returned again in August 1938 and again at Christmas and New Year. 'Far-Away Hill' with its 'clump of gorse' was probably to the east of Morton Road and Conyers Street. It is where Mrs Scott's children are called from in 'The Vigil'. In 'Death of a Dog' it is where the Connolly boys built an underground hut and where their favourite dog was shot and buried. It clearly acquired symbolic importance for Davin after he left New Zealand. See 'Gardens of Exile'.

13

Presents

THE TWO BOYS WERE READING at the kitchen table. Mrs Connolly had set a place at the range end of it an hour before. Now there was nothing for her to do but wait and worry. From time to time she leaned her head to one side, though her hands kept shuttling the knitting-needles, and she listened. When no sound answered she would glance over at the boys and look down at the half-finished sock again, not sighing. They knew she had looked at them and knew why she hadn't sighed.

When the heavy step and the clicking of the bicycle chain came round the corner of the house they all heard it at the same time.

'There he is at last,' she said. 'So he'll be able to take you into town after all. Now out of here with you and let him have his meal in peace.'

Now that she wasn't worried any more her voice was sharp. They were afraid she was trying to get them out of the way to give her a chance to go for him. If he was in a bad mood that would make him worse. If he was in a good mood it might put him off.

'You wouldn't like us to give you a hand washing up the dishes?' Mick said.

'I know you and your tricks, Mr Long-ears. Run on into the sitting-room now, there's good boys. Your father and I want to have a talk.'

But they did not quite close the door.

'What on earth's been keeping you, man?' they heard her say. 'You know you promised those kids you'd take them in to see the Christmas shops tonight and they've set their hearts on it. Where on earth have you been? Is anything wrong?'

'Wrong, Mary? It's the terror you are for worrying. Of course there's nothing wrong. Why should there be anything wrong?'

That was like him, asking one question to answer another. And the voice sounded too cheerful.

'He's had a few in, all right,' Mick whispered.

'Shut up, Mick,' Ned said. There was talking again in the kitchen.

'Well, I only hope you haven't gone and spent that few bob in Joe Shield's pub.' She was poking the range fire to bring the kettle back to the boil and make fresh tea. You could tell from the noise what she thought.

'It's little enough the poor kids get at the best of times,' she went on. 'And you know how much money there's left in the house. Yet you're not content with filling them up with all sorts of talk about Christmas presents. No, you must go and spend most of what money there is down there in the town, buying drinks for strangers, I'll be bound, and forgetting all about your own family. It doesn't look as if they'll get much of a Christmas.'

'Now never you fret, Mary. I'll take them all right. We'll manage, don't you worry. It's not my fault the damn strike[1] is on and you wouldn't be having me a blackleg,[2] would you, Christmas or no Christmas?'

'It's not a question of that. You know I'd never ask you to go against the union. But I would ask you to do without a few beers for the sake of the kids.'

This was a facer.[3] They were afraid he'd get wild. If he did they could say good-bye to Christmas Eve.

'That'd be asking more than you think sometimes, Mary,' he said, quite gently. 'When things are like this the days drag on a man. He thinks of what's best for his missus and his kids and the next thing he knows he's doing what's worst for them. It's the way things are.'

They heard her sniff in the silence. They knew by the sound of it she would be wiping her eyes now on her flour-bag apron. His chair scraped and they heard him get up. He would be putting his arms round her.

'Smooging[4] won't get you out of it,' she said. But her voice was different from the words.

'The poor kids,' she said, 'what do they know about strikes? All they know is that it's Christmas.'

They walked along towards the tram stop,[5] one on each side of him. Mick had the sixpence for the tickets in his hand and it was sweating.

Part of him was still back in the kitchen. The sixpence had come out of his mother's black purse, not his father's pocket. Did that mean anything? And the strike was in his mind, too. Till today it had been quite exciting, something to tell the other kids. Having the old man at home was better still. When he wasn't digging the garden he'd tell them stories about when he was a boy in Galway[6] or show them how to make cradles to catch birds. Everything he made always worked and the very first time they tried it they caught a blackbird and two ring-eyes.[7] And every day he thought of something new that they might never have known about if he hadn't been on strike.

It was different today, though. He'd gone away straight after dinner and as the afternoon went on the fun just went out of things and they could tell from their mother's crotchetiness that she didn't like it and something was the matter. The way she kept looking at the clock at tea-time put it into their heads what she was worrying about and so they began to worry as well. The strike seemed to become quite a different kind of thing, not like a holiday at all.

Still, here they were walking along Centre Street[8] with him and the tram waiting at the top of it[9] to take them into town and see the sights. And he didn't seem to be worrying, not a bit of it.

'Got that sixpence, Mick?' he said when they stopped by the door of the tram. Ned had already climbed up the step and jumped in.

'You bet I have, Dad.' And he almost blurted out that he and Ned had two more sixpences, one each that they'd saved up. But that was still a secret.

'Good for you, then.' And he took Mick's arm with one hand and hoisted him right past the step into the tram. He was very strong.

They got out at the main stop in front of Post Office Square.[10] There were lines of trams there, all lit up inside, empty ones going off to get more people and full ones coming all the time. There were lights everywhere in the streets and shops, Chinese lanterns and strips of coloured paper. What with the lights and the moon you could make people out right across the street as clear as day, even though people said that Dee Street and Tay Street were the widest streets in New Zealand.

'Come on,' their father said, and they crossed to the Majestic side,[11] opposite the Post Office. Behind them sand crackers[12] and bombs were going off in the square and you could hear kids squealing with laughter.

'Can we go and see, Dad?' said Ned.

'Not just yet, Ned. I want to go round to Esk Street for a minute and see a man.'

The two boys looked at each other. The Shamrock was in Esk Street.[13] Of course, Invercargill was a dry town now. Still, even they knew you were supposed to be able to get sly grog at the Shamrock.[14] Once he was in there was no telling when he'd come out. Christmas Eve didn't look much just then.

But he put a hand on the shoulders of each of them and steered them through the crowds and Mick felt how kind he was and how mean it was to be so suspicious.

'Now just wait on this side for a bit and have a look at the shop-windows. I'll be out again in two shakes of a dead lamb's tail.'

They watched him cross over and go in by the back way.

Ginger Timms went by with his father and mother. He was blowing at a long paper snake thing that went in and out and made a crackly noise. They turned to the window behind them and he didn't see them.

The shop was a Chinese laundryman's[15] and the window was full of pink strings of crackers and roman candles. The centre piece was a big basket-bomb.[16]

'I wish we could spend our sixpences on that,' Ned said. 'I'd like to buy the biggest basket-bomb there is and blow up Ginger Timms.'

'But he's not a bad joker,' Mick said.

'I'd blow him up all the same.'

Then they saw Ginger coming back. They crossed the road to the other footpath. It was darker because there was only the Shamrock and next to it the Rialto[17] with its window full of second-hand furniture which nobody thought worth lighting up tonight.

'There he is,' Ned said.

He was standing just outside the Shamrock gateway with his back to the footpath. They recognised him by the way he stood with his hands in his pockets and his shoulders squared back. He was talking to someone just inside. As they got closer they recognised the voice. It was Joe

Shields. They'd often seen their father talking to him after eleven o'clock Mass on Sundays.

'I'm sorry, Ned,' Joe was saying, 'but that's the best I can do. You know I'm only too anxious to lend a hand if only for old times' sake. But all the boys are in the same boat and this is the time of the year when we all feel it. I'll tell you what, though. If you get a chance later on, come back and we'll have something together.'

'That's all right, Joe,' their father said. 'I know you would if you could. Thanks all the same.'

The two boys were at the gate by now. Mick felt as if he'd dearly like to be somewhere else. Neither his father nor Joe Shields sounded quite natural, as if they wanted to get away from each other and at the same time didn't want to or didn't know how to.

Then Joe noticed them.

'So these are the two young sprigs, eh, Ned. Fine-looking kids too, aren't you, eh? But you'll have to be pretty good if you want to be as good as your father, won't they, Ned?'

He patted their heads. Then he stuck his hand in his hip pocket.

'Here,' he said, 'here's something for you.' He grabbed Ned's hand and put something in it, then Mick's. Mick could tell by the feel it was sixpence. He would look later and make sure.

'Thank you very much, Mr Shields,' they said.

'Well, good night, Joe,' their father said. 'And many thanks. A Merry Christmas, too.' His voice sounded much warmer now.

After they had spent Joe's sixpences on some sand crackers and a bomb each and had had some fun throwing the crackers at people's feet in Post Office Square they all sat down on a wooden seat next to the City Library.[18] They were going to keep the bombs to let off next day after the Christmas dinner.

'Well now,' their father said, when he got back from the Gentlemen's underground, 'what would you like to do next? Would you like to come and help me buy your Christmas presents?'

They looked up at him with delight. Ever since the Shamrock they'd been convinced there weren't going to be any presents and had been making the best of the lights and the crowds and the sand crackers. And that was why they'd hung on to their basket bombs, so as to have something for tomorrow. Neither of them could say a word now.

'Come on,' he said, 'tell me what you want and we'll see what we can do. You first, Ned. What do you want for Christmas? Don't ask for a bike though. That'll have to wait for your lucky day.'

That made Ned laugh. The cheapest bike you could get was six pounds thirteen and six with guarantee.

While Ned was laughing Mick was knitting up his forehead. Would there be enough money for what he wanted? Better wait till Ned had had his and then if it wasn't too much and his father was still smiling he would be able to tell whether he should ask for something nice and cheap.

Ned knew what he wanted. 'I'd like one of those fountain pens Pat Rodgers has. They're only four and six at Playfair's.'[19]

'Only four and six?' his father said. 'And what about you, Mick?'

Mick couldn't tell from the way he said it whether four and six was an enormous lot or whether it wasn't. Perhaps he just ought to ask for a pencil. But perhaps his father had the money after all and half-a-crown would only be a fleabite.

'I'd like a printing-set,' he said. 'They only cost two and six.' And he looked down so as not to see how his father would feel if he didn't have enough money.

'Well,' said his father, 'We'll see what we can do.'

All the way to Playfair's their father seemed to be thinking of something else. Once he stopped and talked with a man they didn't know and it looked as if he were asking the man for something. The man shrugged and threw his hands out sideways and said: 'Search me, Ned.' Their father shook his head in the queer, comical sort of way he had sometimes. 'Well, a Merry Christmas, anyway, Jimmy,' they heard him saying. He came back and joined them and they went on.

People were pouring in and out of Playfair's with their arms full of parcels. Everyone seemed to have a kind of dazed grin on his face and to be in a hurry to squash through one way or the other. But when their father went into a crowd there was always room somehow and it was easy if you kept close up behind him to follow along in the tunnel he made.

'Now where are those pens of yours, Ned?' he said when they got inside.

'Over there at the stationery counter.'

There were some real beauties, 'Swans' and 'Onoto the Pen' and 'Watermans' and kinds you'd never heard of with gold and silver all over them and places to get your name engraved. The four and sixpenny ones were in a big tray right at the front.

Their father picked up a beautiful gold one as big as a barrel and showed it to the girl behind the counter.

'Is this a four and sixpenny one?' he said, smiling at her.

The girl was very smart in a tight black dress. She was wearing a real pearl necklace and she smelt of nice scent. But she must have been tired with so many people pestering her and not able to make up their minds what they wanted because she just looked at the pen and not at him and she said 'No,' a bit huffily. 'The tray at the front,' she added.

He smiled more than ever and took one from the tray. 'I thought so,' he said. She looked at him then and began to smile back as she wrapped it up in a bit of fancy paper.

'Which one is it for?' she asked, quite nicely.

'The big one.'

'So he's the scholar?'

'Oh, they're both scholars,' he said. 'Not like their father.'

'Better to be nice than clever,' she said with a special smile.

He held out a half-crown and a two-shilling piece and wished her a good Christmas.

Mick was wonderfully relieved. His father really had had money and he'd been wrong again. Now it would be all right with the printing set. And they'd get their mother a present, too, and it would be a real Christmas.

The printing sets were on a shelf in the middle of the shop. There were all sorts of other things as well and people were pushing and shoving everywhere and asking how much this was and how much that was and there weren't enough girls to look after everybody and kids were blowing toy bugles and wanting to practise with wheelbarrows and tricycles and their mothers were trying to stop them. There was a terrible hullabaloo going on.

Mick opened the box and showed his father how you fixed the rubber letters into the stamp and how you could print your name and everything.

'We'll make a printer out of you yet,' his father said, 'and you can print the *Southland Times*. Now close it up and we'll try and get out of this madhouse.'

They started to move over to the counter.

'I'll tell you what, Ned,' their father said, 'you and Mick get out of the crush and wait for me outside. I won't be two ticks.'

The two boys made for the door. But on the way they stopped to buy their mother the brooch they'd planned to get with their shilling. And while Ned was paying Mick looked through a gap in the crowd to the other counter. His father wasn't there. But Mick saw him going towards the other door and at the same time putting the printing set in his pocket.

They found him outside. When they explained what they'd been doing he said: 'That's good kids. And now I think we'd better get the next tram home.'

Their mother seemed even more pleased to see him than them. It was the first time they could remember seeing her kiss him in front of them.

'And what lovely presents,' she said. 'And a present for me, too. You shouldn't have been so extravagant, Ned. I didn't need anything.'

'You should know me better, Mary,' their father said. 'They saved up to buy you that.'

Mick went to bed that night with the printing set on the chair beside him. 'I don't care if he did pinch it,' he said to himself finally, 'it was better than if he'd bought it, in a way.'

Presents: first published in *Landfall* 7:1 (March 1953): 19–25.

NOTES

[1] strike: the railway strike of 1923. Davin's father was involved as a loyal member of the railwaymen's union. *FW*, p. 26.

[2] blackleg: someone who returns to work before a strike is settled.

[3] a facer: sudden, severe check; unexpected difficulty. *DSUE*.

[4] smooging: flattery, showing affection. *ODNZE*, s.v. 'smooge'.

[5] tram stop: situated at Centre Street which bisects Morton Street, running east-west. Horse-drawn trams were introduced to Invercargill in 1881, electric trams in 1912; they were discontinued in the 1950s.

6 a boy in Galway: Patrick Davin, b. 1877, came from Tonagarraun, a townland about twelve miles from Galway, arriving in Bluff around the turn of the century. *FW*, pp. 3–6; 'Gardens of Exile

7 two ring-eyes: mainly a South Island bird, known also as wax-eye or silver-eye, for the circlet of satiny white feathers surrounding the eyes.

8 Centre Street: from the town end of Centre Street the trams ran north toward Tweed Street, then up Conon Street, west along Tay Street, then to Dee Street and Post Office Square.

9 the tram … it: the tram terminus was on the corner of Centre Street and Pomona Street, parallel to and west of Morton Road.

10 Post Office Square: at Dee Street onto which the Square fronts, facing away from Leven Street, located between Esk Street and the Crescent. See the photo in Holcroft, *Old Invercargill*, p. 117.

11 the Majestic side: the east side of Dee Street, between Esk and Tay Streets, near the Tay Street corner. The Majestic Theatre is directly opposite Post Office Square.

12 sand crackers: small ($^1/_2$ in.) tubular paper packets of sand with a thin layer of powder in one side. When thrown at a hard surface they explode, showering sand everywhere. Crackers are the size of a marble.

13 Shamrock … Esk Street: the Shamrock was on the corner of Dee and Spey Streets. In 1929, according to Wise's *Directory*, Deschlers was the private hotel in that part of Esk Street.

14 sly grog … Shamrock: both the Shamrock and Deschlers are recorded as closing to drinkers at 10 pm on 30 June 1906, the last night of serving alcohol when Invercargill officially became a dry town, but court cases heard the following year confirm that whisky continued to be sold illicitly. See Holcroft, *Old Invercargill*, p. 111; *The Southland Times*, Saturday 29 June 1907: 4; *RfH*, p. 63 and n.

15 a Chinese laundryman's: at 80 Esk Street (in the first block east from Dee Street) was Shing Lee, a Chinese laundryman/tobacconist.

16 basket-bomb: a type of Chinese cracker, also popular in Australia.

17 the Rialto: D.W. McKay's Rialto at 58 Esk Street which ran across the block to Don Street. On Todd's Rialto, see 'Late Snow', 'Gardens of Exile'.

18 City Library: located upstairs on the corner of Dee and Esk Streets, almost adjacent to and north of Post Office Square.

19 Playfair's: probably H. & J. Smith's department store located on the corner of Tay and Kelvin Streets.

14

Roof of the World

THE COAST WAS CLEAR. Mrs Connolly had gone off with Eileen to the Paddy's Market for the Saint Vincent de Paul Society.[1] And their father was on the Dunedin express run.[2]

Their mother had left them to do the washing up so as to make an early start and Ned was to do the churning. Mick and Paddy finished first and left him grinding grimly away – he never stopped the way they did to lift the lid to see whether the butter had come when they knew very well it hadn't.

First of all they went down the garden and filled their pockets with gooseberries. Then they went round the far side of the house where there was a narrow strip of lawn between the house and the macrocarpa hedge but where nobody ever went much because it wasn't sunny. They had a look at the wild cat's kittens but didn't come too close – Mick still had scabs from the scratches he got the last time. Then they climbed up on the wooden tankstand, took hold of the rim of the round, corrugated iron tank, and hauled themselves up to where they could reach the roof guttering. From there it was an easy matter to get right up on the roof.

For a while they sat side by side with their feet dangling over, squashing the inside out of the gooseberries and throwing the skins into the open tank. When they had enough they began to chase each other with the ripe berries they could no longer be bothered eating.

The clatter of their hobnailed boots on the roof brought Ned out onto the verandah below.

'Hey, you kids, cut out making all that noise.'

'Ned,' called Paddy, 'sling us up Dad's bike pump, will you?'

'What do you want it for? I will if you promise not to go squirting me.'

'I promise.'

Ned got the pump from its shelf at the end of the verandah and flung it up to where Paddy knelt in the gutter, looking down into the yard. Paddy caught it neatly.

'Come on, Mick,' he said. 'Let's fill her up and lay an ambush for the postman.' He walked over the roof to the tank, his boots grinding on the iron and making shiny lead streaks through the red paint. He leaned over the tank on his stomach and filled up the pump.

Mick watched with a certain lassitude. He was thinking of the two frogs he had put in the tank the year before with the idea of starting an aquarium. Then he had forgotten about them and by the time he remembered they were floating belly-up on the surface. The water had been too far below the lip of the tank that dry summer and they had not been able to get out and have a rest. They couldn't have had much to eat either. They still haunted him from time to time and at the moment the thought of that murderous failure left him with no heart for squirting the postman. Besides, the postman mightn't have any letters and if he didn't he wouldn't need to come within squirting distance. Even if he did have any letters they'd probably be bills. Or perhaps there'd even be something from the police about Mrs Quelch's broken window.

A sparrow perched on the macrocarpa hedge opposite. Without moving the rest of his body Mick felt in his pocket and pulled his shanghai out gently by the prong. But the leather pouch coming out after the prong dragged a small mirror with them. It fell on the roof with a clatter. The sparrow swivelled a beady eye, twitched its tail and was off. Mick put the shanghai in his pocket. Then he bent and picked up the mirror. He had pinched it and a comb lately from Eileen. They were useful when you went swimming, though why he'd got interested in combing his hair lately he didn't bother to ask himself. Now he studied his face in the mirror and felt his chin musingly. Nothing there yet. Ned had nothing either, though, even though he was two years older.

He sighed and put the mirror back in his pocket. Then he turned to look at Paddy who was now crouching just at the foot of the slope which ran up to the front-room chimney. From this position he overlooked the path by which the postman would have to come.

Mick had an idea. On hands and knees he began to crawl up the slope to the peak of the gable, putting his feet against the lead-capped nails so as not to slip. At the top he lay with only his head showing. His spread weight and the roof nails against his toecaps stopped him from slithering down again.

On the other side of the road Mr Pratt[3] was in his garden, digging weeds out of the lawn with a queer-shaped fork. Mick took out his mirror and manipulated it to catch the sun. The trapped light began to dance obediently about Mr Pratt's head. Mr Pratt moved and the reflection played on the grass below his face. He straightened himself up slowly with one hand on the small of his back in the 'Every Picture Tells a Story'[4] position. He looked about him puzzled. The light flashed in his eyes and then as he began to track it to its source Mick disappeared behind the gable.

When Mick took another look Mr Pratt was bending over his weeds again. Once more the light began to dance in front of him. But Mr Pratt knew his neighbours and this time he managed to stoop right down and look between his legs towards the most likely place.

It was too late to bob down so Mick stayed where he was and grinned. Mr Pratt grinned back and shook his fist.

Well, it was no good trying to trick him any more. Mick looked around for fresh victims. And there was the postman coming along from the direction of Stone's house.

'He's coming, Paddy.'

'Yes, I've spotted him.'

The postman crossed the road towards their front gate, the light from Mick's mirror frisking about his eyes. The front gate clicked and he came down the path. Paddy let him go out of sight to the front door. They heard the lid of the letterbox rattle and the postman blew his whistle. As he came into sight again on the path Paddy let fly with the pump. The water squirted in a long leaping then dying stream, falling short except for the first few drops.

The postman, his face red with the heat and his heavy black uniform, turned and looked up to see their laughing faces.

'At it again, you young devils,' he said. 'I've a good mind to tell your mother.'

He went out the front gate and they could see as his head bobbed along the front hedge that he was grinning. He wouldn't tell.

They joined forces again at the bottom of the slope just as Ned's head appeared above the tank. When he had climbed on to the roof they could see he was carrying their mother's best umbrella. His face had a solemn, absent look.

'What are you going to do, Ned?' asked Paddy.

'I'm going to try out this parachute stunt. I reckon that if I put the umbrella up and jump off holding it I ought to float down gently. Be interesting to see whether it works or not.'

'But it's a hell of a height, Ned,' said Mick.

'Can't help that. If you don't try a thing out how can you ever tell whether it's going to work or not?'

This convinced Paddy. He sat down with his legs hanging over the edge and resting on the tank rim. Mick was still sceptical but he sat down, too.

'He might break his neck,' he murmured anxiously to Paddy. It was no good arguing with Ned, though. When he was like this you just had to wait and see what happened.

Ned had put up the umbrella and taken his stand near the edge of the roof. He seemed to be thinking.

'Go on, Ned, what are you waiting for?' said Paddy. He could already see Ned floating gently in the air. And he was impatient for it to come to his turn.

'Got to wait till the wind's just right,' Ned said. There was no wind of any sort this late summer day, but neither of them for a moment doubted that this was what he was waiting for.

Ned took a deep breath. 'Here goes,' he said and jumped. Both hands above his head and holding the umbrella he dropped like a stone. Not expecting to fall so fast he fell badly with his legs too stiff and then tumbled over on one shoulder. He lay there.

'Are you all right, Ned?' Mick called.

Ned sat up red in the face. 'Of course I'm all right,' he said when he got his breath back.

'Well, that's the end of that, I suppose,' Paddy sounded very glum.

'What do you mean, end? You can't say a thing won't work if you only try it once.' He picked up the umbrella, closed it and climbed back on to the roof.

'The wind might have been wrong, or anything,' he explained as he opened the umbrella again. He wet his finger and held it up. Then he pulled it down again, looked at it, considered. 'It's from the east,' he said. 'I'd better go off at an angle this time.'

He turned half away from the tank side and jumped again. He went down as fast as the first time, only his feet, they noticed, landed the right way and took the force of the fall up to his bent knees.

'Give us a go, Ned,' said Paddy. 'You're probably too heavy. I'm the lightest so it'll probably work with me.'

'It's a bit high for you to be jumping if it doesn't work,' Ned said doubtfully. 'After all, you're the youngest.' But he climbed up again with the umbrella.

'Mick ought to try next,' he said.

'But I don't reckon it'll work whoever tries it,' Mick said.

'Go on, you're frightened, that's what,' Paddy said.

'I am not,' Mick said. 'I'll give her a go if you like, Ned. But I still don't believe it.'

'Frightened,' said Paddy.

'I'll show you if I'm frightened,' Mick said. He got to his feet, walked along the edge, stopped to get his balance, and then jumped without any umbrella, landing neatly with bent knees and bottom sinking to his heels.

'Well, anyhow, let's have a go,' said Paddy.

Ned looked at him approvingly. There was something disloyal about what Mick had done. It took the excitement out of the thing a bit. So he warmed Paddy's faith. 'It'd be interesting to see if it worked with someone lighter. But I don't want you to get hurt.'

'Don't you fret your fat,'[5] said Paddy. As he was two years younger than Mick he had developed a reckless competitive courage long since.

'All right, then. Here you are.'

Mick had climbed up again by now, feeling rather guilty though still sceptical. But it was plain from the way Paddy looked, standing on the edge under the open umbrella with a blissful look on his face, that he didn't doubt for a moment it was going to work for him and that he would float like thistledown.

Paddy jumped and hurtled down as fast as Ned had done. On the way down he dropped the umbrella but it took no longer to land than he did.

'My turn now,' Mick said.

'But it's no go, Mick,' Ned said. 'You saw the way the umbrella fell. It's too heavy. Hold on, Paddy. I'm coming down.' Not bothering any more to climb by way of the tankstand he jumped down on to the lawn.

Paddy was already on his feet, bouncing around, disappointment forgotten. 'I did a jolly good jump, didn't I, Ned. It's the first time I've ever jumped from so high.'

'Yes, very good, Paddy. But come on in to the wash-house and I'll show you my new water-mill. It's got much bigger paddles than that other one that wouldn't go. I think it's going to be a real beaut.'

They disappeared round the tankstand. The umbrella still lay on the grass.

Mick jumped down, too. Just like Ned. Never did anything just for fun. If it didn't work he lost interest until he'd thought up something new.

Still, you could never be sure. Perhaps it might work, after all, especially now when no one was looking. Though of course it wouldn't.

Mick took the umbrella and climbed back on to the roof. Perhaps the distance wasn't great enough to give the parachute a chance? He climbed up the slope to the peak of the gable. That was a good ten feet higher. But it was also a good ten feet higher than he'd ever jumped before. If the parachute didn't work he might break his neck. It made you giddy to look down.

He looked down, all the same. It made him dizzy with a queer feeling in his stomach. Of course the damned thing wouldn't work. And there'd be no one there to pick up the pieces. They wouldn't even believe that he'd ever jumped from so high. So if he didn't break his neck this time he'd have to do the jump all over again to make them believe him. And he'd never get away with it twice.

Just like Ned to get him into such a mess and then clear out without even bothering to watch. Well, he had to go through with it now or he'd never be able to look himself in the face again.

'Hail Mary, full of grace,' he began to gabble as he jumped. The umbrella gave no support. The green ground shot up at him. He just managed to get set in time for the landing. His knees came up at him but he managed to throw himself back just before they hit his chin and he lay on his back with the breath knocked out of him.

'I knew I was right. Just another of Ned's stupid ideas,' he thought, forgetting how until the moment he jumped he had believed right inside himself that this time it would work and he would float down like a spider on a thread. He felt himself over to see if any bones were broken.

Roof of the World: first published in *Malahat Review* 10 (April 1968): 89–95.

NOTES

[1] Paddy's Market … Society: possibly held in St Mary's Hall near the Basilica.

[2] the Dunedin express run: the main passenger line from Invercargill through Dunedin to Christchurch. The Invercargill crew would disembark at Dunedin, which is approximately halfway, in order to take over the express arriving from Christchurch for the run from Dunedin back to Invercargill. On Patrick Davin's employment as a guard see 'First Flight'; 'Failed Exorcism'; *FW*, pp. 8–10.

[3] Mr Pratt: the Davin's neighbour who lived at 49 Morton Road. See 'Milk Round'.

[4] 'Every Picture Tells a Story': an allusion to the advertising slogan of the early 1900s for Doan's Backache Kidney Pills. See Elizabeth Knowles, ed., *The Oxford Dictionary of Quotations*, 5th edn. (Oxford: OUP, 1999), s.v. 'Advertising Slogans', p. 19.

[5] Don't you fret your fat: don't get upset about it. Colloq., 'Don't stew over it'.

15

Goosey's Gallic War

IN THE LAST FEW WEEKS of that summer Goosey's Roman army had been getting a bit beyond a joke. When the Saunders family first came to live in the house next door,[1] we had merely kept up a routine surveillance, checking on the kids' doings through knot-holes in the wooden fence, and we'd decided that Goosey and his swarm of young brothers were mad but harmless enough. Their old man was a returned soldier who'd been at Gallipoli and in France too, people said. He was a black Orangeman,[2] I heard my father tell my mother, and a tiger for the drink, and he had a bad tongue on him. We were told to have nothing to do with the kids. Not that we wanted to. They went to the Georgetown school[3] anyway, which was Protestant, and we looked down on them as strangers, and there were enough of us on our own to keep ourselves amused. It wasn't likely we were going to rush to make friends with this red-headed lot.

Later on, though, Goosey and his bunch began to branch out. Their old man was working on some unemployment scheme, and so he was away a lot, going round the country gassing rabbits for the Government at ten bob a week or working on the new road up at Lake Te Anau.[4] Their mother was a bit of a streel[5] our mother said, and she didn't have much control of the kids, especially in the long summer holidays. So they'd be out of the house as soon as breakfast was over and ranging round the countryside. The trouble was that before long they began to find their way into all our favourite territories. We didn't have the feeling that the gravel-pit, Metzger's Bush, the Faraway Bush, Heidelberg Hill, or Lyons' Swamp[6] belonged to us in peace any more.

The next thing we knew was that Goosey had made himself a suit of Roman armour out of old sheets of corrugated iron. He pinched his father's steel helmet and his bayonet too. He armed his brothers in much the same way, except that they only had wooden swords and javelins instead of the bayonet and they didn't have proper helmets, only cardboard ones. There were some other kids from Georgetown school as well as the three young brothers in his gang and they built themselves a sort of Roman camp in Murray's paddock.[7] Goosey used to drill them in front of the camp every morning before taking them out on manoeuvres.

We watched them from our hut in the macrocarpa tree and there was really something rather impressive about the way Goosey would lead them in a charge on Murray's cows. The cows would be feeding, their heads down and all facing in the same direction towards the wind. Goosey's army would march towards them in artillery formation, with a few light-armed troops skirmishing on each flank with shanghais. When they got within about thirty yards of the cows, Goosey would give the word of command and the two files of infantry would peel off into line of battle. Then another word of command and the slingers would let fly over the heads of the infantry with stones from their shanghais. At the same time the infantry would hurl their manuka javelins and then charge, swords drawn. Goosey would be a few yards in front, waving his bayonet and shouting. The cows would look up gaping with their great eyes and wondering what on earth was happening. Then their tails would go up and, before it could come to close-quarters' fighting, they'd turn round and bolt for it at the lick of their lives,[8] udders swinging from side to side.

Goosey used to call a halt then and regroup his forces and give them a short, martial speech, praising their valour and sometimes awarding a leather medal for some conspicuous act of courage beyond the call of duty. After that, he would give an analysis of the action and explain the lessons to be learnt from it.

Goosey himself didn't look all that impressive, if you just saw him in the street in his school clothes. He had red hair like all that family and his father kept it close-cropped to save paying a barber. Everything he wore had obviously been bought at a jumble sale or handed down by his big brother who was too old for playing soldiers, had a motor-bike and a job in a garage, and was chiefly interested in girls. Goosey's legs and arms were long and thin and his body was short but not stocky. His eyelashes were pink and every part of him you could see was covered in freckles. His neck was too long and he carried his head forward. His nose and his eyes were the things that struck you, though. The nose was a great hooked thing with a white patch on the bridge where the skin was too tight for the bone, like a clenched knuckle. The eyes were a pale blue and they stuck out of their sockets as if they were straining to get round the nose. He had an expression like a goose looking up a bottle, my father said. But they were fierce eyes, a fanatic's, and the grown-ups were fooled by the fact that he wasn't clever at school and didn't have much to say when they were around. In fact, Goosey lived by the imagination and there was something extreme in the way he acted out his loony notions which made him able to impose himself on other kids. They mightn't like being bossed around but the fact remained that when Goosey was about no one could complain that there was nothing to do. He always thought up some mad scheme and he made it seem so real that they just couldn't help getting interested and tagging along, if only to find out what was going to happen next.

Well, we kept a pretty sharp eye on Goosey and his army, thinking that they were up to no good, but there wasn't any real trouble until Goosey's father, Duncan Saunders, complained to the police that our big red cow Rosy had been loose in the Oteramika Road[9] one night and had tossed him and his bike into the ditch. None of us believed it, of course. We just thought he'd been tight and had ridden into the ditch and then thought up a cock-and-bull story. Or else he'd had the DT's we thought, and had seen a horned beast which he'd taken to be our placid Rosy but which was really a foul fiend imagined by himself out of all that Presbyterian stuff he'd probably been taught as a kid.

Unfortunately, though, other people had seen Rosy on the road that night. It was true they were Protestants but then so were most people round our part of the town and we knew perfectly well that quite a few of them, most of them in fact, wouldn't tell lies any more than we would. Not in a court of law, anyway, and that's what it came to. For Duncan sued my father and there was a great old fuss. In the end the case was dismissed but we were given a warning that we must make sure our fences were all right and that the cows didn't get loose.

The whole thing caused a good deal of bad blood, one way and another, and of course religion got mixed up in it. When we passed some of Goosey's lot, if there were enough of them to feel safe, they'd call out 'Catholic dogs jump like frogs'[10] and that sort of stuff. And we had a few things of our own about black Orangemen and so on. A sort of feud built up and after a bit we had to make sure that none of us was ever out in the paddocks by himself or up in the bush.

One evening my young brother and I went up to get the cows and found them looking very wild in the eyes and sweaty in their coats. And we spotted the rearguard of Goosey's Roman army withdrawing behind a gorse hedge. The cows didn't let down their milk easily that evening and my mother was puzzled why they gave so little. We didn't tell her what the reason was but it wasn't hard to guess what had been happening.

When we put the cows up in the hill paddock that night, my elder brother said it mightn't be a bad plan to take a look round the fences. And, sure enough, we found someone had taken down the Taranaki gate[11] on the side that led to the Oteramika Road, the one we didn't normally use. So we put it up again and tied it round with so many strands of barbed wire that it would be a bit of a job for anyone to get it open again.

Then he and I went home and had a council of war with our two younger brothers. Tom, that was my elder brother, said envoys would have to be sent to Goosey to protest against the attack on our cows and the sabotage of our fence and discuss whether it was to be peace or war. I was in favour of peace, because it was going to be a hellish nuisance if you couldn't go out to mind the cows while they fed on the grass roads and you read a book under a tree or in the dry ditch without being in danger of an ambush. But my two younger brothers were all for war and Tom said that probably the only way to get peace was to give Goosey's army a thrashing that would teach them a lesson.

So it was decided that Tom and I would go as ambassadors that very evening after we'd had tea.

Goosey's headquarters was in a big red shed in the far bottom corner of their garden. In the days when whoever lived in the house used to run cows and kept a couple of draught horses, this shed had been divided into two, one part for the horses which you got at through a half-door, and the other part a cowshed open at the front.

When the time came Tom and I climbed over the barbed-wire fence and went up the track towards the red shed. There was a gorse hedge on our left, which hadn't been cut for years, and on our right was the garden with a lot of blackcurrant bushes and raspberry canes run wild. Duncan Saunders never bothered about the garden and it was pretty overgrown.

We knew Goosey had sentries posted because we could hear them moving level with us on the other side of the gorse hedge and caught a glimpse of a blue jersey hiding in the bushes on the right and of a bow and arrow trained on us. When we got within a few yards of the shed the ones who'd been behind the gorse came out in front of us. They stood there in a row with their hands on their swords. As well as Goosey's younger brothers, there were big Tony Tansley from the house beyond,[12] Soapy Stone the boy from the orphanage whom everyone was sick of being sorry for, and Nuggety Daniels who was Goosey's chief lieutenant.

'Where do you think you're going?' Nuggety said.

'Where's Goosey?' Tom asked.

'What do you want to know for?'

This didn't seem to be getting anyone anywhere, what with one side asking questions and the other asking some more, and I was thinking of trying some other sort of diplomacy when suddenly Goosey stood up behind the half-door, opened it and came out. He was wearing his full armour and he passed through his men and stood in front of them about a yard from us.

'What do you want?' he said.

'You were chasing our cows this afternoon,' Tom said.

Goosey frowned. He didn't like Tom's choice of phrase. 'We were conducting a punitive expedition,' he said.

'Call it what you like but as far as I'm concerned it was chasing our cows. And I'm not going to have a pack of bloody kids chasing our cows when one of them's in calf and the rest are in milk. Or any other time, for that matter.'

'You aren't, aren't you?' said Goosey. 'We'll have to see about that. Are you prepared to give hostages or guarantees for their conduct in future? If so, I'm prepared to grant them an amnesty.'

'Even if we wanted your silly amnesty,' Tom said, 'it wouldn't be much use when you start leaving our gates open so that our cows can get out and get into trouble on the roads, frightening the wits out of drunks who don't know a pair of cow's horns from the devil's. So you know what you can do with your amnesty. You'll leave our cows and fences alone.'

'Or else what?'

'It boils down to this. Either you promise to leave our cows alone or your army of kids is going to take a thrashing. I give you fair warning.'

'Then it's war,' said Goosey.

'Call it what you like. But you aren't going to like it when it comes.'

'I give you safe conduct back to the frontier,' Goosey said. 'After that, watch out, that's all.'

'To hell with you and your safe conduct,' Tom said.

'I've given my word and you won't provoke me to breaking it,' Goosey said, with maddening dignity.

'Come on,' Tom said to me.

We walked back down the track. The hairs were standing up on the back of my neck. As we'd been talking I'd seen the rest of Goosey's army forming up in the open front of the shed. They all had bows and arrows except a few who had airguns. The arrows were only long dock stalks but they had nails in the heads and I'd used them often enough to know that they could hurt. There were a few of them with shanghais, too, and a stone from one of those could hit hard. I'd once killed a rabbit with one.

I wished Tom would walk a bit faster but he strode on at a deliberate pace. I wanted to look back to see whether they were following us but couldn't very well with Tom alongside me. He wouldn't have thought much of that.

We got through the barbed-wire fence. As soon as we were on our side I heard the airguns go off and the whine of BB pellets[13] past our ears. And stones fell round us and a dock arrow hit me in the back.

'You have been warned,' Goosey shouted after us.

Back in our cowshed, we found reinforcements had arrived – Les Stokes and Denis Wood. Tom grinned when he saw them. 'Good,' he said. 'Now we can have a proper go at them tonight.'

I still thought it wasn't too late to make peace through some neutral envoy and on a basis of territorial division. I pointed out that there were far more of them than we had on our side and some of them had airguns.

'Don't you worry,' he said. 'Once we get to close quarters we'll soon fix them. Now listen. Here's what we'll do. Goosey will be more or less expecting us any night from now on and the longer we wait the better chance he'll have to build up his defences. So we don't gain anything by waiting. I guess he'll put the blokes with the airguns inside the closed part of the shed because they don't need much room. He'll put the small kids with shanghais on both sides and the big ones in the middle watching the main track. They're the ones that count, Nuggety and big Tony the most. So they're the ones to go for. Soapy will just skedaddle, it doesn't matter about the little kids.

'So Martin and Les and I'll go up the middle. Denis can go on the gorse hedge side and Jack up through the garden. They can keep the kids busy and stop them from pelting us while we take on the big jokers in the middle.'

'What about me?' Pat said. He was our youngest brother and only ten. But he'd have had a fit if anyone suggested leaving him out. And he wasn't a bad shot – he even used to kid himself he was a better shot than I was.

'You follow on behind Jack and get behind a bush with your shanghai and plenty of stones. You're the best shot and if you watch the windows and the doors you can keep the airguns down. Then when we make our big charge at the finish you join in with us.'

So then we collected all our ammunition supplies and weapons. We all had bows and shanghais, the bows made out of strong lancejack[14] and the shanghais with strips of rubber cut from old lorry tubes. Mine had a willow prong notched for everything I'd killed, two notches for a rabbit and three for the hawk I'd once stalked in a swamp.

In case of emergencies we'd been collecting ammunition for a good while back, ever since we got suspicious of Goosey's gang, in fact. We had piles of stones specially chosen from the river gravel, nicely round and shiny and just the right size. And we'd been raiding the old man's toolshed for special flat-headed nails that just fitted into the dry dock stalks that we'd picked from the lower paddock. The nails gave the arrows the weight they needed at the business end to make them shoot accurately and hit hard.

There was still plenty of light to see by and we wormed our way along behind the board fence where we couldn't be seen from the Saunders' place. Then we crawled out and got into position behind an old log. Denis wriggled through a gap on to the gorse hedge side and Jack and Pat managed to get behind some bushes in the corner of the Saunders' garden without being spotted. By this time the light wasn't so good and we would have to get going pretty quickly before it was too dark to aim properly.

'I can see Nuggety and big Tony and Goosey in front of the shed,' Pat called over to us, just loud enough for us to hear him. 'No sign of Soapy, though.'

'Right,' Tom said. 'When I say "Go", everyone can shoot off all his arrows. We're close enough and it's no good taking the bows with us; they'll only get in the way once we get to close quarters and start putting in the stoush.'[15]

We waited for a bit to make sure everyone was ready. Then Tom called out 'Go'. We all jumped up so as to be able to see and started loosing off our arrows. Stones began to fall all round us and you could hear the airgun pellets pinging past. This went on for a couple of minutes and then Tom shouted, 'After them.'

The three of us raced up the track towards the shed, Tom in the middle. We could hear kids squealing on the other side of the hedge and could see some more of them running back towards the shed from the garden, Jack and Pat after them.

Then big Tony and Nuggety were coming towards us. I felt a sharp pain in the flap of my ear and realised I'd been hit by a BB pellet but I didn't care by then. I was feeling full of a queer sort of artificial rage and when a stone from a shanghai hit me next, full in the chest, I didn't care about that either. Next thing I knew Nuggety was in front of me, waving his sword. I went at him hard and got him with my shoulder just below the ribs. He doubled up, properly winded, and I grabbed his sword from him and broke it. I looked round and saw that Les had big Tony on the ground and they were rolling over and over. Tom was in front of me and Goosey was in front of him with his bayonet out but backing away as Tom came at him. Other kids were coming out of the shed to help but at that moment Jack and Denis came out on either side of the track and began to let fly with their shanghais. The kids all ran back into the shed.

I looked round to see how Les was getting on. He had big Tony on his back with his arms pinned but Nuggety had got his wind again and was going to the rescue. I ran in front of him, grabbed an arm and tried the flying mare[16] the way my father had taught me. It worked like a dream and Nuggety went sailing over my shoulder into the gorse hedge.

Tom was still driving Goosey backwards step by step towards the shed. But the bayonet looked pretty ugly and I could tell Tom wasn't sure whether Goosey wasn't mad enough to use it. So Tom just kept after him, waiting for an opening. Suddenly young Pat darted out of the currant bushes and dived for Goosey's legs. He wasn't big enough to bring Goosey down but Tom saw his chance, rushed in past the bayonet and hit Goosey on his breast-plate with the heel of his fist. Goosey went down with a crash and couldn't get up again because of his armour and because Pat was still hanging on to his legs. His helmet had fallen off and rolled away.

Tom grabbed the bayonet from him and threw it into the hedge. Then we left Goosey still on the ground and charged on towards the red shed. Though the three champions were out of action Goosey's discipline was strong enough to keep the others in action and stones and airgun pellets were all round us. Tom got to the shed first and charged with his shoulder against the half-door. It broke open and we were in. All the kids except Soapy who was too fat had bolted by now out through a hole in the back wall and the fort was ours.

'I surrender,' Soapy said.

We looked back down the track. Pat had left Goosey so as to be in at the death with us. Goosey was sitting up and rubbing his head. Nuggety had got out of the hedge and was trying to help him up. Les had let go of big Tony and they were standing grinning at each other, not knowing what to do next.

I ran back and got my favourite bow from where I'd left it. I went over to Goosey, who was standing up now.

'I have a message from my sovereign liege,' I said, 'Richard the Lionheart. It says: "To Robin Hood, of Sherwood Forest. My servants tell me that you have fought nobly in the cause against the usurper John and the caitiff[17] Sheriff of Nottingham. In token whereof I send you by the hand of herald this bow. Keep it and continue to do good service, succouring the poor and pillaging the unjust rich."'

A light came in his eyes. A new vein of fantasy in action had been opened. Besides, it was a very good bow. He held out his hand and took the bow.

'You may tell your master that I shall gladly be his ally. And he can count equally on my brave lieutenants, Little John and Friar Tuck.' He looked at big Tony and Nuggety and I could see they had caught on and were quite happy with their new parts.

'Have you read the books about Robin Hood and all that?' Goosey asked me.

'Some of them,' I said. 'But there are one or two I haven't been able to lay hands on.'

'Come and take a look at mine,' he said. 'I've got them hidden in the wash-house.'

Tom leaned over the half-door, watching us and grinning.

When we got to the door of the wash-house, we heard grown-ups talking and laughing somewhere in the house. Goosey put his finger to his lips to indicate silence and signalled to us to follow him. Tom had gone back home but all the rest of our side were with me and Goosey. We went round the side of the house and peered through the window into the front room. To my amazement I saw my mother and father sitting in chairs round the fireplace. Mrs Saunders was talking to my mother. They were holding glasses of wine of some sort and eating seed-cake. Our sister Norah was sitting on the sofa with Jim Saunders, Goosey's big brother. They weren't drinking or eating but were just looking at each other, as far as I could see. And Mr Saunders and my father were standing by the mantelpiece with glasses of beer in their hands.

Mr Saunders spotted us kids staring in through the window and came over. 'Bring in your cobbers, if you like,' he said to Goosey. 'I'm just showing Mr Cody my souvenirs.'

We went round to the front door and trooped in. The things were all spread out on the sideboard, all sorts of medals and ribbons, a German helmet, a gas mask, a big shell-case, a belt with 'Gott mit uns' on the buckle, and a whole lot of other stuff.

I can't say my father seemed to be taking a great deal of notice and the women just weren't interested. Norah and Jim didn't seem to realise there was anybody else in the room at all.

'Those are my father's medals that he won at the war,' Goosey said to me. 'Was your father at the war?'

'No,' I said and I almost wished he had been, though he'd often said he was glad he had too many kids for anyone to expect him to fight in England's war.

'We'll open another bottle,' Mr Saunders said to my father.

My mother never missed a thing. 'Now, now, Ned,' she said. 'Remember you're on early shift tomorrow morning.'

'Never mind about that, Mary. It's not every day we have an engagement in the family.'

And that was the real way that Goosey's family and ours turned out to be allies in the end.

Goosey's Gallic War: first published in *Landfall* 22:4 (December, 1968): 387–96.

NOTES

[1] the house next door: when the Davins were living at 52 Morton Road in the 1920s, the next door lot to no. 52 was vacant. Davin locates the Saunders family in this space.

[2] a black Orangeman: a Protestant of the Orange Order. 'Late Snow' and 'The Black Stranger' also reveal the diluted meaning of 'black' as found in the transplanted Irish discourses of Southland.

[3] Georgetown school: the local Protestant public school. See 'Milk Round'.

[4] the new road … Lake Te Anau: aiming to put a tunnel through Homer Saddle to open up the Milford area, this roading project for the unemployed began in 1929. Two hundred men used shovels and buckets to create a road from Te Anau township for thirty kilometres (nineteen miles) to the Te Anau Downs station. This was relief work for single men, who lived in labour camps. The road reached the Divide in 1934, then continued down the side of Hollyford Canyon by blasting. Tunnel construction began in 1935 at the head of the Hollyford and the tunnel was opened in 1953. 'Homer Tunnel', *Te Ara – the Encyclopaedia of New Zealand* (updated 26 Sept. 2006), http://www.teara.govt.nz/1966/H/HomerTunnel/HomerTunnel/en (accessed 17 Jan 2007).

[5] a bit of a streel: Hiberno-English pejorative term for a slatternly woman.

[6] the gravel pit … Lyon's Swamp: **Metzger's Bush**: also known as Metzger's Paddocks, near or beyond what is now Metzger Street in the area now known as Heidelberg. Possibly the bush referred to in 'Death of a Dog' (see 'Invercargill Boundary', 'Gardens of Exile'). **The Faraway Bush**: possibly bush near Faraway Hill (see 'The Vigil', 'Death of a Dog', 'The Far-Away Hill'). **Heidelberg Hill**: in Georgetown where St Patrick's Primary School now is, i.e. two blocks east of Morton Street, between View and Metzger

Streets, and Rimu Street to the north and John Street to the South (see Davin, *Not Here, Not Now*, p. 133). **Lyons' Swamp**: not identified.

[7] Murray's paddock: on Robert Murray see 'Growing Up', 'Invercargill Boundary', 'Gardens of Exile'.

[8] at the lick ... lives: at full speed. Cf. lickety split. *DSUE*.

[9] Oteramika Road: see notes to 'The Apostate' and 'Gardens of Exile'. Part of the road is now renamed as Tweed Street; Oteramika Road begins now at Rockdale Road.

[10] 'Catholic dogs jump like frogs': see the full rhyme in 'The Apostate'.

[11] Taranaki gate: simple gate made of No. 8 fencing wire (often barbed) and battens, held shut by wire loops. See 'Growing Up', p. 104; 'The Black Stranger', p. 272.

[12] big Tony Tansley ... beyond: Wise's *Directory* (1929) records Tansleys living at 56 Morton Road, several houses away from the Davins.

[13] BB pellets: lead pellets used in target shooting or hunting small game, here fired from air rifles.

[14] lancejack: this name is not recorded. Possibly it refers to lancewood (horoeka), the wood of which is suitable for making bows.

[15] putting in the stoush: fighting to hit, brawling.

[16] the flying mare: a wrestling throw in which one grabs one's opponent's wrist, turns one's back to the opponent, and flips the opponent over one's shoulder onto the ground.

[17] caitiff: despicable, base, cowardly.

16

The Tree

IT WAS WELL AFTER THREE when Ned and Mick finished bagging the potatoes. Ned got the big stable broom and Mick held the sack open, just below the lip of the doorstep. Leaving only streaks of fine dust behind it on the floor and a wet patch where the heap had been, Ned's broom swept in front of it all the rotten potatoes and the ones that were too small to be any good. Then the two of them caught the sack by an ear each and dragged it into the fowl run. The hens scattered in front of them but when the sack was upended and emptied they were soon back and picking in the mess, grabbing special little morsels for themselves and scuttling off to eat by themselves.

'Well,' said Mick, looking at his hands all smeared with dirt and rotten potato, 'that's that. A good Saturday afternoon wasted. It's too late to take the ferrets out between now and milking time. What on earth shall we do now? There's over an hour to put in before we can bring the cows home.'

Ned felt the challenge. 'We'll soon think of something. Come on and we'll wash our hands first anyway.'

In the washhouse Ned rinsed his hands under the tap and dried them on an old sugar-bag apron of his mother's. While Mick took his place at the tap he sat on the separator bench. His eyes ranged around the walls and fixed on the crosscut saw[1] suspended by its handles from two nails above the copper.

'I'll tell you what, Mick,' he said. 'We'll cut down the tree.'

'What tree?'

'The macrocarpa tree, of course. The old man's always going crook[2] because the thrushes and blackbirds roost there and come down and gobble up his blackcurrants. Well, he'll get a surprise tomorrow when he comes home and finds no tree.'

Mick looked at him doubtfully and then at the saw. The handles made you just itch to get to work on something with it. But he hadn't any grudge against the tree.

'And afterwards we can cut it up for firewood. It'll keep us going for weeks,' Ned went on.

Mick still hesitated.

'Of course, it isn't the easiest thing in the world to cut down a tree. You've got to make them fall the right way and that's easier said than done. You remember how old Andy Keogh brought that big broadleafed[3] down right on top of his own kitchen. Only the real bushmen[4] can do it properly.'

The word 'bushmen' did the trick. Mick climbed up on top of the copper and lifted the top handle off its nail so that Ned could pull the saw out from the wall. They carried it, a handle each, out through the backyard and past the woodheap. The sun caught it as it rippled between them. It made a noise like steel water. There was something fierce about it, like a stallion. It couldn't wait to get at the tree.

They walked down the path and between the rows of gooseberry bushes, long since picked. From his post at the rear handle Mick looked over to the corner of the garden. The trunk of the macrocarpa tree reared up from behind the wooden fence and spread its broad green hands. It had been there longer than he could remember. It was alive and they were going to murder it. Still, it was only a tree.

Ned unlatched the wooden door in the board fence and it swung back by its own weight on the leather hinges. They took the saw through and came up to the tree. Looking up they caught glimpses of the sky through its deep green darkness.

'It leans outwards,' Ned said, 'so we'll start on the fence side. When she crashes she ought to fall just by the gorse hedge.'

They crouched one on each side of the tree and ran the teeth of the saw to and fro until it had cut through the bark. When the colour of the sawdust had changed from dark brown to white they stopped.

'Now remember,' Ned said, 'we've got to keep the saw exactly level or otherwise it'll start sticking and jamming as soon as we get properly into it.'

Mick looked up at the banked darkness and then back down the trunk to the brief white scar where the teeth had begun to bite. It didn't seem possible there was any connection between what they were doing and the life of the tree.

Ned was spitting on his hands. 'It stops the blisters coming.'

Mick spat on his hands too.

They looked at each other along the flat, malevolent saw. Ned's eyes were solemn. They were always like that when he was set on something. It was their way of showing excitement.

'Now,' Ned said.

The saw worked to and fro between them. The white sawdust trickled down below the cut, filtering at first into the cracks in the bark and then, as these filled, sliding straight down and heaping in a little pile at the foot. The teeth ripped and tore closer towards the heart, greedily.

All through milking Ned was making plans. As soon as they were old enough they would get a job at Port Craig.[5] They would be known as the boldest bushmen in the south and as a team they would beat the Aussies at all the axemen's carnivals. Nick milked away in silence and felt the sting in his blisters each time he squeezed.

'Old Con Kelly says you can always tell a bushwhacker[6] by the shape of his arm muscles, the way they're long and supple and not bunched up like the muscles of a man who works with the shovel.[7] We must have a look at ours after we're finished and see if it's made any difference. And we'll get Dad to take us to the Tuatapere sports next year and watch the crosscut competitions.[8] We must try our hands with the axe, too, later on when the trunk's dry enough.'

But listening to Ned wasn't quite the same as working with him on the other end of the saw. It didn't get across to you the same. By the time they had put the cows up, brought the milk to the wash-house, separated and come in to find their mother was home and supper ready, most of Mick's ardour had vanished.

'Did you boys finish picking those spuds?' asked Mrs Connolly.

'Yes, Mum.'

'And how is Strawberry? Does she show any signs of springing[9] at all?'

'Oh yes, she's getting a real big bag on her. I reckon she ought to be about due in a week or two from now,' Ned said.

'Here, Mick, bring over your plate and have some more fried potatoes.'

Mick held out the plate.

'What's the matter with your hand? What's that, is it a blister you've got there?'

Mick looked down at his hand and then looked over at Ned for his cue.

'Yes, we've both got blisters,' Ned said, holding up his own right hand.

'And what have you been up to to get blisters?'

'We've been sawing down the tree.'

'What tree?'

'The old macrocarpa tree. It's a surprise for Dad.'

She looked at Ned, then at Mick, and pursed her lips doubtfully. 'People don't always like surprises,' she said.

But she went on dishing out tea for the others.

'What do you want to cut down that lovely old tree for?' asked Eileen. 'It wasn't doing any harm to anybody.'

'That's all you know,' Mick said fiercely, for this was what he had been coming to feel himself.

'Well, what harm was it doing?'

'It was a real pirates' nest for all the birds that pinch the fruit.'

'The worst pirates live in this house, not in the poor old tree,' she said meaningly.

'And it was choking all Dad's plants with its roots,' Mick said, and then was silent with surprise, for this was the first time he'd thought of that for a reason.

'A fat lot you care for Dad's plants. Look at the fuss you made the other day when he was going to hit Jack for chasing the cat over them.'

'Oh, shut up, Eileen,' Ned said. 'We're cutting the tree down and that's all you need to know about it. You look after the flowers and leave trees to the men.'

'Cissie Francis is going to be a boarder in Saint Dominic's,[10] so Mrs Francis told me today,' Mrs Connolly said quietly. And Eileen thought no more of the tree.

'We'll have to hurry if we're going to get it finished before dark,' Ned said.

Mick had begun to hope that they would wait till tomorrow to finish the job. He should have known Ned better, though. And he wasn't going to complain about the blisters if Ned didn't.

So they fitted the saw into the cut again.

'There's not really any need to push or pull, you know,' Ned said, the next time they paused to get their breath. 'All you have to do is just keep it going and the teeth cut in of their own accord.'

'I wonder if it'll fall the way we want it to.' Mick got up and pretended to study the lie of the tree. His back was very stiff.

'She'll be jake,[11] don't you worry,' Ned said without getting up. Mick bent down again, on one knee this time to see if it was any better that way.

The saw went to and fro.

'What are you jokers doing?' They looked up. It was Tinny MacEwan from next door.

'Just sawing down this old tree,' Mick said casually.

'Can I have a go?'

'Mick might let you have a turn at his end. He's getting a bit tired, I think.'

'I am not.' Mick sawed away harder than ever.

Tinny walked round the tree. 'You're well past halfway. I'll tell you what. What say I get a rope and see if I can lend a hand, giving her a good tug?'

Ned didn't care much for the idea. It didn't sound the sort of thing they would do up at Port Craig. But it was getting dark and he was more tired than he would admit. 'If you want to, you can. But you'll have to hurry. She'll be down in a minute anyway. Get a legrope out of our cowshed.'

In two minutes Tinny was back with a rope and up the trunk. He tied it to a limb near the trunk and came slithering down it.

'Which way do you want her to fall?' he asked.

'She's going to fall between the fence and the end of the gorse hedge.'

Tinny took his rope out, found it was too short, got another legrope and tied it to the first. He walked out and began to take the strain.

Ned eyed him jealously. 'Watch out she doesn't come down on you now,' he said. 'Come on, Mick, a little bit more and the job is done.'

Just then there was a tearing and cracking. The gap above the buried saw blade began to widen upwards. Then the branches above began to heave and sway as if they were trying to regain their balance. It was as if the sky was moving. Watching, Mick suddenly felt as if it were someone like his father beginning to fall. It was the first time he had ever known something permanent change.

'Come on, Mick, let's finish her off.'

They tore to and fro with the saw. Tinny grunted as he strained and hauled on the rope. Suddenly he dropped it and began to run. Mick looked up at the tree. It was listing. And then, seeming stationary, as if it were the world that was shifting and not itself, the tree toppled. The earth came up and met it, absorbing its crash in a smashing softness of broken minor branches that heaved and writhed as if they were alive, while the larger branches that now spanned an incredible stretch of ground bounced at the edge of a green sea. One branch had caught the gorse hedge and a shower of gold followed it down.

Tinny was on the other side, grinning and cheering. Mick looked at Ned who had straightened up and was now staring gravely at the fallen tree.

'There,' Ned said, 'just where I wanted it to fall.' He picked up his end of the saw. 'We must rub this with an oily rag before we put it away. It's a good saw.'

It was still not quite dark when Mrs Connolly and Eileen came to have an awed look. Then they went away again. Tinny was called inside by his mother to finish his homework. Ned and Mick took the saw in, oiled it, and hung it up once again on its nails. They went inside then and Ned began to read a copy of *Wide World*.[12] But Mick could not settle.

Soon he was back at the tree. He looked at the stump. Its surface was smooth except where the jagged pieces on the further side stuck up like stalagmites. Near them drops of gum had begun to exude. Like tears, Mick thought. Like blood.

He and Ned would never climb up into those branches any more, never sew together their father's sacks and make hammocks where you could lie with a book listening to the life going on under you and hearing the world breathe in the wind. Never again sit up there remote with nothing but a green roof between yourself and the sky, feeling the strong, living tree move gently under you. The birds would never nest there again and he would never wake in the morning to hear them singing there. Something that had challenged the sky was gone.

Mick sat on the stump, staring down into green branches. Then he felt someone standing beside him. He looked up. It was his father.

'It was the only tree I left when I cleared this section,' his father said. 'Later on I always meant to cut it down but somehow I didn't want to. It was a good tree.'

And Mick saw that what had added to his own past was taken from his father's.

The Tree: a transcript is held in the Alexander Turnbull Library (MS-Group-0319).

NOTES

1 crosscut saw: a long, two-man saw for cutting across the grain of a log.
2 going crook: becoming angry, complaining.
3 big broadleafed: trees of the *Griselinia littoralis* genus with distinctive broad glossy leaves. See *ODNZE*, s.v. 'broadleaf' for quotation of this passage.
4 bushmen: men who fell bush professionally for land-clearing or timber-getting purposes. See *ODNZE*, s.v. 'bushman' for quotation of this passage.
5 Port Craig: site of the country's largest sawmill camp in the 1920s, on the coast of the western end of Te Waewae Bay, west of Invercargill, deep in the bush and reachable then only by tramlines or boat.
6 a bushwhacker: one who fells standing trees. *ODNZE*.
7 shape of his arm muscles: see allusion to 'big long bushwhackers' arms' in 'Prometheus'.
8 Tuatapere sports: the Tuatapere annual sports events held on New Year's Day at which the crosscut-saw competitions attracted attention. See 'A Meeting Half Way'.
9 springing: calving.
10 Saint Dominic's: the Dominican Priory and College in Dowling Street, Dunedin, which opened in 1871. It offered elementary schooling for children of working-class Irish and at secondary level was a boarding school for Catholic girls, educating them for civil service and university entrance exams. Winifred Gonley was a boarder there. See Anna Davin, 'Davin, Winifred Kathleen Joan 1909–1995', *DNZB* (updated April 2006), http://www.dnzb.govt.nz (accessed 17 Jan. 2007); *FW*, p. 52.
11 She'll be jake: all right, OK. *ODNZE*. See 'A Return', p. 201.
12 *Wide World: the Wide World Magazine: a magazine for men*, published by the Englishman, George Newnes, and edited by Horace Pitt-Kethley. It ran from 1898–1965. A pulp-style magazine directed at 'imaginative amateurs', it purportedly contained the 'true adventures' of its contributors. Among its writers was Conan Doyle.

17

The Quiet One

THE BAND CONCERT WAS OVER and the three of us came out of the Regent[1] into Dee Street with the rest of the crowd.

'I could swear she gave me the eye,' Sid said.

'I'll bet she did.' Wally said. 'One look'd be all she'd need, too. Who did, anyway?'

'That sheila with the black hat on that was in front of us about two seats away. You'd be too busy looking at the statue of the naked Greek dame to notice, I expect. Anyhow she was just in front of me when we were coming out and when I pushed the swing door open for her, she turned round and gave me a real grin. Look, there she goes.'

He pointed the way we were going, and, sure enough, we could see a black hat bobbing along a bit in front where the crowd wasn't so thick.

'Come on, boys,' said Wally, 'Here we go.'

'But, look here,' I said, 'I thought we were going to the Greek's.'[2] All the same I changed my pace to keep up with theirs.

'To hell with the Greek's. Who wants to be sitting down to eggs and chips when there's a chance of picking up a sheila, eh, Sid?'

Sid just grunted. You couldn't see the girl because of the crowd and he was staring straight down the footpath, towards where we'd last seen her. You wouldn't have needed to know him as well as I did to guess from the sour way his mouth was closed that he didn't fancy the shape things were taking much. Wally was a tiger for the girls, and a good-looking joker, too. And old Sid hadn't had the same confidence in himself since the dentist made him have all his top teeth out. Wally didn't give him much chance to forget about it, either, calling him Gummy all the evening.

Not that there was anything in it for me, anyway. If there was only one girl I wouldn't be the chap who got her, that was certain. And, as a matter of fact, though I'd have been the last to say so, I'd have been scared stiff if there'd been the least danger of me being the one. I never really knew why I tagged along with them those Sunday evenings. I must have hoped some sort of miracle would happen, I suppose, and that some sheila or other would fall for me and put me into a position where one move had to follow the other in such a way that my mind'd be made up for me. At the same time I was terrified that just that would happen, knowing in advance that at close quarters with a girl I'd be like a cow with a musket. Anyhow, I needn't have worried. Nothing ever did happen and by this time I think I was getting to realise only I wouldn't admit it, that nothing ever would.

That didn't stop me, though, from putting off going home till the last possible moment in case some sort of miracle turned up and when I finally left Wally or Sid at Rugby Park corner[3] of a Saturday or Sunday night I'd trudge the rest of the way home in the rain or the moonlight, cursing myself and the town and everything in it and wondering what the hell was the matter with me, whether I was a different breed or what, and why it was always me that was left, and thinking that in some other country somewhere things mightn't be like that at all and people would see what I really was instead of what I'd always been.

So, with all that at the back of my mind, and Wally rampaging alongside with about as many afterthoughts as a dog has after a rabbit, and Sid on the other side getting down in the mouth already at the thought that Wally was going to pinch his girl, I didn't think much of the night's prospects. The upshot'd be that Wally would get her all right and I'd have to spend what was left of the evening at the Greek's trying to cheer Sid up by encouraging him to skite about all the girls that had fallen for him and pretending not to notice how much Wally going off with this one had got under his skin.

Well, after a bit the crowd got thinner and most of them started to cross over to where the last tram was waiting, towards the Majestic side.[4] So we could see better what was in front of us. And there was the girl all right, about twenty yards ahead, all by herself into the bargain, and pacing along at a fair bat.[5] Good legs she had, too.

'I reckon she knows we're following her,' Wally said. 'The trouble is, there's too many of us.'

'That's right, Wally.'

It was very sarcastic the way Sid said it but that didn't worry Wally.

'Go on, Sid,' he said, 'don't be a dog in the manger.[6] A fair fight and let the best man win, eh?'

Of course, that was just the trouble, the way Sid looked at it. It's always the best man who says these things.

Anyhow, before Sid could think of an answer, or before he could think of something that wouldn't have given away he knew he hadn't a hope against Wally whatever kind of fight it was, the girl started to cross the road and so, us too, we changed course like a school of sprats and over the road after her, only about ten yards behind by this time.

She stepped up onto the footpath on the opposite side of the road, us tagging behind like three balloons on a string. She looked behind just then and saw us.

'Now's our chance,' Sid said, getting quite excited and nervous, I could tell.

Wally didn't say anything but he took advantage of his long legs and he was up on the pavement a good yard in front of us.

It was darker on the footpath because of the shop verandahs and because the nearest street-lamp was a good distance away. At first I couldn't see what was happening, owing to the notion I had that if I wore my glasses when we were out on the pick-up on nights like this I'd spoil my chances, such as they were: but I felt both Wally and Sid check. And then I saw what it was. The girl had stepped into a shop doorway and there was a chap there waiting for her.

The girl and her bloke came out of the doorway and walked off towards the other end of Dee Street, her hanging on his arm and talking a blue streak[7] and laughing the way we could tell the joke was on us. And the bloke looked back once as if he'd like to have come at us. But, seeing Wally and thinking he had the trumps anyway, I suppose, he turned round again and kept on going.

'Well, I'm damned,' Wally said.

'Foiled again,' Sid said. But he didn't sound narked at all,[8] really, and I knew by his voice he'd sooner have had it that way so that the laugh was on Wally instead of on himself as it would have been if things had gone differently.

I was pleased, too, for that matter, though I couldn't help envying that bloke a bit with a good-looking girl on his arm and a nice new blue overcoat and Borsalino[9] and never a doubt in his head as to where he was going and what he'd do when he got there.

Still, envying him made it easier to pretend I meant it when I cursed the girl up hill and down dale like the others. For it wouldn't have done for me to show I was really relieved. It was sort of understood that even if I didn't mean business like Wally and Sid I had to go through the motions just the same. They really weren't bad blokes in a way, Wally and Sid, because they knew all the time I wasn't a serious competitor and yet they always treated me as if I was, thinking I'd be hurt if they didn't, I suppose.

And I would have been hurt, too. Somehow, if there hadn't been this kind of agreement about the way we were all to behave, I'd have had to drop the game altogether. I could tell that, because when, as happened sometimes, other blokes joined us who didn't know the rules or didn't care if there were any and they began to pull my leg, I always pushed off after a while. Which was what these other chaps wanted, I expect. 'The Wet Napkin,' I heard one of them, Ginger Foyle it was, say once after I'd gone and he didn't think I could hear him, because I hadn't got my glasses on, perhaps.

No, Wally and Sid weren't like that, especially Wally. They knew I was all right once you got to know me and, besides, I used to be able to make them laugh when we were by ourselves and get them to see the funny side of things they'd never have noticed if it hadn't been for me.

Well, anyway, there we were left standing in the middle of Dee Street and all cursing our heads off in the same way.

'Nothing for it but to go over to the Greek's,' I said.

'Listen to him, will you, Sid,' Wally said. 'Him and his bloody Greek's. And us all whetted up[10] for a bite of something tastier than old Harry could ever put under our noses.'

I felt a fool immediately, because I might have known that was the wrong thing to say, the way they were feeling. Once Wally had got the idea of skirt into his head it wasn't easy to put him off. And Sid, for all

I don't think he really liked Wally, would trail along with him all right, knowing that was his best chance. That was what fascinated him about Wally, he could always have what Wally didn't want. But it was what made him hate Wally's guts, too.

Besides, I suppose they felt I'd sort of broken the rules by not being keen enough and waiting a bit longer before giving up what we all knew was a bad job.

'Well, what'll we do now, Wally?' Sid said.

'Let's take a stroll as far as the Civic[11] and back,' I chipped in, trying to establish myself again. 'You never know, we might pick up something.'

'That's more like it,' Wally said. And then, because he wasn't a bad bloke, a better chap in many ways than Sid would ever be, he added: 'After all, if there's nothing doing, we can always go over to have a feed at the Greek's later on.' Which showed he wasn't really fooled by what I'd said.

So away we went, down past the Majestic where Len Parry and Alec Haynes and all that bunch were as usual, pretending they were talking about who was going to win the Ranfurly Shield[12] when all they were interested in really was the girls who kept scuttling by on their way back from the band concert. I took a look at the Town Clock[13] on the other side as we went by and there it was, half-past ten already, one more Sunday evening just about over and nothing happening, only the same old thing. Already everyone who had anywhere to go was going there and soon the only people left in the streets would be chaps like us who couldn't think of anything better to do and soon we'd be gone home too and the streets would be empty and another night would be gone out of a man's life and him none the wiser one way or the other.

'Was that your cousin Marty I saw all by himself in the doorway next that bloke who met the sheila, Ned?' Sid suddenly asked.

'I didn't notice.'

'It was him all right, poor bastard,' Wally said.

I pricked up my ears at that. My cousin Marty wasn't the sort of chap you talked about with that particular tone in your voice. He was rather a big shot in the eyes of our crowd. A good five or six years older than any of us, he must have been twenty-two or twenty-three, and he used to earn good money before the slump. A plasterer he was, by trade. But he'd been one of the first to be turned off when things got tough because, though he was good at his job, he had a terrible temper and was too handy with his fists. A big joker, he was, with reach and height, and they used to say that if only he'd do a bit more training there wasn't a pro in the business he couldn't have put on his back for the count. As it was he'd made quite a name for himself round the town as a fighter and once when I was at the barber's and got fed up with the way slick little Basset kept taking me for granted because I didn't know what was going to win the Gore Cup[14] I'd managed to get in casually that Marty was my cousin and after that Basset could never do enough for me.

'What do you mean, "poor bastard"?' Sid was saying.

'Didn't you hear? The trouble with you, Sid, is you never hear anything now you've got your teeth out.'

'Come on, come on, know-all. What's it all about?'

'Yes, what was it, Wally?' I asked; for I could tell Wally was wishing he'd kept his mouth shut, knowing Marty was my cousin.

'Well, it's only what they're saying, Ned, and there mightn't be anything in it, though I have noticed Marty hasn't been about much lately. You know how you'd always see him and Dulcie Moore round together of a Saturday and Sunday night?'

'That's right,' Sid said, glad to get in on the inside again. 'I saw them coming out of the Rose Gardens about two in the morning the night of Ginger Foyle's keg-party and they were always at the Waikiwi dances[15] together.'

'Well, they say he put her up the spout.[16] And then he got some old dame who hangs out in Georgetown[17] to fix her up. Of course, that's happening all the time all over the place, you know, and nobody ever thinks a thing about it as long as no one gets caught.' This was for me. 'But the trouble this time was that something went wrong and she got blood-poisoning or something, and now she's in hospital and they say the johns have been at her all the time beside her bed trying to find out who did it and who was the man. But so far she won't say and the odds are she won't pull through.'

'Jesus,' said Sid. 'I thought he looked a bit down in the mouth.'

'Wouldn't you be?'

'But, look here, Wally,' I said, 'who told you all this?'

'I heard Marty's crowd, Jim Fergus and all that lot, talking about it yesterday after the game. And when I was shaving in the bathroom this morning and they didn't know I was there, I heard Mum telling the old man about it. It was her that told that bit about her not being expected to live.'

We'd got as far as the Civic and turned back by this time and the crowd was getting very thin by now, everybody making for home, feeling much the way I'd been feeling, I expect, that they might as well be in bed as hanging round. Only I didn't feel like that any more. Things happened, sure enough, and even to people you knew, even to your own family, near enough.

Sid and Wally kept talking about it all the way back up Tay Street. It was queer the way they seemed to get a sort of pleasure out of discussing it. And what was queerer still was that I liked hearing them talk about it. It must have been partly how old we were and partly the town we lived in. You felt the place wasn't quite such a dead-alive hole, after all, and you felt you really were grown up when things like that, terrible things but things all the same, happened to people you even knew.

Anyhow, just as we got to the Bank corner,[18] two girls came round it the opposite way and we almost banged into them. While we were dodging around them to let them pass and show what gentlemen we were they cut through between me and Wally and we could hear them giggling as they went on.

'Sorry,' Wally called back in an extra-polite voice I hardly recognised, he could put on the gyver[19] so well when he wanted to.

'Don't mention it,' one of the girls said and giggled again.

We stopped at that and Sid made a great show of lighting cigarettes for us while we all had a good dekko[20] back to see what the girls were up to.

'They've stopped in the doorway next the jewellers,' Wally said. 'Come on, Sid, here we go. We're home and dry.' He was so excited he forgot to pretend I was in on it too.

The two of them cut back the way we'd come, like a couple of whippets at first and then as they got closer with a sort of elaborate stroll as if they might just as well be walking that way as any other. I followed after them, trying to catch up and yet not to catch up. I knew I ought to have gone away. There was no good just tagging on, being a nuisance. But I kept following, all the same.

'Hello,' Wally was saying as I came up to the doorway. 'Going anywhere?'

'What's that got to do with you?' the girl who had called back to us said.

'Well,' Sid said, 'it's getting late for girls to be out by themselves with all the roughs there are about this time of night and we thought you might like to have an escort on the way home.'

Sid could always talk well when it came to the pinch, especially if he had Wally with him. I of course couldn't say a thing, being as nervous as a cat, although I knew already that it didn't matter much what I did, me being only the spare part.

'You know what thought did,'[21] the girl said.

'Come on, Isobel,' the other girl said. 'It's getting late.'

'Will you have a cigarette, Isobel?' Wally said. And he took out his case. It was the one he kept his tailor-mades in, not the one he used for home-rolled ones and butts. In that light you'd have taken it for silver.

'Don't mind if I do.'

'Come on, Isobel,' the other girl said again.

'Now, Jean, don't be an old fusspot. There's heaps of time really. Why don't you have a cigarette, too?'

'That's right,' Wally said, and so Jean took one from the case, a bit nervously, I thought.

'We don't even know your names, do we, Jean?' said Isobel when Sid had flourished his lighter for them. You could see them trying to get a look at us while the flame was there. But of course we had our backs to the street-lights and they couldn't have made out much what we looked like.

'That's easy,' Wally said then. 'I'll introduce us. My name's Wally Radford and this is my friend Sid, Sid Cable. And this is Ned.'

'He's a quiet one, isn't he?' Isobel gave Jean a nudge and giggled at me.

I tried to think of something very witty to say, the sort of thing that would have come to Wally or Sid in a flash. But I couldn't think of anything at all and I could feel myself blushing. I hated that Isobel then.

It was always the good-looking ones that made me feel most of a fool. The other one, Jean, I didn't mind so much because I could tell by her way of giggling that she was nervous, too. She wasn't anything like such a good-looker, though.

There was a bit of a silence then. They were all waiting for me to say something. When I still didn't say anything I felt them all just give me up. Wally got into the doorway close to Isobel and tried to get his arm round her. She kept fending him off and looking at him and then at Jean in a way that said as plain as a pikestaff: Wait till afterwards when we can get away by ourselves.

Sid was talking a blue streak to Jean so as to give her a chance to get over her shyness, I suppose, and to shut me out of it and make me see I was being the gooseberry,[22] in case I didn't see it already.

There was nothing to do but leave them to it. I was only holding Wally and Sid back from doing their stuff, hanging round like that.

'Well, I must be getting along,' I said.

'Why don't you come with us?' Jean said. Her voice sounded quite scared. But I could tell Sid wasn't going to get anywhere with her and I wasn't going to have her use me as an excuse to keep him off and then have him putting the blame on me next day.

'I'd like to,' I said, 'but I live up the other end of the town.'

'OK, Ned, good night,' Wally said in an offhand sort of way and Sid said good night too, in the friendly voice he always used when you were doing something he wanted you to do. That was one of the things Sid liked about me, that I always did the expected thing. It wasn't one of the things I liked about him.

So I set off by myself up towards the Bank corner again, feeling like a motherless foal, as the old man would have said. I thought I'd better give them plenty of time to get clear and so I decided I'd walk a few blocks up Dee Street and back again.

The town clock was pointing to nearly eleven by now. All the crowd that'd been in front of the Majestic was gone and Dee Street was as empty as the tomb except for a bobby standing in the library doorway over the other side, just in case there should be a row at the Greek's, I expect.

Seeing the Greek's lighted windows gave me the idea of going in for a feed, after all. But it was pretty late and I couldn't face going in there all by myself, with the blokes eyeing me and guessing what had happened. So I crossed Esk Street and went straight on up.

But it wasn't nearly so bad being by yourself when the whole street was empty like that and you didn't have to wonder what people were thinking about you. I quite liked striding along under the shop verandahs as if I were going nowhere in a hurry and listening to my heels hammer on the asphalt and seeing my reflection pass dark on the windows. It was better feeling miserable by yourself and not having to put up a show any more. Or else the kind of show you put up when there was no one but yourself to watch was more convincing.

'Hullo, Ned.'

I stopped in my tracks and looked round to see where the voice came from. Then I saw him. He was in the same doorway that the sheila had met her bloke in earlier on. He was standing there, all stiff like a sentry, and in that light you'd have thought his eyes were black they were so dark. A Spaniard, he might have been, with the long sideboards halfway down his cheeks and his straight, thin nose, that had never been broken for all the boxing he'd done.

'Hullo, Marty,' I said.

He didn't say any more, just went on looking at me. I didn't know quite what to do because it struck me it was probably only the suddenness of seeing someone he knew that had made him call out and probably he wished he hadn't now. Besides, knowing what I did, I felt uncomfortable.

I went up to him all the same, not knowing how to get away without it looking awkward and as if I'd heard about his trouble and was dodging off so as not to be seen with him.

'Have a cigarette,' I said, and I produced a packet of ten Capstan.

'Thanks.'

I lit them for us both and when that was over there I was still stuck and unable to think of anything else to say. The only things that came into my head sounded quite hopeless compared with the things that he must have in his mind.

'All the crowd gone home?' I said in the end, for lack of anything better.

'Suppose so,' he answered and took a puff of the cigarette. Then he added in a voice so savage that it gave me a real fright. 'Who the hell cares what they've done? Pack of bastards.'

I didn't say anything. I was trying to work out what he meant by that. Had they done the dirty on him and talked to the johns? Or was he just fed up with them?

He gave me a look just then, the first time he'd really looked at me since I stopped.

'You've heard all about it, I suppose?'

That stumped me properly. I didn't want him to get the idea the whole town was talking about him. Especially as that was what they were probably doing. I was scared of him, too. He'd be a bad bloke to say the wrong thing to.

'Hear about what?'

'You know.' He'd guessed by the time I took to answer. 'About Dulcie.'

There was no good pretending. 'Yes,' I said. 'How is she?'

He didn't answer but he kept on looking at me in the same queer way that he had been looking at me before. And then, as if he'd been sizing me up, he got down to what was on his mind.

'Look here, Ned,' he said. 'What about doing something for me?'

'All right,' I said. 'What do you want me to do?' My heart was in my boots because I didn't know much about the law but I felt sure this was going to be something against it.

'It's like this. I can't ring the hospital to see how she is because the johns are there and they keep asking me my name and they know my voice, too. What about you ringing for me?'

'All right, Marty,' I said. 'But what'll I say if they ask who I am? If I give my name they might come poking about home trying to find out what I know about it.'

'Say your name's Eddie Sharp. That's a friend of her young brother's and it'd be quite natural for him to ring. Will you do it?'

'I'll just see if I've got any pennies.'

We walked back towards the Post Office square. But the john was still in the library doorway and so I told Marty to go back to the place where I'd met him and wait for me there.

The john gave me that hard look that policemen give you but I went straight past him without giving a sign of how nervous I was. It was being so sorry for Marty that made me able to do it, I think.

'Southland Hospital,' a woman's voice answered when I'd got the number.

'I want to inquire about a patient, Miss Moore, Miss Dulcie Moore.'

'Will you hold on, please?'

There was a lot of clicking at the other end and I could hear whispering. Then a man's voice answered.

'The patient died an hour ago. Who is that speaking?'

I didn't answer. I just rang off and came out of the phone box.

How was I going to tell him, I kept asking myself as I went back past the john, hardly noticing him this time.

Marty was standing in the doorway, just as he had been the first time.

'How was she?'

There was nothing else I could do. I out with it.

'She died an hour ago.'

He stood there without saying a thing, just looking at me and yet not seeing me. Then he took a deep breath and his chest came out and he stood even straighter.

'So that's how it is,' he said. 'She's dead.'

I didn't say anything. I just stood there, wishing I was anywhere else in the world.

'If only I'd known,' he said. 'Christ, man, I'd have married her a hundred times, kid and all.'

He stopped. His mind must have been going over and over this ground for days.

He gave a laugh suddenly, such a queer, savage sort of a laugh that I jumped.

'If it'd been twins, even,' he said.

I had enough sense not to think that I was meant to laugh at that one.

'And those bloody johns sitting by the bed.'

'Did she come to?' I asked.

'Yes, she was conscious a lot of the time. But she wouldn't talk, not Dulcie. Not her. She was all right, Dulcie.'

Then there was silence again. I didn't know what to do or say. It was getting late. They'd have locked the door at home and there'd be a rumpus if they knew what time it was when I came in. How queer it was: here I was in the middle of something that really mattered and worrying about what my mother would say if she heard me climbing in the window.

All the same I wanted to get home. And then I had to admit to myself it wasn't really that. It was that I wanted to get away from Marty. I think it must have been the first time I was ever with someone who felt as badly as he was feeling.

'I remember her,' I said. 'She was a stunner to look at.'

'Wasn't she?' Marty said. And the way he said it made the tears come into my eyes.

'Why don't you walk my way?' I asked him. If he did that I could be making towards home and at the same time wouldn't feel I was ratting on him.

'No, I'm not going home yet,' he said.

I shuffled from one foot to the other, wondering what to do next and a bit worried what he would do after I'd gone.

'We always used to meet here,' he said. 'In this doorway.'

'Oh,' I said. 'Well, look here, Marty, I've got to be getting home now.'

'That's all right.'

I tried to think of some way of saying how sorry I was. But there was no way of saying it.

'Good night, Ned,' he said, and then, as I began to walk away, he called out: 'Thanks for doing that for me.'

So that's how it is, I was saying to myself all the way home. That's the sort of thing that happens once the gloves are off. And by the time I'd got to the front gate and opened it with one hand on the latch to stop it clicking and sat on the front verandah to take my shoes off I think I'd taken it all into myself and begun to wake up to how we only kid ourselves we can tell the good things from the bad things when really they're so mixed up that half the time we're thinking one thing, feeling another, and doing something else altogether.

The Quiet One: first published in *Landfall* 3:3 (September 1949): 228–40.

NOTES

1. the Regent: cinema on Dee Street, just past Don Street.
2. the Greek's: a fish and chip shop in Dee Street.
3. Rugby Park corner: outside Rugby Park, Invercargill's main football ground, on the corner of Tweed Street (formerly Oteramika Road) and Elles Road.
4. Majestic side: the east side of Dee Street between Esk and Tay Streets where the Majestic Theatre was located.
5. at a fair bat: a fast pace.
6. a dog in the manger: churlish. *OED*. See 'A Meeting Half Way', p. 145.
7. a blue streak: at full pace. Equivalent to 'flat out, ten to the dozen'.
8. narked: annoyed, irritated. *ODNZE*.
9. Borsalino: type of fedora hat named after the founder of the company based in Alessandria, Italy, Guiseppe Borsalino (1834–1900).
10. whetted up: sharpened up.
11. the Civic: the Civic Theatre on Tay Street (part of the Town Hall).
12. Ranfurly Shield: trophy for interprovincial rugby union, named after the 5th Earl of Ranfurly, Governor of New Zealand 1897–1904, and patron of the New Zealand Rugby Football Union.
13. Town Clock: above the Government Buildings on the west side of Dee Street.
14. Gore Cup: climax of the annual race meetings held at the Gore Racecourse on Labour Day, the fourth Monday in October. *RfH*, p. 171 and n.
15. Waikiwi dances: located three miles from Invercargill on the main North Road, Waikiwi was the first Catholic suburban parish. The electric trams stopped there at the end of the Northern line.
16. put her up the spout: slang for 'made her pregnant'.
17. Georgetown: area southeast of Tweed Street and east of Rugby Park, to the south of Oteramika Road.
18. Bank corner: on Tay and Dee Streets where the ANZ, BNZ, and NSW banks were located.
19. put on the gyver: airs, affectation, 'side', excessive show. *ODNZE*, s.v. 'gyver'.
20. a good dekko: a good look, stare. *DSUE*.
21. you know what thought did: allusion to the aphorism, 'Thought planted a feather and thought it would grow to a hen' (i.e. ideas are ineffectual unless proven in practice).
22. the gooseberry: the unattached third party in a lovers' tryst.

18

A Return

OF COURSE I DIDN'T SHOW IT but it was all a bit of a shock to me. I'd heard bits and scraps of news from time to time while I was away – that Martin's old man had died[1] the year I left, that Martin had come back[2] and had married the O'Halloran girl whose father owned the stud farm up at Morton Mains.[3] But none of it meant much, what with Munich and a war brewing and then the war itself. It didn't prepare me, anyhow, for a new house[4] in what used to be the front paddock, with an electric stove and a washing machine and all sorts of things Martin's old man would have sweated blood to see.

So I was rather relieved when I got outside with Martin by himself. Though for a start neither of us had much to say; picking up the threads, I suppose.

It was seeing old Glen that gave me the first link; apart from Martin himself, of course.

'Surely it's old Glen,' I said, as I bent down to pat him. 'Do you remember me, Glen, old boy?' But he didn't know me. It was too long.

'That's him all right,' Martin said. 'Nearly blind now, poor old chap, aren't you, Glen? I'll let him off the chain and he can come with us.'

We walked on down the drive and Glen came along behind us, close at Martin's heels. Don, the new dog, a smart black and tan collie, heard us and came frisking out from behind the woodheap.

'Now there's a dog for you,' Martin said. 'He knows more about sheep than I do myself.' And he began to tell me stories of Don's brains, much the same stories that used to be told about Glen, except that in the old days it was always cows, not sheep, that gave a dog on this farm a chance to show his intelligence.

But I was only half-listening. My mind was on the past and I seemed to be seeing things double, as they were now and as they once had been. This drive under our feet still ran down to the old house[5] I could see ahead of us, crouched among its trees the way it used to be, but empty now. To that house, built with his own hands, and along this drive old Martin must have come when he first brought his wife[6] there in the years before I, her sister's son, was born. And along it, after she had had young Martin, the last of her sons,[7] the old man had driven her in his trap[8] that cold November morning when he took her to the dentist in town, twelve miles away. They had come back the same night, she with all her teeth out and muffled – but not enough – against the bitter wind. Her last journey till the one not long after when they took her to the cemetery, dead through the chill she caught.[9]

And in the years that followed, as one child after another grew old enough to rebel, each of them had come along this drive in the night, just before daybreak, making his way to the gate, the main road and freedom. At the last the old man himself had come along it to join his wife, worn out by work and his own harshness to himself. Only Martin had come back, alone of all that family. And now the old house was empty, the drive was a path that led only to the past. Grass grew between the wheel ruts.

'What's happened to the gorse hedge that used to be here?' I asked. For the wind came straight across the paddocks, ruffling the backs of the ewes and cutting at us through the bare, wire fence.

'Had it all yanked out,' Martin said. 'I got the tractor on to it. You can't beat a good wire fence. Tight wire and sound totara straining posts[10] and you're jake for ten years.'

I looked at the hedge that wasn't there. The thrushes used to fly out of it bursting with alarm as the ferret threaded his way in and out among the dry, twisted roots before vanishing down another burrow. In spring the whole hedge was saddled in gold.

'That fixed the rabbits, too,' he said. 'Not one on the whole place now. No, I'm well rid of the hedges.' He changed his voice suddenly. 'Get along with ye now, what way is that to cut a hedge? It's as crooked as a dog's hind leg.[11] Give me that slasher.'

He had his father to a T. I gave a jump when he said it. For I'd had the lash of the old man's tongue myself in my time.

'Remember?' he said. 'And he wouldn't be satisfied, either, till you could have run a spirit-level along it. By God, what a tiger he was for work, the old tyrant.'

'Well, I've changed all that,' he went on. 'No hedges, and no cows either. Sheep, that's the thing. No more slavery for me. Look at that mob of sheep now out there, worth four guineas a crack, every blasted one of them, not counting the lambs they'll have.'

I looked at the sheep, bunched out in the paddock, heads down and backs to the wind, cropping.

'Here, Don,' he said to the dog. 'Way back.'

Don ran out towards the sheep and, answering immediately to every whistled command, shuffled them about for me to get a good look at them.

'Hullo,' Martin said. 'What's the matter with that one?'

We got through the taut wire and went over. The ewe didn't move as we came up. There were two lambs beside her.

'She's had it, poor bitch,' he said. 'Still, we'll rear the lambs all right. We'll pick them up on the way back.'

Out on the drive old Glen, who hadn't followed us into the paddock, fell in behind again.

'I suppose I ought to shoot him,' Martin said. 'But he was a good dog in his day. He's never been the same since I got rid of the cows. Once a cattledog always a cattledog. Though he'd be too old for that now, anyway.'

I said nothing. The Glen I remembered was a young dog, out in the morning chivvying the cows in for the milking, the dew flying up at his heels.

We were coming into the backyard of the old house now. The kitchen garden on the right was wild. There was no movement in the macrocarpa hedges that once bustled with hens. No trail of geese came marching in convoy from under the five-barred gate. The cartshed seemed to have staggered, got smaller. What had been the stand for the milk cans was a crumpled heap of boards with docks growing round. The old spring-cart[12] we used to drive in with the milk to the factory had fallen on its knees.

'We'd better take a look at the old house,' Martin said, 'before it gets dark enough for ghosts.'

He fished out the key from under the tankstand, the old hiding place.

The door gripped a bit on the floor but gave to a shove. We went in, Glen following.

We wandered from room to room, our feet echoing. And in all the rooms it seemed as if the old man's presence dominated still. In the kitchen where the family used to eat, his fearful silence still ruled over the absent table. In the sitting-room the emptiness, the bare boards, were less real to me than that clear picture from the past where he sat with his legs stretched before the log fire, boots still on, the boys scarcely daring to whisper over their homework and no other sound but the occasional knock of a pot out in the scullery where the girls would be washing up.

But most of all you felt him still in that room where Martin and all the others had been begotten and born, where their mother had died, where the old man himself had died, reconciled to no one and alone.

Something about the timid way we peeped into it, as if we half-expected him to stare up at us with his fierce, green eyes, roused Martin to the defiance which was the mainspring of his life.

'And what brings ye in here peeking?' he suddenly shouted. 'Can't ye find anything better to do than hang round here waiting to see when your father will die? Aren't there cows to be milked and pigs to be fed? Is there no ploughing that you can be idling away the good days that God made for the land? Get away with ye now to your work before I get myself up from this bed and show ye who's the master here.'

Glen looked up at Martin uneasily and went skulking down the passage to the back door.

'You were always a devil for the mimicking, Martin,' I said.

He grinned. 'Wait and I'll give you another one.'

He crossed the passage to the room where old Paddy used to sleep, his father's only friend. We used to hide under the bed in there and frighten him, pretending to be ghosts.

There was silence for a minute and then I heard old Paddy's high-pitched brogue.

''Tis the fairies, Martin, 'tis the fairies that are after the living soul of me,' the voice shrieked and Martin came rushing out as if he were indeed Paddy and were fleeing from all the ghosts of Ireland.

I followed him down the passage and through the thickening memories.

At the next door on the left a new voice awaited me. It was Norah this time and how well I recognised that passionate storming of God that you might have heard any night and any time of the night in the years when this house lived so long ago.

'Oh God in Heaven,' the voice was surging, 'have mercy on us all, have mercy on us all, all of us, oh God, except those wicked devils, my own flesh and blood, that never leave off tormenting me with their teasing and talking and tattling, and you, oh Holy Mother, do you save me from that lost soul, O'Connor, who's forever watching me at the dances and in the very church itself in the middle of Holy Mass is moving his terrible eyes at me.'

But another voice took its turn now, the voice of Rose, the bold and domineering daughter of her father, a strong voice full of jeers.

'For Heaven's sake, Norah, won't you be quiet now and leave us in peace with your O'Connor. It's ashamed you should be howling and praying at all hours and all over a man that's nothing but a red-haired gorilla when all's said and done and would never have looked at you twice if you hadn't put the idea into his head yourself by asking him to dance in the Ladies' Excuse Me, if it's in anybody's head but your own, that is, and him a married man and all.'

There was an even wilder shriek from Norah at this and as the door flung open it was all I could do to believe that it was not Norah herself I saw holding it closed and shouting back through it.

'Not a minute longer will I stay in this wicked house, I swear to God I won't. I'll go to him now with all I have which is myself and tell him I've been driven out of my own house by my own sister. I'll disgrace the lot of you, that's what I'll do, but at least I won't have to stay on here among a lot of scheming, jealous devils that have the making of nothing in them but drunkards and old maids. So put that in your pipe and smoke it.'

All the men were out of the house that night at the lambing, I remembered. She had gone, and I wondered that the memory of that alone and what had happened to her afterwards was not enough to quieten Martin. But he was in the grip of his art now and perhaps, too, there was something in all this that helped him shake off the past that had driven him to the new house and new ways, bold man that he was ever to have come back to that place so full of terrible memories.

'Look,' he was saying now, having drawn me into the back bedroom where he and his two brothers, Neil and Con, used to sleep, after Ned, the oldest son, had gone off to his death in the first war, and before Neil cursed his father and went off to Australia[13] and Con shot himself in the back stables. 'Look,' he said, 'there's the window we used to climb in at after the dances long ago or after all night round a keg or a bottle of Hokonui whisky,[14] and sometimes we'd hardly be under the blankets before he'd come roaring in with that whip of his.'

He began to shout in his father's voice again.

'Up with ye, up with ye, ye lazy omadhauns.[15] Isn't it nearly daylight already and the cows out there with their bags bursting and devil the one of you caring a tinker's dam[16] but lying there like gentlemen pensioners.[17] Oh, it's a fine parcel of useless brummocks[18] and Lady Janes[19] I'm rearing and no mistake. Out of bed with you now before I tear the blankets off you and lay this whip across your bare backside.'

Martin leaned against the wall and looked round the empty room, bemused.

'Ah, poor Con,' he said. 'Will I ever forget that night? It was after the milking and I had just put the cows out and come up with the buckets from feeding the calves when I heard the clamour of it. "And what brings you home from the seminary, my lad?" the old devil was saying when I got in. And there was poor Con, still in his black suit the way he'd walked up from the station, leaning back there in the corner by the window. "I've decided I haven't got a vocation," he said, as quietly as I'm speaking to you now. And the old man came up on him, and little fellow though he was, it was frightening, I tell you, because of all that devil was in him.'

'"So that's it," he says at last, quietly this time. And then he suddenly lets out a bellow. "I'll give you vocation," he says and hits Con across the face with his open hand. Well, you know how I liked Con, I wasn't going to take that. And poor Con was the last man in the world to stick up for himself. So I caught the old man by the shoulder. And what does he do then but take a crack at me, if you please. So I hit him. And hit him hard. That was the night Con shot himself. And I lit out for the North that same night, not knowing.'

'Aye,' he went on. 'And Rose wasn't long after me and none of us have heard so much as a whisper of her from that day to this, whatever happened to her. Aye, there was a devil in that man, even though he'd whip you for not knowing your prayers. Comfort was a sin for him and he died as hard as he lived. Well, I hope he has a better time in hell than he gave us. And yet, you know, when I look back on it all I feel sorry for him. God only knows what was the matter with him, but I think he was fond of us in his own queer way.'

He led the way towards the back door.

'Yes,' he said, looking back into the dark kitchen from the failing light outside. 'He was a queer old fellow. But he was a hard worker and we were a wild lot. It was a good farm he left behind him at any rate. And he made it out of nothing. Perhaps if she had lived things would have been different. It might have been the devil in himself that he was trying to whip out of our backsides.'

When we got through the fence to pick up the lambs he bounced his hand on the wire. It didn't satisfy him and he took hold of the straining stick[20] to give it a couple more twists. 'I'm glad I got rid of the hedges,' he said. 'A man's got to keep up with the times.'

And as, each of us with a lamb under his arm, we walked up the drive again towards the roughcast house where the electric light was already shining and where hot water and a meal and a wife were waiting, I saw that it was not only Glen and I whom the times had left behind, not only us for whom this new, efficient factory, its wire fences and its sheep, were not quite real, not only us for whom youth meant the old place behind us where there used to be room for gorse and rabbits and ghosts and where life had toiled and twisted round its own frustrations, a coil of passionate wills driven not by comfort but by love and appetites and dreams.

A Return: first published in *Arena* 19 (December 1948): 72–8. Davin wrote this story after revisiting the Woodlands dairy farm of his Concannon cousins on his first trip back to New Zealand after twelve years in August 1948. He had stayed there often as a child and was close to his cousin, Michael Concannon (see Tom Hogan's reminiscences, *IS*, p. 31). It recalls the situation of the family after Ellen Concannon (née Sullivan), Davin's maternal aunt, died suddenly of pneumonia in 1917 aged forty-three, leaving nine children, the youngest child, Peter, being only six months old.

NOTES

[1] Martin's old man had died: 'Old Martin', Martin Junior's father, refers to the widower Michael Concannon, who brought up the children after his wife's death until his death at the age of sixty-four in 1927. A Gaelic-speaking Galway Irishman, he has been described as a 'hard man with a short temper and a complete workaholic'.

[2] Martin ... back: Davin's cousin, Michael, third youngest of the Concannon sons, who left the farm for Australia in the mid-1920s, returning at the family's request to manage it in 1929–30 after his father's death. Michael Concannon married in 1935, and bought the farm from the estate. See Denise Beerhens (daughter of Michael Concannon Junior), *St Patrick's Church Rakauhauka, Southland*, pp. 25–6.

[3] Morton Mains: approximately twenty-four kilometres from Invercargill, and eight kilometres northeast of Woodlands.

[4] a new house: probably built after Michael Concannon married in 1935.

[5] the old house: this house was accidentally burnt down in the 1950s, two years after the composition of this story.

[6] his wife: Ellen Sullivan, Mary Sullivan's older sister, who married Michael Concannon in 1895. After farming at different places they settled at Woodlands in 1905.

[7] young Martin ... sons: Peter Concannon was the youngest son, not Martin.

[8] trap: two-wheeled cart on springs, gig.

[9] Her last journey ... caught: Ellen Concannon in fact died in Park Hospital, Invercargill.

[10] straining posts: a strong post against which the wires of a fence are tightened.

[11] as crooked ... leg: very crooked.

[12] spring cart: trap.

[13] Neil ... Australia: Michael left for Australia in the mid 1920s; the two younger brothers, Peter (b. 1917) and Paddy (b. 1911) in c. 1950. See *IS*, p. 31.

[14] Hokonui whisky: whisky illicitly brewed in the Hokonui hills when Invercargill was a dry town. See 'Late Snow'.

[15] omadhauns: fools, idiots.

[16] tinker's dam: proverbial. *OED*, s.v. 'tinker'.

[17] gentlemen pensioners: 'playing at being pensioners'. *ODNZE*, s.v. 'gentleman colonist, gentleman farmer'.

[18] brummocks: possibly a dialect form or corruption of 'brummel', as in the English socialite and dandy Beau Brummel (1778–1840).

[19] Lady Janes: probably another aristocratic name. Martin is chiding his children for idleness, fearing that they will become 'dandified layabouts'.

[20] straining stick (or strainer): a tool used to stretch or tighten the wire in a fence.

19

First Flight

1

IT WAS THE LAST DAY OF MY VISIT. After my mother's death,[1] my father had sold the old house and nowadays he lived in digs. So, to be independent of friends, I'd put up at the Grand.[2] That way, I'd been able to get around by myself a bit, though I'd been seeing a fair bit of the old man as well. He really was something of an old man by now, just how much over seventy[3] I wasn't sure, but wearing well. Retirement didn't seem to have got him down at all, though he liked talking about the old days on the railway – especially the time that I could remember best, nearly twenty years before, when he used to be on the Invercargill-Dunedin run.[4] He didn't really miss it, though, and he was quite happy, as far as I could make out, living on his pension and keeping his hand in by digging gardens for people who knew what a slogger he was with the spade.

This last day of my visit he was having lunch with me at the hotel before I caught my plane – only I called it dinner when I was talking to him in case he'd think I'd got stuck up all these years away in England. When coffee came, he sat back in his seat and watched me light a cigarette.

'You ought to throw off that rotten habit,' he said. 'It'll do your lungs no good at all. Expensive, too.'

I didn't answer. I was working out how long it was till the plane left. This was probably the last time I'd ever see him. And I couldn't think of anything to say. It didn't seem worth while to argue about smoking. I was too old myself now, and had been too long my own man, to get annoyed by that sort of advice the way I once would have.

'You know,' he said, 'I've got a bally[5] good mind to come with you as far as Dunedin. I've never been up in an aeroplane. I nearly went once, just after the other war, when they were charging a fiver a time out at the racecourse. But your mother wouldn't let me. A waste of money and you might get killed, she said.'

He was like me, the way he often seemed to be coming out with a sudden idea when he'd really been turning it over in his mind for a long time. I guessed this one must have come to him when he saw my plane coming down to land three days before. He was like me another way too, or perhaps like any man who's been married a long time. The reason he would give for wanting to do something wasn't always the real reason, or at any rate the only one. If you gave your real reasons, you often found yourself landed in unnecessary arguments.

'Why not?' I said. 'I'll pay your fare. You could do with a holiday. Or a bit of a change, anyway.'

'There's nothing to keep me here since your mother died. I could look up a few old friends.'

'Come on, then,' I said. 'If we get a taxi now there'll be time to pick up whatever you want from your digs. I expect there'll be no trouble about getting a seat. There was only one other passenger when I came down.'

I waited in the taxi while he went into the boarding house in Tweed Street to get his bag. I used to pass the same house on my way to the school in Clyde Street[6] when I was a kid. It looked even more the worse for wear than I did.

There was an east wind blowing across the airfield from the estuary.[7] I remembered the tidal flat that used to be there before they reclaimed it; the mud and the little crabs scuttling to their holes. The whole of Invercargill and the people who lived there were like that, I used to think in those days. Not only Invercargill, I knew now. My father didn't seem to feel the cold but I did. Autumn coming. But it would be spring when I got back to England.

There'd been no trouble about getting a seat on the little Rapide.[8] The only other passengers were a young man and a girl with confetti in her hair. We had seen her mother crying at the edge of the field, and a lot of other people cheerful with wedding breakfast. They were calling out now and the girl was looking back. Eurydice, but not for the underworld.[9]

We were both wide, heavy men. They stowed us up front, my father in one seat on the left of the gangway and me across from him and just behind the pilot. The young couple were right behind us. The man watched me show my father how to fasten his seat-belt and then leaned across to show his wife. She had been waving a wet handkerchief at the window but now she turned to him and let herself be taught. His hands were red and strong. They looked as if they were used to harness. But I remembered things had changed since I left New Zealand. It would be tractors he knew about, not horses.

The pilot was a large man, too. He worked his way along the narrow gangway and took his seat at the controls. He took off his cap and loosened his tie. He'd probably had a good lunch. He didn't close his door. The instrument panel in front of him didn't look much more complicated than a motor-car's.

We took off without much fuss. My father was looking out his window, with that sort of fixed grin he had when he was excited and interested. I watched Invercargill's rectangular blocks turn into an almost vertical plane and then go flat again. I was not sorry to be going. My life there had been over long before I returned. The house I had been born and reared in was surrounded now, hemmed in by other, new, houses.[10] Other people lived in it, unaware of all that had happened there. Thinking of this, I realised we were over the cemetery already, with my mother's grave.[11]

He shouldn't have married again, so soon after Mum died, my sister had said. It was an insult to Mum's memory.

She felt too much, poor Nora. She had loved him, perhaps even more than she loved her mother,[12] if that was possible. She had probably been jealous, too, without knowing it. There had been no point in trying to explain, and anyhow she had a nice nature. She'd get over it. I thought I knew how it must have happened myself, though I hadn't been there and with a man as reticent as my father you didn't get much to work on. I guessed he was in a state of shock when he found that everything was over and he was by himself in that empty house, the house he'd built himself when they were first married.[13]

He was hard in many ways and probably while she was ill[14] he thought he'd be able to take it all right when the time came. And then the time came and he couldn't take it at all. So when the widow, Maisie, turned up, at some euchre party or other, and they'd taken a bit of a shine to each other that must have seemed the answer. It wasn't an insult to Mum at all but a compliment, if anything, thinking that was the only way for a man to live.

Besides, it must have looked quite a promising set-up. She had a pretty good farm out Edendale[15] way and her only son was doing well in Australia with a family of his own. The old man had always wanted a farm and he was good with animals. At the time, he was still only in his early sixties and still as tough as a goat's knees. It must have looked like the answer all right. It might have been, too, if the son hadn't taken fright about the property and come tearing home.

I took another look across at him but he was still staring out and down. He hadn't talked to me about the big quarrel, only about my mother. He behaved as if the thing with Maisie had never happened. He knew he could count on my not asking questions. That had never been my method of finding out about things. In a way, I suppose I didn't care enough, either. I liked him, as I knew he liked me. Whatever had happened, it was his business, and it probably made plenty of sense once you saw his side of it. So best leave it at that.

I looked away from him again and found myself staring at the pilot's back. An old RNZAF man, to judge by the glimpse I'd had of his medals. In his middle thirties now, with a married set to his shoulders. Beefy tanned neck, and a honeycomb of deep lines above the collar. In quincunxes.[16] Had Sir Thomas Browne[17] thought of that one? Pity the way one couldn't help thinking in literary allusions. Occupational syndrome. You had to keep that sort of thing to yourself in this part of the world. People would think you were showing off.

I felt my father was looking at me and I turned towards him. He spoke but the noise of the engine was too loud. I cupped my left ear and leaned over. He raised his voice and it came through as a shout.

'These aeroplanes don't go anything like as fast as I expected.'

'Faster than you think,' I said, and I looked nervously at the pilot. Blood had flooded into the tan network of his neck. He probably hated having to fly this miserable little machine for a living anyway. In his own mind he'd always regret that he wasn't back in a Spitfire or a Wellington or whatever he'd flown when he was a youngster, the speed and dash of a fighter or the mighty throb of a bomber. He'd mix it up with regret he couldn't acknowledge for the days when he was a kid, the tension before a mission, the extreme, excited calm of being up and over the target, the relief afterwards, the mess and the drinks, the fast cars across the tarmac, the beer and the popsies[18] whose tomorrow you didn't have to worry about because you probably wouldn't have one yourself.

Or else he'd resent being wakened up from a fantasy of flying a Thunderjet[19] or a stratocruiser[20] or whatever was the latest thing. Perhaps WAAFs on the tarmac in Korea or BOAC stewardesses[21] in smart uniforms, with disciplined but promising breasts. And millionaire passengers aboard, of whom he was master.

And perhaps anyway he was devoted to his little crate. They were probably things you could get fond of, like a pony that understood you and answered all your hinting movements.

My father was looking out the window again. I thought of the book in my pocket. But he had always hated me reading. And even if it was too difficult to talk over all the noise, and there wasn't much anyway that either of us could say, I felt it would be rude to cut myself off from him by reading. Silence, for him, was still a way of talking, so long as a book didn't spoil it.

What plans did he have, I wondered. I'd been going to take a room at the Majestic. He'd probably want to stay somewhere cheaper and less showy, even if I offered to pay, as I easily could. Would it be all right if we went to different hotels? And would he let me pay in any case? He hadn't made any objection when I bought his ticket and I didn't suppose he had much money, though he'd probably picked up all he had when we stopped at the boarding house to get his traps.[22] I had no notion of whether my mother had left a will. Anyway, whatever savings they'd had would have been in common. I seemed to remember that even in the depression years she had always managed to stow something away in the Building Society Savings Bank. She was one of those who always think that there'll be even worse rainy days. And he must have got a bit of hard cash when he sold the house. He'd probably come off pretty badly when the thing with Maisie went bust but he couldn't have lost much and he didn't have to support her, since she had plenty of money and she was the one who'd technically deserted him. Well, if he needed money I'd know soon enough.

The plane was losing height, I noticed. We couldn't be as near as all that to the Dunedin airfield, could we? I peered out the window, and down. That wonderfully clear New Zealand air. Perhaps I missed that more than anything, expatriate in a country where even light was a compromise. My father was tugging at my sleeve. When I looked at him he gestured downwards. I went across and looked down over his shoulder.

The pilot had flattened out again and we were coming in fairly low over what must be Wingatui racecourse.[23] The grandstand was full and the rails crowded. My countrymen and their religion. A race was on. We were too high to upset the horses but flying in line with the course. There were three out in front, the rest bunched, except for a straggler or two. As we watched, the shadow of the plane, about a hundred yards wide of the course, drew level with the horses and passed them. Then they were out of sight behind the wing. It had all happened in the second or two I stood beside my father. I went back to my seat and he grinned at me gleefully.

In front of me the pilot was immobile. He must have been tempted to look round and grin but he didn't. Then my father was plucking at my sleeve again and pointing.

I looked down. We were flying above the main trunk railway. Away in front and below, a train was moving towards Dunedin. We overhauled it quickly and left it behind.

'That must have been the Express,'[24] my father shouted across to me. 'To think I spent all those years on her and I thought we made a fast run.'

Something in the pilot's back told me he had heard; I guessed he was satisfied. The plane was gaining height again. Soon he began to turn into the wind, getting ready for the final drop into Taieri airfield. We were to fasten our safety belts, the pale lights told us. My father didn't need any help this time. His fingers had always been quick to learn things. I took a look over my shoulder. The young man was helping his wife into hers and she was letting him. But I could tell she didn't really need help, either. He let his hand lie a moment across her upper thigh and smiled at her. She saw me looking and flushed. I looked away.

The plane landed smoothly and taxied to the arrival point. It stopped, breathing, and we waited for the steps to be brought and the door to open.

'I'll never go by train again,' my father said in the same loud voice he had used when we were in the air. 'It's a sheer waste of time. Isn't it great the progress there is nowadays? You've got to move with the times, there's no getting away from it.'

The door opened and we all got up, standing awkwardly between the seats and waiting for our turn. The pilot had turned in his seat and looked at my father, smiling.

2

My father and I stood in the bar at Mrs Blaney's.[25] It was Saturday evening and the five till six rush hour.[26] He had insisted we both stay in the same hotel and whenever he was in Dunedin he always stayed at Ma Blaney's. They both came from the same part of Ireland,[27] I discovered. Something I'd never known in the days, twenty years before, when I'd drunk there as a student on Saturday nights after football. She was busy now, helping with the rush, a little old woman with high white hair, brisk and fierce in all her movements, though she must have been rising eighty. She had noticed us in the bar and sent two more of what we were having.

A man of about my own age, but greying and with more of a paunch, came up to me. 'It's you, isn't it?' he said. 'I'd heard you were paying us a visit.' Kevin Hickey's face emerged from under the face in front of me, young, devout. For some reason I remembered him at the altar rails, eyes closed, tongue out, waiting to receive the Host. He had a vocation, we all said, and was going to be a priest. Then he met a girl and took to the law instead. His father had felt disgraced and went to bed refusing to get up. Kevin's brothers were said to have lit a fire under the bed and smoked him out. What difference did it make now?

I introduced him to my father and of course my father had known his. There was a time when my father must have known everyone. But after a bit we were an island of silence in the middle of all the noise and I knew they must be thinking of the bed business and all that, as I was.

So I said something about the old days and then got Kevin to tell us a bit about his law firm. Things got easier and we had another round. The noise was terrible, even after you got used to it. The usual subjects, what they always talked about. Football, the races. My father began to make a story out of how we'd won at Wingatui but Kevin caught only half of it and looked puzzled.

My father gave up trying to explain. 'Excuse me a minute,' he said. 'I've got to use the telephone.'

I marvelled. We had never had a telephone at home and somehow I'd assumed he wouldn't even know how to use one. There'd been great progress, all right, in my long absence.

When he came back, Kevin had gone. The barman was calling time. Men were buying their last-minute bottles to take away.

'She's invited us out after tea,' my father said.

'Who has?'

'Maisie.' It was the first time he'd mentioned her name but he knew I would know it. He wasn't one to waste time on explanations. When I came to think of it, he'd never written to me since the letter he wrote after my mother died. We were in the middle of the Cassino battle then,[28] and so many were dying. I had read the letter and put it in my battle-dress pocket, meaning to read it again. I never did, though I often thought of my mother, that night and afterwards. She had been good to me and I was guilty that I had not been more grateful. After she died it was always my sister Nora who wrote the letters.

'We'll go and get a bite to eat somewhere,' my father said, 'and we'll go out there afterwards.'

'Let me shout you a meal at the City,'[29] I said. 'I'd like to take a look at the place for old times' sake.'

'It's not as good a table as it was in Mrs McCormick's day, God rest her,' he said. 'Still, it'll be good enough, I dare say.'

We waved to Mrs Blaney as we went out.

'Don't you boys be late now,' she called to us. 'You've got to get to Mass in the morning, mind.'

I hadn't thought of that one. It was going to be awkward. But I'd find some way round it when the time came.

3

It was latish when we got away from the City. There were a lot of people in Dunedin for the races and we had to wait for a table. That meant a few more drinks in the lounge, and as usual the old man kept running into people he knew and old-timers of one sort and another. Everyone wanted to buy a drink, of course, for their old friend Paddy – they always called him Paddy though his name was Ned – and that meant me as well. They'd ask me a few questions for politeness' sake and because, being back from the Old Country and all that, I was a bit of a nine days' wonder. But nobody really wants to talk to a nine days' wonder and my answers, like their questions, were just a sort of social sparring to show willing. They soon got back to talking about the old days with my father. After all, it's only your own life that's real, the realest part about it is the time when you were young, and the best way of being sure you haven't just dreamt even that is to talk with someone else who remembers the same things and can be trusted to remember them in the same sort of way, with plenty of detail but not too accurately.

Like a lot of Irishmen my father had always been better at talking to acquaintances, friends as he called them, than to his own family. He'd always been pretty silent at home, not necessarily in a grim sort of way, but in a way that suggested that it was only women who always had to be going on about something. When men weren't doing things, they were thinking. It wasn't till I was well grown and old enough to have seen him drinking with other men, that I realised he was really a rather talkative man. But he was good at listening, too, and he had a way of identifying with the other people while they were together which made them feel easy with him. It was quite genuine, too, I think, though afterwards when they'd gone, he'd become different again, and he'd go over what they'd said with a sort of amused mockery, often. I suppose it was a way of having his own back for the energy he'd spent in being partly inside their skins for a bit.

He was back on the old caper tonight properly and when the waiter came to tell us there was a table I had a bit of trouble getting him away. When we got down to it, though, he tucked away one of those big South Island meals without any trouble – soup, fish, roast beef, cabbage and potatoes, and a great wodge of apple pie.

Then it was coffee in the lounge and two or three rounds of whiskies with the pals who hadn't eaten yet and didn't look as if they were going to. So I began to think we were stuck there for the night, what with most of them being residents in the hotel and so no trouble about opening hours. I didn't much care myself, as I rather enjoyed listening to these tough old fellows. I'd have been bored to tears when I was a youngster, but by now I'd learnt enough to prefer long yarns about the early days to the average conversation about books which had once been my idea of how an intelligent chap should pass the time.

My father hadn't lost sight of his objective, though, as we used to say in the army and it wasn't as late as all that before he had me out in George Street again and striding north. He'd gone quiet again, in spite of all the drinks and I guessed he was working out how the evening was likely to go and how much he ought to brief me or how far he could rely on me to sort the situation out for myself.

It wasn't until we turned into Pacific Street[30] and began to climb the hill that he evidently decided to give me a grudging clue or two. 'She's got a nice little packet salted away somewhere,' he said. 'But she's pretty near[31] with it, though she likes to live comfortable.'

There was a flight of stone steps up to the front door. It was freshly painted and the doorknob and the knocker were shining under the light. My father didn't seem nervous, but a little bit tense and almost mischievous at the same time, I thought, as he rang the bell.

The door opened and I saw a woman, it must be Maisie, standing in the hall.

'Hello, Maisie,' my father said.

'Hello, Ned. Come in. And so this is that famous son of yours.'

'That's the one.' I realised that it was only when we were by ourselves that he took me for granted. It was one of those moments when you suddenly know that other people talk about you when you aren't there and you become a counter in their games instead of always being banker in a game of your own.

She had a service flat on the ground floor of one of those houses that used to be lived in by a single well-to-do family when I was a student. The sons were usually in the family business or medical students and the daughters were always in the social column of the *Otago Daily Times,* giving farewell parties before they went Home[32] to be presented at Buckingham Palace, or getting engaged to young men from the same sort of houses as their own. For some reason or other, it always seemed to be important what dress they were wearing on these occasions and who else had been present.

My father never wore an overcoat unless it was actually raining, but

I took mine off in the hall and she hung it for me, using a coat-hanger. She then led us along a wide corridor to the living-room, where there was a good log fire burning under a massive mantelpiece. I noted, out of the corner of my eye, glasses and a bottle of brandy on a sidetable. There were deep, comfortable chairs, not too modern, a grand piano with photographs in frames, a procession of diminishing elephants on the mantelpiece, various brass objects, and pictures from which one immediately averted one's affronted eyes. And there was a cabinet wireless which she went over to and switched off.

She stood in front of the fire and faced us. Black hair, probably tinted, bright dark eyes, a full-fleshed neck and bosom, figure well preserved though thickish and the lines controlled by corsets. A dark red dress. A lot of jewellery. Probably in her late fifties.

'Now sit down and make yourselves comfortable while I get you a drink,' she said. She was addressing herself to both of us, but looking mainly at me. And when I offered to help she put a strong hand on me and pressed me to sit down. 'Would brandy be all right?'

'That'll do us fine, Maisie,' my father said, winking at me like a showman as she went over to the table.

I had the feeling she had been thinking carefully about the evening, what was likely to happen, what I was going to be like, what my father might be up to. She had decided brandy would make the right impression on me. It was probably her own favourite drink, as well.

They talked about people who lived near the farm, which ones were doing well and which were just working for the mortgagees, and who had sold out. He asked about her son John, who'd brought his family back from Australia and was now running the farm. It seemed he'd settled down well but the wife wasn't too keen.

I didn't say much. I just sipped away at my brandy and water, warning myself that I'd had a good deal already, and I watched and listened. My father gave no sign of what his real reason for coming might be. He managed to give a general impression that he had simply wanted us to meet each other. As I watched, I could see that there was still a physical attraction between them. They were people whose vitality had been less slowed down by the years than was usual for their age. Her bare forearm along the arm of her chair was only a foot or so away from him. The flesh of the under side, though it was rather full and flattened a little too easily, was still the flesh of a woman, not just the neutral flesh of one who had reached the age where the sexes merge. She had kept herself well and was turned out well, even if flashy and provincial. The rings on her fingers were too many, too big, and too costly. She had on her left wrist one of those bracelets which have a lot of charms and knick-knacks dangling from them. Her necklace might have been a real diamond one and the turquoise cross at the end of it hovered over the crevasse of her full breasts. She was rather heavily made up, but the lipstick and the rouge went well with the dark skin, not turning it magenta.

At the end of the day my mother used to sit, tired, at the kitchen table. She'd have her old slippers on, because of her poor feet. She carried too much weight and was too short for this to suit her. Her hands were red and swollen, the skin shiny over the knuckles. Her hair hadn't been near a hair-dresser for years, perhaps never. She wouldn't have changed her dress – too tired, and nothing but her Sunday dress to change into, anyway. She never wore make-up and she and my father scoffed at people who did, especially older women.

In my mother's idea of marriage, there was no need for these things. The tactics of femininity were for girls or fast women. Absolute devotion to her family, her man, to the house and her work, this was the weapon and the armour of her simplicity. An equal loyalty on my father's part she took for granted. Her love was unthinking, inarticulate as far as I could judge and expressed mainly in worry about him in his absence and too much fussing when he was at home, but confident and quite free of coquetry.

She was right, while she lived. But my father, though he depended on her as she was and would not have expected her to be different or have been pleased if she had tried to be, must have missed all the rest – the effort to make him seem more than he was, even to himself, the little extra gestures that might give him the sense that he could be desirable to others, hard to be kept, the attention to appearances as well as the reliance on realities.

It was clear how Maisie must have attracted him: an obviously sensuous nature, a determination not too laboured to remain attractive as a woman: the alertness of the widow who still needs a man and must be attentive, flatteringly predatory. She had a kind of energy, too, and a sort of readiness of response to a man that might have looked like warmth, an affectionate nature. To my father she must have seemed rather sophisticated as well, someone who had been brought up in a convent, had seen a good deal of the world afterwards, and had travelled in the North Island and Australia when she was young. She would have seemed rather a cut above him, somehow, a way of improving himself.

That was the trouble, though, I decided, looking round the room which I gathered was called the lounge. It was furnished in a way that suggested an attentive reading of the woman's page of any and every New Zealand newspaper. For such a taste, in ruthless pursuit of refinement, my father must have seemed too crude, too rough, once the first animal drive had slackened and could no longer sustain the machinery of illusion necessary to keep two people living together in harmony.

I looked at him now. His cards weren't really very strong. He was still very much a man, it was true, and his blue eyes were lively with a sort of intelligence and life. But he was not polished, not educated. The hands that rested from the wrists on his knees were those of a man who used the axe, the shovel, and the spade. His back was too straight, his laugh too unguarded. He was not quite the stereotype of the New Zealand working-man because there was still in his bearing and manner the peasant Irish culture of another world, a dignity, a pride in being a man rather than that harassed and embattled masculinity. But his wasn't a dignity or a culture that she was likely to discern or value if she did discern it. It was the kind that a woman of her sort would be able to sense and appreciate for a while where both were alone or in an environment proper to it. It would not show to advantage in the world where she would like to shine. So she would have wanted to change him, civilise him, make him a middle-class husband in the New Zealand pattern, as she would have aspired to be a middle-class wife, superior and more genteel than he, but not too much so. And the very strength in him which attracted her, the pride, would have ruled that out. There could never have been any real prospect that the thing would have worked.

My father had been steering the ball my way, I became aware. It was time I took my cue. She was good at listening, I found, and all the drinks we had had were beginning to take effect. She herself must have had quite a few by then, and perhaps before we came, too. But she showed very little sign of being anything but the better for it.

I told stories about London, about Paris, about the war. My father led me on to something about Dublin. Her father had been a Dublin man, it seemed, and her mother had come from the North. We had more drinks and I remembered nice things about Ireland, the Old Country to both of them. There was a suspicion of tears in her eyes, a faraway look, and she folded her hands in her lap and sat up straight without realising it. So, as a little girl, she must have listened to her father.

My father took the opportunity of telling stories about his own boyhood in Galway but I could see she had heard them before and he sensed too that this wasn't what she wanted and left the going to me again. I knew somehow that I was in the vein he wanted. I sang one or two songs – my tenor was good enough to pass so long as people had had a few drinks. My father's chair seemed to have got closer to hers and their arms were nearly touching. As if their bodies at any rate were more or less ready for a *rapprochement.*

'Ah, it'd be great now to see the Old Country again,' my father said. 'I hope I'll get there once at any rate before I die. It'd take no time at all in one of them planes.'

He looked at me as he said this, but I knew it was meant for her. She just sighed, as if in sympathy, but non-committal. I said nothing. The old people I'd known who'd gone home to Ireland had found no place for themselves there and, when they came back to New Zealand and found themselves without a dream, they usually died fairly soon. You cannot emigrate twice.

I asked where the bathroom was. 'Come and I'll show you,' she said.

When I came out again into the corridor, she was still there, waiting for me. She took me by the arm and I realised there was still a passionate woman there. A bit tight, though. She had been drinking drink-for-drink with us.

'Martin,' she said, 'I don't want you to think it was my fault that things went wrong between your father and me. He's the one who was to blame.'

'I'm not blaming you,' I said. 'Or anyone else. It's no business of mine. You're old enough, both of you, to know your own minds.'

But it wasn't good enough. She insisted and kept hold of my arm, with a grip surprisingly strong. 'No, Martin. He's a very cruel man, your father. He had me and John in fear of our lives. He didn't tell you he went for my son with an axe, I'll bet.'

'He didn't tell me anything at all. And perhaps you shouldn't, either.'

'You're a very nice man, Martin, and you've seen a lot of the hard world, I know. And it's only natural you should stick up for your own flesh and blood, don't think I don't understand. But I wanted you to know how awful he'd been to me. He's a very hard man, Martin, real hard. I couldn't ever live with him again. I'm sure of that.'

'Well,' I said, 'that's up to you to settle between you. And no one's going to make you live with him if you don't want to. We'd better go in now or he'll think we're smooging with each other out here.'

'Fancy even thinking of such a thing, you naughty man.' But her face had changed and she looked pleased at being still thought possible.

As we came in my father gave her and then me a quick, curious look. He would have guessed that she was telling her side.

We couldn't get going again, somehow, after the interruption. It was after midnight and I for one had had enough, of the brandy and the situation in general. Somehow that bit about his being cruel stuck in my gizzard. He might be a hard man, and unfeeling sometimes, but whatever else he was he wasn't cruel. If he really had taken the axe to John, it must have been to scare him, and even then they must have driven him to the end of his tether.

'Well, Dad,' I said. 'What about it? We mustn't keep Maisie up any longer. It's time we got going.'

'Yes, son, it is that. Well, Maisie, it's been very nice seeing you again.'

'You're very welcome. But you can't go off and leave that little bit in the bottom of the bottle.'

She filled up our glasses, all three of them. But she didn't sit down again, and neither did we.

'Here's to your health on your travels, Martin, and I hope you go on making a name for yourself over there. It's a fine young man you've got for a son, Ned. Someone to be proud of.'

'He is that, Maisie.' And he looked very pleased.

4

My father wouldn't hear of getting a taxi and so we walked back along silent streets, silent ourselves. Only a taxi sped past us now and then, an occasional policeman on rubber-soled boots tried the locks of shop-doors, and once a drunk student was kissing his girl goodnight outside the Excelsior. Dunedin was already in its Sunday sleep. I forgot to wonder what my father might be thinking and thought of the early mornings long ago when I had hurried along these same streets, from a girl's bed to my own.

The front door of the hotel was closed. I was going to press the night bell when my father stopped me. 'Come round this way,' he said.

We went down a side passage and at the back of the hotel there was an iron fire-escape. My father led the way up, and on the bedroom floor a window opposite the landing was open. Mrs Blaney leaned out and looked at us. She was still dressed as she had been earlier.

'A fine time of the night to be coming home,' she said, 'for the pair of you. Shame on you, Ned, to be setting your own son such an example. Come in with you, now, and don't wake the whole hotel with your noise.'

She stepped back and my father climbed over the sill. I got in after him, half-expecting to be slapped.

'Sure, we were only visiting a few friends,' my father said, and I could tell he was as scared of her as I was.

'Fine friends they must be that would keep you and the boy up drinking to this hour of night. Off to bed now, the pair of you, you scallywags, and don't be late in the morning.'

My father came as far as my room with me and sat on the bed. 'She's a great old stick, isn't she?' He grinned a bit ruefully.

For a moment I thought he meant Maisie and then realised my mistake in time. He didn't want to talk about Maisie at all, and he was using Mrs Blaney to fill the gap.

'Yes, she's a great old character,' I said. 'She's hardly changed a bit since I was a student.'

'Well, good night,' he said. 'I'll call you for breakfast.'

I was desperately tired and a bit tight. I went straight to sleep, leaving it till tomorrow to puzzle things out.

I woke about eight, pretty thick in the head and cursing Maisie and her brandy. I went along the passage to the bathroom and let the cold tap run in the bath while I cleaned my teeth and shaved. Then I stood in the bath and lowered myself in gingerly, gasping. I lay back in the cold water and splashed about till I'd had enough. Then I got out and dried myself, feeling a bit better.

Outside the bathroom I found my father standing in the passage fully dressed. He looked cheerful and none the worse for wear.

'I thought that was where you must have got to,' he said. 'Come on now and get dressed. I managed to get her to open up the bar and I've brought us a couple of double-headers.'[33]

Sure enough there were two full whisky nobblers[34] on my dresser.

'Drink it up now. It'll do you the world of good and give you an appetite for breakfast.' He took one of them and drank it off.

I sipped mine and the taste and smell of it at that time of the morning and the way I felt made me toss my head and almost whinny like a horse. I put it down again.

'I'll get dressed first,' I said. 'I'll see you downstairs.' Funny, I had some sort of shyness at getting dressed in front of him. Because he was my father, I supposed, though that didn't really explain much.

He went out and I began to put on my clothes. Even that little sip of whisky had begun to act now, though. I took the glass and gulped the rest. Then I finished dressing and went downstairs.

There was a sign pointing through the bar to the dining-room. But in the bar I found my father talking to a large red-faced man. They each had a long beer in front of them. 'This is Pat Plunkett,' my father said. 'My son Martin, the one I was telling you about.'

We shook hands and my father went behind the bar and got me a bottle of beer. 'That's what you need now, my lad,' he said. 'A chaser. Drink that up and you'll be as right as the bank.'

In spite of the whisky the idea of breakfast was still not at all acceptable. Coffee and a bit of toast and marmalade at the most. But I drank down the beer. Somehow it was all a bit like one of those wartime mornings in the mess, when you were making an early move back to the desert.

'Well, cheerio just now, Pat,' my father said. 'It was nice running into you after all these years.'

He led me into the dining-room and we sat down at a round table in the corner. Someone had already breakfasted there. The maid came and cleared the table and laid two fresh places. 'Bacon and eggs for two,' my father said, and I shrugged inwardly.

Mrs Blaney appeared in the entrance from the kitchen and saw us. 'Good morning, Ned,' she said sternly to my father, and she managed a faint smile for me. Then she looked down and saw the crumbs on the table. She clicked her tongue. 'These girls you get nowadays,' she said.

She went away and I listened for a row in the kitchen. But instead she came back with a little tray and curved brush and swept up the crumbs from my part of the table. She didn't bother about my father's place, though, but went off again and came back with a clean linen napkin which she handed to me, ignoring him.

He didn't appear to be at all offended or puzzled by this but just grinned at me, showing white even teeth, not one missing. You could have guessed from that alone he hadn't been brought up in New Zealand.

'You can't beat old Mrs Blaney,' he said, 'for knowing how to keep a good table. Fancy her being on deck at this hour of the morning. It must have been going on for two when she let us in last night.'

To my surprise I had no trouble eating the bacon and egg after all. And the coffee was very good.

Afterwards, we sat in the lounge while I had a smoke. My father sat still and silent the way people can who never read and don't feel conversation necessary. I thought he might be trying to make up his mind to talk about the night before. But it wasn't that.

'It's time to be thinking of getting up the hill to the Cathedral,' he said.

I noticed the neutral way he'd put it. No doubt it was well known in the family that I didn't go to Mass[35] any more and he was leaving it to me to make the running.

'I don't think I'll go with you,' I said. 'I've got some people to see and some letters to write.'

I could feel him disappointed. Perhaps he'd hoped it wasn't true that I'd left the Church. And I suppose he'd rather have liked meeting people he knew, the way he always did, after Mass, and introducing me to them. But he made no comment. 'I'll see you here about twelve, then. We'd better have something to eat here before you catch your plane.'

5

Travelling out to the airfield on the bus, I looked at the broom with its twisted black pods. When we were kids we used to hear the sharp crack they made in the summer heat when the time had come to scatter their seeds. You could hear quite small noises in those days. Now there was always a roar of engines between you and small noises, and a screen of motion between yourself and stillness. I thought of the people I'd seen that morning, after my father went off to Mass. They had all got older except me, it seemed. Their hair was grey, you had the feeling of fixed habits, minds preoccupied with the unknown experiences that lay between now and the time we had been friends. They remembered different things, or remembered the same things differently. I shouldn't have come back. They were blurring the outline of the past. It was only the broom, and the gorse, the sun on the hills, and the wind, that didn't change.

'You know,' my father said, 'she took rather a fancy to you.'

This time I knew he meant Maisie, but I couldn't think of anything to say. Looking back on last night, I'd decided I didn't like her. She obviously didn't see that my father was worth two of her and rather looked down on him. And if she'd made a fuss of me it was only because I had prestige value for discussion over tea with her friends, having come back from abroad and having my name in the papers.

'I've been thinking that one of these days I might talk her into shouting the pair of us a trip to the Old Country,' he said. 'It'd be great to see where you live and meet the children. And I'd like to go back and see who's still left in Galway.'

'We'd love to see you,' I said. 'The children have heard so much about you. When they were small, they once started to dig a hole in the garden, so as to get through to the Antipodes and meet you.'

If it ever came off, I was thinking, it would be worse for him than it had been for me. At least I had been warned by books that you could never go back.[36] I knew what to expect not to expect. There was no need to fear, though. He'd played his cards well enough, but the hand was too poor. I was his only trump and there wasn't much he could do with me against her sort of player. Perhaps I should have taken a hand myself.

'It's not money that'd be the trouble,' he said. 'She's got plenty of that.'

I didn't much like the idea of a proud man like my father scheming to use the woman's money, even if she was his wife, more or less. I began to wish, as I did once in a while, that I'd paid a bit more attention to making money myself. It would have been nice to be able to say, 'Come on, Dad, don't worry about her, I'll shout you the trip myself.' But I'd never treated money seriously enough to have it in that sort of quantity. So there was nothing to be done.

When we were in the little departure lounge I saw a hire car pull up and Maisie get out.

'I thought I'd come and see you off,' she said when she found us.

'That was very nice of you. But you shouldn't have bothered,' I said.

I looked at my father. He was smiling to himself as he bent to pick up the luggage. 'How are you feeling today, Maisie?' he asked.

'Fine, thank you, Ned. It was such a nice day I thought I'd come out and find you both. It might be a long time before we see him again, after all, that young man of ours.'

'It might, at that.' My father spoke shortly. He wouldn't have liked that suggestion of ownership. And he was probably thinking that the likelihood was he'd never see me again.

'Your poor mother,' he said to me, 'if only she'd lived to see you come home. She always believed you'd come home some day. Even in the thick of the war, when they said you were missing, believed killed, she always said you'd come home. You were like a cat, she used to say, always so quick and quiet, and with nine lives and all.'

Passengers had been called. The others had gone out already the short distance across to the plane. I half-embraced Maisie. She wasn't a bad sort, after all. She'd lived in a hard world where you had to look after yourself, or else. I shook my father's hand.

'Goodbye, son. Forget what I was saying about that trip. I wouldn't want it to happen that way, you know.'

'I know,' I said. I did too, in a kind of way.

'I may see you some day over there myself,' Maisie said. 'You never know.'

I knew it was quite likely she would come. But I knew, after what he had said about my mother, that if she did come it wouldn't be with him, whether she wanted it or not.

When the plane was in the air, I looked back and down. There was no one waving from the airfield now, and I could not tell whether he had gone back in the car with her or was in the bus which was crawling minutely out to the main road.

First Flight: first published in *Landfall* 23:1 (March 1969): 12–33. Like 'A Return', this story is also based round Davin's return to Invercargill in August 1948, and his reunion with his father.

NOTES

[1]   mother's death: Mary Davin died suddenly of a cerebral haemorrhage on 10 May 1944.

[2]   Grand: licensed hotel off Dee Street, at that time the city's premier hotel.

[3]   over seventy: born in 1877, Patrick Davin was approximately seventy-one in 1948. See 'Black Diamond'.

[4]   Invercargill-Dunedin run: the express train to Christchurch on which Patrick Davin worked as a guard. The crew stopped off in Dunedin and returned on the Christchurch-Invercargill train. See 'Roof of the World', 'Failed Exorcism'.

[5]   bally: euphemism for 'bloody'.

[6]   the school in Clyde Street: from February 1921 Davin attended the Marist Brothers School in Clyde Street; it moved from there to Mary Street in 1925. See 'Failed Exorcism'.

[7]   airfield ... estuary: Invercargill airport is located three kilometres west of the City Centre, across the New River Estuary.

[8]   Rapide: probably the DH89 Dragon Rapide, introduced to New Zealand in 1934, or the improved version, the DH89a (introduced in 1937), which had flaps outboard on the lower wings. It was used for commercial passenger operations until the 1970s, and had room for the pilot and eight passengers.

[9]   Eurydice ... underworld: an allusion to Eurydice's descent into Hades, after Orpheus broke the condition that he not look back to see if his wife was following. Davin reverses the Greek legend; this young woman will make an ascent from the earth in the airplane.

[10]   The house ... houses: the house in Morton Road to which the Davin family moved from Gore in 1920 was then on the edge of town, surrounded by gorse-hedged paddocks.

[11]   over the cemetery ... grave: Eastern Cemetery in Rockdale Road. See 'The Vigil'.

[12]   She had loved ... mother: after Patrick Davin's second marriage broke up he lived with his daughter Molly in Dunedin for the rest of his life.

[13]   the house ... married: Patrick and Nora Davin married in 1907. Patrick Davin purchased the property at 36 Morton Street and possibly built the house himself in 1909. See 'The Apostate'.

[14]   she was ill: Mary Davin suffered a mental collapse before she died, due to deep anxieties about the family. She was taken to Seacliff Mental Hospital on 27 April 1944.

[15]   Edendale: between Invercargill and Gore, on the main road. In reality the widow was a wealthy publican, Mrs Bolt, who owned the pub at Wrey's Bush about ten miles north-west of Winton. See Father John Pound's memoir in *IS*, p. 28.

[16] quincunxes: patterns of lines forming a rectangle or square with a fifth line at the centre.

[17] Sir Thomas Browne: an allusion to the seventeenth-century writer and mystic Thomas Browne's belief, presented in *Religio Medici* (1642), that formal patterns in nature like triangles and squares are proof that the world is divinely ordered, that man is a microcosm of the world, made in the image of God.

[18] popsies: Australian slang for girl, sweetheart.

[19] Thunderjet: the F-84 Thunderjet, turbo-jet fighter bomber built in the US between 1947–54, used in the Korean Conflict, and then supplied to Allied Nations participating in mutual security programmes. It was the first jet to carry a nuclear bomb.

[20] stratocruiser: the Boeing Model 377 stratocruiser, with an upper deck, the first of the post-war luxury airliners.

[21] WAAFs ... BOAC stewardesses: acronyms for Women's Auxiliary Airforce and British Overseas Airways Corporation, now British Airways.

[22] traps: personal belongings, luggage.

[23] Wingatui racecourse: the main Dunedin racecourse, situated near Mosgiel.

[24] the Express: the Invercargill-Christchurch train on which Patrick Davin worked as a guard on the Invercargill-Dunedin leg.

[25] Mrs Blaney's: Mrs Annie Blaney, proprietor from 1917–54 of Tattersalls Hotel on the north side of Stafford Street, above the Provincial Hotel, and a legendary figure by the 1930s.

[26] the five ... hour: Six o'clock closing was introduced as an economy measure in 1917; but the last hour's drinking became known as 'the six o'clock swill'. Opening hours were extended to 10 p.m. in October 1967.

[27] the same part of Ireland: this is unlikely. Ma Blaney was born in Inchclutha/Stirling, South Otago in 1890. Her father, James Blaney, may have once lived in Ireland but she was probably Scottish and a Protestant. James McNeish (*Tavern in the Town*, p. 257), says she was 'a spry Scots landlady'.

[28] the letter ... Cassino battle: according to Ovenden it was his brother Tom who wrote. The letter reached Davin on 3 June 1944, almost a month after his mother's death, when the New Zealand Div. was advancing on Avezzano. *FW*, pp. 187–8.

[29] the City: the City Hotel on the corner of Princes Street and Moray Place, founded in 1864 and still standing.

[30] Pacific Street: in Maori Hill, a prosperous suburb of Dunedin.

[31] near: (arch.) niggardly, mean.

[32] Home: England, or the Old Country. See *ODNZE*, s.v. 'home', 1.

[33] double-headers: twice the standard nip of spirits, served in a single glass. *ODNZE* s.v. 'doubler'.

[34] nobbler: the glass in which a measure or nip of spirits is served. *ODNZE*.

[35] I ... Mass: Davin evidently gave up the faith after he arrived in Oxford in 1936 but news of this filtered only slowly back to his family and relatives in Southland.

[36] I had been warned ... back: Sir Thomas Malory's *Morte D'Arthur*. See 'Bluff Retrospect'.

20

Bluff Retrospect

IT WAS A STIFFISH CLIMB to the top of Bluff Hill[1] but he took it pretty fast, remembering how steep they had found it as kids when they had come to the Bluff for Regatta Day and the rows they used to get into when they finally came down again and found the family with the picnic things all packed and his mother and aunts and the girls all sitting round having a last cup of tea and wondering where on earth all those boys could have got to.

He sat on the top and looked out over Foveaux Strait.[2] Three miles away he could see Dog Island[3] with its black and white lighthouse, tallest on the coast. Then Centre Island[4] away to the west, an old burial place of the Maoris. He could barely make out Puapuke Island[5] which used to be Bloody Jack's hide-out[6] and could only guess where the Orepuki cliffs[7] must be, Papakihau was the Maori name, 'slapped by the wind'.[8]

How strange that a few years should have made the difference between what he was now and the kid he used to be. The preparations for those picnics.[9] His mother making fruit cake, sponge cake and marble cake days beforehand, and deciding how many tomato sandwiches, ham sandwiches, tongue sandwiches, corned beef sandwiches, chicken sandwiches were going to be needed. The packing of tins and baskets, the search for bathing suits and sandshoes. Julia[10] putting a statue of Saint Joseph on the front doorstep the night before, to make sure the weather was fine. The alarum loud through the house in the early morning and the rush to the window to see whether it was going to rain. The last minute panics about what had been forgotten, the ceremony of closing all the windows and locking the doors, the despairing look in Roy's eyes at the front gate, hoping to the last, though he knew better from the sorrowful way they spoke to him. His anguished yelp when the front gate closed with a click and he was left behind. Then they all trooped down the street to the early tram and waited listening for its whining throb to turn into action, his mother already worrying whether she'd forgotten anything and whether they would be late for the train.

Then the gathering of the clan at the station, his mother greeting sisters from Makarewa[11] and Woodlands;[12] the girl cousins at once making friends again and comparing dresses and whispering and giggling; the boys[13] looking at one another more suspiciously before merging and boasting about what they had got for Christmas and how good their ferrets were and how they had a new Winchester .22 rifle. The wild struggle for seats on the train; the mothers worrying about boys hanging halfway out the windows; the mud of the Invercargill estuary as the train went south through Clyde Street and Clifton.[14] Then, as Greenhills[15] approached, there was the warning to look out for old Auntie Wyatt[16] and this time the children could have only corners of the windows while the full bosoms of the mothers were framed in them, handkerchiefs waving. And there she was, sure enough, at the gate set in the middle of the tall macrocarpa hedge, her eyes as keen as ever for all her eighty years and her spotless white handkerchief waving as the family went by. She was the one who had sent his father the fare to bring him across the world out of Galway which she had herself left twenty years before that.[17]

They would settle back into their seats again, his mother's handkerchief a ball now and dabbing at her eyes, as she thought if it hadn't been for old Auntie Wyatt's money long ago she would never have met her man, and poor Auntie an old woman now with not long to go, the Lord have mercy on her. But soon it was Ocean Beach, the sea mysteriously on their left now instead of the right where there were only the ugly meat works you didn't like to think about. The women were beginning to stuff things back into baskets, the napkins that had been changed, the sandwiches that had been sampled, the thermos flask that go-ahead Uncle Jack had bought as a Christmas present for Auntie Nellie.[18] And now they were coming alongside the Bluff platform and everyone was getting up to disembark and his mother was calling to them to be careful and not to get out before the train stopped.

Out on the platform the boys always made a vain attempt to escape without carrying baskets but were always caught and the family convoy went at a snail's pace through the barrier and out into the hot sunlight of the street and the smell of the sea. As they trooped untidily along the street, the boys up and down the outside gutter like sheepdogs, the men dropped quietly out of the column and disappeared. His mother would look significantly at Aunt Nellie and the older girls would solemnly imitate the clicking of their tongues. From the open doors of the pubs you could hear the glasses chinking against the clatter of talk.

In Argyle Park[19] the women spread blankets and rugs while the older boys were sent off to get hot water from the big coppers with fires under them that lined one side of the paddock. At least one boy usually escaped while the tea was being made and search parties would be sent out in case he got himself drowned in the Devil's Pool.[20] Then there would be a mighty lunch and the men would arrive back in the middle of it smelling of beer and looking sheepish but in better tempers than they had been since they started out that morning.

Afterwards, the grown-ups would sit up against the old oyster sheds[21] and chat and go to sleep, the men meaning to make off again as soon as things got quiet. And sometimes, if the sparkle of the sun on the sea was especially tempting, husbands and wives would go down to the beach. The women would take off their shoes and stockings and go paddling, giving little screams at the onset of a wave or the coldness or their own daring. And the men, after watching and scoffing for a while, would be jealous at being left out and would roll up their trousers and follow. And the children looked shyly at them and then looked away, embarrassed because their parents had become somehow like them, only their flesh was a pallid white, and the men's legs hairy and on some of the women's there were varicose veins which they themselves would never get. The girls and boys would break up. The younger kids would be off paddling and looking for crabs or spending their pocket money on a trip round the harbour in the *Skylark* or the *Waterlily.* The girls would go looking at the shops or if they were old enough would set off in twos and threes round the Point,[22] telling one another secrets and throwing their chins up and shaking their plaits when strange boys whistled at them. The older boys went off into the bush to cut supplejacks[23] and throw down stones at the sea. It was there that Martin and his brothers first learnt to look at girls, though they never got much further than looking at likely pairs and following them in the vague hope that something would happen. Only it always seemed that the girls of their own age were too old for them and the younger ones too young.

And sometimes, if there was time, they would climb Bluff Hill to where he was now and speculate about Bloody Jack and the Maoris and tell one another they could see Slope Point,[24] the point of the South Island nearest to the Pole. And they would dream of themselves as whalers and castaways and explorers and prisoners of the Maoris who became tohungas and chieftains because of their bravery and wisdom.

There was the time, too, when his mother and Aunt Nora and the rest really had missed the first train. By the time they got to the picnic place it was too full. They had gone on a bit further and found a nice dry place under some stunted pine trees. They had stretched the rugs over the pine-needles and were just settling down when a gaunt old Maori woman, with blue tattoo markings on her chin and lower lip, came up and began to harangue them fiercely in Maori.[25] No one could make out what she was saying except that she was obviously furious with them for being there. Neither his mother nor Aunt Nora, especially Aunt Nora who was no mean scold herself and had a very strong sense of her rights, was the sort of person to be easily persuaded to budge once established. But there was something about this old woman that carried passion and authority.

Sheepishly but angrily they gathered up their things and moved back into the crowded paddock, the kids trailing after them, feeling miserable and defeated and somehow guilty. The old Maori, hands at her sides and head up, watched them go, dark eyes still fierce. When they had settled again she disappeared through the trees.

An old man in a fisherman's jersey and wearing a peaked cap had been standing by the road and laughing to himself.

'What was she making all that palaver about?' Aunt Nora asked him. 'Anyone'd think she owned the place.'

'She does in a way,' the old fellow said. 'That's an old Maori cemetery[26] you picked on. There's always hell to pay if she catches anyone there. She's even after the loving couples at night if they curl up there for a canoodle on their way home from the dance.'

'Poor old thing,' said Martin's mother. 'I can imagine what she feels. Only she ought to have seen we wouldn't have gone there if we'd known.'

'Ah well, she's a funny old stick,' the man said. 'She'd be a chief if she had her rights, they say. But it's all old stuff now and who knows or cares about chiefs any more, or Maori cemeteries for that matter. Half the Maoris themselves, even, don't know what they are.' He went on his way, chuckling.

Martin had felt guilty and terribly embarrassed. He hated his mother and his aunt for not getting away quickly. And he hated the old man for laughing at them, and at the old woman. Now, coming back to it, he still found himself blushing. Only now it seemed worse that it should have been his family, Irish people who were in this country because life in their own had been made impossible, their priests proscribed, their chiefs dispersed and their graves forgotten, who had even innocently violated the soil of another conquered race, especially that part of it which was sacred to the dead. By now, probably, the old woman herself was dead and buried, as like as not in the Anglican or Methodist or Presbyterian churchyard instead of in the burial place of her ancestors. It wouldn't be long before the cemetery without its guardian, its tapu forgotten,[27] was grabbed up by the new people, its memory as dead as those who lay under it. In fact, now he came to think of it, he could not remember seeing that patch of the pine trees on the right of the road as you went towards Tom's place,[28] though that was where it used to be.

He remembered how his father had merely laughed when they told him and said it was time for the Maoris to forget about all that old stuff, now that they were Christians anyway even if few enough of them were Catholics. Would his father feel any differently about it now, the older man who had replaced the laughing black-haired active man of those days? Probably not. Time that had caught up on the Maoris was catching up on him. Martin thought of his father as an object for a moment, a man outside himself. He saw him sitting across the table at Tom's, so like himself, so different. The same hands as his own, except that his father's were stronger, more worn, the veins on them heavy, the fingernails seamed and black at the ends. The same shoulders, wide and square, the same set of the chest, the same strong neck and heavy head. Only his father's neck was tanned a deep red, with grooves along the lines of the muscles, and a sort of greenish stain from the times when he wore a collar and the stud pressed. The same nose and the same blue eyes, coming down to them through Heaven only knew how many forgotten generations, generations which the Maoris would have remembered and named, and the Irish also, until the confusion of a new language, and the scattering of Cromwell, and slavery to the desperate business of keeping alive compelled them to forget.

But, from his mother perhaps or from the luxury of not having to use all his energies in keeping body and soul together here in an easier country, he, the son, had managed to develop a new sensibility, both a weakness and a strength. To his father, the Maoris were just a poor shiftless lot, who wouldn't do a decent day's work, were rotten with consumption, and spent any money they had buying booze or flash clothes. For himself, they were a persecuted people, robbed of their country and wasters from despair. And the English had seen the Irish in both these ways.

His father would have shrugged if he had said this to him. And rightly. For there was something false in it. Maori and pakeha alike had been driven to what they did and were by forces beyond the mastery of any individual. It was life that had been at work. It was all very well to be 'enlightened'. What was he going to do about it other than indulge the sort of regret that had lain behind their own dreams of being chieftains long ago? There was nothing he could do about it. Nothing whatever. King Arthur never came back.[29]

Bluff Retrospect: a transcript is held in the Alexander Turnbull Library (MS-Group-0319).

NOTES

[1] Bluff Hill: also known as Motupohue. Its height of 265 metres gives unobstructed views of Stewart Island, Foveaux Strait and Southland.

[2] Foveaux Strait: sea-way twenty-six kilometres wide which separates the South Island from Stewart Island.

[3] Dog Island: low-lying island in Foveaux Strait, just off Bluff, which contains New Zealand's tallest lighthouse, built in 1865.

[4] Centre Island: low-lying island in western approach to Foveaux Strait between Stewart Island and the South Island. Its lighthouse was built in 1878.

[5] Puapuke [sic] Island: Ruapuke, an island of 3500 acres, on the eastern approach to Foveaux Strait.

[6] Bloody Jack's hide-out: the stronghold of Chief Hone Tuhawaiki (1805–44), called 'Bloody Jack' by whalers and traders, also known as 'King of the Bluff'. Tuhawaiki ambushed Te Rauparaha (1831) and as leader of Ngai Tahu inflicted losses on Ngati Toa in 1835 and again in 1836 near Mataura. He signed the Treaty of Waitangi in April 1840 and converted to Christianity. In 26 July 1844 he and other chiefs, sold the Otago block for £2400; later that year he drowned in suspicious circumstances off Timaru. Robert Ritchie Alexander, 'Hone Tuhawaiki', *Te Ara – the Encyclopaedia of New Zealand* (1966; updated 26 Sept. 2006), http://www.teara.govt.nz/1966/T/TuhawaikiHone/en (accessed 17 Jan. 2007).

[7] Orepuki cliffs: further west along the coast, gold was found in the black sand in 1865 at Orepuki, and a gemstone beach is nearby.

[8] Papakihau … 'slapped by the wind': Marjory A. Smith in *Orepuki: from Goldfields to Fields of Green* (Waimahaka: M.A. Smith, 2003) defines Aropaki as 'a pathway where the sound of clapping hands is heard'. Another theory is that Orepuki is a corruption of Aropiki, meaning 'cliff washed by high tides'. The connection here between Papakihau and Orepuki has not been verified.

[9] those picnics: annual picnic excursions by train to Bluff, put on by the railways for their employees.

[10] Julia: probably an allusion to one of Davin's sisters, Molly or Evelyn, known for their piety.

[11] Makarewa: 7.5 kilometres inland from Invercargill, home of Davin's grandparents, Nora and Daniel Sullivan. Of Mary Davin's (née Sullivan) four sisters, this probably refers to her younger sister, Annie, who lived with her husband Harry Dooley in Flora Road, Makarewa, before moving to Oteramika. Their brother Dan Sullivan and family also lived at Flora Road. See *IS*, p. 31; 'The Black Stranger'.

[12] Woodlands: an allusion to Mary's sister Ellen Concannon who lived at Woodlands. However, this picnic probably occurred after her death in September 1917 and after the Davin family had moved to Dunedin in 1920.

[13] girl cousins … boys: the Concannon boys, Michael, Pat and Peter, Esmond Dooley who stayed with the Davin family in Invercargill during the week while attending Marist Brothers' School, and his sister Florence, a special friend of Davin. *FW*, p. 22.

[14] Clifton: southernmost district of Invercargill. The train would have passed through Clifton en route to Bluff.

[15] Greenhills: a small community about five kilometres from Bluff near Greenpoint.

[16] old Auntie Wyatt: Nora Davin, married to John Wyatt, had migrated to New Zealand and settled at Greenhills.

[17] She was the one … that: Auntie Wyatt sent back to Ireland the five sovereigns that paid for Patrick Davin's journey out. *FW*, p. 5.

[18] Uncle Jack … Auntie Nellie: probably fictional relatives.

[19] Argyle Park: near Argyle Beach, bordered by Athelney, Gregory and Burroughs streets.

[20] Devil's Pool: now known as Devil's Pond. Situated on Bluff Hill near the reservoir, it is reached by a track at the end of McDougall Street.

[21] oyster sheds: the retail fish and oyster trade began in Bluff in 1884. Bluff oysters were exported to Melbourne and Sydney and kept the town prosperous through the depression of the 1890s.

[22] round the Point: probably Stirling Point, at the end of Marine Parade, off Ward Parade.

[23] supplejacks: woody plant or liane with strong tough stems.

[24] Slope Point: with the same latitude as Dog Island, Slope Point in the Catlins is seventy kilometres east of Invercargill and not easy to identify even with good visibility. It is the southernmost point of New Zealand's South Island.

[25] a gaunt ... Maori: a local tradition. A Bluff resident remembers that in the late 1940s or early 1950s he encountered in the same place the Maori lady Rena Spencer, who expressly forbade the children to mark or damage the land.

[26] an old Maori cemetery: a burial ground uncovered after excavations to build a Senior Citizens Centre in Onslow Street.

[27] tapu: Maori: forbidden or sacred.

[28] Tom's place: a friend of the narrator's father. In *Not Here, Not Now* (pp. 276–7) the hero, Martin Cody, visits Tom Fallon in Bluff with his father who had been at school with him in Galway; they had come out on the same ship together as young men. See 'Late Snow', 'The Black Stranger'.

[29] King Arthur ... back: a sceptical reference to the prophecy with which Malory's *Morte D'Arthur* concludes, that Arthur would one day return from Avalon to rule again. Davin's decision not to return to New Zealand permanently was made about this time; he believed that once severed, the ties to home and nation were unable to be reforged. Towards the end of 'First Flight' the protagonist Ned thinks, 'At least I had been warned by books that you can never go back.'

PART III

Previously Uncollected Stories

Invercargill Boundary

Oh, Conyers Street,[1] there was a time
When you divided the sinful men of town
From the busy men who farmed.
Mr Murray,[2] brave and drunken,
Raced his spring-cart chariot
And his homing mare
Against invisible, fuming, snorting odds.
While we, dreaming like the drips from Rosy's nostrils,
One hand leaning on her dung-scarred flank,
Brought the cows home across the ghost dawn
Metzger Street[3] – gravelled grass between ditches –
A Pompeii that never had been inhabited
And existed only in that Metzger mind
Which once had brooded from Heidelberg Hill.[4]

March 1984

Invercargill Boundary: this previously unpublished poem is in the Daniel Marcus Davin archive in the Alexander Turnbull Library (MS-Group-0319).

NOTES

[1] Conyers Street: before the Davins moved to Morton Road, Conyers Street marked the edge of town – a boundary between the urban and rural worlds of Invercargill.

[2] Mr Murray: Robert Murray, contractor, a neighbour in Conyers Street. See 'Milk Round', 'Goosey's Gallic War' and 'Gardens of Exile'.

[3] Metzger Street: running parallel to and east of Conyers Street, and so outside the town boundary, it came into existence in c. 1912. Sections were auctioned in 1914, but it remained mostly 'gravelled grass'. By 1929, according to Wise's *Directory*, only five houses had been built. On Metzger's Bush see 'Goosey's Gallic War'.

[4] Heidelberg Hill: in Georgetown where St Patrick's Church is now, near the suburb of Heidelberg.

21

Prometheus

JACK PETRIE slumped across the wet wharf-approach, picked his way gingerly in the intricate criss-cross of rail-points and slouched to his place among the others under the shelter. If this drizzle kept up there wouldn't be much work done today. And the Port boat[1] was taking on meat mostly, too. But the weather would probably clear with the turn of the tide.

The town clock struck a doleful winter's morning eight, and the foreman began to call labour.[2] The non-union men crowding forward to catch the foreman's eye drew contemptuous smiles from the sophisticated unionists. Petrie lolled back against the wall, watching them with jaundiced gaze. There was that fellow who biked eighteen miles every morning on the off-chance of a job. Had a wife and kids, so they said, and no work. Petrie as a union man was sure of a job, but he envied that man. He knew why the union had taken him on. Not because he could work, but because he couldn't. His father before him had worked out a wild thirty years on this wharf in the days when there was a fight every night on the foreshore, and when the policeman went home to bed while ships'men and oystermen fought it out. He'd been a good man, too, that father of his, before his feet gave out.

And here was his son, gaunt and useless, racked with his ceaseless cough, an object of contemptuous commiseration. There were times when he cursed his certainty of a job, because it was pity that gave it to him. But mostly he took it and felt lucky to get it.

He was told off to work on number five hatch. As usual the foreman was considering him. The trucks for number five stood over the points and every time there was a shunt[3] the gang had a spell. They would be putting him in the covers gang[4] with the boys and old men next.

By the time the hatch was ready and a rake of trucks alongside the drizzle had gone off, the meat could be handled. It was still bitter cold, and the wind drove up from the wharf through the spaces between sleepers and pierced right into a man, in spite of thick underclothes.

Though the chutes were now ready against the meat wagon, he still had time to kill. There was only room for one man to work at first, and his mate took first turn to 'break down'.[5] Jack smoked and watched morosely. A man was forever killing time in this place.

His cough recalled him to his more immediate miseries. He remembered things. The day before he had noticed for the first time how the men were extra careful to wash the mug at the tap after he'd had a drink. He had overheard them saying he'd been up to Waipiata.[6] Damn them, he envied their caution. He wished it weren't too late for him to take precautions.

The same thing day after day, the same petty reminders, and the same eternal cough. The same drizzly dreary wharf, the same monotonous work and always the same cough. As monotonous as the work of his hands was the onerous daily treadmill of his thoughts. Always to be brooding, and always envying the men who did not even know they had lungs; and worst of all, always to be fretted by a persistent irrational hope.

'Room enough for two, now!' A yell from his mate broke in on his brooding. He climbed awkwardly into the wagon and began. It was even colder in here, and the ice fell heavily from the frozen carcases as he dragged them from their tiers and thrust them one by one into the chute. Two hours of this till ten o'clock. Quarter of an hour's smoko, then at it again till twelve. Home for lunch and dreary argument. Back again till five. Home for tea and more argument, and back again till ten. Day in, day out, the same. He supposed it was lucky the wharf was so busy. And after all it wasn't quite so miserable as sitting at home with an empty wharf and an empty pocket. Or trying to while away the day in the pub, listening to the same yarns and nursing his beer for an hour at a stretch. Friday was the best day. Collect your pay and then off to the pub. But even in the pub he was out of place. For some strange reason the genial obscenities of the others made him uncomfortable. With every drink he seemed to become more unpleasantly aware of the grim shadow between him and his fellows. And he hadn't a stomach like theirs, either. As like as not he would be sick or go out on his back. The last had its consolations.

Up and down the truck, up and down, dragging the cursed mutton over the slippery floor. Strange to be sweating, and yet feel the ice crunch underfoot. An occasional rest for a shunt. His turn to 'break down' and then up and down again, further and further, as they worked back to the ends of the wagon.

His mate was a big Irishman who had been working in the quarries during the slack season. He would carry two sheep sometimes if he thought Petrie was not looking.[7] For in his blunt, rough way he was conscious of Jack's sense of weakness, and would not knowingly force on him its realisation.

Between shunts while they rested in the doorway, swinging their legs, Tom O'Connor smoked an illicit cigarette, listened to the rattle of the winches, and watched the nets of fifty frozen carcases go swinging up, with an interest not apparently dulled by familiarity. Petrie looked at him out of the corner of his eye. Big thighs with the trousers taut across them. Powerful arms folded across a heavy chest. And there was Conaghan, bending over the returned net with his big long bushwhacker's arms,[8] tall and lithe and tireless, full of easy profanity. How difficult was their vitality from his! They lived gloriously because they took living for granted. They were careless and prodigal of life because it was rich in them. They had life and to spare. His vitality he had to hoard feverishly and husband like a miser. He must always conserve his energies, put forth the minimum of effort. And there were those careless powerful men, unthinking and hard-drinking, men on whom monotony had no effect, whose highest ambition was to win an Art Union,[9] and whose greatest joy was to get fighting drunk.

The day dragged through. And as an incessant companion to his cough nagged at him the need for a decision. He could not go on like this. He was engaged to his girl. She was prepared to marry him. Could he marry her? Apart from the uncertain work, could he get married with that cough? He knew he could not. And yet he would. Every time he saw her he meant it to be the last. But he always came back. And sometimes he raved and cursed as he came home. How could he give her up? He damned well couldn't. He wouldn't. He was a pariah in society, though men met him with a smile. Why should he concern himself with them?

Please yourself and please somebody, his mother used to say – she, poor devil, had never pleased anybody, least of all his father. And she was dead – but always he remembered the girl. He couldn't risk passing this on to her. It wasn't fair. Nothing was fair. Something had to be done. Yet he knew nothing would be done. And what was the use of making up your mind to do things? Circumstances arranged everything finally.

It was his mate's turn to break down again. He stood on the wharf's edge and looked up at the vast bulk of ship looming above him. He felt frailer than ever. Clouds scuttled before a sickly moon now, and the huge derricks stuck out from the ship and cut across the sky. Lights shone at intervals down the length of wharf. He saw Banjo Patterson,[10] the hatchman,[11] leaning back over the rail and cursing in voluble cockney at the winchman.

He looked down at the water, swirling in dark oily filth between the ship and the wharf piles. One of the wharf horses, not properly broken, had been frightened by a shunter once and jumped clean into that water. But it had been fished out again. And so would he be if he jumped in. Fished out ignominiously, dripping and sodden. But he wasn't likely to. He was caught in a trap. Couldn't marry because he loved her. Couldn't leave her because he loved her. And even if he could leave her, and leave the poor broken devil of a father whom he kept in food and beer, he knew he was too tenacious of life, however wretched, to do it. There were times when life was good, when the sun shone and the steam rose from the rails; when the strength about him was not the text of his own weakness, and when he did not envy the gulls that swept about the wharf. At such times the powerful men who worked about him, and the strong thrust of the shunter's pistons, and the great wharf horses no longer stung him to the consciousness of his own weakness, but seemed a part of him, and in their strength he shared. For such moments, however rare, life was worth while, and he had weathered worse moods.

Life would drag on, the bad outbalancing always the good. But he would live fiercely, if desperately, with always a decision to be made which he would never make, and problems which he would never have the heart to solve.

He spat over the wharf's edge and returned to the truck. Another hour and they were finished for the night. His mate left the truck and, preparing to follow, Petrie paused for breath in the doorway. The moon struck out from the clouds and outlined the figure of one more lank Christ on yet another Calvary. He coughed and spat. There was a taste of blood.

Prometheus: First published in the Otago University *Review* (Vol. 48, September 1935: 26–9), this short story won the Literary Society's Competition of that year. It draws on Davin's experience of casual holiday work as a wharfie in December 1932, May 1933 and the summers of 1933–4 and 1934–5 (*FW*, pp. 67–8, 81, 91). The title refers to the classical legend of Prometheus, punished by Zeus for his hubris in giving fire to mankind. Prometheus was tormented by an eagle eating his liver, which then renewed itself daily and was eaten again at nightfall. Davin's protagonist, suffering from a progressive illness (TB), endures psychological torment over his questionable future and that of his fiancée: the present impasse from which there is no future release recalls the bondage of Prometheus.

Davin recasts the story in *Not Here, Not Now* (pp. 273–7), switching the point of view from the TB sufferer, Jack Petrie, to that of the novel's hero, university student Martin Cody. Cody helps out his weak offsider on the shift by sometimes carrying two sheep. Cody's father points out that such efficiency might encourage the company to fix new time schedules (p. 276), in contrast to the focus in 'Prometheus' on the plight of Petrie.

NOTES

[1] the Port boat: sheep carcasses arrived at Bluff from the Southland Frozen Meat Company's works at Makarewa, Mataura and Ocean Beach, destined for London.

[2] Jack Petrie ... labour: see *Not Here, Not Now* (p. 273); Cody, like Davin, gets work because his father, a railway wharf foreman, tips him off when there is a glut of shipping (see *FW*, p. 67). Unlike Jack Petrie he is a non-union man.

[3] a shunt: see 'Black Diamond'.

[4] the covers gang: gang in charge of the framework coverings for the hatches. The implication is that these are easier jobs.

[5] 'break down': possibly a term for separating carcasses to be loaded onto ships.

[6] Waipiata: the Waipiata Sanitorium (est. 1914), originally a Maniototo railway camp.

[7] He would carry ... looking: in *Not Here, Not Now* (p. 274), this is the hero Martin Cody helping out the famished, impoverished Hobbs, his offsider on Number Five Hatch.

[8] his ... bushwhacker's arms: see 'The Tree'.

[9] Art Union: a government-regulated lottery run from 1932 until 1961.

[10] Banjo Patterson: 'the nick-name of anyone whose surname is Patterson.' G.A. Wilkes, ed. *Dictionary of Australian Colloquialisms* (Sydney: Sydney University Press, 1978).

[11] the hatchman: watersider who directs the winchman in loading operations.

22

The Albatross

WHEN WE WERE KIDS, me and Colin and Elsie, our old man was farming about three hundred acres a few miles south-east of Otautau,[1] not far from the Aparima, just where it gets ready to go out to sea.[2] Our great hero in those days was Hawk Metzger.[3] He lived in one of the rouseabouts'[4] huts and was a sort of head sherang[5] to our father, who had married late, having waited, I suppose, to have the bush cleared and a reasonable farm in good nick before he'd get spliced[6] and start a family. He was like that, sort of slow and cautious when it came to anything he really thought important. I don't think he paid Hawk much more than his keep and enough for tobacco and an occasional binge in Otautau, but I think he at heart thought of Hawk as a sort of adopted son and relied on him for doing most of the hard grind; and he didn't take many decisions about what to do next on the farm without talking it over first with Hawk. Hawk was a terrific worker and there wasn't anything he didn't know about cattle which was what the old man mainly specialised in just before the Depression, the time when you could still get a decent price for beef and for butterfat both. Hawk could even mend the milking-machine because he somehow understood electricity, just the way he understood cows and horses, and people for that matter.

When Hawk came back after the Great War my old man had built him what was almost a proper house, two living rooms lined with T and G boarding[7] and a window at each end, a lean-to kitchen and wash-house, and corrugated iron roof painted red that the old man swore would keep out the worst winter gales that came blasting in from the Foveaux Strait,[8] more or less straight from the South Pole.

You might think it was odd of the old man to do this. He wasn't a sentimental bloke and there wasn't much money to chuck around anyway but he'd missed Hawk a lot during the war and Hawk had fallen for some pommy sheila while on convalescent leave in London and the general idea was that he'd bring his loving bride to live with him on the farm. Hawk had joined up with the New Zealand infantry when the war started but later had himself transferred to the Royal Flying Corps because he rather liked, so he said, the idea of flying. It was no wonder this sheila had taken him on, for even now, ten years or so later, he was the real cut of a man, just over six feet tall, wide-shouldered but lean below, and with a slightly dark complexion stretched over a hawk-like profile. That's how he got his nickname. The only thing wrong with him was that he'd got hit in a dogfight with a German Fokker[9] and had come out of it the worse for a gammy left arm, though it didn't seem to handicap him much with a sheep-shears or a pitchfork or anything else that needed handling round the farm.

From what we could gather listening in on the grown-ups, it wasn't the damaged arm that bust up the engagement, because he'd got it before he met her. She had come out on a ship later than his to New Zealand and on board had fallen for some other hero. She had written one of those Dear John letters – the sort we got to know about later when our own war came – and that was the last Hawk or anyone else round our gap in the bush[10] ever heard of her. So Hawk had taken against the nice new house and stayed on in the rouseabouts' shack. The new one never got painted and the old man used it for putting up passing swaggers,[11] or a couple of shearers, or anyone else who dropped in – our place was pretty well in the back of beyond and we didn't get many visitors. When we did, they were always on their way somewhere else. Still, I suppose everyone always is.

When us kids gradually pieced together all of this about Hawk from bits of gossip we overheard, I often used to look at him, when I thought he wasn't looking – not so easy because he was the sort of chap who notices everything but usually doesn't let on about it – and I'd try to guess if it made any difference to him and how he felt. I'd never have dared to ask him, of course, and I never did make out how big a knock it had been for him. I was only fourteen or so at that time, mind you, but the old man was fond of saying I was a real deep one, and as I look back I reckon I probably was pretty sharp for my age. I certainly was damned inquisitive.

I could never see any change in Hawk, though. He was always calm and good-natured and he was more tolerant than most men of his age would have been of kids always badgering him to tell us over and over again the story of how he'd shot down the German but nearly didn't make it back to base himself.

Well, I seem to have got a long way from the point, which is really not about Hawk at all but about this albatross that got blown in on to the high ground in one of the early winter storms that plagued the hell out of us and still, I dare say, plague Hawk and my sister Elsie who in the end got married. Colin had been shot down in the RNZAF, and so they took over the old homestead, making sure that the old man till he died had a decent supply of beer and grub, living in the little house that had been meant for Hawk, strange to say, and that Hawk had at last got painted and done up for him. I, of course, had fled the coop long before and came back only very seldom.

Anyhow, this albatross had been forced down in the gale and some of our half-wild Herefords had rushed it. Hawk had spotted it and seen what was happening. He'd dashed off up the hill, with us kids trailing after him, and chased off the cattle. When we caught up with him he was squatting on his haunches rolling a fag and looking at this bloody great bird, which was facing into the wind and towards the sea a good few miles away.

'What is it?' I asked. I'd never seen such a huge, strange bird before – it must have been about four feet from the beak to the tip of the tail.

'An albatross,' he said, and kept on looking at it, rather strangely. 'I've seen them from the troopships during the war,' he went on. 'They used to follow us. The blokes in the crew told us that seagulls were the souls of sailors but the souls of captains became albatrosses.'

Hawk grinned when he told us this and then licked along his cigarette. Looking at the live bird I thought it might be true but I was also remembering, now, having seen a stuffed one in the Invercargill Museum[12] one rainy Sunday a couple of years before. You wouldn't have thought it was the soul of a captain; this one, though, was the same as that stuffed one but different. It was very much alive, for one thing, and it had a fierce, long, hooked, yellowish bill; and the rest of it, except for the almost black wings, was as white as my mother's washing on the line on Mondays. It had sturdy, reddish legs but it didn't seem very happy standing on them. The cattle had damaged its left wing – broken it, we found out later – and it kept trying to lumber out with both wings. In a clumsy, flapping way, it could get the right one moving a bit but the left one wouldn't work at all. I went round to the front of the bird, keeping a safe distance, and looked into its large, dark eyes. I had never seen anything so wild, so remote from anything I'd ever known, steely in a way but a steel that might have been made of the sea. It looked through me as if I wasn't there and as if it was watching something a thousand miles away.

'It's beautiful,' I said, forgetting to feel embarrassed at using a word like that.

Hawk didn't laugh at me. 'Yes,' he said. 'Beautiful. I think it's a Royal Albatross.[13] An admiral[14] perhaps. We'll have to do something about it. We'll have to fix that gammy wing somehow.'

Our two collie dogs started to circle the bird warily, trying to make out what kind of sheep it was, I suppose. 'Get out of that, you bastards,' Hawk shouted at them. I was startled. He didn't usually use words like that in front of us kids, especially Elsie. The dogs were startled, too, they cringed back and lay down watching him. Beyond us and the dogs the cattle stood in a circle, also watching. They were even less used to strangers than we were.

Hawk finished smoking the cigarette he had rolled, threw the wet stub away, and stood up. He put the dogs on to the cattle and drove them down to one of the lower paddocks. Next we helped him get some barbed wire and stakes and we made a four-yard fence round the bird that gave it room to move but would keep the cows out. Then we went back to the homestead to consult the old man.

It turned out he didn't know any more about birds than we did. So we telephoned the local vet, Bob Dodds. He suggested that the Acclimatisation Society[15] might be able to come up with something. And he'd come over himself next day. According to the bloke at the Society, there were some chaps away north on the Otago Peninsula who'd been trying for years to raise a colony of albatrosses.[16] He said he'd get in touch with them and see if they had any advice to give.

Hawk had taken over telephoning: the old man was a bit hard of hearing, always got cross because he thought the bloke at the other end wasn't speaking loud enough, and one way or another used to get everything the wrong way round and lose his temper. Anyway, after all the telephoning, which took most of the rest of the day – party lines, with everyone else listening and even horning in[17] and long distance which wasn't so hot round that time – the upshot was that if we could keep the bird alive for a fortnight or so its wing would probably mend. Albatrosses usually fed on surface fish, they said, and some stuff called krill,[18] but as we weren't in a position to provide the right kind and quantity of fish, we'd better try feeding it with chunks of raw steak – only fair since we had plenty of beef and it was the cattle who'd done the damage in the first place. If the bird got better, they told us, we'd have to take him to some high point over the sea and do our best to encourage him to take off. He'd be all right once he got into the air, because albatrosses were much better at gliding and soaring than ordinary flying and needed the help of winds and waves to get going.

Next morning, as soon as the milking and the separating were done, Hawk took us with him up to where the bird was and I had the tricky job of holding its beak open while Hawk chucked pieces of raw meat down its throttle. After putting up a hell of a struggle at first, it seemed to get the general idea. Then the vet turned up and me and my brother Colin and Hawk held the bird more or less still while the vet fixed a sort of splint gadget on the broken wing. Once the splint was on the bird stopped fighting back and just turned his eyes on to us. Something I'll never forget, those eyes were – and I've seen some pretty weird eyes since then.[19]

I don't suppose Albert – that was the name we gave him – had ever eaten steak before, unless he'd snatched a bite of whale, but he certainly seemed to thrive on what we gave him and he could put away as much as any shearer after a morning's work or any Texas cowboy. Luckily for us kids, since we were crazy about him by now, it was the school holidays and the old man didn't worry how we spent our time as long as we did our share of the milking twice a day and fed the pigs and hens and all that. If it hadn't been for Albert we'd have been out all day after rabbits with the dogs and the ferrets and our Remington .22 rifle. Mum was none too happy about that rifle – she was a worrier and always afraid one of us would get shot or we'd get drowned in the Aparima or fall down a well or something like that. So she was quite pleased that we were spending so much of our time and energy on looking after Albert. We used to squat on our heels and admire his great, proud head and beautiful white body and argue what sort of a captain he had been and whether his wing was getting better or not. One thing you could be sure of – he wasn't settling down for good and he always had that queer look in his eyes as if he were seeing something miles and miles and miles away. It was a look that reminded me sometimes of the look in Hawk's eyes, after we'd had him talking about life in the Flying Corps and drawing quick sketches for us of battles between our fighters and the Germans. He'd go silent suddenly, and refuse to talk any more about the war and pretend to be reading the *Southland Times* or something. But we knew Hawk would never go back to flying, whereas our whole aim in life – Hawk's too – at this time was to get Albert up on his wings and into the air again.

The Acclimatisation Society bloke and the other experts were very much in favour of the same thing and they were always ringing up to ask how Albert – they didn't know we called him Albert – was getting on. They were very pleased indeed when we told them how we'd got him used to feeding on a diet of raw steak, though we didn't tell them what hell's delight it had been, that first time or two, to get his beak open and get the meat far enough down. It was just as well Albert had such a huge appetite and was such a quick learner.

Well, this went on for a couple of weeks or so and Albert began to stagger and totter about in a way he hadn't done before and even though a bit lop-sided still. We used to worry lest he bust his splint and we were always careful to keep the dogs away from him for fear of their driving him to efforts beyond his strength. And Hawk used to feel the wing round the splint every day with his long, brown, muscular hands until the time came when he asked Bob Dodds, the vet, to come out and take a proper look at things. So Bob came and he agreed with Hawk that Albert was just about ready for having a real go at a take-off.

By then the idea of losing him had begun to worry Colin and Elsie and me, because we'd got used to having him as a sort of constant occupation. At first we'd been a bit upset that we could never get anything out of him except that fierce glare. We were rather proud of the way we'd learnt from

Hawk how to get on with all sorts of 'birds, beasts, and fishes' – we were collecting that series of cigarette cards the old man got with every packet in those days. And we used to notice, though we weren't really jealous, that Hawk seemed to be able to get along with Albert better, even if you couldn't say exactly how. Albert's eyes glittered and glared as they had done from the beginning but there was an odd look about Hawk's own eyes often that seemed to have something in common with Albert's. You had the feeling that the two of them had somehow gone everywhere, been everywhere, and would always know what they had to do and wouldn't let anything short of being killed stop them from doing it. And they'd always know when the right time had come to do whatever it might be.

Anyway, whether we liked it or not – and we did and we didn't – we knew from what Hawk and Bob Dodds said that there was no point in putting the day off much longer. So the next Sunday, when they'd decided the wind was blowing the right way and strong enough, out towards the Antarctic, they got out the big farm truck and hitched a trailer behind it with a sort of wooden railing all round that we used sometimes for moving calves or a few sheep. Hawk and the old man and Bob took down a gap in Albert's fence and they carried him, struggling a bit, into the trailer.

Hawk drove, with the old man and Bob in the front seat beside him. Colin and Elsie and me rode in the back, keeping an eye on Albert and the trailer. We drove quite a few miles south-west till we came to some very high cliffs not far from Orepuki,[20] and Hawk took the truck as close as he safely could to the edge.

We all got out and we unhitched the trailer and hauled it even closer to the edge. Then the grown-ups carried Albert out of the trailer and Bob Dodds took off the makeshift splint. Albert didn't put up any sort of a struggle this time: he seemed to have a shrewd idea of what was happening, or so I thought. Then we manoeuvred him like an aircraft till he was facing out to sea and the wind was behind him. We stood back from him and watched and waited for a big gust to come. It came, he got both wings moving and managed to get airborne. We had a bad moment when he seemed to veer downwards on some sort of thermal, I suppose, and his glide kept declining till he settled on the water. He seemed to ride there for a while as if to assure himself that he really was back in both his elements. Then we saw the wind coming hard across the sea and Albert zig-zagged from wave to wave and then rose nobly from the biggest wave and glided, turning into the wind and out of it again. As he flew out to sea he seemed to get smaller and smaller and before long he was out of sight altogether.

None of us kids said anything but I think there were tears in our eyes. I know it was then I thought for the first time I might myself glide away some day magically like that.

'Well,' Hawk said, 'he's made it, he's free.' I felt a grief in his voice that, though he too was free, he had done with gliding and flying for ever.

The Albatross: first published in the *New Zealand Listener*, 2 March 1985.

NOTES

[1] south-east of Otautau: situated at the confluence of the Otautau stream and the Aparima river, Otautau is about forty-eight kilometres north-west of Invercargill.

[2] where it gets ready … sea: the Aparima is one of the main rivers of Southland. It rises in the Takitimu Mountains, and flows 104 kilometres south to enter Foveaux Strait at Riverton. As the distance from Otautau to Riverton, mouth of the Aparima and Pourakino Rivers, is about thirty-two kilometres, this topography is not entirely realistic. The farm's location, south-east of Otautau, is considerably further north from the mouth of the Aparima.

[3] Metzger: Davin's preoccupation with this name (Metzger Street was founded in the late 1920s) is illustrated in the poem 'Invercargill Boundary'.

[4] rouseabouts: general hands or odd-jobbers on a farm. See 'A Happy New Year', 'The Black Stranger'.

[5] head sherang: the boss, person in authority.

[6] get spliced: colloq. for 'get married'.

[7] T and G boarding: Tongue and Groove boarding. See 'A Return'.

[8] Foveaux Strait: sea-way twenty-six kilometres wide which separates the South Island from Stewart Island. See 'Bluff Retrospect'.

[9] a German Fokker: planes designed by the Dutch aviation pioneer, Anthony Fokker (1890–1930), and built for German army during the First World War.

[10] our gap in the bush: our small space, i.e. settlement.

[11] swaggers: itinerant tramps carrying a 'swag'. See 'A Happy New Year', 'The Black Stranger'.

[12] stuffed … Invercargill Museum: there is still today a stuffed albatross in the Southland Museum in Invercargill. See 'Late Snow'.

[13] Royal Albatross: one of the Great Albatrosses (*diomeda*), a black-and-white seabird of which both species – the northern and southern royal – breed in New Zealand. Examples

of the species which now breed at the Taiaroa Heads albatross colony on the Otago peninsula have wing-spans of up to three metres and are capable of speeds of 115 kilometres per hour.

[14] an admiral: possibly a sub-species of the Royal Albatross.

[15] Acclimatisation Society: originally founded in the 1860s in order to import English wildlife to New Zealand, ensuring acclimatisation of the different species, now called Fish and Game New Zealand, with numerous regional branches. Terry Hearn, 'English', *Te Ara – the Encyclopaedia of New Zealand* (Updated 26 Sept. 2006), http://www.teara. govt.nz/NewZealanders/NewZealandPeoples/English/en (accessed 10 Jan. 2007).

[16] Otago … albatrosses: the Taiaroa Heads albatross colony at the tip of the Otago Peninsula is the only mainland breeding colony in the world. Albatrosses landed there between 1914–19, the first egg was sighted in 1920, and the first Taiaroa-reared chick flew out in 1938. The colony has over twenty breeding pairs, some of them hybrids, and is now a renowned ecotourism area.

[17] horning in: butting in, intruding into.

[18] krill: small shrimp-like animals that grow up to six centimetres in length and live about five years. They are an important food source for fish, penguins, seals, whales and some seabird species such as the albatross.

[19] those eyes … weird eyes since then: an allusion to *The Rime of the Ancient Mariner*. See 'Late Snow'.

[20] Orepuki: cliffs overlooking Te Waewae Bay. See 'Bluff Retrospect'

23

Black Diamond

ONE OF THE ODD THINGS, though natural I suppose, about war is that because – or that's how I'd explain it – your future looks somewhat unpromising, you tend to get sudden shocks of memory of the times when you were young and lucky enough to feel secure. I remember how the first time I really noticed, as distinct from seeing, that the New Zealand Division's[1] special sign in the desert was the Black Diamond.[2] The Provo blokes[3] always went ahead of the foremost troops and planted steel or wooden poles with a black diamond-shaped figure on top[4] and as long as you found your way from one of these to the next you knew you weren't too far away from your own chaps. But what struck me this day I'm talking of, when I first really noticed, was how loaded for me personally, in the rather extensive and neglected backyard of my mind, and not too full of blooming lilacs at that, this black diamond sign was. For when I was a kid Black Diamond[5] was the best coal you could get round Southland.[6] Here we were in a waste of sterile sand, but the sign evoked at that moment, in a most sovereign way, memories of a landscape almost unimaginably different in its green, wet expanses, from the perilous and lethal territory, sown only with mines,[7] over which we were now travelling.

Though I had left Southland years before, my recollection of my early life[8] in Gore[9] was intense. Sitting beside my driver in late 1942[10] as we headed towards Tripoli,[11] in my retrospective musings, I used to revert in a large part of my mind to early childhood. I remembered how we thought, my brothers and sisters and I, that grown-ups were a pretty odd lot and it was hard to know what they'd be up to next. Now, of course, I can see that this was because we didn't spend much time working out how their minds worked, and why. Anyway, we simply didn't know enough to understand it all. We did, though, have enough grasp to stop them from stopping us from whatever it was that we might want to do, and stopping them from making us do things we certainly didn't want to do.

The old man wasn't too much of a problem for us. He was a railway guard on small branch lines running out of Gore[12] and he was away most of the time; and when he was at home he spent most of his time down in the back paddock planting spuds or digging them up again, according to the time of the year. Come to think of it, that's what we're all doing, one way or another, but of course I didn't think of it then – just concentrated on keeping out of the way in case he wanted you to lend a hand.

Driving all those hundreds of miles through the Western Desert[13] and beyond, I began to reflect a lot about those days and about my father. He had what you might call a princely memory, an Irish one: he tended to recall disaster – Cromwell, the great Irish famine, the flooding of the Mataura[14] – but he didn't blame anybody but himself. He won't remember now – over eighty[15] if he were still alive and remembering different things or the same things differently. And I haven't the ghost of an idea whether he'd remember as I do those years, about 1918 or 1919, when we were living in the cack-coloured[16] railway house we'd moved to after the big Mataura flood.[17] Well, the facts – however he might have remembered them or might have come to see them – didn't much matter. After all the past is the creation, or the making up or whatever, of those who survive long enough to be the only witnesses of its future, or of the next generation, inexperienced in the facts, who have to devise a past and a present for themselves.

Anyway, however historians might fiddle around with the plasticine of truth, those were hard times in Gore, at least for some of us. My father and mother, at the time I'm speaking about, had only five kids but my mother had begun to bulge a lot – which puzzled us since she ate the least meals because she always served herself last – and she'd begun to spend more time in bed than we could remember. Also our Aunty Mollie[18] had come down from where she lived in Auckland on a visit, bringing her daughter Nora, our cousin, whom we boys didn't like much, though our sisters did.

Keeping the home fires burning,[19] an expression the grown-ups seemed to have a sort of relish for in those years of the Armistice and all that, was a real problem. The way we kids saw it, next to getting porridge and sausages and stuff to eat, keeping warm was the worst problem of the lot, that winter. We'd used up the totara logs our old man had spent his fortnight's holiday cutting out of the bush on the hilly side of the Mataura. We were always competing for who could get his feet first in the kitchen oven or get the best place near the fire in the sitting room. We burnt lignite[20] there mainly, but it needed a bit of decent wood or coal first to get it going and I've never forgotten my fury when I discovered that our Cousin Nora had broken up the wooden chocolate box in which I used to keep my treasures, bits of magazine and *Buffalo Bills*[21] and that sort of thing, and she'd used it to start the fire one morning when I was out milking our half-Jersey half-Shorthorn cow so as to get enough milk for our porridge.

Looking back on it I can't find the heart to blame Nora, however much I remember how I felt. Aunt Mollie was a sort of infatuated mother, having only the one child. Whenever one of us kids looked a bit peaky or went off his food – not often – she'd say to my mother 'Give him malted milk like I gave my Nora.' And when she was cross with Nora about some awful behaviour she'd say 'Black man want Nora', which made us feel at least then on Nora's side since we didn't see much wrong with being wanted by a black man and of course didn't realise that Auntie Molly was using 'black' as a direct translation from the Irish 'Dhu' which took you into quite a different world, that of the 'black stranger'[22] with which my mother used to threaten us as the representative of the outside world, the world outside the light and the family.

The fact remained, though, that the lignite we were having to rely on for the range and the fire was bloody slow and bloody cold. It especially got on the nerves of Auntie Mollie. She felt the cold more than most of us. Though she'd been born and brought up in Southland, she had got used to the cissy, thin-blooded climate of Auckland where she was always telling us about how you could grow lemons and oranges and grapefruit and how her husband, Andy, never had to wear woollen underpants, and all that sort of thing. So it was she who said to my elder brother, John, that us kids ought to get cracking and do something about the cold. John's own way of dealing with the cold was to play football or go exploring into the hills around Gore. So his first reaction was to say 'Go to Hell', or 'Go home to Auckland', except that, being like all of us a well-brought up Catholic child – we went to the Sisters of Mercy School[23] – he probably wouldn't have spoken quite like that. As far as I remember, that winter, Hell, though, didn't seem such a bad sort of place.

On thinking it over, though, John decided that Aunt Mollie was right. He remembered that, down at the shunting yards where the coal trucks came and went, there were bits of coal on both sides of the rails, stuff that had fallen off in the shunting. Good coal at that: Black Diamond from Nightcaps[24] and places further down south. He was a very determined bloke, my brother John, and the following Sunday after Mass he set off to inspect the site and see what catches there might be, inquisitive policemen or railway inspectors or whatever. That night he told me it was worth giving her a go.

His next thing was to get two pairs of old pram wheels from the town dump and then make a kind of trolley out of old apple and tomato boxes. He had a natural feeling for things like nuts and bolts and sprockets and so on and he even managed to make a steering wheel with reins of fencing wire to the front wheels. The only thing he couldn't manage was an engine. Only people like Doctor Pottinger[25] could afford to run a car and John had been looking at it closely – it was an Armstrong-Siddley[26] I seem to remember – in the hope of inventing one for himself on the same model. He had some good opportunities for watching it lately because Doctor Pottinger for some reason and to our vague alarm and sense of self-importance had been coming to our house a lot these last few weeks.

Anyhow, it wasn't like nowadays and John's closest inspection of the town dump didn't produce handy wrecks the way it might nowadays or anything you could cannibalise – not like the Western Desert by 1942 – so John was forced to fall back on the other and easier source of energy, me and my young brother Matt. Luckily Gore was so low-lying in the Mataura valley and the railway yards[27] more or less followed the course of the river so there were no great slopes to climb – and no downward slopes to give us donkey engines[28] relief either. And the railway yards were only a mile away from the house we'd moved to after the big flood.

When he'd at last, like a one-man Swiss Family Robinson, got the damned trolley into a going concern – me and Matt functioning as Man

Fridays, if you'll forgive the confusion[29] – we waited under starter's orders for the next Sunday, and then we hauled and pushed our vehicle along to the shunting yards. Because every grown-up was at church, or at home sleeping Saturday night off, we didn't have to worry about nosey-parkers or sticky-beaks. So all we had to look out for was where the blokes who'd been shunting the rakes[30] of coal-trucks had juddered a bit on the rail points and the jolt had made a few chunks fall down on the track. You got quite good at it after a bit, the way you learnt where was the best place for catching eels in the creeks or crawlies[31] in the flooded gravel pits, or in the flood pools round the Mataura. I must admit, though, that I felt a bit queasy once or twice, when I remembered how Sister Mary Benedict[32] had held up poor Tommy Bates[33] as an awful warning to us when he got drowned in the river because he went swimming on a Sunday instead of going to Sunday School and how Billy Dryden[34] had been struck by lightning for the same reason.

Still, that didn't last long and I don't think we wasted much worry about whether the Devil stoked up Hell with the very best Black Diamond on Sundays. We were more interested in keeping warm on week-days than being fried in Hell for what we'd done on Sundays or Holy Days of Obligation.[35] And, anyhow, Tommy Bates had been a bloody fool for taking a swim in the trickiest part of the Mataura just to show off his breast-stroke and Billy Dryden was in for it anyway because he'd stolen a ham from the Presbytery's larder and was scoffing it under a tree when the lightning struck.

It wasn't too hard to spot the places where the biggest chunks of shiny black coal were and John and I had no great problem manoeuvring our machine into the right bit of territory just alongside a rake of big trucks that, even though they were covered with those large tarpaulins my father used to scrounge sometimes to save himself the trouble of thatching his haystack against the winter, still had a lot of spillage between the lashed-down corners.

It wasn't long before we got the trolley loaded more or less to the top. So then, with John whipping us on, we pushed and pulled her back home. It was a bit tougher, that return trip – it felt like two miles as against the half-mile or so we'd felt it on the way to start with, that morning. We made it all right, though, pretty pleased with ourselves once we'd got there. We dumped the coal behind the wash-house and put a lot of old lignite and other piss-awful scrappy coal in front of our dump, just in case the old man went out there in daylight and happened to notice. We were rather counting on his having been put on a night-shift just about that time. He was always going to and fro from places like Waimea and Hedgehope[36] and had to spend most of the daytime having a kip, with Auntie Mollie bringing him a bit of grub at mealtimes. And he spent a lot of his waking-time talking to our mother in a sort of whisper, obviously not wanting us kids to hear whatever it was. Auntie Mollie herself, being from Auckland, didn't have a clue and I suppose Mum, who seemed to have to spend a lot of time lying down, was too busy wondering what would happen next to be able to spot, as she otherwise would have done, that there didn't seem to be any problem about keeping the coal range and the sitting room fire going.

We thought we'd give it another go the next Sunday but there we made a mistake. The shunters[37] wanted the coal trucks off that track so as to let a big load of gravel get through for a new road they were making towards the Mataura.[38] So the points[39] had been changed and the shunters were working overtime instead of observing the Sabbath. I've an idea that the bloke in the signals box towards the Mataura station had seen what we were up to the previous Sunday and because he was a North of Ireland Proddy Presbyterian dog was out to spoil our doings. I expect he thought we ought to be at Sunday School. Anyway, there we were, John and the other two of us, scrabbling away under the wheels of the coal trucks, going like hell as if it were real diamonds we were after, when, bang, and the whole rake of trucks was suddenly on the move – not very fast, luckily, to start with, but too bloody fast for safety, or at least our safety.

The sort of coal we were getting was nothing to the real coal under the tarpaulins which bulged. The coal these trucks had in them was your real diamond coal, not just black but Ethiopian,[40] glinting and sparkling at every edge and angle. It was real dinkum[41] coal, with corners on it. In fact it was rather queer, now that I look back on it, because it made you want to touch it and yet it wasn't like skin, the way you got the feel of someone else's skin, a good many years later.

This was still in 1919, though, and none of us was old enough to be puzzling about skins except our own and how to save them. And the first forward jolt of the shunting engine at the other end – a cobber of my old man's was driving, I found out later – brought down a huge chunk of Black Diamond, bigger and heavier than a camel's hump, and right on the top of John's back as he was grubbing for smaller lumps underneath.

John was pretty strong for his age, luckily, but it was a heavy wallop he had to take. I was watching from the next track, because I had that awful instinct for seeing when something terrible was about to happen and was always, as I see it now, both an accomplice, or accessory, and witness for the defence. The way it seemed, that moment, he looked as if he was up the creek[42] for good, and I was somehow responsible. Still, people who expect the worst aren't always right, can be feeling disappointed even, and after I'd gaped at him for a bit, useless bastard that I felt, I saw him do a sideways roll. The great hunk of Black Diamond came off his back. He wriggled clear of the moving trucks, back to where the points were.

My next brother, Matt, by this time had seen what was going on from the other siding where the bits of coal weren't too heavy for him. Our eyes met across the sidings, the middle rake of trucks having gone, and his were even more frightened than mine. How would we explain it all to our mother, if he'd been killed, and how would we get on without him? And, anyway, we were completely bushed,[43] not having him to tell us what to do next.

We didn't have to worry for long. The trucks were out of the way and the line was clear, the shunter not seeming to have noticed anything. There was John, on his feet, as good as gold, and carrying in his arms that bloody great chunk of Black Diamond I'd have sworn would have killed anyone else.

'You silly little sod,' he said to me, 'why didn't you tell me the bloody engine was starting up?'

I said nothing back because there didn't seem anything much worth saying. He knew it wasn't my fault and he was only saying what he felt which doesn't necessarily have anything to do with logic or things like that. When you've made a mistake it's natural to try and put the blame on someone else. Young Matt must have felt the way I did, because he just peeled off a few of the smaller lumps from our trolley, to make room for John's huge Black Diamond.

Down south, it got very dark very quickly in the winter. By the time we'd sweated the bloody trolley out of the yard and on the way home, there was something nice about the gas lamps lit in our house, at a distance that didn't seem all that impossible. We'd tried to make John lie down on the top of our load and take it easy but of course he wouldn't have any of that and insisted on dragging instead of pushing the way we were doing.

We did manage, though, to talk him into nipping round the back of the house especially as we could see Dr Pottinger's Buick pull up just after us and him get out carrying a black Gladstone bag. It didn't seem a good idea for us to show ourselves just then, whatever he might be up to.

Cousin Nora spotted us, though, and she said Dr Pottinger had a baby in the Gladstone bag. We weren't much impressed by that story but when I went to the front of the house to make excuses for being so late back, as soon as I got into the front hall I could hear awful noises, moaning and that, and it was my mother's sound I could recognise, and yet the sound of an animal being hurt. So I ran towards the kitchen – we never went into our parents' front bedroom except sometimes exploring when they were both out – and there I found Auntie Mollie with great pots and pans of water boiling on the range and herself running around like a scalded cat.

Just as Matt came in through the back door she seemed to get the idea that we existed and had to be coped with.

'Your mother has just given you a little brother,' she said.

We weren't much worried about little brothers as long as Mum was all right and Aunt Mollie said she was fine now. Then she noticed that John was missing and wanted to know where he was.

'He's bringing in a bucket of coal,' I explained. Then, to distract her, I said, 'What's our new little brother like?'

'He's the jewel of a boy,' Aunt Mollie said. 'Very dark hair, and a lot of it, like your father. Your mother wants to call him Donal Dhu.'

'What's that mean?' I asked her.

'Daniel the black,' she said. 'Like a Black Diamond'.

Black Diamond: the final draft of this story is dated 26 October 1984. It was published in *Islands* 37 (August 1986): 42–4, accepted for broadcast by Radio New Zealand on 1 April 1987, and produced in 1988 (actor Peter Vere Jones). 'Black Diamond' first went to air on National Radio on 1 January 1990 and concert FM on 1 October 1990 (both networks of Radio New Zealand). As the events refer to Davin's childhood in Gore and his experiences during the war, and as the characters resemble members of his family, references have been correlated to his biography.

NOTES

1. New Zealand Division's: Davin was fighting with the 2nd New Zealand Expeditionary Force (2NZEF), of which the Division ('the Div') was its fighting arm.
2. special sign ... Black Diamond: the tactical sign of the NZ Div. after which its trail through the Western Desert was named 'The Diamond Track'. In the Div's campaigns in the Battle of North Africa, during which Hitler and Mussolini suffered a major defeat in Tunisia, the 'black diamond signs marked the axis of our thrust line from the frontier of Egypt to the final battlefield in Tunisia'. B.C. Freyberg, Lieutenant-General commanding 2NZEF, foreword to the *The Diamond Track: from Egypt to Tunisia with the second New Zealand Division, 1942–1943* (Army Board: Wellington, 1945).
3. Provo blokes: military police and traffic control.
4. steel ... diamond-shaped figure on top: diamonds were cut from petrol tins, painted black and mounted on iron standards. See Freyberg, *The Diamond Track*, p. 6.
5. Black Diamond: another name for anthracite, a steel-black coal composed predominantly of carbon, having lost most of its water and gas by natural processes; it has the greatest heating power of all. New Zealand has no true anthracite but a variety of anthracite-like types. See Alan Sherwood and Jock Phillips, 'Coal and Coal Mining', *Te Ara – the Encyclopaedia of New Zealand* (updated 30 Jan. 2007), http://www.teara.govt.nz/EarthSeaAndSky/MineralResources/CoalAndCoalMining/en (accessed 10 Feb. 2007).
6. best coal ... Southland: from mines in the Ohai/Nightcaps area comes a hard, black shiny coal with similar qualities to anthracite.
7. sown ... mines: minefields throughout the desert in the North African campaign (e.g. north of Bir Hachim) meant that the battle of El Alamein was scheduled for a moonlit night, 23 October 1942, so that corridors could be cleared between the belts of German minefields. See Francis de Guignand, *Operation Victory* (London: Hodder, 1947), pp. 115–7, 131–2, 157, maps 20 and 21.
8. early life: from the ages of one to seven. In spring 1914 the family arrived from Makarewa, where Davin was born on 1 September 1913. They returned to Invercargill in spring 1920.
9. Gore: a town and borough of Southland. Gore is bisected by the Mataura River.
10. in late 1942: a reference to the North Africa campaign. Davin had been working in Intelligence for GHQ in Cairo, which was evacuated by the British in June 1942 as Rommel advanced. He was then seconded on 6 October 1942 to J Staff Information Service, being promoted to Captain on 26 October. 'J Squadron' was a new mobile network of reporting centres which gathered and relayed information by wireless direct to the HQ of the Eighth Army. *FW*, pp. 164–5; de Guignand, *Operation Victory*, pp. 144, 146.
11. Tripoli: following the second battle of El Alamein and Montgomery's Allied Offensive from November 1942–3, in which he retook Egypt. After Rommel and the Afrika Korps withdrew, there was a motorised advance (which included J Squadron) from 5 November

across Cyrenaica and Tripolianicia towards Tripoli, which fell to the Allies on 23 January 1943.

12 branch lines … Gore: the Waimea Plains Railway running west to connect with the Kingston Branch in Lumsden, the Waikaka branch which connected with the Main South Line railway from Dunedin to Invercargill (which ran through Gore) in nearby McNab, and the line to Waikaia. See 'The Black Stranger'.

13 the Western Desert: the North African or Egypt-Libya Campaign in the Libyan desert.

14 Cromwell … Mataura: Cromwell's massacre of Irish Confederate troops at the siege of Drogheda in 1649 (see 'Death of a Dog'). The Great Famine was due to the potato shortage in Ireland from 1840–50 during which many Irish emigrated. The river Mataura which runs through Gore has flooded several times, in 1913, 1914, 1917, and 1918. *FW,* pp. 9, 13.

15 over eighty: Davin's father, Patrick, was born in 1878 and died 3 January 1958.

16 cack-coloured: the colour of excrement. In the unpublished story, 'The Unjust and the Loving', this is the house that was moved as 'It used to be in a different street down near the Mataura River'. It was 'a sort of muddy tan' , 'the railway colour … which I did not like'.

17 the Mataura flood: the Davin family temporarily evacuated their railway house, located either in River Street (close to the Mataura River) or more probably in Jacobstown, close to the Waimea Railway line, after the 1918 flood. The family rented another house and sometime later their old house was relocated to Hyde Street (Patrick Davin is listed in Wise's *Directory* for 1920 as 'Shunter' from Hyde Street, Gore). In 'The Unjust and the Loving' Davin writes: 'we were in a rented house on higher ground for a while. Then our old house was jacked up, while we kids watched, on to a flat transporter thing and hauled around the corner to the Main Street. The new section where they put our house fronted on the Main Street … and it was between the road and the railway which ran past our backyard. Dad was a guard on the railways and we used to sit on the corrugated-iron roof of the garden lean-to and wave whenever his train passed on the Dunedin-Invercargill shift.' In this story it is not clear whether the family home is the original railway house which had been moved to Hyde Street or the temporary accommodation.

18 Aunty Mollie: a fictional counterpart to Davin's mother, Mary Sullivan's younger sister, Maggie Gunn (née Sullivan). She is 'Aunty Mag' in 'The Black Stranger'.

19 Keeping … burning: a pun on the title of a popular song from the First World War, with music by Ivor Novello and lyrics by Lena Guilbert Ford.

20 lignite: coal in which plant material can still be readily identified, and which has a relatively low heating capacity. It is mined at Charleston (Buller) and in many parts of Canterbury, Otago, and Southland, including Ohai and Nightcaps.

21 *Buffalo Bills*: Buffalo Bill Stories, a weekly concerning the adventures of Colonel William Cody, aka Buffalo Bill (1846–1917), published by Street and Smith, New York, 1906–10. They were part of the Dime Novels Library (USA) or Penny Dreadfuls (UK). See 'Failed Exorcism'.

22 'black stranger': this term comes from the 'Manichean diction' of the Irish Troubles. See Akenson, *Half the World from Home,* p. 103; 'The Black Stranger'.

23 Sisters of Mercy School: St Mary's Convent School which Davin attended when he turned five. See 'The Black Stranger'.

24 Nightcaps … south: Nightcaps is seventy kilometres northeast of Gore and approximately

ten kilometres west of Ohai, where the major Southland coalfields are located. Approximately four kilometres from Nightcaps at Tinkertown, the mine known as the 'Black Diamond Mine' was being worked out about fifty years ago. This confirms that the name had by then become associated with the region's coal.

25 Doctor Pottinger: a doctor based in Invercargill rather than Gore, whose surgery was located on the corner of Kelvin and Don Streets and who was possibly the Davins' family doctor. See 'Dee Street Plan, 1928–9' in John Meredith Smith, *Southlanders at Heart* (Invercargill: Craig Printing Co. Ltd., 1988).

26 Armstrong-Siddeley: an anachronistic reference. Armstrong-Siddeleys were not produced until the 1930s (on page 262 the car is described as a Buick).

27 railway yards: these covered a large area from Hyde Street intersection to the Gore Bridge, but the freight and locomotive sheds near the shunting yards were located at Mersey Street, close to the main railway station, and not far from where the family were living, which by then was probably in Hyde Street.

28 donkey engines: human, portable engines. See *ODNZE*, s.v. 'donk'.

29 Swiss Family Robinson … confusion: the narrator has mixed up *The Swiss Family Robinson* by Johann Wyss with Daniel Defoe's *Robinson Crusoe*, in which Man Friday appears as Crusoe's servant.

30 shunting the rakes: pushing the rows or series of wagons to connect them to trains.

31 crawlies: children's name for freshwater crayfish. *ODNZE*.

32 Sister Mary Benedict: in 'The Unjust and the Loving' she straps Mick for throwing a stone at Dolly Holmes.

33 Tommy Bates: a school friend, the same age as Davin, who drowned in the Mataura River on 1 November 1923 (*Mataura Ensign*, 1 November 1923: 2). See 'The Black Stranger'.

34 Billy Dryden: possibly a fictional name and incident.

35 Holy Days of Obligation: 'Holidays of Obligation', the days when Roman Catholics are obliged to attend Mass. In Australasia these were all Sundays: 1 January – The Circumcision, Ascension Day; 15 August – the Assumption; 1 November – All Saints; 25 December – Christmas Day.

36 Waimea and Hedgehope: on the Waimea Plains Railway, see 'The Black Stranger'.

37 shunters: involved in the operation of shunting a train from one track to another or from a main track to a siding. Davin's father, Patrick Davin, is identified as a shunter of Hyde Street, Gore, in Wise's *Directory* 1920. See 'Prometheus'.

38 a new road … Mataura: River Road. Known locally as 'The Back Road to Mataura', it runs along the east side of the Mataura River from McNabs. The beginning of River Road would have been a short distance from the railway siding in East Gore; the date it was built has not been ascertained, but it was later than Old Coach Road.

39 points: 'The tapering moveable rail by which vehicles are directed from one line of rail to another'. *OED*.

40 Ethiopian: hyperbole. i.e. densely black.

41 real dinkum: absolutely genuine, first rate. *ODNZE*, s.v. 'dinkum'.

42 up the creek for good: slang for 'in dire, terminal diffculties'.

43 bushed: baffled, bewildered. *ODNZE*.

24

The Black Stranger

WE HAD TO LEAVE PADDY BEHIND at the first railway fence,[1] that Saturday afternoon. He wasn't really old enough to climb over all that barbed wire and stuff, and we reckoned we had a long way to go. We'd had a pretty good feed at dinnertime at half-past twelve sharp, because Mum and Aunt Mag were both mad about punctuality. So were we, except that our bellies were our clocks. Anyway, the fact was that Paddy was only five[2] and he would get tired too soon and make himself a nuisance. He yowled like hell when we left him behind but he couldn't get over the barbed wire by himself and so we cracked on the pace and got out of earshot as fast as possible. We just had to dump everyone and anything that was going to get in our way. This was our great exploration that Ned, my elder brother,[3] and I had been planning for ages and we couldn't take the risk of having Pat on our backs, though he was a good kid otherwise.

Mind you, it wasn't as if we hadn't had enough trouble getting away to begin with. It wasn't so bad dodging Mum, because she had her hands full, her lap full for that matter, with Peter our youngest brother,[4] who was just old enough to blow bubbles when he got at Mum's breast – she didn't know we'd seen – and made a frightful noise if he didn't get at it when he wanted. Thank goodness, he spent most of the time sleeping and pretending he was some kind of Holy Child.

No, the danger wasn't Mum or even the Sacred Infant, but Aunty Mag.[5] She'd come all the way down from Auckland, all-night express through the North Island, and then the ferry across Cook Strait at its roughest, and then the Christchurch-Invercargill express, which dropped her off at Gore, where we were living then. She spent rather a lot of time telling us about the hardships of the journey and how terribly slow Gore was, compared with a great city like Auckland, and how worried she was that her darling daughter, Mona, who'd come along with her and was about my age, might not survive the dangers of the Southland winter and the dampness of the Mataura plain[6] and the flu that was killing everybody off like flies that year of 1919.[7] To be fair, though, she had taken the risk of coming because Mum, her favourite sister, was worn out with having got us all through the flu, Dad included, and having a young baby to look after as well.

She and Dad didn't get along too well. He didn't like all that gabble about Auckland, he couldn't understand why she'd called her daughter Mona – what sort of an Irish name is that for a girl? – and he didn't like the way she was always going on about what good husbands Englishmen were and how considerate her husband Bill was. Looking back, I now see that there was an underground argument going on about birth control and my father was probably resenting implied criticism of his own Catholic Irish ways.

Anyway, Mum was still recovering from the flu, Dad was well again but was away most of the time on railway shifts to Waimea and Hedgehope[8] and places like that. So Aunty Mag ruled the roost and we had to be very careful how to deal with her and young Mona. Aunt Mag had a nasty habit of asking you to go to the grocer's or the butcher's on some message or other, just when you were planning to do something quite different. So we'd planned to sneak off that afternoon with as little fuss as possible and that's why we'd taken Paddy as far as we did.

Mona had nearly wrecked things, though. She wasn't a bad kid, or wouldn't have been a bad kid, if it hadn't been for her mother. Her chief trouble seemed to be that she thought she was a boy, like us, even though we'd all shown each other the differences one night when the grown-ups were still sitting over their last and then next-to-the-last cup of tea. Nobody with eyes in his head could deny that there was something different between her and us when we took our pants off in the bedroom with the door shut, but somehow she wouldn't admit it made any difference and always wanted to do whatever we were doing – except milk the cows – and she wanted to go with us wherever we went.

So she was a blasted nuisance that afternoon when we were setting off on our expedition and she saw we weren't going to take her. She made a frightful hullabaloo, bawling and screeching and crying, until Aunt Mag came in and grabbed her and said, when she went on yelling, 'Black man want Mona, He'll take her up the Chimney.' For some reason that always seemed to work and frightened the kid out of her tantrums. Our own Mum I don't think liked this way of going on much. When we were being pests and she'd had about all she could take from us, she'd say, 'You wait till you go out into the world and have to deal with the black stranger.'[9] I suppose both she and Aunt Mag, though, were really using the Irish word, perhaps not knowing they were, as they did in phrases like 'a black Protestant', 'the black North', and a lot more expressions like that, where they weren't really thinking of colour but of how intensely dark and dangerous some parts of their world might be. I think it may have been just a stronger way of saying 'very', except that you only used it for something you didn't like. When I come to think of it, they used 'dark' on the whole for what they did like – my dark Rosaleen and that sort of thing – and my mother used to call me, when she was in a good mood with me, 'the dark one of the family'. I think she meant that I was thought to be a bit secretive, the 'old-fashioned' way I had of watching people and not saying anything, and she also meant that I had a very dark smooth skin. 'Yellow as a duck's foot', though, was what she said when she was in a bad mood.

Well, there we were at last, Ned and me, Pat's yelling far behind. We felt a bit the way Noah must have done when the rains began to fall and people began to sawney[10] up to him in order to get a ticket on the ark. We'd got across the railway – the one Aunt Mag had come by and the troops coming back from the War – and over the second fence. We were heading south under a long stretch of pine trees in a double row that we knew, from what people said, went all the way as far as the racecourse, territory we'd never explored before. Once I stood on an empty blue egg with freckles, a thrush's egg, and I hoped that the younker[11] had got out of it safely and was now flying overhead somewhere. And there were lots of pine-cones we kept throwing at each other, though they were too light to hit you hard. It was great getting away at last from the house and the kids and Aunt Mag saying to my mother, who never seemed to have the time nowadays for Ned or me, 'Give him malted milk, like I gave my Mona.' My Aunt Mag knew the answer to everything and, though we were only kids, we could tell by the way Mum smiled and said, 'Yes, Mag,' that she didn't believe a word of it.

Well, there we were and, in spite of our running up and down and chucking the pine cones, believe you me it was cold, bloody cold. The day was bright with the brightness of a Southland white frost. There was no darkness in it at all and no wind. Only the blue sky and the sun that had no heat in it. Jesus it was cold. We hadn't really noticed until we'd got over the two barbed-wire fences, either side of the railway but, now we'd run out of pine cones, we looked at each other and blew on our fingernails. It was September already but the Southland winter didn't let go easily and this was a real stinker of a frost. You could still see it lying on the shady side of the gorse hedges and every patch where the sun hadn't been able to reach it. And if you went out from under the pine trees into the open paddock the grass crunched under your feet like fresh lettuce from Dad's garden.

Of course, we hadn't brought our overcoats – it would have attracted too much attention when we were escaping from Aunt Mag and, besides, it would have made us look like softies. Explorers don't like to look like softies. Even so, though, when we stopped, there under the pine trees and feeling so cold, Ned and I looked at each other. If he'd said, 'It's too bloody cold, to hell with it, we'll go home, come on,' I'd have been glad to say, 'Yes, we're mad, I want to go home.' But all Ned did was look at his nails and knuckles and blow on them to keep off chilblains. Then he said, 'I'll race you to that macrocarpa.'

He won, of course. He was two years older than I was, after all, and I'm not sure whether it was on purpose or by accident that I found an old blackbird's nest that slowed me up just at the last. The race warmed us up, though, and by the time we'd climbed a few trees and had another race – Ned won that one, too – we'd forgotten how cold it was. So we kept pushing on, in a snakes and ladders sort of way, but what was really driving us was that Ned had some maggot in his head about finding a treasure. Anyone with any sense would have known that you didn't find treasures in Southland but Ned had been reading the Tusitala edition of Robert Louis Stevenson[12] that he'd won as a school prize. And, though

I didn't believe in treasure in those days, I always seemed somehow to go along with people who did. Nowadays, of course, nobody my age believes in treasure and so there's no one to go along with.

After a bit more slogging it out under the pines, we came to a little creek that, if it lived long enough, would feed into the Mataura River. The ice was mostly melted so we forgot about treasure for a while and tried to catch cockabullies[13] instead. I couldn't keep my mind on the cockabullies because I kept thinking of my friend from the Sisters of Mercy Convent,[14] Tommy Bates. He'd been drowned in the Mataura[15] three weeks before our expedition: the nuns said it was because he'd gone fishing instead of to Sunday School. I was a bit doubtful about that: the Kenny brothers had broken into Father O'Neill's[16] presbytery, stolen his Sunday lunch of cold roast lamb and his whisky, and were caught by him that afternoon drunk on the school roundabout and swings. He'd whipped them with a horsewhip but they didn't die of it. They hadn't been drowned in the Mataura. So what about poor Tommy Bates? Well, puzzling about all this, I saw Tommy's eyes looking back at me through a sort of skim of icy water and I could hear him say: 'Why pick on me? I bet you didn't go to Sunday School either.' And of course he was right.

Ned didn't like not succeeding in whatever he did and so he said it was plain stupid what we were doing. Anyway, what would we do with the cockabullies even if we did catch them? You couldn't eat them. So we pushed on and there was a big paddock to the left of us with poplar trees like soldiers in a line down to the creek behind us. Here and there in the paddock there were some miserable-looking cabbage trees. Whoever burnt off the original native bush must have left them there, the way the Spaniards might have spared one or two ancient Inca ruins. I suggested this to Ned but he said, after thinking gravely for a while, 'No, I bet they didn't.'

On the far side of the paddock, under the sunny side of a gorse hedge, there were a lot of heavy ewes that someone must have brought down from the high ground, the Catlins or the Hokonuis[17] perhaps, so they'd be on good flat grass for the lambing. And, sure enough, there were a few lambs here and there, scampering in the thick Southland grass, and bouncing as if their skinny legs were on corks.

'That's a black one,' Ned said, as if I hadn't noticed. This black one had got hold of his poor mum by one of her tits and was properly doing her over. His brother or sister, or whatever it was but it was white, looked on for a while as if it were bellyaching 'My turn'. But the black one paid no attention to that. 'He's going to get on in life,' Ned said. 'It'll get him to the meatworks all the sooner,' something in my nature made me say. 'In time for Christmas!' So we laughed and went on.

I reckon we must have walked two or three miles by then – well, two miles, say. Ned had a theory that if we walked far enough we'd come to a creek that had not just cockabullies and minnows but real rainbow trout. And, what's more, we could pan for gold. He said they were called rainbow trout because they spent their lives swimming in the gold that came down from the Takitimus or the Hokonuis,[18] I forget which, and anyway, because I privately thought it was all fairy gold, I didn't much worry. I don't know how it is, but when people, especially your own family, go in for imagining things and keep themselves going because they think they're going to get to the end of the rainbow, I always feel I have to look as if I'm going along with them. Even though I know, though I don't know how I know, that there isn't any rainbow. And what the hell would you do with that pot of gold anyway? Still, I could see they wanted someone outside themselves to believe in rainbows and trout and pots of gold and that Southland would win the Ranfurly Shield from Otago and Dad would win on his ticket to Tattersalls[19] and take us all home to Galway[20] where he'd come from. I don't know why I never felt any of these things were going to happen, it must have been just my nature; but I was an obliging sort of joker – when I was six or seven, I mean – so I did my best to look as if I went along.

Well, on we went, and things were getting a bit monotonous and there was a sort of sharpness about the air that even began to get at the lobes of your ears. Once a rabbit flittered her bum and her cheeky wee tail and two bunnies raced with her into the gorse hedge, one yellow and the other black. No wonder the bloody rabbits were the curse of New Zealand, the way they could breed right through the winter, and couldn't care less what colour their babies were. After that, I found a dead seagull. At first I thought it was the Holy Ghost, its wings were so beautifully folded, but then I remembered not to be superstitious. It took us quite a while, with only our pocket-knives Dad had given us last Christmas, to give the poor bird a decent burial but we got it under the ground in the end, safe from the hawks and the blue-bottles. We put a pyre of pine needles on top but we decided not to light it but just leave it as it was.

Then we came to a wooden gate – not just an ordinary barbed-wire Taranaki gate but a real one with five bars and two cross bars and lichen growing all over. It must have been there before the railway went through because it opened onto the railway just as if the line weren't there. It was like an old man who'd got somewhere first and was still there but no use any more, just staring at whatever passed by.

So we by-passed that gate and the next thing was that there, in front of us, at the head of the big paddock, was a big, two-storeyed building. It was like a picture out of the *Boy's Own Paper*[21] or *Chums*,[22] except for the weather-boarding and the corrugated-iron roof. It was a real big stables.

Apart from being leery of something we'd never seen before except in pictures, we were suspicious that there might be all sorts of racing people about. Still, the only horse we could see was a tired-looking old mare, not up to the shafts any more, let alone a racing sulky. She stood freezing in a resigned sort of way in the only bit of the paddock where the late afternoon sun could get through to her. We looked around for stallions but there weren't any. The mare wouldn't have been in danger even if there had been. It was obvious that the stables were no more meant for her than she was for them. Come to that, there wasn't much sign of life in the stables either.

We were very careful, though, the way we came at the place, in a sideways sort of fashion, stopping behind each tree like Redskins and peering forwards and around, looking and listening the way the signs at railway crossings told you to. No sight or sign of any human beings. No dogs either, which was strange because there are always dogs around stables. Round the front there were a few huddled ewes, ewes that hadn't lambed yet, lying with their knees knuckled up under their throats and looking out at the world without seeing anything, the way those stupid bloody sheep always do. I suppose, like cabbages, they were quite satisfied with what was going on inside. Perhaps it was just as well for them that they couldn't see what we could see. Perhaps if we could see far enough we weren't all that different.

Then Ned said, 'I reckon she's safe.' So we ran across the open gap – it was at least twenty yards – till we got to the front half-door of the stable, where once a horse would have been poking his head out. The door had a padlock on it but it was only a rusty bluff. Ned wrenched it from the chain without any bother. Even the sheep didn't do more than lift their champing heads and gaze on us with their green, serene eyes as we quickly, backwardly glancing to see we hadn't been spotted, got ourselves inside.

It took us a minute to get used to the dusk when the door was closed but there was damn-all to see, anyway. And it was as cold as hell because the frost hadn't lifted all day in here, the stables being in a shelter-belt of macrocarpas and pines that hadn't been cut back or meddled with in their whole lifetime. When we got used to the half-dark we saw that the ground floor had been used lately by cows for a shed during the winter at its worst, and we had to watch out where we put our feet. But there was a step-ladder against the inner wall and we could see it led to a trapdoor in the ceiling. Otherwise there was nothing but a row of stalls for horses, though there wasn't even a smell of horsedung and you could feel that the horses were gone for ever and the whole place was done for.

We looked at the ladder and the trapdoor and we looked at each other. Ned was very quiet and still for that moment. I could feel the excitement coming out of him, like heat from a red-pine fire. I didn't know where I was, so to speak, but I knew that he had somehow got me into some deep dream of his own mind and that neither of us knew the plot but that he would insist on going through with the action, whatever it was.

Then he nodded, to himself not me. He pushed me aside – as if I were going to be such a bloody fool as to try and get up the ladder first. I watched the gristle on the back of his legs, each side behind the knees, stretch and relax with every upward step he made, and the way his calves bulged and slackened inside the elastic garters that kept his stockings up. I was following him at a distance just safe enough to keep out of the way of his heels and his hob-nailed boots and I was to dodge if a rung broke and he fell. But nothing broke and, as I looked up, I saw first his top half and then the rest go through the trapdoor and disappear. So I stopped for a second and listened in case anything went wrong.

I heard nothing, so I went up the rest of the ladder and got myself through the trapdoor. I took a quick glance around, just enough to see the place was as bare as a baby's bum, except for one corner, the one near the only window, that in the old days had been the way they hoisted up the tucker for the horses. It wasn't just the bit of frosty light that managed to get through the cobwebs, or Ned's fixed stare, that drew my eyes. On the floor, under the window, there was a sort of shakedown[23] – you know, the kind of lair you associate with rouseabouts[24] in the shearing season, or tramps and swaggers[25] and sundowners[26] in bad times. We had a lot of them in that year just after the War ended and the men came back and started drifting, I suppose because they'd got out of the habit of living in one place or just liked being their own bosses for a change. Anyway, at the bottom of this shakedown there was an old cow-cover, with the tartan woolly part upwards and the canvas underneath. Alongside but thrown off, it looked like, was some kind of overcoat without buttons, dyed black it was, but now the khaki was showing beneath the dye.

'It's Uncle Tom,' Ned said, lifting his eyes away from the floor and looking at me with those clear blue eyes.

I knew he didn't mean our real Uncle Tom, who was running a pub in Wellington, and used to come down for Christmas and have wrestles with Dad, his elder brother.[27] Then I realised that on the top of that heap of stuff there was a man's body. I hadn't spotted it at first, because the great thing about people's bodies is that they're always moving even when they think they aren't. So it was the deadness that really struck me. At first I thought that the kind of stiffness you felt in him, even without touching him, might be that he was just freezing cold. Perhaps he was; but he was dead all the same. It was only then I noticed his face and hands were the colour of milk chocolate and there was a frizzy greyness on his head. I'd never thought before that black men could have white hair. Come to think of it, though, old Tom was the only real black man I'd ever seen. And I recognised him and knew what Ned meant.

Ned meant he was the black man who used to come down our street in Gore that last winter, trying to sell my mother some stuff called Bulldog Glue or Monkey Brand Shoe Polish, where the ads showed a monkey admiring himself in the looking-glass of a frying-pan. My mother always said that she'd rather stick to the little money she already had and would sooner use elbow grease to make things shine. All the same, she used to give him whatever was going, a plate of soup or a pig's trotter or something like that. And she would make him sit down with her in the kitchen while he ate it and would tell us kids to get out of the way and stop staring, because it was bad manners to stare.

Afterwards, when he'd gone, she would satisfy her worrying conscience by running him down a bit. 'He's a bit of a blatherskite,[28] you know, full of soft sawder,[29] very suave. Thinks he can get round me by calling me Madam and thanking me for not calling him Sambo. Which reminds me, Ned, you mustn't call him Uncle Tom just because you've been reading that book.[30] Anyway the poor man fought in France with them Yanks and little thanks he's got for it, having to walk the roads of a far-off country in the bitter winter and beg for a living from the black stranger.'

This way, she was defending herself from Aunt Mag who, given half a chance, would have said there was no sense, when you didn't have much to come and go on, doling out to wasters, especially black wasters from the devil knew where. Luckily Aunt Mag didn't know that the pig's trotter Mum had given the poor bloke was one she'd been saving for when Dad came home. And, in spite of Aunt Mag, though she didn't bother to argue, Mum wouldn't be tormented at night by the thought of that poor man along the road in the black winter night and nothing in his swag to eat and keep out the bite of the frost in the bitter small hours.

And it had been like that, the last time we saw him, on a Saturday when we were home from school and he was wrapping up whatever Mum had given him in a big red handkerchief, and he put on a big black hat he had and then took it off again with a great princely flourish and said, 'You are a queen, Madam, a royal queen.' 'Get along with you now,' Mum said, 'you and all your fine talk.' But after he'd gone and she was resting for a while beside the hot range where our dinner was getting ready, she said to Aunt Mag: 'I wonder if he knew our mother was an O'Connor[31] and we were kings and queens, long before Black Bess and Cromwell,[32] that was.'

Aunt Mag said, 'Of course he didn't know. And, true or not, it's no time for that nonsense now.'

But my mother was on a different tack by then. 'Poor fellow,' she said, 'how could he know? You see, he doesn't even know he's black.' And I could tell that somewhere in her she had been stirred by that rich Old Man River voice.[33]

And now, we stood on the floor of the stable, near a spilt heap of chaff, the great black hat on top of it, and the dirty old shakedown of a bed. There was an old black pipe with the tobacco ashes spilling out of it just out of reach of where it might have started a fire. And Uncle Tom was lying, a spilt man, like a sack of oats that had been dropped and burst. He was still in the scuffed-out old blue suit and a shirt I recognised as my father's that Mum must have given him. His shoes were on either side of the shakedown where he must have kicked them off. He was lying on his back, his eyes glazed over like a dead rabbit's, the life gone out of them, and staring up at the roof where the sparrows, now they'd got used to us, were bundling about and trying to jump on each other as if they'd had some special message that winter was as good as over, and they'd better get their nests into proper shape before the starlings got in before them and grabbed everything.

I didn't want to but I couldn't help looking down again at the dead man. I saw his hair was white and frizzy at the sides and his white eyebrows. His mouth was gawping open a bit.

'Heavenly Powers,' I said. 'Jesus, Mary and Joseph save us.'

Ned looked at me as if I'd gone mad. But, of course, I was only saying what Mum would have said. Ned dropped to it at once and there was no need for me to explain. And I didn't ask, 'What'll we do now?' because I knew that if there were any way of handling the fix we were in he'd find it.

He stood there thinking for a minute. Then he went over to the body and, as if he were doing a thing that something inside you tells you to do, the way a thrush builds a nest or a dog buries a bone, he pushed up the man's jaw and so closed the mouth and then pulled down his upper eyelids and closed off that dreadful glazed stare. I felt he was saying to the man, 'Now you don't have to look outward any more.'

He straightened up again and said, without looking at me, 'We'll have to search him.' Just about the last thing I'd have thought of, let alone wanted to do.

'Have we got to?' I asked. The late Southland afternoon was dying and I was cold. But I knew, while the air was still blue with my breath, that I was wasting my time.

'Of course we've got to.' Ned stuck out his chin and went over to the body again and went through the poor old fellow's coat pockets, jacket pockets and trouser pockets. He even hefted the stiff body up a bit and onto one side so as to get at the hip pocket. There was bugger-all to be found, of course – a hole in the lining of one trouser pocket when Ned pulled it out to make sure; a dirty hanky – the red one I remembered him wearing round his neck instead of a tie – and a half-crown in the other. That was it. Nothing in the hip pocket at all. And nothing in the pockets of the old waistcoat we found beside the bed, except a dirty old comb with a lot of teeth missing.

I didn't want to be there any more. The air was full of the frost, today's and the one on the way. It was very cold. Even my feet were cold and that didn't often happen, in those days. It would soon be dark. Inside the stable it was nearly dark already. Ned looked down on the body, when he'd finished his search, and I began to think to myself what a queer word 'body' was. Somehow it was as if we were sneaking a read of our parents' Sunday copy of *Truth*.

Ned, without looking at his hands, was chucking the half-crown from his right hand to his left and then back again.

'I reckon the poor old sod is done for,' he said.

'I reckon he is,' I said. 'So what'll we do?'

Naturally, Ned had already decided that. 'We'll smartly get back home, as fast as we can lick.[34] We've still got the blasted cows to milk, remember. We'll tell Mum as quietly as we can, with that Mona and Mag on our backs. And we'll get Aunt Mag to nip over to Mrs McGibbon's and tell the police.'

'What about the half-crown?'

'I reckon I'll just hang on to it for the time being.' I didn't say it but it crossed my mind that he might have been thinking of it as a bit of the treasure we'd set off to find that day. Anyway, he put the half-crown into the hip pocket of his shorts. He was very proud of those shorts, good dark-blue serge and a size too big for him so that he could grow into them. They were real quality serge because my mother, who hated having to buy clothes, always said it paid in the long run to buy the best. I was still wearing shorts that she'd made herself out of an old suit of Aunt Mag's, and they had a patch instead of a fly with buttons like Ned's and there was no hip pocket. But when Mum saw me thinking that when Ned got too big for his she could hand them down to me, she got soft the way she sometimes did and said she'd give me a real shop-bought pair like Ned's for my next birthday – though it was still nearly a year away.

We belted back at a pretty fast clip because we were none too sure, not having a watch, what the time was. No looking at old bird's nests now or having fun with pine-cones. We had to be back by five at the latest, because that was milking time, but we knew we weren't far out because the 4.30 ballast train[35] to Waimea hadn't gone through yet. Still, the dusk closed in behind us every step we took, like a dying ghost.

There was nobody in the kitchen and we went bursting into Mum's room. She was lying on her bed and she had her breast out and the baby was sucking it. Aunt Mag was in one of the chairs and looking as if she'd rather like to have a baby sucking at herself. And Mona was in the other chair watching Mum and the baby with fascination.

Mum quickly put back her dress over her front and said, 'How dare you boys come busting in like this?' I think she was blushing. And the baby was red with rage. And Mona, I could see, was laughing at us because we were boys and not supposed to know about these things. Aunt Mag just looked as if nothing like this would ever have been allowed to happen in her house in Auckland. I don't suppose it would have, because she only had the one daughter then, anyway.

Even Ned saw we were in a sticky position and so we raced out into the kitchen again. After a bit, the baby had stopped making a bloody awful noise and Mum and Aunt Mag came in and Mona sneaking behind them, still laughing at us, I could see, in a prim, girly sort of way.

Then we told them all about it. Or at least Ned did. It wouldn't be any good to have two versions of the same story and, besides, I always preferred watching.

'Oh,' Aunt Mag said, 'I can't believe it. Dead men and all that. It's more like Auckland, not Gore.' I think it was then that I understood why Aunt Mag had left my grandparents' farm in Makarewa, years ago and before I was born. Their photographs hung on either side of the fireplace in the sitting-room and they looked as if they would never forgive anybody anything.[36] When we were saying the family Rosary at night I always tried not to look at them. But they were always looking at me. Anyway, when Aunt Mag got so excited about a dead body I saw why she'd had to get away and gone right up into the far North, to Auckland, to seek her fortune. This was the first time she'd ever come back, and the nearest to Makarewa, I found out much later, though I felt it then. She hadn't dared to bring her husband with her, though Grandad and Grandma were forty miles away from Gore.[37] She'd married a Protestant, whose father and mother had been English. Even Dad didn't like that much but if she thought she was being criticised she'd say before anyone actually said anything, 'Even the black stranger Mum cursed me with when I went out to service was better than the sawney[38] Irishmen from Galway that we used to meet, drunk, at the Bachelors' Ball in Makarewa. They all wore blue suits with slanting pockets and tan boots and they couldn't dance the Canadian schottische,[39] only some queer hopping around of their own.'

We didn't have a telephone in those days – we didn't even have electric light, come to that, or gas. Dad used to be an expert at fiddling with the oil lamps and all that but he didn't see why people needed anything else, let alone gadgets that gave women a chance to keep on gabbing even when they were by themselves. Aunt Mag was a real bustler,[40] though, just like an Australian or even an American. First she and Mum, without Mona this time, went back into the bedroom, where they were surrounded by all those holy pictures, the Holy Family, the Sacred Heart and all that. I expect Mum was quite glad for Aunt Mag's sake that there was some 'news' for a change – in New Zealand when we were kids everyone always seemed to be longing for something to happen, preferably frightful and to someone else.

The upshot of their consultation was that Aunt Mag went bustling over the Main Street to Mrs McGibbon's where there was a telephone. Apart from Mum not being very well, it was better for Aunt Mag to go, because, according to her anyway, nearly everyone in Auckland had a telephone. Mona skited that she quite often used to ring up people herself, but we were none too sure we believed her.

By this time, Ned and I had begun to wish Dad was home but he was away on the night shift to Waimea[41] that week and, even if he did get back, he wouldn't get away from the railway shed till very late. If he'd been there he'd have somehow or other calmed down all the fuss. He didn't go much for Aunt Mag's way of making a sensation out of everything and, when he was around, Mum didn't seem to be so up and down with us kids or getting herself into a mad fuss about nothing. Besides, if he'd been there we'd have felt a bit less frightened by the idea of police coming. And he'd have given us a hand with the milking as well.

Anyway, what with one thing and another, and Mrs McGibbon coming back with Aunt Mag and a present of parsnip wine in case she and the wine might come in useful, there was a great kerfuffle and Aunt Mag even got it into her head that Ned and me and Pat should go to bed early, after tea. But Ned pointed out that we still had the cows to milk, unless she and Mona wanted to milk them instead. So we had no more of that nonsense. But the baby had started howling again by then and Mum said Ned shouldn't talk that way to his Aunty and we'd know better how to behave when we grew up and, instead of our own loving family, had to deal with the black stranger, the way she and Aunt Mag had to do when they went out to service.[42] But Ned and I had heard all that stuff before and we just thought it was lucky that Mrs McGibbon was there and so we didn't have to hear Mum shouting in that voice of hers that you hear streets away, when she was scolding us. Anyway, we knew we held the trumps because who else was going to go out and milk the cows?

So, in the end, it turned out that the poor old black man had felt the flu coming on and had holed up in the disused stables, all by himself, poor sod, and he'd curled up there and died. Later on, when Dad came in earlier than he'd been expected, Mum kept worrying to him that perhaps if she'd known and taken the black man in he mightn't have died. But Dad just said, 'Don't be a bloody fool, Mary. We've only just come through the flu ourselves, thank Heaven. We've got five kids and another one on the way.[43] What would we want with a poor old black stranger who was bound to die anyway? And what would we have done with him if he didn't die?'

When we got back from the milking we knew the police were there, because we could see their big Raleigh bicycles leaning against our fence. Ned insisted on telling them about the half-crown. It didn't do any harm, though. They gave him a reward of five bob for his honesty and he gave me half. The paper next day had a long story about it, which was very nice for Aunt Mag. She and Mum, the two of them, the day Aunt Mag and Mona left for Auckland, kept gabbing on about our real Uncle Tom, my father's brother. 'Poor silly man, he's married that girl, and though she's a good Catholic, God be praised, she comes from the black North!' We knew by now they didn't mean the North Island.

And then Mum said, 'And that poor old black man, dying there all by himself, not even the black stranger to help him or a priest to confess to, no kith or kin, just like a lonely Protestant.'

The Black Stranger: first published in the *New Zealand Listener*, August 29, 1987. Some correspondences between these characters and members of the Davin family are noted.

NOTES

1. railway fence: this story is set after the great flood of the Mataura River on 25 June 1918 (see 'Black Diamond'). The family were living in a railway house on the corner of Hyde Street and Main Street, which fronted onto Main Street, 'between the road and the railway which ran just past our backyard' (from the unpublished story 'The Unjust and the Loving').

2. Paddy ... five: corresponds to Davin's brother Martin, younger than him by one year.

3. Ned: corresponds to the oldest of the Davin boys, Thomas Patrick, born 7 May 1911.

4. Peter: corresponds to the baby named Daniel Dhu in 'Black Diamond', a fictional counterpart to the youngest Davin, Patrick, born 15 September 1917.

5. Aunty Mag: corresponds to Aunt Mollie in 'Black Diamond', a fictional counterpart to Davin's aunt, his mother's younger sister, Maggie Sullivan, who married a Jack Gunn and moved from Makarewa to Auckland.

6. the Mataura plain: the plains of the Mataura river and its tributary the Waimea, stretching northeast of Invercargill, inland as far as Gore.

7. the flu ... 1919: the Asian flu pandemic brought to New Zealand by the soldiers returning from war. Ovenden (*FW*, p. 14) reports that the entire family came down with it.

8. Waimea ... Hedgehope: the Waimea Plains Branch Railway running northwest from Gore to Lumsden (fifty-nine kilometres away), a secondary railway line to the Main South Line from Christchurch-Dunedin-Invercargill that ran through Gore. Other branch lines from Gore went to Waikaia and Waikaka. The Hedgehope branch (also known as Browns Branch) was a branch line railway which connected with the national rail network in Winton on the Kingston branch. Hedgehope is forty-two kilometres west from Gore. At that time, to get there from Gore via Winton required a detour through Invercargill or Lumsden.

9. the black stranger: these terms come from the 'Manichean diction' of the Irish Troubles. See Akenson, *Half the World from Home*, p. 103; 'Black Diamond'.

10 sawney: approach solicitously, sidle up to, wheedle. See also n. 39.

11 younker: youngster, young bird.

12 the Tusitala … Stevenson: the most popular collection of Stevenson's works, published in thirty-five volumes by Heinemann in 1923–4. Possibly a reference to *Treasure Island* (1923).

13 cockabullies: small freshwater fishes. *ODNZE*.

14 Sisters of Mercy Convent: St Mary's Convent School on Ardwick Street. Davin began attending on 1 September 1918 with his older brother Tom and sisters, Evelyn and Molly. See 'Black Diamond'.

15 Tommy Bates … Mataura: Dan's classmate from kindergarten days who drowned in the Mataura aged ten in 1923. See 'Black Diamond'; *FW*, pp. 14, 361.

16 Father O'Neill's: in 1969 Davin made enquiries of the borough librarian of Gore about this incident, and was told the priest's name was Father O'Donnell. *FW*, p. 361.

17 the Catlins or the Hokonuis perhaps: the Catlins, a hilly region on the coast east from Bluff, is too far distant; but sheep could have been moved down from the Hokonui Hills, four miles northwest and east of Gore.

18 the Takitimus or Hokonuis: the Hokonui hills are one source of Gore's rivers and creeks, but not the Takitimu mountains, a distant mountain range about ninety-six kilometres to the northwest of Gore, east of Fiordland.

19 ticket to Tattersalls: Victorian lottery/gaming company, the main lottery in Victoria, Northern Territory, Australian Capital Territory and Tasmania from c. 1895.

20 Galway: Patrick Davin had migrated to New Zealand around the turn of the century from Tonagarraun, a townland about twelve kilometres north of Galway. See 'Late Snow'; 'Bluff Retrospect'.

21 *Boy's Own Paper*: see 'Saturday Night'.

22 *Chums*: a weekly illustrated paper for boys, published from 1892–1934.

23 shakedown: any makeshift bed, especially one made up on the floor.

24 rouseabout: general hand, odd-jobber. *ODNZE*. See 'A Happy New Year', 'The Albatross'.

25 swaggers: itinerant labourer carrying a swag. *ODNZE*. See 'A Happy New Year'.

26 sundowners: swagmen who arrive at a homestead at night for shelter, too late for work.

27 Uncle Tom … brother: the much younger brother of Patrick Davin. According to Wise's *Directory* of 1929, J.T. Davin was running the Railway Hotel in Lower Hutt, and by the 1930s a public house at Opunake in Taranaki. *FW*, pp. 3–4, 69, 97.

28 blatherskite: boaster, blowhard.

29 soft sawder: flattery, blarney.

30 reading that book: i.e. *Uncle Tom's Cabin* by Harriet Beecher Stowe (1852).

31 our mother … O'Connor: the maiden name of Nora Sullivan, Davin's maternal grandmother. She married Daniel Sullivan and they emigrated from Cork on the *Cory Castle* in 1874. O'Connor was the name of the ancient kings of Ireland.

32 Black Bess and Cromwell: another reference to the siege and massacre at Drogheda in 1649. Cromwell sold the survivors, and the children of those Catholics whose land he confiscated, as slaves to the sugar plantations at Barbados, such as the Black Bess Plantation, the first Banyan Tree resort in the Caribbean.

33 Old Man River voice: an allusion to 'Ol' Man River', a song composed by Oscar Hammerstein, in the 1927 musical *Show Boat*, of which the most famous version is Paul Robeson's.

[34] as fast ... lick: at top speed. See 'at the lick of their lives', 'Goosey's Gallic War'.

[35] the 4.30 ballast train: a train which maintained railway lines or for new lines by dropping onto the track special gravel (ballast) through a slot along the bottom of special Y-shaped wagons. A spreader plough at the back would distribute the ballast, into which the rails are embedded, across the width of the track.

[36] Their photographs ... anything: a photo of Daniel and Nora Sullivan taken c. 1916 is reproduced in *FW,* p. 234. The caption, taken from *RfH*, describes 'the hard nose and the hard undoubting eyes' of his grandfather.

[37] Grandad ... Gore: Davin's maternal grandparents, Nora and Daniel Sullivan, were small farmers living in Makarewa, about twelve miles north of Invercargill on the road to Winton. They had seven children in order: John ('Uncle Jack'), Ellen, Mary, Annie, Nora (Honora), Maggie (Margaret), Daniel (*FW*, p. 6; letter from Delia Davin). See 'Bluff Retrospect' and notes.

[38] sawney: 'simple'. See also 'A Happy New Year', n. 2 ('a sawney'), and n. 10 of this story. The precise meaning of the usage here is unclear.

[39] the Canadian schottische: old-time dance featuring the fiddle, popular in the 1850s, but still around now.

[40] bustler: someone who bustles or displays fussy activity.

[41] the night ... Waimea: possibly on the Waimea Plains Railway which linked Lumsden and Gore. The trains only ran on Tuesdays, Thursdays and Saturdays. Waimea is thirty-four kilometres from Gore.

[42] she ... service: a reference to the fact that Mary Sullivan and her sisters left school at the age of fourteen. Mary worked as a parlour maid in a hotel, probably in Wellington.

[43] We've got ... way: the four children in this story are all boys (corresponding to Davin and his brothers). In real life two older sisters, Molly and Evelyn, made up the number to six.

25

Gardens of Exile

WE WERE RUNNING LATE and still had a mile or so to go before we got home. We were pretty done, too, all four of us kids. Still, the day had started well enough, with hard, white frost and the likelihood of a bright and very cold day. We'd reached Black Jack Fahey's Farm,[1] about six miles from home and a bit this side of Waimatua,[2] about eleven o'clock that morning. By mid-afternoon we'd got thirty-three rabbits with the ferrets and the dogs had got three more. And Ned had copped a couple with the .22 Winchester. To save carrying weight, we'd skinned them all except for a couple of young bucks for Mum to cook for us and a couple of elderly bucks for the hens. The hawks that kept following us were having a good day, because the meatworks these days of the Depression were giving nothing for the carcases. The skins still fetched a decent price though.

There'd been no sign of Black Jack until about noon, when we saw him cross the valley driving his spring cart full belt over the patch that used to be the vegetable garden when his wife was alive. He was standing up in the cart before he did a flash turn, came to a halt, unharnessed the horse and put it in the stable, and then went in to have his late dinner. He didn't see us because we were hiding behind a dead tree in what used to be the bush until, years ago, they took out all the big timber and burnt the rest, leaving it for someone else to clear up the blackened logs and stumps and turn the ground to grass. By the look of Jack and the way he walked, staggering a bit, it'd have to wait a good deal longer. He'd be in the Waimatua cemetery before those acres were in grass. The pub where he'd probably just been was where he'd be growing the grass in his mind and under his feet. Still, that was his problem and, after his dinner – McConachie's[3] tinned herrings in tomato sauce, probably, or some bully beef – he'd go and have a kip and sleep the booze off. So we counted on being pretty safe for the rest of the afternoon.

We weren't though. That big black ferret we'd bought the week before, at Todd's Rialto Auction Mart[4] in Esk Street, had us stuck.[5] He'd bailed up a tough old buck at the end of one of the underground runways and if you put your ear to the ground you could hear the thump of his clawing at the rabbit's backside, trying to make him bolt. The burrow was under the thick root of a burnt-out totara, pretty tough. It was hard going with the adze, and Ned and I took turns, trying to dig down and haul out both ferret and rabbit. Both of us soon had a sweat up, though it was now late afternoon and getting on for another hard white frost.

As if that weren't bad enough, Bessie, the cocker spaniel, had sneaked off to the green patch of bush left in the swamp and she started barking after a rabbit she hadn't a hope in hell of catching, given her short legs. The noise, though, was enough to waken Jack half a mile away. We saw him come raging out onto the verandah of his unpainted wooden shack, trying at the same time to button up his flies and braces and shake his fist at us. We could hear him quite clearly in that frosty air.

'You bloody little bastards, wait till I flaming well catch up with you,' and a good deal more of the same. He was well-known in those parts for being a hard man. Besides, in those days the only way his kind of cow-cocky[6] could lay hands on ready cash was by selling rabbit-skins – the big mortgage companies had the small farmers well and truly by the throttle[7] and had first call on any regular money that came through meat or wool or butterfat.

By now he was roaring across the swamp hell for leather and we weren't prepared to wait and discuss the New Zealand economy with his big boots at our behinds. So we bolted over the barbed-wire fence down on to the yellow clay road and raced down the hill to hide in a patch of gorse. Luckily we'd had time to grab our nets and the adze and the rifle and two of our ferrets; so there was nothing left there except the bloody black ferret, and Jack wouldn't have bothered about that even if he knew it was there.

He pottered about for a while, getting his breath back, and cursing and snarling. Then he gave us up and marched home again towards his shack. We had crept back up to the fence and could hear him still swearing a quarter of a mile away. He disappeared into the shack again. We waited for a few minutes and then, with Bessie on the lead this time, we dodged behind the logs back to the burrow. We coaxed that rotten ferret back to the mouth of the hole by putting a freshly skinned rabbit down it. Then I grabbed the brute by the neck and put him in a sugar-bag sack separate from the other two ferrets we had trained not to play dirty tricks on us like this half-wild bastard. One of the two was a jill[8] and we wouldn't trust this one with her.

It was getting on to dusk by then and we had about six miles to walk home, along the clay road to the Puni Creek crossing near Rimu,[9] then along the avenue through Maple Grove,[10] then past the Sunday School some sanguine and crazy evangelist had built, miles from anywhere. And then the final stretch down Oteramika Road[11] with its high hawthorn hedges the dogs were by now too tired to investigate.

'Just as well the old man's got the day off,' Matt said. 'At least he'll have got the cows in and fed, and there's only Silky in milk.'

'Yes, but he had great plans for getting on with his digging today,' Ned said. 'He was going to put in some cabbages as well and wanted to finish off the clamp[12] for the parsnips and the swedes. You know what he's like about that garden of his. He says we don't know how lucky we are here in New Zealand. Back in Ireland the bailiff put the rent up if you tried to plant anything.'

I wasn't worrying much about how the old man would take our being so late, but more how Mum would be feeling. She'd have got herself into a fine state. It was pitch-dark by now, except for a miserable sliver of moon. She'd have got it firmly into her head that one of us had come to grief, hit by a bullet from the Winchester, most likely. She'd be having visions of whichever one it was – Paddy, probably, because he was the youngest of us and her pet – lying under a stump out in the freezing cold somewhere or else being carried home on a gate, bleeding frightfully. Or even dead. We could never make out why Mum always imagined the worst, unless it was a sort of superstitious precaution to prevent it from happening, the kind of prayer that the Irish monks used to say in their wild evenings of storm against the coming of the Vikings.

On the whole, it seemed best not to raise this side of things just now. Our morale was enough on the low side already. We'd been off first thing after we'd milked Silky that morning and fed the cows and put them up in the Faraway Paddock.[13] We'd had only a few sandwiches to eat and must have walked the better part of fifteen miles all told,[14] climbing in and out among the burnt stumps and fallen logs and having to halt every now and then to scrape the bidi-bidi off our socks and trousers with our knives, all the time looking for the right ferreting ground, and doing a good bit of digging after that bloody polecat[15] as well – not to speak of running like hell with Black Jack after us.

'And that damned thing calls itself a ferret,' Matt said with disgust.

'He seemed to think we carried him all that way so that he could have a good feed,' Ned said. 'Back he goes to Todd's next Saturday so some other poor sod can deal with him.'

Without relish, Matt chanted the schoolboy rhyme:

Todd, Todd, the auctioneer,
sold his wife for a bottle of beer.
The beer was bad
so Todd went mad.
Todd, Todd, the auctioneer.

Paddy didn't manage a half grin like the rest of us. He was getting pretty done. He'd insisted on wearing the new boots he was so proud of, boots Mum had bought for him at Scully's the Catholic shoeshop,[16] the day we bought the polecat. He knew that, after the warnings we'd given him, he wouldn't get much sympathy for the state of his feet; but we were sorry for him and wouldn't let him carry anything, not even the adze – and still less the rifle which, in spite of his blistered feet, we knew he was longing to carry so that he could imagine himself a soldier or Hopalong Cassidy or Buffalo Bill – two more Redskins bit the dust.

So on we went, doing our best with the help of that bloody feeble moon to avoid stumbling on the big stones and the wheel ruts and the shoals of loose gravel that the county put down so as to stop the corduroyed wooden cross-ribs from the original bush road coming through the hard standings[17] that had been put on top.

We had the consolation, though, of saying to one another what a good day it had been, about forty rabbits altogether and no ferrets lost or nets forgotten, and we reckoned up what we'd get for the skins when we sold them at Rabbit-Skin Black's in Dee Street.[18] The bottom hadn't dropped out of the market yet, and you could get a bob and a half for the skin of a good young buck. We were saving up to buy another .22, a Remington this time, and Matt had visions of owning a Bowie knife which you could buy from McCarthy's sports shop,[19] fairly cheap.

Then, as well as the skins, we had those two young bucks for the kitchen and two more for the hens and we thought that after the first furious explosions of relief they'd help to mollify Mum a little. She was a bit like the opera singers whose arias we used to hear on the old horn-fitted His Master's Voice gramophone that Cousin Jim[20] had bought at an auction sale and given to us. The big bursts of shouting and reproach usually calmed down before long into something smoother.

We were over halfway and we kept passing landmarks which were more and more familiar and showed we were within striking distance of home. We weren't so hungry either by now because we'd pinched some swede turnips at Graham's paddock as we passed. The dogs didn't like swedes and they were even more anxious than we were to get home. They'd eaten even less than we had because they were spoilt and liked their rabbit cooked, wouldn't look at the raw carcases. Still, they knew where we were and it wouldn't be long now and they padded quietly behind us, without bothering to rummage in the hedges. They kept that even, easy jog, shoulders and head slightly to the right, the way dogs do when they're tired and taking it steady.

There wouldn't have been anything for them to go for, anyhow, by now; for all along the right of Oteramika Road were the Chinese market gardens that ran right down to the Puni Creek,[21] and the Chinese seemed to have some sort of magic formula for keeping rabbits off their stuff. Not that they could have much that was worthwhile for a rabbit at this time of the year: these Chinamen didn't seem to go in for root vegetables much – not our kind anyway – though they always managed to have a special kind of cabbage that could stand up to the frost, and some other hardy green stuff.

At the end of the gardens nearest Scott's Paddocks[22] they'd lately built a long wooden shack. It wasn't much more than a kind of barracks, really, with two small windows and only one door: the sort of place, they might have been thinking, that ought to be able to stand a siege. About a dozen of them lived in it and I don't know that any of the white townspeople ever got a foot inside, but those who didn't like Chinamen and used to talk about the Yellow Peril[23] said it was a disgrace, so many Chinks living in so small a space. But people like Mum and Dad said, 'Poor things, what else do you expect, everyone against them because they aren't the right colour, and them not even allowed by law to have womenfolk and wee babies of their own, and they work so hard to help their families back in China.' The wowsers[24] in Invercargill also said that they gambled, playing pakapoo[25] and that they were a danger to young white girls, but on the whole people had too much sense to take that rubbish seriously. Why shouldn't they gamble if they wanted to? And no one had ever seen a white girl near the place, or any other shade of girl.

There was deep shadow on the near side of the hut as we got closer, the moon being on the Puni Creek side. As we came alongside we saw someone stir in the dark, stand up and come towards us, giving us a bit of a scare. But the dogs didn't growl and the hair didn't go up on their backs. Instead they started to wag their tails and ran forward to whoever the bloke was, as if they knew him.

Then our old man's deep voice said, 'Is that you boys?' And he himself moved bulkily out of the shadows, on to the road in front of us. He was wearing his cloth cap, I noticed, but hadn't bothered about a jacket, making do with his old saddle-tweed[26] waistcoat, its pockets full of nails and fencing staples, and his saddle-tweed trousers, with the side pockets in front. He never felt the cold, or said he didn't, whenever we complained. Behind him now we could hear the sing-song voices of Chinamen, talking nineteen to the dozen, though they obviously hadn't heard us. We never made much noise when we were on the road, and my father hadn't spoken loudly.

'I'm sorry we're so late,' Ned said. 'We got stuck up by our new ferret. Blast him, he's still no better than wild. And so was Black Jack Fahey when he spotted us.'

'Be cripes, you shouldn't have worried about him,' our father said. 'Weren't he and I at school together, with the monks, way back in Galway, in Tonygurrone?[27] Pretty rough, poor Jack, since his wife died, but if you'd told him who you were he'd have said take all the rabbits you can catch and come home and have a cup of tea. He talks Irish as well as I do, nearly, the old rascal.'

We weren't so sure, and the Irish wouldn't have been much help because we didn't know more than a phrase or two, since we'd been too busy fighting other kids at school because they laughed at our brogue, and anyway we were setting up to be New Zealanders and only a few of the Marist Brothers who taught us knew Irish, and even they were all set on making good English speakers of us.

Anyway, if we'd made pals of Black Jack that would have kept us later than ever and we wouldn't have felt able to go rabbiting on his land again, since he would have been a friend then and we knew he lived on the smell of an oilrag, or what he got from the rabbit-skins and selling back his empty bottles. He didn't even have a garden any more, since his wife died, nothing but a tangle of gorse and blackberries.

Our father, after a few seconds' silence, had the gist of our thinking, if only because we didn't say anything. He and my mother were both very quick to guess what silence meant, though only my father was good at keeping what he thought to himself.

'Probably just as well, though,' he said now. 'Your mother's been getting herself hysterical with worry. You should hide that gun when you go out so it won't put these silly ideas into her head. I knew you'd be all right but nothing would do but I must come out and look for you after I'd got Silky milked and the cows put up and the hens and pigs fed. She did the separating herself and I've never heard her turn the handle so hard. It's a miracle the cream didn't come out sour. Though I knew you'd be as right as rain I was glad to get myself out of it all. There are times when it's more peaceful to have your ears out of reach of your mother's tongue. All my fault for letting you have a rifle. Why didn't I get you interested in the garden, and all that sort of thing? She's got a real tongue on her, that one. I expect that's where you got yours, much good may it do you.'

'You seemed to pick on a babble of tongues yourself, all the same,' said Ned, the eldest of us and his favourite, though he didn't go in much for pets, except for one or two of the cows. Ned was gesturing towards the Chinamen's hut. 'I expect you preferred to listen to something you couldn't understand, after what Mum had been saying.'

That was a clear hint of curiosity, as near as we could risk, about why Dad was sitting under the wall of the shack listening to a language he couldn't understand. He'd probably been there since darkness fell, his ears stuck to the wall.

He would have been well aware of our curiosity but he was always inclined to take a pleasure in being silent about his reasons for whatever he did. It saved argument and he hated argument, especially as Mum was one of those people who could never hear a proposal made without wanting to improve on it or throw cold water on it. My father had always thought over his plans very carefully before he disclosed them and didn't take kindly to suggestions for alteration. He was one of those people who don't want advice even on the rare occasions when they ask for it. And my mother was one of those who can't resist giving advice even before they're asked for it, and whether or not it's welcome.

As for the Chinese, his curiosity was unusual. No one ever took much notice of them, except the sex maniacs and professional haters of foreigners, especially of those with different-coloured skins or different native languages or different religions. Irish, Poles, Dalmatians, Indian hawkers, Catholics, Chinese, we were all much the same, except the Chinese because you could see their different colour. Jews were under suspicion but there weren't many of them and they were generous to public causes. So they weren't so bad. They didn't breed fast like the others, either, and though they had queer taste in music and pictures they used to subsidise concerts and found art galleries. And, at A.B. Wachner's shoeshop,[28] Mum said, you could get real bargains.

Anyway the Chinese didn't take much notice of us either and, looking back, I suspect that they thought we were a pack of relatively harmless barbarians. Anyhow we thought we had them taped. They ran the laundries in town where you got your stiff collars starched and all that, and the older kids at school said you could buy french letters[29] from them. We younger kids weren't at all sure what french letters were but knew enough not to mention them in front of grown-ups. Once Fatty Ratcliffe brought one to school in a matchbox. It wasn't very impressive, I thought.

Well, the Chinese were great ones for fireworks, too, and at Christmas and New Year they had the best crackers and basket bombs.[30] They owned most of the fruit and vegetable shops, too; at least in the main streets.

Even the women who thought they were heathens and went in for dreadful sexual goings-on with white or Maori women they hid in their basements, and spat on their apples before polishing them, still bought from them because their stuff was cheaper than anywhere else and looked so clean, whatever doubtful methods for getting them so shiny might have been used. They were always smiling when they sold you things, and lots of us liked it that way, though other people who read the stories of Sax Rohmer[31] said it was all a bit sinister, like Fu Man Chu.[32] We kids didn't care, except that the more timid and suspicious ones used to spit on the apples they bought and wipe them with their handkerchiefs. Kids like that always had handkerchiefs.

Then a Chinese conjuror and magician called Long Tak Sam[33] came to Invercargill and everyone went to see him at the Civic, though some said afterwards it was all phony tricks. But there were enough who were convinced, especially by the juggling and by the sawing of a woman in half – she was very pretty and wasn't very much damaged, or even at all – and Nugget Brown, though he was younger than the rest of us, said she gave him the horn. A lot of people had their toothache cured when Long Tak put his finger on the sore spot. The lads of course said it must be wonderful when he put his finger on the spots that weren't sore. They said he had miraculous sexual powers, greater even than the ordinary Chinese. I never met anyone with hard evidence on this; but perhaps I was too young. The Chinese gardeners didn't get much chance to show their powers. And the people with toothache were soon going back to the dentist. Long Tak had gone north again by then and the posters were half-torn on the hoardings and flapping in the wind.

My father scoffed at all the stories about the Chinese, Long Tak Sam and all. Sometimes he used to get up early and walk alongside their fences and look at their gardens in case he could pick up a hint or two, being a mad gardener himself. And my mother sometimes sneaked away from the Catholic fruiterer in order to buy from the Chinese. She used to smile back at them, in a charming way she had, and they'd often give her an extra orange or apple or cabbage and smile back at her, which made her blush, though she took the presents all the same. I think my mother and father, having had a bit of the dirty end of the stick themselves, had a genuine sympathy for Chinese, Indians, Dallies, black men, and anyone else who had to struggle to rise in the world.

Well, that particular night by the market gardens, there were the lot of us except Mum and my two sisters. We went marching on, all of us speculating, I think, how these Chinamen spent the time at the end of the day's work, without women to cook for them or scold them or go to bed with them and no children to play with and put hopes in. They were a peaceful lot and didn't go looking for trouble, even when schoolkids passed them in the street and called out 'Too le Mani'[34] which was popularly supposed to be a deadly insult in Chinese. The real trouble, of course, was that no one knew Chinese and so we were clueless about what they really thought and felt about things.

What was puzzling us now was how our old man could sit there and listen to those high-pitched, up-and-down voices with such concentration when he had no notion of what they were saying.

Ned took courage, at last. 'What were they saying, Dad?'

'I didn't understand a word of it, not for the life of me.' He paused then, as if he too was asking why he had been listening so intently to what was gibberish to him.

'Was it like listening to music?' Ned persisted, knowing that Dad, though he could sing Irish melodies and play the jew's harp and liked listening to my sisters singing High Mass, couldn't read music and in a way understood it no more than he understood Chinese. Or Latin, for that matter.

'I wasn't thinking of music,' Dad now said. 'I was thinking about these poor Chows thousands of miles from home and no one except themselves, just a dozen or so of them, to understand what they're saying. By now every one of them must know all about the others and there'll be nothing new to say. I suppose they just go on night after night wondering what's happened to their mothers and fathers and brothers and sisters and asking themselves if the rice crops have been good, and whether there will be dumplings or whatever they eat for tea, and whether the new bridge over the river has been finished yet, what the taxes are like, how many kids have been born and who's married whom and all that. And they'll be asking themselves, if ever they get out and home again, whether their parents will still be alive and if they'll still be young enough or be rich enough to find girls to marry them. And they'll be worrying whether they'll have to spend the rest of their lives in this barbarous bloody country instead – if only St Patrick had been buried here – not allowed to have families of their own and neither kith nor kin to see them to the grave.'

His voice was quite level, though he didn't usually say as much as this, at least to us. But what he had said seemed to be quite natural thoughts for a man to be thinking who'd been away from Ireland twenty or thirty years himself by now, and only twenty years old when he left. He must have had a cud of memory that wasn't always good to chew on.

We were well down towards home by now and from Conyers Street[35] we could see across Murray's paddock[36] where the peat-fires were smouldering, like history, under the burnt gorse to where the light was glowing from our kitchen window. The thought of the food that would be waiting for us was enough to make us forget the tongue-thrashing we'd have to listen to before we sat down to table and we stopped wondering about my father and his listening to the Chinese.

I dreamt that night of Fu Man Chu with his evil moustaches and his tong[37] but just when he was going to get me he turned into Billy McNab,[38] the old Chinaman who lived up at the end of Metzger Street,[39] in a one-room hut. He'd been a cook on the McNab sheep station[40] years before and got his name by answering an ad in the *Otago Daily Times* for a cook and, although he was Chinese, signing his letter Billy McNab. He got the job, even though the boss McNab[41] was startled to find his new cook was a Chinaman. He asked Billy how he got his name, and Billy truthfully replied it was because he knew he'd never get the job if he used his own real name. Anyway, it was too late to advertise again because the shearers were arriving that day and McNab Station was miles from anywhere – it still is. So Billy cooked there for thirty years and when he was too old for the job the McNabs gave him a pension and he retired to our territory. His hobby was going to all the auction sales and buying up bits and pieces of rubbish, and he was, in that line, my Cousin Jim's chief rival. The ground all round his hut was covered in empty bottles he never got round to selling. My father used to call it Billy's glass garden, but we kids were the ones who pinched the bottles and sold them. Billy was good-natured and never held it against us. He didn't go near the market gardeners either and would never speak Chinese. We all looked on him as a pet rather than a real stranger.

Now in my dreams, though, he had Fu Man Chu's moustaches and he had a long knife and terrible grin instead of his usual sweet smile and Jack Fahey was there as well, also with moustaches and shillelagh,[42] and they had me bailed up in a cowshed and they were coming at me for stealing what they lived by. And my father sat on the milking-stool with a grim smile and you couldn't tell whose side he was on, mine or theirs or everybody's.

Then I woke with my mother shaking me and telling me it was time for us to get up and get the cows milked if we weren't going to be late for early Mass. She always went to early Mass herself on Sundays so as to have breakfast ready and see my sisters all set for eleven o'clock Mass when they sang in the choir. My father had to be seen off too in time to hear them sing from down below and doze through the sermon till everything was over. Then he'd go outside the Basilica[43] and meet all the latest arrivals from Ireland, especially the Gaelic-speaking ones with the latest news from Galway. We boys usually went to nine o'clock Mass, after we'd dealt with the cows and fed the pigs and hens.

These new Irishmen were all big, powerful fellows, in their early twenties usually. They soon got jobs in the quarries once they'd arrived, the wool-stores, on the wharves or up at the saw-mills at Port Craig.[44] They generally tried to get into Invercargill over Saturday and Sunday for a bit of a change and they stayed at the Criterion Hotel[45] which, although the town was dry, always managed to be pretty wet, with no nonsense about closing time either. Saturday nights were a bit rough but the young men usually tried to look their best on Sunday mornings and they came to eleven o'clock Mass in their blue serge suits with sloping side pockets and wearing tan or oxblood-coloured boots. They were somehow unmistakable in a crowd, with their wide shoulders and their high cheek-bones, blue eyes and red complexions – you'd never be misled into thinking they were home-grown Kiwis. I always admired them for their size and their respect for themselves but my cousins born in New Zealand, though of the same generation, used to imitate them mockingly, when the victims were not there.

They all took a great shine to my two sisters and my mother rather encouraged this, thinking they were good Catholic boys and knowing they were tigers for hard work. After all, she'd married one of them; from out of the previous migration. I suspect my father felt the same about them and my sisters, but he didn't talk about that side of things, at least to us kids, and he seemed to be mainly interested in talking Irish to the suitors. My sisters themselves were rather disdainful: they were a bit flirtatious with them whenever they were around but scoffed at them when they were absent because of the way they dressed and their 'homey' accents and their rather simple ways. 'Sawnies'[46] my sisters called them, which always made me feel a bit uncomfortable because I didn't feel that my sisters had all that right themselves to be so superior.

Anyway, it usually ended up after Mass on Sundays that Dad would ask some of them home to Sunday dinner and Mum, guessing what would happen, would have cooked an immense roast of beef and huge gooseberry or plum or apricot pie or a treacle pudding. What with the cabbage and carrots and parsnips from Dad's clamps down in the garden and the swedes he'd have pulled the night before it was staggering the amount those spalpeens[47] could eat.

After the washing-up my sisters would disappear – they had to go to music practice or they had one excuse or another to go visiting. My mother would retire to bed for a rest. We boys would usually go rabbiting or push off to Metzger's Bush[48] to build manuka huts or something. My father would first take the Irishmen for a walk round the garden and skite a bit about his rhubarb or whatever. And I remember once, big Kevin Manion[49] took out his green handkerchief from an inside pocket and showed my father how it was full of earth: 'Good Galway ground,' he said, 'and I'm the spud that's going to grow in it when they spread it on my grave.'

After the ritual round of my father's garden he would shepherd them up to the front sitting-room – the parlour, as Mum and the girls called it – which wasn't used except on special occasions. The blinds were made of green slats, acrosswise, and they were usually kept shaded. But when my father used the room he'd jerk the cords back and let the sun in, not giving a damn about the fading of the carpet, of which Mum went in terror. And there the lot of them would sit all afternoon chewing the rag in Irish about the Corrundullah[50] and Bally this and Bally that and Tonygurrone and Castle Craven,[51] where most of them came from.

On this particular Sunday I felt inquisitive over what they talked about and in general how things went. So instead of going off with Ned and the others I made some excuse and, when the coast was clear, I settled myself in the passage outside the door. All I could hear was intense excited conversation in Irish, sometimes the long monologue of someone telling a story, sometimes great bursts of laughter I couldn't know what at. I noticed that my father talked more than anyone and they all seemed to listen without impatience as if he were a recognised story-teller. In fact, he talked far more than ever he did at home with us in English, except occasionally when he came home a bit tight. Yet somehow, perhaps because I could only guess at what it was all about, I felt something sad in the background, like what you feel when you listen to some music.

Eventually, I heard a shuffling and knew they would be coming out. I darted out of sight and when I reappeared my mother was up and about again and giving them tea and big slabs of fruit-cake. They reminded me a bit then of how it was coming out of the pictures after a Tom Mix film,[52] feeling as if you were in two worlds and the one you'd come out of was somehow more suitable for you. And when they'd all gone my father looked a bit downcast and faraway and I saw then why he'd listen outside the Chinese gardens, as he heard voices far away and outside his, even though it flourished only a few yards from our house, and I know now he understood the inside of what the Chinese were saying, even if he didn't know a word of it.

Gardens of Exile: first published in the *New Zealand Listener*, January 7, 1989.

NOTES

[1] Black Jack Fahey's Farm: Davin's comment that 'he used to chase us when we used to go on his ground chasing rabbits, because in the Depression it was all a hard-up farmer had to live by' (interview: Dan Davin to Dave Arthur) suggests a date for this incident of c. 1929. Wise's *Directory* 1929 lists Jack Fahey as a farmer at Waimatua. Fahey is the model for Jack Lardner in the war story, 'The Dog and the Dead', whom the protagonist recalls helping blow up stumps of burnt-out bush with gelignite. He was buried in the Waimatua Cemetery and his sheepdog Glen died by his grave. See 'The Vigil' and *Salamander*, pp. 59–68.

[2] Waimatua: approximately nine kilometres southeast from Georgetown. See 'Late Snow'.

[3] McConachie's: brand name of tinned food..

⁴ Todd's Rialto Auction Mart: see 'Late Snow'.

⁵ had us stuck: one is 'stuck' or 'stuck up' by a ferret when it corners a buck rabbit it cannot dislodge, as in this case, or alternatively kills a rabbit in the burrow, eats it and goes to sleep there. See *RfH*, pp. 132 and n., 261; below, p. 289.

⁶ cow-cocky: colloq. a dairy farmer. *ODNZE*.

⁷ by the throttle: colloq. 'by the throat'; i.e. the big mortgage companies were throttling the small farmers.

⁸ a jill: a female.

⁹ Puni Creek … Rimu: Puni Creek crosses Rockdale Road, flowing west along Oteramika Road before ceasing; Rimu is a further mile or so east. Returning via Rimu village would have been a considerable detour involving a journey of more than twenty-four kilometres altogether. More likely they passed where the road to Rimu starts, near Kennington.

¹⁰ Maple Grove: according to a note from Davin to Lawrence Jones, it was a fruit farm on Oteramika Road half a mile past the turn-off to Mill Road Station. *RfH*, p. 142, n. p. 261.

¹¹ Oteramika Road: see notes to 'The Apostate', 'Death of a Dog'.

¹² the clamp: mound of earth lined with straw for potatoes, parsnips, etc.

¹³ Faraway Paddock: like Faraway Hill, this was probably located to the east of Conyers Road, and south of Oteramika Road on the way to Rimu. See 'Faraway Hill'.

¹⁴ fifteen miles all told: from Georgetown to Waimatua, they went further east towards Rimu, before embarking on the ten-kilometre journey home.

¹⁵ polecat: a polecat ferret is a brown variety of the ferret.

¹⁶ Scully's … shoeshop: Scully Brothers were bootmakers at 61 Tay Street.

¹⁷ standings: standing base, foundation. In *Roads from Home*, it is a corrugated patch in the road, the ends of totara spars protruding at the verges. Ned's father says '"They've neglected it and the crown's wearing thin. It used to be the old bush tram when I first came to Southland."' See *RfH*, p. 142.

¹⁸ Rabbit-Skin Black's in Dee Street: a possible conflation of several local rabbit skin merchants: The Invercargill Rabbitskin Co. of Liddel Street or J.H. Kirk and Co. of Don Street, Invercargill, and the Robert Black who sold rabbit skins in Stafford Street, Dunedin.

¹⁹ McCarthy's sports shop: A. & W. McCarthy gunsmiths, located at 86 Dee Street.

²⁰ Cousin Jim: Jim Walsh, a retired surfaceman on the railways, who was a kind of second cousin to Mary Davin. See *FW*, p. 29.

²¹ Chinese market gardens … Puni Creek: the market gardener, Chin Lim, was located in Tweed Street, on the southern corner of Tisbury Road (now Rochdale Road). Wise's *Directory* 1929.

²² Scott's Paddocks: see 'The Apostate'.

²³ Yellow Peril: the Chinese menace; the fear that the East Asian hordes would overrun the rest of the 'civilised' world.

²⁴ wowsers: people censorious of the habits of others; spoilsports.

²⁵ pakapoo: illicit gambling game played by marking a number of Chinese characters on a ticket to try and match those on a master ticket.

²⁶ saddle-tweed: strong woven tweed, associated with colonial lifestyle. 'Original "Petone" saddle tweed trousers of 100% wool' is a brand name in New Zealand.

²⁷ Tonygurrone: i.e. Tonagarraun.

[28] A.B. Wachner's shoeshop: a shoeshop upstairs in Don Street, on the south side, near the corner of Dee Street. Wachner later became a popular mayor of Invercargill and attended the concert and banquet of the 50th Jubilee of the Marist Brothers in 1947. See *Jubilee Magazine of Marist Brothers' School Invercargill 1897–1947*.

[29] french letters: condoms.

[30] basket bombs: a type of Chinese cracker, also popular in Australia. See 'Presents'.

[31] Sax Rohmer: pseudonym of Arthur Henry Sarsfield Ward (1883–1959), prolific English mystery writer and author of the Fu Manchu novels, the first being *The Mystery of Fu-Manchu* (1913), whose heyday was in the 1930s. He was the most popular magazine writer in the English language in the 1920s and 30s.

[32] Fu Man Chu: fictional character. Rohmer's Oriental master criminal, through whom he expressed racist fears and introduced the concept of the yellow peril. He soon became a cult figure. Davin may have read the Fu Manchu stories which were published in *Chums*, the weekly British Boys paper, in 1923–4 or seen the film, *The Mystery of Fu Manchu* (1923), starring Harry Agar Lyons as the sinister Chinese doctor. Cards in cigarette packs featured scenes from the film.

[33] Long Tak Sam: Chinese magician, entertainer, and acrobat troupe director in vaudeville. A friend of Orson Welles, who opened for the Marx Brothers, he toured an exotic variety show in the 1920s becoming an international celebrity. The documentary, *The Magical Life of Long Tak Sam*, was made in 2003 by his grand-daughter, Anne Marie Fleming.

[34] Too le Mani: 'I curse you most viciously', the equivalent to 'May you rot in hell' or 'The curse of Cromwell upon you'.

[35] Conyers Street: runs parallel to Morton Street on the eastern side. In the 1920s, before Metzger Street was created, it marked the town boundary.

[36] Murrays Paddock: on Robert Murray who owned Murray's Paddock in Conyers Street, see 'Growing Up', 'Goosey's Gallic War' and 'Invercargill Boundary'.

[37] tong: secret society. Fu Man Chu boasted: 'I command every tong in China'.

[38] Billy McNab: Sandy McNab who lived near what would become Metzger Street in the late 1920s, behind Morton Road. He took a Scottish name in order to improve his chances of employment as shearers' cook. *FW*, p. 29. In *Not Here, Not Now* (p. 59) Martin Cody lets the cows in through the Taranaki gate opposite 'Billy McNab the Chinaman's old shelter'.

[39] Metzger Street: in Georgetown, parallel to and east of Conyers St, running south from Oteramika Road. Davin's preoccupation with this name (Metzger Street was founded in the late 1920s) is illustrated in the poem 'Invercargill Boundary'.

[40] McNab Station: the area, formerly known as Waikaka, named after Alexander McNab, and located at Knapdale (north/northwest of Gore). It was the first sheep run in the region. See Herries Beattie, *Otago Place Names*, p. 92.

[41] boss McNab: probably Robert McNab (1864–1917), son of Alexander, a noted politician, lawyer and historian and author of *Murihiku: A History of the South Island*, 1907, 2nd ed. 1909. See J.E. Traue, 'McNab, Robert 1864–1917', *DNZB* (updated 7 April 2006), http://www.dnzb.govt.nz (accessed 17 Jan. 2007).

[42] shillelagh: Irish cudgel of blackthorn or oak.

[43] Basilica: St Mary's Basilica on Tyne Street, the main Roman Catholic church, consecrated in 1905. It was designed by Francis Petre after the Byzantine style of late Greek architecture, and modelled on St Sophia, Constantinople.

[44] saw-mills at Port Craig: Port Craig was the country's largest sawmill camp in the 1920s, on the coast of the western end of Te Waewae Bay, deep in the bush. See 'The Tree'.

[45] Criterion Hotel: the Criterion Private Hotel on Don Street, like the Shamrock and Deschlers, was one of sixteen hotels which officially closed to drinkers on 30 June 1906; it became a 'sly grog' pub. In *RfH* it is fictionalised as the Metropolitan (p. 63 and n.).

[46] 'Sawnies': simpletons or fools. See 'The Black Stranger'.

[47] spalpeens: young labourers.

[48] Metzger's Bush: see 'Goosey's Gallic War'; 'Invercargill Boundary'.

[49] Kevin Manion: a familiar name in Davin's oeuvre. See 'The Vigil' and 'Death of a Dog'. *RfH* refers to one of the 'Manions of the Turi' (p. 147).

[50] Corrundullah: i.e. Corrandalla, a townland about five kilometres north of Tonagarraun.

[51] Castle Craven: probably Castlecreevy, a townland situated between Corrandalla and Tonagarraun. In *RfH* (pp. 143, 147), Larry O'Daly, fictional counterpart of the itinerant Irish storyteller of Davin's youth, Larry Hynes, is mourned as 'the 'last [bard] of the Castle Craven O'Dalys'. *FW*, pp. 24–5; Davin, *Closing Times*, p. 273.

[52] Tom Mix film: screen idol (1880–1940), known as 'King of the Cowboys'. See 'Late Snow'.

26

Failed Exorcism

MOST OF THE KIDS IN OUR CLASS, Standard Four,[1] were away for the St. Patrick's Day Concert Tour in places round Invercargill like Winton and Otautau.[2] Out of our gang only Hap Nelson – we used to call him Half Nelson[3] – and I were left behind: Hap because he couldn't sing at all and me because, when Brother Anastasius[4] got me to try 'Proudly the note of the trumpet is sounding,/ Loudly the cry on the vale',[5] my voice broke in the middle and he wouldn't let me get to my favourite part, the beginning of the second verse, 'Princely O'Neill to our aid is advancing.' He just stopped me with a wave of his thin, white hand and said 'That'll do, Michael, you can sit down again now.'

Of course, all the big blokes, Fatty Crawford,[6] his brother Hughie, Jack Reidy, and the rest of them, were bogged down in Standard Four because they were no good at lessons. And, as their voices had properly broken, they weren't on for the concert tour either. Their gang hated our gang because we were, most of us, small and slippery and clever and, without meaning to, always made them look stupid in class. I can still remember how poor old Jack Reidy got into trouble when he started to recite 'Lord Ullin's Daughter'[7] and said 'bony lass' instead of 'bonny'. Brother Anastasius, who didn't have much notion of what school life was like outside the class-room, asked me to recite it instead, while everyone was still laughing at Jack. It didn't do me any good at all, getting it right, but I couldn't bring myself to put myself on the safe side by making the same mistake.

So that Saint Patrick's Day I won't easily forget. At the lunch-break Hap and I got out of the class ahead of them and ran for the Invercargill estuary,[8] where we hid among the tussocks and ate our sandwiches. But then we realised, too late, they'd surrounded us. Hap got away, because they were fixing on me as the one who was strong and best at running and because of the bony lass. There was a good deal of sun that day, though it was getting on for autumn and a cold wind was blowing across the Oreti River and the estuary[9] straight down from the Takitimus,[10] which still had plenty of snow on their peaks.

Fatty Crawford sat on my chest and his brother Hughie on my legs. The rest just stood around and watched, except for Jack Reidy and Skinny Thompson. Skinny had a magnifying glass and he used it to get the heat of the sun on his face and bare arms. Jack had grown his fingernails especially for torture and he was busy tattooing crescent-shaped ditches in my forehead. I was pretty helpless but I was determined not to give them the satisfaction of crying and I was saving my strength. When they were getting a bit tired of the game themselves and Fatty had rolled off me laughing I suddenly gave a heave, threw Jack off me, got up and shoved Hughie off my ankles and bolted like a bat out of hell.

I could run much faster than any of them could, except perhaps Jack, but once I'd beaten him in a wrestle and nearly smothered him in the wood-shavings the Marist Brothers used to get from the sawmill opposite the school[11] so the playground wouldn't be too sodden after the floods. So Jack wasn't all that mad keen to catch up with me all by himself and have another go.

I got through the hole in the back fence and made for the school. I was more pleased to see it than usual. The safest place, I guessed, was the class room. They wouldn't think of looking for me there. It turned out that Hap had had the same idea. There he was sitting on the fender in front of the fire, measly but all the Brothers could afford, as I now see. But by then, although it was still early afternoon, the Southland frost was setting in and the fire of lignite kept going by a few bits of Nightcap coal[12] wasn't putting up much of a fight, especially as us kids over the years had punched holes in the rotten wood of the inner walls and sparrows had left great gaps where the ventilation hole in the roof used to be.

Anyway, Hap seemed relieved to see me still alive but he was a bit down in the mouth all the same; he felt the cold more than I did. He used to get chilblains. So, to cheer him up, and myself too I suppose, I went over to Brother Anastasius' desk and felt underneath it for where he kept the cane.

I had a particular dislike for that cane. The week before, I'd read all our set books for the year – Longman's Reader[13] with yarns about boys lost in the Australian bush and found safe and alive by black trackers, and settlers who'd been bitten by poisonous snakes but saved their lives by laying the bitten finger on a tree-stump and chopping it off with an axe, and a few more books like that. Some of them were history where Brother Anastasius would make us write in the margin and change what the book said from 'In this year England conquered Ireland' to 'In this year England once again failed to conquer Ireland.'

So I was reading under my desk one of those Buffalo Bill stories about the Pony Express[14] or whatever and I was deeply absorbed. I didn't notice Brother Anastasius sneaking alongside suddenly until I heard that sarcastic voice of his.

'If your book's so interesting it seems a shame to keep it from the rest of the class,' he'd said. 'So I want you to come up on the platform to show them how Buffalo Bill used to ride.' He called up Hughie Crawford and Jack Reidy from the front row and got them to carry a form up to the platform. Then he made me sit astride it and he jogged the top end up and down to imitate the movement of the horse while I sat blushing in what was supposed to be the saddle.

The kids laughed at first but uneasily and soon they stopped. Brother Anastasius was satisfied by then and felt the fun had gone out of the thing anyway. So he got out the cane, gave me two cuts on each hand and sent me back to my seat.

Now Brother Anastasius was well out of the way, off on the Concert Tour, and Brother Tarcisius,[15] the Head, would be taking us for the afternoon's lesson. There was a good half-hour before afternoon class yet, though. So I got out my pocket-knife, the one I used for skinning rabbits, and I cut the cane into six pieces, each about six inches long, and threw them on that miserable fire. They gave a nice little blaze, even if it wouldn't last long. I'd saved one piece, lighted at one end, and Hap and I took turns having a smoke from it. The smoke tasked horrible and burnt your throat but it was fun all the same, as we laughed at the faces we pulled when it was our turn.

Then I had a sudden feeling that someone was watching us. I looked up at the door to the next classroom, just in front of me. Its upper half was all glass. Brother Tarcisius was looking through it, straight at me. Then the door opened and he came in above us, towering. He was a tall, powerful man. He had a sort of fixed smile on his face. After one look at him I lowered my eyes and all I could see was his lower half and the thick black folds of his cassock. He didn't seem to be paying any attention to Hap but to be concentrating on me.

'Well Michael,' he said in his ordinary, level, controlled voice with that tenseness in it that made you feel he was a volcano, always nearly ready, but not quite yet ready, to explode.

There's not much you can reply when someone says, 'Well, Michael,' and then stops. You know there's plenty more where that came from. And so he went on: 'There's a lot of devil in you, I'm afraid, Michael,' he said. I didn't look up but kept staring at the fire as if expecting to see the devil in the image of myself jump out of it. I noticed bits of the cane hadn't quite burnt out. Brother Tarcisius was not the sort of man who'd fail to spot them. I said nothing.

'Next year you'll be in my class,' he said. 'I intend to use the opportunity to drive the devil out of you.'

The cassock swished and the black boots left, smartly, like a soldier's. He moved like one of those territorial officers we used to watch marching their men to and fro from the Drill Hall.[16]

The door closed behind him and we stood up to watch him crossing the next classroom to go through another glass door on the other side.

Hap said 'Cripes, I'm glad my Mum and Dad are moving to Australia next year. So he won't be able to get at me. But we were lucky it wasn't worse. He didn't say anything about the cane, did he? He must have been watching us smoke that piece of it and spotted what was in the fire.'

'It's me he's after,' I said. 'He won't forget about the cane but he'll tell Brother Anastasius on Monday and will leave all that to him. That'll mean the cuts for us with a new cane. I don't mind that much. It's next year I'm worrying about. I don't know what he meant by that stuff about driving the devil out of me but I don't like the sound of it at all. Not one bit I don't.'

Luckily, I need not have worried. Old Tarsy was transferred during the holidays to Sacred Heart College in Auckland the next term. I was relatively safe with Brother Vergil,[17] in the new school on the Elles Road, where we moved to in 1927.[18] Brother Vergil had black curly hair and his growth of whisker was so fast that he had to shave twice a day. He was mad about the Irish and used to maintain that it was an Irishman, St Vergil, who wrote the *Aeneid*. He taught us Latin which I took to like a duck to water. He also inadvertently taught me the relativity of our history: in the textbooks like *Our Race and Empire*[19] that we had to use for lack of anything better and because of the national syllabus, whenever we came to anything like 'in this year the English conquered Ireland', he would make us cross out and substitute 'in this year the Sassenach[20] once again failed to conquer Ireland'. I guessed the truth must lie somewhere in between and worked on that principle from there on.

So that year went on happily enough. But the next year, 1928, when I was in Form Four, I got back from the summer holidays to find that Brother Tarcisius was back again, and was now the head of the Secondary School and had taken over the top form, the Fifth.[21] I couldn't help wondering whether he had forgotten about me and his promise to drive the devil out of me. I hoped he had forgotten. I was reasonably satisfied with the way I was, devil or no devil.

Monday to Friday began to crawl by, the same old way, and as I was by now in Brother Egbert's form[22] and looking forward to getting the Matric. exams over and then getting myself some sort of job, I wasn't specially worried about Brother Tarcisius or the devil either for that matter. Brother Egbert himself was all the trouble I wanted. Piety was his great thing. He kept a weekly table of how many of us had gone to early Mass and Communion on Sundays, which to second Mass and Communion and which to eleven o'clock Mass when there wasn't Communion. This got on my nerves so much that I always said eleven o'clock no matter which Mass I'd really attended. He used to give me a wounded look each time but, after all, he'd asked for it.

I expect the Brothers talked about this sort of thing at their mealtimes, though in those days I never thought of them as existing outside school hours. If they did I saw no sign of it and Brother Egbert anyway didn't go for me at all. I was the favourite for getting top marks in Southland in

Matric.[23] and the Brothers were anxious that I should make a name for myself because I'd also be making a name for the school which, starting from scratch as it had done, needed all the success it could get so that Catholic parents who still sent their children to the Southland Boys' High[24] would learn to know better and send them to a school where they'd not only get as good an education but have a proper Catholic education as well.

Then it was announced one day that Bishop Whyte[25] and Judge Gilfedder[26] were to come to the school and lay the foundation stone of a new wing that they had been building for nearly the whole of the last year. There was to be an illuminated address and I was commanded to give it. I didn't want to do it, of course. I was terribly shy in those days and I just couldn't face the idea of standing in front of the whole school and reading out anything, let alone something I'd written myself. So there was a big argument about this and, to my terror, Brother Tarcisius was to have been brought in to clinch it, but luckily he got a bad go of the flu at the critical time and I was able to win a compromise: I was to write the blasted thing but Bandy Kempton, who'd won a prize for Recitation in the Invercargill Competitions, would read it.

The day came and there were seats in front of the Fifth Form room for Bishop Whyte and Judge Gilfedder and Brother Egbert and Brother Tarcisius who'd got out of bed to be there. Bishop Whyte had his ring kissed by the two Brothers, and then he made a speech, full of the usual things about a good Catholic boyhood and all that. Then Bandy read my piece, reasonably well, because he had a loud, clear voice, but missing the craftier parts where he should have paused for a bit then changed his voice to go more slowly.

Afterwards we all clapped and Judge Gilfedder made a neat little speech and at the end of it he and Bishop Whyte said that we were to have the afternoon off and could go home there and then, though it wasn't yet twelve o'clock.

As I was going out I ran into Brother Tarcisius in the corridor. He patted me on the back and said how well-written the address had been and what a pity I hadn't been willing to speak it myself. He said nothing about the devil, though the opportunity must have been very tempting, so I thought he must have forgotten all about that day he caught me and Hap smoking the cane. It was years since that had happened, after all, and I was probably the only one who remembered that threat of his.

A week or so after this, though, one of the boys in Form Four knocked at our classroom door. Then he poked his head in, tiptoed up to Brother Egbert and said something. Superego,[27] as we used to call him now, frowned and then looked at me and crooked his finger. So I went up and he said 'Brother Tarcisius wants you in Form Four classroom.'

This gave me the shivers, properly. Had someone seen me smoking in the gallery of the Civic[28] with my arm round Ellie Cunningham? Or having a snort of scotch out of the bottle we'd paid a taxi driver to fetch from the White House pub[29] five miles away and outside the boundary of our dry town?[30] Or perhaps it was the fight I'd had behind the Civic cinema with two jockeys? Or the bloke I'd thrown into the Puni Creek for trying to get away with my girl in the City gardens when I'd left her for a minute while I had a piss behind a tree? All sorts of deadly sins I'd committed came vividly before me. And I had a healthy respect for old Tarpot's gift of knowing all about everything that happened.

I walked along the passage with Ted Mullen, the kid who had come for me. I didn't ask him what it was all about – he was too young and it was beneath my dignity. I knocked at the door and went in. Brother Tarcisius was standing facing me, with one side to the blackboard and the other to the class, so that he could keep an eye on both. Behind him were my two brothers, looking a bit sheepish, though Matt gave me a wink from where Tarsy couldn't see him. Good Lord, I said to myself, perhaps he thinks they've got devils too.

'So there you are Michael,' Brother Tarcisius said. 'I want you to take this piece of chalk and write in big letters on the blackboard the word "Guard".'

I took a quick look at the board and I could see where the word spelt 'Gaurd' had been written twice and rubbed out. You could just manage to make out the two ghosts.

Not that I needed to know the wrong way of spelling it. But it gave me a glimmering of what old Tarsy was up to.

I wrote in capital letters 'GUARD'.

'That's right,' Tarsy said. I couldn't tell whether he was pleased or disappointed. Perhaps he thought the devil had come to my rescue. If so, all the worse for me, sooner or later. Still it was a relief that he didn't seem to be after me for something really serious.

Then he said to the class. 'So now you know how to spell the word, thanks to Michael here. I thought there must be at least one member of that railway family who could spell the name of their father's job correctly.'[31]

Matt and Paddy didn't show a sign of what they must be feeling. But I knew how they felt. In our family we weren't encouraged much to show on our faces what was in our feelings. I was pretty furious myself: Old Tarsy had tricked me. If I'd known what it was all about I'd have spelt it 'gaurd' the way they'd obviously done. Better still, Tarsy would guess that I could have spelt it the right way and had spelt it wrong on purpose. He'd have thought I did it to spite him. Well, no. To be fair, he wasn't like that. He'd have known I was simply standing by my brothers. As it was, though, I was going to have a hard time with them when they said, as they'd be bound to say, I'd been smarming up to[32] Tarsy.

'Right,' he said now, with that maddening, tight look[33] of his. And he sent Paddy back to his place and Matt back off to his class.

Then he turned to me and said. 'I haven't forgotten my promise. I'll attend to you and the devil when you're in my class next year ...'

I had no difficulty in not showing gratitude for this promise to turn me into a lily-white boy.[34] I said nothing and just stared at him. I dare say he saw the devil glinting out of my eyes.

'Off you go, then,' he said.

But that next year it turned out that I'd won a scholarship to Sacred Heart College in Auckland.[35] Before Tarsy was appointed there again, I'd won a university scholarship[36] and so escaped any further assault on my character – at least from him.

I was on my way to Oxford a few years later[37] when I happened to be in Invercargill to say goodbye to my parents and to the home town which at that stage of my young man's conceit I regarded as a death-hole. There was a Marist Old Boys' annual get-together and as I'd been playing rugby for the Old Boys' Marist team[38] I thought it would be small-minded not to attend. It turned out that Brother Tarcisius was the guest of honour[39] – his fiftieth anniversary as a Marist Brother or something like that.

After the formal business we had fried oysters and saveloys and beer which, except for the beer, had been fetched from Café de Kerbstone in Post Office Square.[40] Tarsy was in his element and all sorts of chaps whose memories ought to have been better or who were a tribute to a Christian upbringing were gathered around Tarsy – who didn't look as much changed as they did. I tried to keep away but towards the end he broke away from his amnesiac former victims and came over to me. He was very genial. I began to feel the same sort of affection for him that had displaced the memories of the others. But there was a remnant of recollection, not to say vindictiveness. I reminded him of how he had failed in his undertaking to expel the devil in me. I said he might have had to expel me from the school instead.

'Good Gracious,' he said. 'Fancy you remembering that. I must apologise.'

He didn't explain, and I didn't ask him, whether he was apologising for his bad memory or for his dereliction of duty.

Failed Exorcism: the draft of this previously unpublished story is dated 15 February 1989. Held in the Alexander Turnbull Library (MS-Group-0319).

NOTES

[1] Standard Four: Davin's biography sheds light on the chronology and events of this story. It begins in 1922 when at the age of nine he was in the Marist Brothers' Junior School in Clyde Street and concludes with his farewell to Invercargill before leaving for England in 1936 at the age of twenty-three.

[2] Winton and Otautau: approximately thirty kilometres north and northwest of Invercargill.

[3] Half Nelson: word play, referring to the wrestling hold, a half-Nelson.

[4] Brother Anastasius: teacher at the Marist Brothers from 1918–23. He was first President of the Marist Brothers' Old Boy's Cricket Club in 1919. The club continued until 1926–7. *The Church in Southland ... 1856–1956*, n.p. He may be the same figure as Brother Athanasius in 'Death of a Dog'.

[5] Proudly ... vale: 'O'Donnell Abu' by Michael Joseph McCann c. 1843. Known as 'The Clanconnell War Song' because of the hatred of England expressed, it is another popular Irish migrant tune.

[6] Fatty Crawford: see 'Gardens of Exile'.

[7] 'Lord Ullin's Daughter': the classic Scottish ballad by Thomas Campbell (1777–1844), published by Palgrave in the *Golden Treasury* in 1875.

[8] Invercargill estuary: the school known as the Catholic Boys' School until 1897 when the Marist Brothers arrived, then as the Marist Brothers Junior School, was located in Clyde Street in 1922, and thus close to the New River Estuary.

[9] the Oreti ... estuary: the Oreti flows south from the Thomson mountains near Lake Wakatipu, entering the New River estuary near Invercargill and then the Foveaux Strait.

[10] the Takitimus: mountain range to the east of Fiordland's Lake Monowai.

[11] the sawmill ... school: the school was on the west side of Clyde Street between Tweed and Ettrick Streets. Two blocks away and on the east side, opposite the school at 43 Clyde Street, and on the corner of Clyde and Tyne Streets, was a sawmill run by McCallum and Co.

[12] Nightcap coal: see the notes to 'Black Diamond'.

[13] Longman's Reader: probably an elementary reader in the early colonial history of New Zealand and Australia.

[14] Buffalo Bill ... Pony Express: Bill Cody (aka Buffalo Bill) had a brief, illustrious career as a Pony Express rider, beginning in Kansas in 1857 aged twelve.

[15] Brother Tarcisius: named in *The Church in Southland 1856–1956* and by J.O.P. Watt in *Invercargill Marist Brothers' School 75th Jubilee, 1897–1972*, as a Brother Director of the school from 1922–4 and again from 1931–3 (succeeding Brother Egbert). By 1939 he was the first Director of Palmerston North High School; see Patrick Gallagher, *Marist Brothers in New Zealand, Fiji and Samoa*.

[16] the Drill Hall: then located in Victoria Avenue, near the A&P showgrounds.

[17] Brother Vergil: Brother Virgilius taught at the Marist Brothers' School in Invercargill from 1925–6; he had been at the Boulcott School in Wellington in 1911, at Sacred Heart College in 1913, and he founded the Marist Brothers School Rugby Club in 1908. Patrick Gallagher, *Marist Brothers in New Zealand, Fiji and Samoa*, pp. 82, 87, 165; J.O.P. Watt, *Invercargill Marist Brothers' School 75th Jubilee, 1897–1972*.

[18] the new school ... 1927: Davin has confused the opening of the new school in Mary Street in 1925 with the commencement of the Marist Brothers' secondary department in 1927. He entered in the first secondary class (Form Three) with about nine other boys. *IS*, p. 228.

[19] *Our Race and Empire*: i.e. *Our Race & Empire: A concise history based on the Public Service Entrance, Intermediate, and Senior National Scholarship syllabus*. Auckland: Whitcombe & Tombs, 1930. According to *Te Ara – the Encyclopaedia of New Zealand*, it stresses the racial superiority of New Zealanders' British identity. See Jock Phillips, 'The New Zealanders', *Te Ara – the Encyclopaedia of New Zealand* (updated 13 April 2007), http://www.teara.govt.nz/NewZealanders/NewZealandPeoples/TheNewZealanders/3/ENZ-Resources/Standard/3/en (accessed 17 April 2007).

[20] Sassenach: a Saxon, Englishman or Lowland Scot.

[21] 1928 ... the Fifth: as the secondary school had only begun with the Third Form in 1927, there was no Fifth Form in 1928.

[22] Brother Egbert's form: Brother Director of the school 1928–30. Egbert was a great character, took Davin under his wing, and coached him. According to Patrick O'Farrell in *Vanished Kingdoms* (pp. 203–24), he was a pro-Irish enthusiast who used his Latin classes to teach Irish history and verse. A public crusader, he wrote pro-Irish journalism and envisaged publishing a collection of quotations called *Ireland the Valiant and the Virtuous* in the 1950s. *IS*, pp. 25–6, 228–9; *The Church in Southland 1856–1956*, n.p.;

J.O.P. Watt, *Invercargill Marist Brothers' School 75th Jubilee, 1897–1972.*

[23] top marks … in Matric: Matriculation or the University Entrance Examination was taken in Form Five in the 1920s and 30s until 1944 when the UE exam (or accreditation), taken after four years of secondary schooling, was introduced. Davin sat Matriculation in 1929 when in the Fifth Form; he came top of Southland, fifteenth in New Zealand, and was dux of the school.

[24] Southland Boys' High: most Catholic families did not expect their children to continue to high school. Before 1927 those who did, like Tom, Dan Davin's older brother, attended the secular school, Southland Boys' High. *FW*, p. 27; *IS*, p. 228.

[25] Bishop Whyte: His Lordship Bishop Whyte was the third Bishop of Dunedin. An Irishman from Kilkenny he had formerly been parish priest of Stanmore, New South Wales. He was consecrated with Bishop Liston by Archbishop Redwood at St Joseph's Cathedral, Dunedin on 12 December 1920; he opened the new school in St Mary's Street in 1925; *The Church in Southland 1856–1956*, n.p.

[26] Judge Gilfedder: Michael Gilfedder, originally a lay teacher in the Catholic Boy's School at Clyde Street in 1885–6. Gilfedder later joined the state school service. He had a spectacular career, representing the Wallace constituency in Parliament from 1896–1902, and qualifying as barrister and solicitor. He was appointed a Judge of the Native Land Court, holding this position for many years. He held the degrees of MA and LL.M. He died before 1947. See the entry by J.J. Forde in the 1947 Jubilee Magazine, *Marist Brothers' School Invercargill 1897–1947.*

[27] Superego: a sobriquet alluding to the eccentricities for which Brother Egbert was known. On his problems in teaching see O'Farrell, *Vanished Kingdoms*, pp. 212–4.

[28] the Civic: on the Civic see 'Late Snow'.

[29] the White House pub: i.e. outside the dry area in what is now known as Lorneville, this hotel was the main venue for legal drinking. *RfH*, p. 34 and n.; Denis Lenihan, 'Roads around Home: Dan Davin Revisited', n. 1.

[30] our dry town: on the closing of the pubs in 1906, see 'Late Snow', 'Presents', n. 13.

[31] that railway family … correctly: on Patrick Davin's employment as a guard on the Dunedin-Christchurch Express see 'Roof of the World', 'First Flight'; on the Invercargill branch lines around Gore, see 'Black Diamond' and 'The Black Stranger'.

[32] smarming up to: toadying up to.

[33] that maddening, tight, look: a pent-up knowing look which infuriates Michael, the visual equivalent to the suppressed rage in Tarcisius' voice alluded to on page 304.

[34] a lily-white boy: possibly a reference to that 'pale lily-white lad' of A.R.D. Fairburn's poem 'Rhyme of the Dead Self' (1930).

[35] a scholarship … Auckland: Davin sat for the scholarship in 1928 but failed to get it (apparently one of his examination papers was lost and never marked). Brother Egbert intervened on his behalf, and he succeeded the following year. He spent his sixth form year at Sacred Heart College in 1930, then located in Richmond Road, Grey Lynn, in Auckland. *FW*, pp. 33, 35; *IS*, pp. 26, 229.

[36] university scholarship: Davin came top of the VIB class at Sacred Heart and was awarded the Gold Medal for Latin. In the New Zealand Entrance Scholarships examination he was thirty-fifth in New Zealand. Recognising his place would have been higher had he performed better in Mechanics, the examiners awarded him a special University National Scholarship. *FW*, p. 43.

[37] Oxford ... later: Davin returned to Invercargill in July 1936 to farewell his family before leaving New Zealand for Oxford on 14 August, on HMS *Akaroa*; *FW*, pp. 97–8.

[38] Old Boys' Marist team: the Marist Brothers' Old Boys' Rugby Club was founded in 1920. Davin played for the third fifteen at Sacred Heart College in Auckland; in Dunedin in 1933 he played for the University D (i.e. fourth) fifteen, and he was Captain of the C Fifteen in 1935. He may have played for the Old Boys' Marist team in the winter university holidays – but there is no evidence he did. *FW*, pp. 40, 70, 91.

[39] Brother Tarcisius ... honour: i.e. the Marist Brothers' School Reunion dinner in July 1936 at which Davin was the guest of honour. Brother Tarcisius is not recorded in the *Southland Times* as being present; he had left the school in 1933. *FW*, p. 97.

[40] Café de Kerbstone ... Square: local argot for a piecart or 'white lady'. A variation is 'Restaurant à la Gutter'.

Day's End

The hens are fed, the pigs are fed.
The cows are milked, and out for the night.
So are the stars.
The Building Society's bill is paid.
We haven't lost the land beneath us.
The night is light,
And so is the moon.
And down by the gorse-flamed hedges
You and I lie prone on the sky
And grow up at our edges.
And that's the way it was.
That is the way it will always be,
Because.

Day's End: Published in Robert Welch and Susheila B. Bushrui, ed. *Literature and the Art of Creation: Essays in Honour of A. Norman Jeffares* (Gerrards Cross: Berkshire and Barnes & Noble: Totowa, NJ, 1988), p. 241.

This poem has no obvious setting but the 'gorse-flamed hedges' suggests Davin is thinking of the Georgetown district of Invercargill where he grew up. As in 'Perspective', written at the beginning of his career, here, nearing the end of his life, he associates gorse with mortality, showing resignation to this fate.